FLYING

ON THE

GROUND

FLYING
ON THE
GROUND

H.D. MAXWELL

Cover illustration: Tami Tsark
tsarkart.wordpress.com

Cover design: Carol Webb
www.bellamediamanagement.com

Author photo: GJ Spiller Photography
www.gjspillerblog.com

Editing: Laura Taylor
www.laurataylorbooks.com

Print Formatting: By Your Side Self-Publishing
www.ByYourSideSelfPub.com

DEDICATION

This book is dedicated to all who wander but are not lost. My wife Jolynn put up with this and many other obsessions, and my daughter Jordan was quite helpful to the end. My son Max is the best guy in my life; being his stepfather teaches me much.

ACKNOWLEDGMENTS

I was encouraged by some really offbeat teachers to go my own way, since I and the world around me did not match. I have never forgotten the unsung hero of that overpacked noisy-ass classroom. Me being the loudest.

The first person to look over my work seriously was Mike Foley of Writers Review (writers-review.com). After two rewrites, I had something that was tolerable to read. My now wife and I met at a writers' group, one of several I have gone to. Thank you to all who run them.

Laura Taylor, a powerhouse author in her own right, finally agreed to help me shape this work into the best it can be. It's been really difficult but worth it. She went through it twice—tough lady, but kind from the bone out. Dana Delamar of By Your Side Self-Publishing also went out of her way to help me do this.

My daughter Jordan had some amazing insights. Thanks to my sister Alice, who one day said, "You write beautifully." Thus began the journey to share what I have lived through. Everything you are about to read happened to a degree.

1
SONS OF AVARICE

It's my fault for being here. Why hurt the little ones? David Dryer thought, looking sixty yards down the field at goal posts pointing to a black heaven. He tried to focus on poetry. *They're like bones poking up from a sun-blanched desert carcass.*

Any chance he had of winning this game, going on to regional, and perhaps a free ride to college would stay on the other side of the fifty. He could run there in seconds, but not with the ball. Not with that big brutal team his Rangers faced off against.

Pete, his right tackle, came up. "They are really good, I can only take on two man."

David nodded and pushed down that sick feeling one more time as the rest of the players came close. He turned to his wide receiver, a tall skinny kid. "Weasel, can you break free or what?" He looked through Weasel's face-mask and saw his answer. *No, and please let this be over…*

Weasel turned his head away. "Your cousins are fast and mean."

"Three yards…" David said. "Weasel, get out fast, then double back. This time everyone pile toward Pete." *God, they look awful. Please let me give something.* Another incomplete thought trailed off and floated away while his players lined up to face the larger, meaner team.

The center snapped the ball to David, who faded back and feigned left, then right to throw off the oncoming line-backers. David knew that low bullet pass would keep it out of sight. He fired off the ball before an opening collapsed just to Pete's left, the ball nearly grazing him. Weasel caught the bullet pass at the forty-eight and landed two yards later, curling his body around the ball as he hit the ground. *Good one, bro!* First down had been secured for the first time past the fifty. David felt relaxed as he took steps in Weasel's direction toward their field goal. *Crossing the fifty is going downhill,* he thought to himself. An opposing player kicked Weasel in the back. David felt a bolt of anger. He was about to take off toward them when the ground slammed up into his face. He felt a kick to the back of his head that would have been lethal without his helmet. He rolled over to see his

1

cousin Bob spit into his face-mask. David felt another kick to his side.

"I own you, boy. Don't bother getting up." Bob walked back to his high-fiving teammates.

David's mind raced around so fast he felt sick. He tried to clear his thoughts enough to find the brainpower to get up. *You die, Bob.* Pete came over to help him.

A young referee drew closer, but was pulled back to the open part of the field by the older one. David heard him say something about staying out of the fight. *Losing this game was inevitable. The pumas had a bigger line.* Pete pulled him up to his feet. His team was already behind by a touchdown and field goal they could not prevent. *Barley slowed them down.* Everything slowed down. He scanned the bleachers that he and other volunteers had helped to repaint and repair. To his left, his hometown supporters. He spotted Jan, a long-time friend of his mother's and her carbon copy daughter, little Jan. Both looked worried. He could just about smell her clean scent and feel that hug she gave until he stopped resisting. Just thinking about it warmed him. To his right the visitors from up North. He knew some of them. Bob's parents were too important to attend, but some of the other assholes were there to cheer and jeer, delighted to watch him fail and his team get punished for even trying. A cool sensation washed over him, like taking a swim in a spring river, the water washing away all the confusion and all that heat in his head, going down stream never to be felt again. It always felt that way when he really focused and did something stupid. The Rangers huddle came up to David at the forty-six yard line. He was putting his helmet back on after wiping his face; the boys crouched down facing him. Normally he looked at his player's eyes, reading them, and then choosing to go in the direction of the one who had the brightest fire in them. They looked scared from play one, except for Pete, who was too big to hurt. Now, he was staring straight down, fingers clawed into his thigh pads. "Pete, make a hole. Let that shit straight back to me." His voice had a tremor. His jaws were tight.

"Forget that! You need more?" Pete said, looking right at David.

David nodded. "Let him straight back. Everyone block in two directions away from the center. Get ready for a short pass."

"BREAK!" They barked in unison.

Bob Lundberg took the bait. He went straight for David. David acted like he was going to pass a long bomb over Bob's head, but ran up on him. Bob jumped up with his arms overhead to block the pass. David shoved his knee into Bob's crotch, smashing into his thigh and then up. As Bob came down, he looked folded over. David made sure his shoulder pad met Bob's descending chin. Bob rolled off David's hip and slumped to the ground. David found Weasel at the twenty-five yard line, another first down assured. His thirty yard bullet pass was a wonder to the cadre of attending press, who watched the game with the scouts that came to recruit for the colleges.

Dr. Richman, an independent reporter on the sidelines, snapped the action. He was duplicitous. He also worked for the university that wanted to see if David was worth looking into. *Ballet, fire hydrant, rhinos.* He sketched the words as best as his arthritic hands would allow. He would send in his new film, T Max to the press service and phone in the story.

The huddle reconvened.

"Pete, can you manage the other idiot? I want to run up on him," David said, getting close to Pete's face.

Pete stood, glancing toward the medics removing Bob from the field.

"Like what? Hold him down so you can stomp his nuts? You got some ill going on, Double D man. Really ill." Pete, the second tallest and definitely the strongest, was also one of the fastest on the field.

David motioned for the rest to get close and spoke when they were touching shoulders.

"Okay make a hole on the right. Pete will break off and go left."

"BREAK!" They yelled in unison and waited for the game to restart.

"PLAY BALL!" The older referee shoved a young defense coach back to the Pumas' side with the help of their head coach.

David scanned the backfield as he took position behind the center.

"Down. Ready. Pull!" He took the ball snapped at him and feigned a pass. He ran side-to-side, throwing off the read the defensive backs were trying to get. His offensive line collapsed quickly. Their players were bigger and faster, except for Pete, who toyed with a running back waiting for the call.

"BREAK! BREAK… NOW!!!"

Pete shoved him to the right and came back to the left to make sure the hole was wide open. David was less than a full step away. His perfectly planted foot turned his whole body into a ram. He crashed his shoulder upward into the defensive back's ribs, lifting him off the ground. He heard his lungs evacuate and the mouthpiece pop out. He would have heard the cracking of ribs except the melee of clashing plastic and the roar of the crowd drowned everything out but his thoughts. The other player toppled like Bob as David ran the ball in for the Rangers' first score.

The second quarter was half over. David now stood on the sidelines, his coach quiet. The Rangers' field goal made the score even.

"Coach Johnson," David said to the head coach. His mind began to race then hyper focus. Both stared at the field.

"David." The coach floated.

"Well, sir, unlike the other time in the beginning of the season, we could win today and go on to regional." David waited to see if the coach would actually listen to him. The Pumas were gaining yardage, but too slowly. He kept a half gaze on the coach's face. *Oh God, he is going to listen!*

"Go on." The coach nodded to him.

"I've noticed the passing game is as bad as usual. They keep running the ball in. They get really tired around the fifty. So, I'm thinking get aggressive at that time, take the ball or force downs so we get possession. I can make touchdowns from there." David waited a minute, observing another short run. "Those receivers are missing. The good ones."

"Nice observation, David. Yeah, the twins are in Europe with their parents. We got stomped so bad last time, I guess they just didn't care." The coach remained silent for a minute, watching the game. "So what do you really see here?"

With his helmet off, wiping his head with a towel, David scanned the field. His mind became a focused fire. "The right side is strong, but very slow. Our defensive backs could crash the line together. One hits the QB, the other takes the ball and downs it or runs it in if he can. Whatever. I get that ball and it's touchdowns from here on out. No shit." David put his helmet back on.

The coach's face lit up. He pulled over the defensive coach, and they began to talk. The conversation turned loud. The coach said "Not like you have a great plan, do it."

The Rangers had possession at the 35 after a turn-over. The huddle came in very close to David. The next target, Woodley, a Puma running back, screamed taunts.

"Get on back hea, bitch! I own you, boy! Ya bitch! Make ya my own!"

David looked up at his player's faces.

"He's next." He turned to Pete.

Pete's expression was bland. "He's next for what? He's faster than anyone else. By far, he is the fastest. You got Nike messenger of gods out there in cleats, David."

David brought his face closer to Pete. "Notice the bandages on his hand?"

One of the other players said "He gets that by punching others. He hit me on the back of my helmet."

David turned to him. "Not any more. I know he won't go near Pete, so open a hole on your side. Left side fade back fast. BREAK!" They yelled with him.

There were disadvantages to David's build. He was stocky, not lanky. It made him a poor choice for quarterback. He had powerful legs, the strongest on the team. His lungs never let him down, his heart could get out and push it was so strong. Woodley was about to find out what 'turn on a dime' meant.

The center snapped the ball and the lines clashed; the left side faded back toward David like he wanted. He made a hole by bouncing off a Puma lineman and headed straight up the middle of the pocket where Woodley waited. He feigned twice and got past him. Woodley was suddenly in hot pursuit of David.

David made full strides until his speed reached a no return limit. He saw virgin turf and ran as quiet as he could. His ears picked up the steps and heavy breathing of Woodley. When he thought Woodley would go for the stick by straightening his body and lunging at him with arms out and shoulder pointed toward his back, David turned mid-stride and spun around.

Woodley was already committed. He flew through the air like a deformed Superman. He could do nothing as David made himself an instant pillar against which Woodley was throwing himself. David turned slightly as he landed, catching Woodley just below the rib cage. He folded over and back up as David shoved against him with everything he had. Woodley flipped over David's shoulder. As he started to land on his feet, David lunged low and hit hard just above the collarbone, knocking the wind out of Woodley and out of the Pumas. The game soon ended. The Rangers took home a victory of avarice.

David's father ran up on him. "That's game over, man!" He slung a drunken arm around his shoulder. "Way to fuck over the northern cousins, my man!"

David broke away without even looking in his direction. "Okay, Dad. See you at the house." He melted into the crowd and headed for the showers.

Two older men on the sidelines with cameras talked about the game for the first time despite standing next to each other.

"Are you Mackie?" Dr. Richman asked.

"Am I that famous?" Mackie put a hand out to Dr. Richman.

"Afraid so. I heard about this David Dryer. Never saw him play before. A real overlooked gem. Throws a bullet. Never saw such a ferocious player." Dr. Richman shook his head as he spoke.

Mackie's bushy white eyebrows raised up like he was trying to pull his old skin tight. "Oh, that's the half of it. It was a family feud out here tonight. I'm surprised there wasn't a riot. Two of the guys he downed in the pocket were cousins. The other he didn't know, but he took him out anyway. No one ever played like David. He's slower, shorter and stronger than any quarterback I know. He also has a gun like no one else. With a proper line, he will gain yardage. No doubt."

Dr. Richman nodded in agreement. "I never saw anyone turn on a dime like that. His forward speed won't impress anyone. If he carries this rather thin team to state, he will get recruited everywhere. Probably will after tonight, anyway. Everyone else came out to see the three from the Pumas. They're done. In two weeks, David's going to be in the hot spotlight."

The two men walked off the field, chatting. The field and surrounding bleachers emptied quickly. A short time later, the small town of Leduc became swollen with angry, drunk relatives.

———

Dr. Fisher was on patrol. He had retired to Leduc, opening a small clinic primarily to assist his dear friend Gahl, the town pastor, with his charity work. He always delighted in the reminders that more came with the package. As the 'town doctor', he possessed the authority to bring in more help or to transport serious cases to the county hospital. He kept walking, deliberately scanning in every direction for drunk trouble-makers. He spotted a pickup full of northern losers looking for a fight. A strong breeze, Gahl in the middle of it, moved past him.

David's father, Harry, threw an empty beer bottle at the pick-up truck of the offensive Lundbergs.

"Ya fuckin go home! It was all settled, bitches! Ya get!"

Gahl grabbed Harry right off his feet. "Over here, my man, over here!"

Harry swung around to hit Gahl in the face; the hand of Gahl quickly absorbed his smaller fist.

"Ya fuck off too, man bitch!"

Gahl was a foot taller and wider than Harry. He was also far more sober.

Dr. Fisher stepped up just in time to see Harry fall backwards. Out cold. "Bring him to the clinic." When Gahl looked at him like he was next, he said, "I said you. I mean now!" He held his ground, leaning back to keep his gaze locked onto Gahl's face.

Gahl did as instructed. Honking, yelling, swearing came from the pickup truck. Dr. Fisher motioned Gahl toward the clinic. Gahl dragged off Harry.

"Hey, that shit has to pay for my windshield!" shouted the Lundberg behind the wheel.

Dr. Fisher walked up to the passenger side window, leaned in, and made eye contact with the driver. "There are two ways of leaving. Right now, before my friend the Sheriff puts your hide in the county lock up. Or next week. I know you don't live here."

The stunned driver clenched his teeth and spittle came out while he swore through the gaps.

Dr. Fisher caught up with Gahl at the clinic.

"Put him over on that cot." Once Gahl followed his order, he put a blanket over the snoring drunk. "I know we're raising David. Do you mind if we do it right?"

Gahl spun around and stood tall. "Some of us are doing the heavy lifting here. I don't mind. It's my assignment. I get that. Don't jump on me about doing the dirty work you can't or won't...."

Dr. Fisher nodded, feeling a bit lost, not just sick and chilled by what happened on the field. "It is the cycle of violence we need to break. You told me when a young man first kills in combat, he has two ways of going. One way is enjoying it. I'm worried that's what we might have here."

Gahl made sure Harry's airway was clear, finished cleaning his face, and then worked a pillow under his head. "Infuriating crap pile," he said, poking hard at Harry's chest. "He has had a taste. I'll ask him when we talk. I think he'll let me know. I promise no preaching. I will listen and let you know," he said.

Dr. Fisher drew in his first deep breath since the game and released his thoughts. "His strength unites many. Please make us strong in Your ways to teach and nurture him as You see fit." Peace seemed to flood the room and so warmed him.

Gahl caught up to David, who was walking slowly toward the gas station with his head bowed. "Hey, David, everything is fine with your dad. Dr. Fisher will watch him tonight. Nothing serious. Let's make sure you eat." He redirected David with a hand to his shoulder.

They went to the Corner Cafe. Mrs. Milnarcheck emerged from the restaurant with her daughter Jan, who ran up to David. "David! You were awesome!"

"Jan! Please go straight home." Her mother was never harsh. Jan walked away, looking shame-faced.

"David, your mother..." Her tone was low and absent its normal reserve.

Gahl stepped between them. "I got this. Dr.. Fisher's orders, okay?"

She watched David's face. He looked at her with dejected eyes. She glanced back at Gahl with fear and anger in her expression. She turned slowly and walked away. A mild breeze removed her clean smell and brought in the musky scent of newly plowed fields.

Gahl and David sat opposite each other in as quiet a booth as the Corner Cafe allowed. It was oversized for just the two of them, making conversation more difficult. Gahl spoke first. "Sometimes it's necessary to kick some asses, David. That was a real animal you let loose on the field. What do you think about what happened?"

David stared deep into the mid-western night through the window. A few people looked in his direction with a mix of fascination and horror. Gahl shot back a quelling look.

David sounded parched as he said, "I told the coach we could win. He listened to me, and he followed my ideas. That's how we won, Pastor Gahl. Me and Pete are nowhere near enough against the bigger teams. The Pumas were the hardest to play against. We can go all the way to regional and beyond, if we play smart." David's focus shifted back out to a thousand yards distance. He arched his eyebrows and unclenched his fists before he turned to Gahl. "It's like I was a coach for a minute. Can you imagine... me coaching? My miserable dad... he..." His words trailed off.

Gahl, quick to respond, locked his gaze on David. "You will write your own future. You'll make a great coach when you're ready. You're a natural leader, David... compassionate and understanding." Gahl felt his appetite come on full force. He would tell Dr. Fisher that the desire to kill could be separate from the killer instinct. David, he felt certain, would not surrender to hate and avarice.

The next morning David sat alone eating breakfast. It was a hungry man lumberjack breakfast; the biggest they made. He needed it and didn't bother digging into his empty pockets. Long ago, Gahl made it possible for David to walk into the Corner Cafe at any time and be served a meal. After breakfast, he stepped out into the mid-western morning and headed for the bus stop one block down. It was such a short ride to school, he often preferred to walk. That wonderful clean smell he loved faded through the morning musk of the fields.

Little Jan Milnarcheck sheepishly looked up at David as she passed him on her way into the restaurant ahead of her mother. The clean smell and safe space stopped right in front of him. She looked into his eyes and placed her hands on his shoulders. He was unsure as to whether or not he was about to get lectured. She spoke calmly, the way he was accustomed. "There is so much love surrounding you. I know after you leave here and find yourself alone, you will remember this town as your home and us as your family." She placed a warm, soft palm against his face.

"I won't forget." His hands locked together, he nodded quickly.

She wrapped her arms around him in the way she had so long ago, when he'd been a hollering boy angry at the world for taking his mother too soon. He breathed in the scent of her, so much like his mother's: clean, safe, and warm. She held him until he began to relax. "Okay, David, see you Sunday for sure." She released him, following after her daughter without a glance back.

He felt warmed but now empty. *Moving on.*

David caught up to John near the bus stop. David appeared cheerful when he walked up to John, who was tall, black, and one of the fastest humans on earth. They were as much brothers as two boys could ever be when born into different families. John was stately, calm, and did his homework. David listened carefully to anything John said, and it helped him maintain a B average in his classes.

"My brother, you don't look so ass-kicked as I would have thought." John smirked, causing a dimple to form along the deep crease on the side of his mouth.

David straightened up. "Dish out more, my man! That's the fat secret." *Thank God for John.*

They boarded the bus. Pete sat in the back, saving two spaces for them like always. As he walked to the rear David noticed the other students avoided his gaze. They stared straight ahead like it was an order not to acknowledge the pariah.

"The hell..." David trailed off.

Pete looked directly at David with a furrowed brow and serious expression. "Cracker-ass northerners were tearing around in pick-ups last night." Pete was brown; no one, not even he, knew why. He was so large, giving him a seat meant for two was just practical. "They say your daddy was beat up, man. Them sophomores are scared. They heard rumors of more people coming tonight because of what you did. You might want to..."

John cut him off, stood and looked at each face. "There was one, repeat, one pick-up in town last night. David's dad went to the clinic after Pastor Gahl took him there from falling down. Everything has been settled. You guys just think about the Rangers going to state for the first time ever, all because of David and Pete here..."

The driver cut John off. "YEAH, MAN, PREACH IT UP!!!! SSSSTAAATTEEEE!!!!!" The driver pulled the air horn all the way from town into the high school after he made an unnecessary detour through the county parking lot for the courts, hospital, and motor vehicles department. He hollered, "STATE, STATE, ALL THE WAY TO STATE! RRRAAAANGEERS!" while pulling the air horn until pedestrians waved back. He did the same in the high school parking lot, transforming a group of students into a happy mob.

David turned to John and Pete, beaming at both and unable to speak the words in his heart. He stood tall and took long strides to the front of the bus, smiling and nodding at every student. Pete looked worried. John nodded, reassuring him that all would be okay.

"I got this one, John. RANGERS!!!" The crowd erupted as the driver again pulled the air horn. "We are victorious! We shall reign in glory and go to STATE!!!" The crowd surrounded him. Pete was almost dragged off the bus. John pushed.

The three of them were taken to the principal's office after students failed to stay in first period, David told to tone it down until regular classes ended. "State, state, state," was quietly murmured all over campus for a week. If one student started it, the rest joined in.

A fire swept through the other players, every game fought for and won. The world was coming to Leduc. David wasn't ready.

2
THE BIG LEAGUE

David's sudden status as a football hero had serious drawbacks. He always thought that the path to your doorstep would be paved in a nice straight line, but it proved to be the more of a crazy quilting of ants on crack and searching for dropped morsels. His head reeled from reporters delaying him from getting breakfast and accosting him at the bus stop. Recruiters hung out at Pete's garage and intermingled with the reporters.

On a dreary, cool morning, David stood with John and waited for the bus. "What a mess," he said noticing Johns placid face growing a smirk. "The fff!!!" A presence behind David made him spin around.

A small man with deep wrinkles stood behind them. "Am I supposed to quote that?" Wrinkles became laugh lines when the man grinned wide.

David bolted straight up. "That's what I mean, who the fff…"

John cut him off. "This is Dr. Richman, David. My dad and Gahl both know him."

"Rich-man here, John!" He beamed. "My, you're as stately as your father! Glad to see academic acorns don't fall far from the tree."

David extended his hand. Dr. Richman took it. David, noting the bent, puffy fingers, gently squeezed.

"Well, sir, sorry about the reaction. I've had strangers crawling all over me. Gonna find them up my ass soon. Yep, John here is amazing with books. He's the fastest man on the planet, outruns my bullets. Sorry we never played together, but he likes track and field. We're going to university together." David felt proud to say that.

Dr. Richman tossed up his eyebrows. "That's a tall order, Double D man. How do you think you're going to drag him along?"

"Well, sir, in three days I've had enough offers to cover everything anywhere. All of them overlap where John is going, so that's the deal. If I get a big offer that does not include my brother here, well… fuck 'em." David shrugged and glanced at the oncoming bus.

Dr. Richman looked at John, then at David. "Okay. Well tonight, Head Coach Saltier has a meeting with you. I'll explain that condition."

"I like you, Dr. Rich-man! You're the kind I trust. So, no offense?" David patted him on the shoulder.

"None taken, Double D man! Plain spoken and fair warning and all!" Dr. Richman's smile broadened. He managed a crooked wave to both as they took the bus for the three-minute ride to school.

On the bus, David and John sat next to each other in the back, Pete lounging in his own bench seat.

David turned to John. "So what is stately, John?"

"A description. Like the way someone looks if they're royalty or the president." John shook his head as though it did not apply to him.

"Hey, Pete, John here is stately. I never knew what his description should be, but it works, no?" He beamed at Pete, waiting for confirmation.

"Yes, that's quite the adverb, John. Do you have a license for such an accolade?" Pete smirked.

John sat up straight and looked far ahead, as though above it all. "Doth ye challenge me status, Brutus?"

Pete leaned back and raised his voice. His ape like arms stretched out wide. "I doth dither on wither ye earned it or by inheritance ye donned it sans effort. For ye sound sage and yet from practice all can be so trained." Pete tried to hold back a laugh.

A long pause drew in the attention of the seats around the three of them. John finally spoke. "It's known ye dither for me as to wither. It would be from ye bescumber habit nay so fervent, but that it sprays into the wind, so blown to ye!"

Everyone knew it was time to laugh, because Pete went into hysterics. Not too many people could say you throw poop into the wind and right back on yourself the way John could. They both relished the Elizabethan language, often taking the lead roles in Shakespearian school plays.

David waited until the laughter subsided. The bus pulled into the school parking lot. "So this adverb thing, writers use that?"

John patted his shoulder. "Yes, my man. Adverbs are the ones with the 'ly's.' Good recognition."

David felt happy and content. "Glad I'm not a writer. Too many rules and so on. Hey, Pete, what school you going to?"

"Ah, man, the one out in California. They can give me an MFA with sculpture, just like I want. All I gotta do is play some ball and throw discus and shot put for track. Easy breezy, my man. Where you going? Lots of choices for an all-star!"

"With John. I don't really care. It won't matter. I wonder if the three of us could go get MFA'd together?" He looked at John, who was gathering stuff for school.

"The world is wide open. I have one-tenth the offers of either of you, but they are all in the bag so it's just a matter of choosing. Glad to know David is also on all the same lists, even for the one school that has no football."

Pete smiled. "No one could ever see you two separated. I dunno, you're like two-thirds Three Stooges or something. Gonna miss you guys, sort of."

John looked ahead, smiling broadly. "Too bad we can't take the third with us."

"Cut!" David said.

They got off the bus and faded into the campus.

———

The living room in John's house was the largest in Leduc. Four couches. Two faced each other, fit five normal adults each, and were paired off to face each other. There were end tables and lamps. Just above two ceiling fans with lights kept the space well lighted and comfortable. They were separated only by a Persian carpet. David knew that it was where important conversations took place. The other two surrounded an open area near the entrance and those faced the long space between the couches where the elders, along with David and John, sat. Young adults were seated at the other two and children played on the open floor until Mr. Kemp motioned that discussion would begin. Everyone went quiet. Fifteen or so people could be in there and it was felt cozy; past beyond twenty-five sitting and standing made it difficult to traverse the room. It always reminded David of a hotel lobby. Gahl and John's father sat together with Coach Saltier and an assistant coach. They were almost touching, thanks to Gahl taking up the space of a man and a half.

Opposite them were John and David. Their couch was empty it seemed, compared to the two boys. David scanned left to right, Pastor Gahl was nearly six and a half feet tall, slightly pudgy, very broad in the shoulders, and as red and white as one can be naturally. John's father was nearly as tall, always in a suit, had sleek facial features, a pointy chin, and was the shade of ebony. Then there was the irritated looking coach, Saltier, with that windbreaker and hat on like he'd forgotten he was indoors. His assistant to his left looked pleasant but also had the countenance of someone who wouldn't linger.

John's father talked about Dr. Richman, about how they were both friends who had known each other through MENSA for a long time. He, along with Gahl, had brought David to his attention. They discussed academic subjects, wondering out loud if the University would be the right one for both boys.

Head Coach Saltier sat upright, his posture almost exaggerated, as he attempted to dominate the room. He tried to speak with finality as he said, "I can't make a package deal, David. Everyone will understand wanting a quarterback with such heart and backbone..."

David snapped, "Because your team has no line. It's a meat grinder out there. You don't have a line, because the university went for passing games."

Saltier was quick. "I have the fastest line in the league. I got them nimble. They listen to me. That's what I need, players who listen. David, you don't have the statistics to make a lot of demands. You're too short and slow..."

"...And a gun that'll drill a hole in someone over 60 yards away!" Gahl exploded with laughter, shaking the walls and startling the children. David's father backhanded him on the knee.

David added, "I can smash over a can at 60 yards and punch holes past any line. My bomb is, within a yard, RE–LI–A–BLE! John decides where I'm going. I don't know about making pro, but I do know I have to make a deal to get a degree I can use to at least work for the county when I come home. If I end up all fucked over and can't do shit for nothing else…" John slapped his knee. "John is the man you need to make a deal with. Sorry about the language, Pastor Gahl."

"Normally, David is quite polite." John's father studied Saltier. His expression made David shrink a bit.

Saltier looked around. "Okay, so what is it? The deal, I mean."

As he spoke, his assistant coach handed him a Pee-Chee folder. Saltier looked inside of it.

John drew in a slow breath. "You have an academic program that I find quite suitable. I gave your assistant what I needed and the list provided by Pastor Gahl for David. Pastor Gahl is taking the place of David's father and can sign in his absence. Your assistant said he would phone it in." John's voice drifted off.

Saltier looked over the brown bi-fold and lifted his head. "All right, I wonder if this can work." His assistant tapped him on the knee and nodded.

He looked back at the two as if they were in some sort of trouble. "I guess I can welcome the two of you to university life. Orientation is next week. Plane tickets for two round trips coming up."

David stiffened, distress like a surge of electricity coursing through him. He appeared mortified.

John spoke up. "We take the train."

The assistant nodded yes as he made a stirring motion with his index finger pointed straight up. The room became empty.

———

A few days later, an early Saturday evening found John, David, and Pete at the county fair. The sun was setting and strings of lights drooped from pole to pole. Gaul made sure David had money in his pocket for a job he would surely forget to remind him to do later. Little Jan was there, anxious as always to be near her self-appointed big brother.

Mrs. Milnarcheck allowed Jan to run up to him. "Wow, what are you guys doing? Are you going to college for real, David? How far away is it?"

He cut in before it became 50 questions. "Well, Jan, we are going to a university, which is bigger than college!" He beamed at her. She could only smile and blink in return.

John was quick to get involved. "Is that any way to treat a family member, David?"

Turning to Jan, John smiled softly. "Hi, Jan. What brings you here?"

Her mother walked up, a question in her eyes for David, and smiles for John and Pete. "We're just getting out and meeting her friends a bit later…"

A loud man and the ringing of a bell interrupted her.

"A prize for only five rings! Look yonder, three stronger men there could never be! What about winning something for the ladies, men?" The man was slight, wiry in frame and loud in mouth.

David glanced at Mrs. Milnarcheck and then her daughter. Both looked at the man with a big mallet. *They had that clean smell; it cracked right through the popcorn,*

BBQ, and fried food. The wiry man demonstrated his technique.

David noticed the crack of the wrist when he let the large mallet fall after lifting it up over his head. Zzzziiiip… BING rang the bell as the weight shot up a long, loudly painted board. "Well, fellas? We can't let that go unnoticed. John, you first."

"To show how it's not done?" John looked tense.

David got close to John's ear. "It's bait, my brother. Pete will pooch it, too. Just trust me on this…"

John paid a dollar for three swings; the mallet fell and the weight came up short three times.

"Oh, my! Where is the champion for the ladies?" The man's voice grew even louder.

Pete took the bait. The mallet made a swooshing sound going over his head. The ground shook three times from the pounding. The weight went up less each time. He began to look as exasperated as the little man looked calm, taking two swings and ringing the bell twice.

David felt like the trap was ready; he walked up and confidently gave the little man a dollar. "Five in a row for the polar bear. The one the size of the girl with red hair." In quick succession, David rang the bell three times; the third time, one-handed.

"It's 50 for the polar bear. They make 'em out of real fur."

"Oh, yeah. Rabbit fur, I know…" David handed him another dollar.

The mallet went over his head and fell. The bell rang even louder than before. "Ladies and gentlemen! Step up and let me show you the simple trick of ringing the bell every time! Notice how I let the…"

The man bumped David on his way to handing Jan the bear. He frowned while shoving David to one side.

Pete tried not to roll across the ground while fighting fits of laughter. "How could anyone get tired of you, man!"

Mrs. Milnarcheck helped Jan carry the huge, soft bear and permitted her daughter to hug David excitedly. He began to cringe. He was twice as tight on the inside as the grip from little Jan. He forced a smile. Mrs. Milnarcheck let it go on for a minute. She stroked the soft and realistic fur on the bear. She hugged David and the boys and then managed to persuade her daughter to come with her. They disappeared into the crowd.

The carnival was barely clean; country clean one might say. Unlike the nearby city, the dirt in Leduc was safe; it grew things; it was nurturing. So a thin dusting of it over everything was okay. The drooping wires on which round bulbs hung began to swing gently. They were bright and white amidst the mid-western night. It was a clean night. Not like the city where the air became fouled by the moisture of one too many bodies stacked inside of buildings, producing an unnatural fog as it clung to the floating brake dust and burned fuel. *City fog is illuminated like a huge, dysfunctional, filthy neon light that was just enough to pollute the view of the stars.* David thought about that and now the too-near future.

Pete would attend school on the outskirts of Los Angeles for several years. He was going to a place that accepted him as being brown in the way that Leduc did.

He stood straight and put his arms out with palms up like he was receiving something from heaven. "Oh, man. We are weeks away from leaving this podunk pleasure behind. I'm soaking this up."

John and David watched the huge man float on his feet and move gently like the breeze was actually drifting him about. They failed to notice Bob Lundberg.

"A nigger for a brother," Bob said with fiery eyes and clenched fists.

Normally faster and definitely stronger, but having been preoccupied with floating around like a balloon, Pete could not stop David in time. He was in Bob's face, ready with a fist faster than a wink. With perfect timing, Bob whipped a metal chain at David's head. It was rigid from the speed with which Bob swung it. David managed to duck down fast enough only to receive a grazing blow.

His first shot at Bob was clumsy and slid off an ear. Bob was able to whip the chain again. This time made he solid contact across David's back. David found his feet again and went for Bob as he flew backwards.

Pete grabbed Bob's free hand and sent him into a trio of trash barrels as if he were tossing a rag. The barrels were empty and gave way when the wiry teen flew into them. If they'd been full, Bob would have died.

A security guard was fast enough and smart enough to restrain Bob from getting up. Sheriff Bosche showed up in time to keep the fight under control. Many families from the North and South were there.

A short while later at the town clinic, David sat on the examination table. Dr. Fisher needed to see the depth of David's cut, and he ordered a nurse to buzz his hair to the scalp. Nineteen Eighty-Two was an odd time for very short hair. David sat on the exam table, fists tight on his knees, erratic breaths, chest heaving in anger, and jaw clenched.

Dr. Fisher spoke to David. "Nothing permanent, David. You're going to spend the next two days and nights with John's family so they can watch you. I told them what to do. Just listen and try to be calm."

His words melted through David's wall of self-protection. He stuttered, "I can... can't... won't... fff!! He dies! He, dies! Dead, fucking dead, Bob!"

Dr. Fisher stayed calm. "You're a bigger man than that now, David. So many people look up to you. Jan and all of the younger kids. David, please tell me you can think about them, too?"

David pulled in such a deep breath, it forced him to sit up straight from the hunched over, wolf-man like state. The words cut in like ice. "Am I really that bad?"

Dr. Fisher took a moment to finish dressing the wound, then looked directly into David's face. "No, David. This is normal for people who hold back and do the right thing. You're a good man."

Like the truth from God, David let it soak in, wrap around his bones, and radiate out. Dr. Fisher was right.

A short while later Dr. Fisher spoke at length with John's parents about how to keep watch over him day and night. He explained some signs and symptoms that should make them call immediately. He felt suddenly funny talking to John's father that way and fumbled an awkward apology. It was smoothed over with brandy in the living room and a long intellectual talk the kind only a few could have. He left when he realized Mr. Kemp was doing the reassuring.

Over two days, John's family refused to take their eyes off of him, even when he slept, per Dr. Fisher's instructions.

David focused on regaining control over himself. He opened his tired deep blue eyes. Confusion. He was lying on his side in a guest room that he recognized as being in John's house. He felt a presence near the bed and began to focus. A small, dark, cherub face stared back at him. She was just tall enough so that her shoulders were the height of the mattress. Her gaze was like that of a soldier on vigil.

His awakening caused her expression to turn to surprise. She ran from the room to report his change in status. Mrs. Milnarcheck came in, sat on the bed's edge, and stroked his brow. He drew a deep breath as she spoke, and relaxed in the clean fragrance.

"Hi, David. Do you know what day it is?"

"I smell Sunday afternoon." He felt peaceful and did not mind her attention.

She smiled warmly. "That's right. Dinner is early today. On Tuesday, you can go back to school. How do you feel? Want to come out?"

He began to stir and tried to roll out of bed. "Yeah, eat. I can help."

She helped him to the table.

He ate with John and some extended family. Jan was allowed to sit next to him and help place food on his plate.

A state away in a cold bed at a top-rated hospital, Bob Lundberg lay on a hospital bed. Anger oozed from his pores. An MRI cleared him from any permanent damage. It also confirmed that he could no longer play football. His mind went over every possible mistake.

He can stand his ground. He can stop fast. He is hard to damage. He will be hard to kill. Take it. Take his legacy and his inheritance. Play nice and take his birthright. Murder David slowly….

Nurses chatted about music-television and popular bands. They did not even look Bob in the eyes as they went over his medication, checking his fingers and toes per doctor's orders; nothing more and nothing less.

Bob's father had made an ass out of himself the day before. Everyone was cautious not to upset the congressman's son or to make any medical mistakes. Bob lay alone in his private room stocked with cable TV, flowers, and candies he was not allowed to eat. His mother was at a social engagement, accepting empty sympathy from phony friends as if it were real.

———

The next few weeks passed quickly for David and John. John had traveled to and from the university campus without David, mapping the layout he would need to help him become oriented. When and where to get to class, a proper head's up regarding tutors who would learn to step back and just talk David through what he actually needed to know.

The campus represented a cacophony of sounds, and would likely become a serious headache until it became his home. It would be the biggest place David had ever seen.

A small parade was held in honor of John and David as they stood in the back of an old stake bed truck. It was a 1948 Ford F5 restored to its original condition by Pete, who owned the corner gas station and garage. The truck made its way around the streets while John's father sat in the front, making sure the awooga horn, not original, was in constant use.

Just two miles away, where the highway and railroad tracks came together, the truck stopped to let out the small town heroes. The small crowd slowly disbanded as the sun set.

Jan was allowed to give both of them a hug. She was hard to let go of, David thought as she clung tightly to him. "Oh, I'm coming back. Look at you, becoming such a big girl now!" David reached down to remove her gently from his mid-section.

"You're going so far away!" she cried, once more burying her face in his stomach.

Her mother's hands were on one side of her red, tear-stained face while the other was firmly planted against David. The three of them held each other until David relaxed and hugged them back.

———

The midwestern night settled over the landscape as everyone else left John and David at the old train station. John knew better than to strike up conversation. He saw how terrified David was as he sat slightly hunched over. His hair was growing in. John thought David looked like someone just out of prison or the Marine Corps.

He was happy to be David's friend. He could be such a funny, boisterous, pain-in-the-ass. He was genuine because he was not smart enough to lie. Getting him to say anything would help. "Hey, my main man. What ever happened to the poet?"

A long pause as David glanced toward John. "Like who, what poet do you mean?"

John looked up into the Milky Way. "The one you used to be, like the time that poem you wrote won the whole school contest not just fourth grade but like you beat out everyone including high school, the Japanese one."

David looked up, too. "The Haiku."

John nudged him. "Yeah. All about love, we love each other something…"

"Jeez John, get it right. Who has memory issues now?" David shifted in his seat and hung his head.

> "I like you
> You like me
> We like each other
> Love."

John felt the smile on his face and thought David must have the same. "I hope you explore more of that talent. Eight years old and you kicked ass all over kids ten years older. Amazing, my man, amazing." He looked over to find David back to his hunched-over state.

It was a warm evening. The two would arrive in Los Angeles by morning. John wondered if David would like Olivera Street and Mexican food as he watched him with his fists tightly clenched, fighting a future that would come whether he wanted it or not. Aside from the anxious breaths escaping David, the train whistle was the only other sound. John sat just close enough to feel him shiver.

3
THE HERO DIES

Three weeks later John nearly danced around a sullen David. "You got everything worked out, my man!"

David nodded without looking at him. "I am grateful, John. It's just still a lot now."

"You have a ways to go, but don't look so beat down. You gotta lighten up." John bounded off with a group of mixed people, always popular and a friend to everyone.

David looked ahead and down without meaning to be arrogant. He used his hyper-focus to get to classes. It was easy to feel overwhelmed. He felt so lost. Being a sudden nobody hurt. Tutoring sessions were a huge relief. He fell in love with books on tape, and the quiet times were good. The library also had fresh air, something all of Los Angeles lacked. The air outside was a concoction of dried puke, burning tires, and sweaty anxiety. Nineteen Eighty-Two was a bad year for smog, and it was hot. David thought, *What the hell is this hot?* He was just steps away from relief when Coach Saltier caught sight of him.

"Hang on there, all-star!" The coach stepped into David's path.

"Yes, Coach." David floated mournfully; he was so close to his sanctuary.

"You're the front man now." Saltier got right up into his face, his own looking grim. "A car accident has left me without a quarterback and two others. The entire offense is gone now. You're taking over. Sorry, David, but we're all in shock right now. You'll need to do something to get the team behind you. Meet me in my formal office, the one by the dean, after 5:00 p.m. Just try to remember to make a strong effort to support your team. See you then."

The coach turned and left a stunned David, who swung away from the library and headed back to the noisy campus. He immediately searched for Absolon, the wide receiver who, like him, had been brought on as a second string player. They'd only scrimmaged, and now they would learn to be brothers of the field.

Absolon was not difficult to find. Something about him reminded David of

John except the funny accent and a bit more meat around taller bones. He was 6'7, just slightly uncoordinated, and powerful. He, like David, was a wild card, his mother from Pakistan, father from Uganda. His name meant 'reward of the gods.' Girls flocked around him David didn't believe it was for his looks. Absolon was flummoxing, really, and not much of a talker. He walked in a way that exaggerated his height. David knew his persona was part of his culture.

This Goliath needed to be brought on board now. "Absolon, we are needing to make talking and things."

David's fearless dig made him smile. "Oh look, a quarterback is what they call such a small thing." Absolon could make himself laugh, and did often. A spare hand lowered to the top of David's head.

"Yo, lank." David quickly pulled out from under his enveloping hand. "It's insulting in some countries to palm someone on the head."

Absolon looked down in mock astonishment. "My goodness, so much talking but nothing done. Tsk. David, are you a punk?"

"I'm a who?"

"A punk." Absolon pointed to the buzz covering David's head. "I am seeing these on music television Billy Idol and such. I was wondering about the short hair."

David made motions like a cop would directing traffic. "Okay, ladies. I hate to break up the session, but I got to get through to Godzilla here and I'm short of time." The girls went off, looking a bit irritated.

"It's like this, Absolon. The whole passing game got into a car accident. Right now, you and I are it. The front line might as well be a drunken mud wrestling team. We have to learn to dance together and unify the team."

Absolon quickly agreed. David hadn't expected his reaction, but felt warmed by it.

"My goodness, David! Yes! Let's get as many players as we can and show the school that we are unified and can make a team. Also, the University has a dance coordinator who coaches professional players. What she has taught me is without comparison. Let's go see her, too."

Odd, David thought. This gargantuan dark man spoke like someone from deep Minnesota. He began to look around and used his loudest voice. "Football!!! I need a football!!! Hey, anyone, got a football?!" He motioned for Absolon to follow. He took his two-man parade through the campus and waved over anyone who looked in his direction. So many faces looked grim.

A 5 foot Asian man, wearing a tight, white T-shirt, gold chains, spiked hair with purple ends, and oversized glasses produced a brand new football. He gave it little twirls atop his fingers, walking up to David with a swagger and big grin. "Yo, Double-D man! The shiz iz up wit ya!"

David tried to process the one-man scene. "Pardon me, kid. Is that an actual pig skin we have there?"

The Asian man cocked his eyebrows up over his large framed glasses and produced a smiling, shocked look. "Cha! You sign it and give it back later. It's my pleasure, big D! I'm Tony. They call me 'Scratch' at the clubs."

David could not help but like whatever the hell this was. "Scratch, I accept your terms with indubitable enthusiasm!" He smiled and bowed a bit.

The ball was given a short toss to him. David pitched it at Absolon, who instinctively caught it with one hand.

"Aw man, a pitch? Dude, you gotta break it in betta then that!" Scratch said, shrugging his shoulders and pointing all his fingers downward.

David had no idea of what the hell all that meant. He smelled a challenge and motioned Absolon back a bit. He fired off a mild bullet. Absolon caught the ball like it was magnetically drawn to his hand.

"Oh, so we're powder-puffing now eh, David? Please don't embarrass us both with this pussy footing. Pepper now if you would." Absolon spoke with a huge smile adorning his face. He lobbed the ball back while running away a bit.

A large crowd grew shortly after Scratch pulled a bulky cell phone from his oversized back pocket. David felt the anguish he saw in some of the faces that gathered. For the first time, David accepted the entire campus as his new place to live. He felt like a leader and rocketed the ball toward Absolon. It whistled a bit after leaving his fingertips, which made a sound like gouging tree bark. Absolon caught it with both hands. The thud from the impact could be heard across the quad, which began to fill fast as morning classes were letting out. As if they had seen a large firework display, the crowd cheered in approval. None of them had ever been close enough to know the sounds of throwing footballs so fast. The whoosh of air, the breathy grunts. The ball came back to David slowly overhead by comparison to his delivery.

"Damn, bro! That's what it is! Yo bullet is the bomb!" The crowd laughed with Scratch. Some knew he was a musician and DJ, many more knew of his persona at the clubs.

David stood up straight, beaming at Tony *they call him scratch for some idiot reason.* "Okay, Scratch, this one's for you!" David faded back three steps and bounced forward one. He kicked his right foot forward, arching his upper body backward like he had seen in ballet. Like he was trying to reach for something up high his body began to whip forward and up. Memories flooded in complete detail within the tenths of seconds it took from planting his foot to snapping the ball forward. *Not a quarterback? Fuck you for sizing me up as a linebacker, Mr. Idiot Coach, sir.* His motions resembled that of a tennis player while serving, the ball heavy and wanting to leave the hand he kept over it. His deft grip on it allowed him to use fingertips as guides. Like someone who plays trumpet without looking, he could more or less press or relax a finger and change the height and direction. All four fingers were solid, this pass snapped straight out.

FOOoooSH snap! The ball screamed across the quad within feet of student's faces. Absolon caught the flat flying bullet and danced like he made a touchdown, nodding and hopping about, waving around the ball like a trophy.

A surprised looking Scratch beamed at David. "Shah, bro! Bomb?" Scratch got the crowd chanting, *bomb bomb bomb!*

"Bomb? ABBEY, GO LONG!" David retreated as far into the corner as the expanse of grass would allow. Absolon followed suit into the opposite corner. David threw with unneeded height. The crowd followed it all looking straight up then arching over. TOCK! Absolon received it after having spread his arms out wide. He looked back with a huge smile, tossing the ball to someone nearby. They threw it in David's direction. Two more tosses and David gripped the ball again.

"Bullet, buuuullet bullet, bullet, BULLET!!!" the crowd began to chant.

Absolon crouched down like a catcher for baseball. David was really starting to like him. The student's quickly arranged themselves along two sides of a path from David to Absolon.

He faded back, keeping his eyes forward. His body became a whip. "FWOOSH!" he exhaled. Anyone near him also heard the ball leave his hand. The whole crowd could hear the ball make the odd whistling sound as it barely got above head height then down to the waiting hands of Absolon. Tock was the sound when he caught it. The crowd erupted at the sight and sound of the off-field practice.

The lead cheer had gathered the three kings. They had just gotten back from visiting the boys who were in the accident. They walked up with Absolon and the football. The largest, Gordon, spoke. "Well, what in business have we got here? You gonna be the new man, little man?" Everyone looked little compared to Gordon, a gentle giant.

"I tell him he is little, because that is a quarter of a back, you see…" Absolon, at least, did not laugh at his joke.

"Mr. Huge, can my friend here have his ball back?" David motioned to Scratch.

Gordon's mouth was pursed on his large, dark, fat-cheeked face that looked like it belonged in an advertisement for baby food, and that forced out his lower lip. It was usually the face he made when forced to think more than average. He had to wonder about the little spiky, purple-haired Asian in a tight, white T-shirt wearing huge glasses and a fat gold chain. He reached out to him and turned over his hand, revealing the football.

"Psyche! Yo, can the three kings, Double-D Man, and Absolon sign it? That would be church, bro!" The crowd broke into laughter as Scratch made exaggerated nods and a big smile.

Someone poked David with a felt tip pen and motioned toward Scratch, and then the other four players.

David began to speak loudly enough for the whole crowd to hear while the other players signed the football and shook Scratch's hand. "I have a meeting with Coach Saltier. I think it would boost morale and help unify the team and school if some of you would come with me." He explained when and where.

Five p.m. came quickly. If David had asked beforehand if it was okay to bring with him a few hundred friends, he would have been told no. They arrived orderly. Noisy, but orderly. It took about an hour for them to finish filing by as the hundreds turned into thousands. Luckily for the administrators, the hallway could handle a crowd twelve wide. They started on one side of the building, climbed the half flight of stairs, and flowed into the other. Word had gotten out. For most who heard what was going on, just the fun of it was too much to resist. Others, emotional over the remaining injured players, felt grateful to have a place and time to grieve without shame.

THE GAME

Four brutal games into the season taught everyone that David Dryer was no fluke. For a quarterback, he was slow, short, and tough as nails. Sports writers used "Double-D man with a gun" to describe his bullet passes down the field. He could bomb the ball over the entire field to the waiting arms of Absolon, whose reach lofted off his 6'7" frame. It was impossible for one man to cover him. He was often doubled and tripled.

Football has its rivalries like Army versus Navy, and a number of blue blood and Mid-west annual contests that were older and more steeped in the psyche of the average fan. None was more popular and filled with infamy than the 'freeway series.' Barely a good bicycle ride separated the schools. David so frothed up both campuses with his mouth, police from five jurisdictions made their presence known.

He would stand on anything that got him seen by a crowd and start to preach.

"I can only say the fortunes of our way of life hang in the balance! Who would go forth from this institution, knowing that all was not done by you? As the philosopher of the Aegean said: Be not among them, but with them. Be not with them merely to observe, but as a victorious people reveal the true nature of your society as opposed to theirs. Do you hear me?! O brethren, where art thou? Can you let another day pass while your players march into contest? I say, no. Ask not what your team can do for you, but what you can do for your team! Graduate from this institution, knowing you deserve the victory of the field as much as the contestant who will endure it!" If television cameras were present, he would go on longer and get louder.

Coach Saltier and Richman tried to get him to tone it down. He did, sort of.

At the behest of law enforcement, the game was held in a neutral location, the Rose Bowl in Pasadena, California. Both teams were bused in, the stadium packed with an overflow topping-out near 90,000 fans. The game was streamed live on Air Force One, Ten Downing Street, and U.S. forces. The world watched. David's mouth was familiar around the globe.

It seemed so deep and cave like below the stadium. The locker rooms shook from the fans' roar above. They clapped and stomped in unison. It became a spectacle fueled by one over-the-top personality.

Coach Saltier tried to be heard, but the minds of each player focused on the rabid gathering. "Stick to playing the game and forget the noise." The coach tried to get into the heads of his players being made nervous by the thumping heard in the concrete catacombs below ground. "You guys look like your trying to survive Dresden..." The coach floated. He suddenly realized their thin knowledge of World War II. "That's it. Out we go. Captain, make this happen!" He was looking at David, who stood quickly.

"All right, seniors, that's enough rest. Let's kill people." David bolted up and headed out to the tunnel that led up and out. He looked over his shoulder, expecting the senior players to jog past him. They looked up at the light and kept a slow pace towards the noise. The 'three kings' of the offensive line motioned him to go ahead. Absolon was about 10 players back, waving him to lead the way. David laughed as he pulled on his helmet, clasped the strap, and jogged toward the sunlight into the deafening roar. *So born for this.*

The rest of the team hustled out behind him and broke to the left, heading toward their sideline. David went straight down the field and stopped at the thirty. *Field goals easy from here.* He spotted his colors in the stands. They took up half the stadium. He raised his hands together in their direction. They stood, yelling and cheering wildly. He turned to the other side, clenched his fists, squatted down and growled in their direction. They booed and growled back.

He went back to his side and then to the other until the entire stadium happily played the cheer and growl game. Three referees came over and started nudging him over to his side. Coach Saltier waited angrily, sort of.

As he approached his spot on the sideline, he noticed in the stands John Kemp, his life-long friend from Leduc, and Dr. Richman. They sat next to a small boy, a lighter carbon copy of a much larger man who had that Pacific Islander look with curly hair. They pointed their index fingers at him. He pointed back and made the 'number one' gesture. Forty-five thousand fans did the same as the man hugged the boy. They both beamed at David.

The game was hard fought and close to half time. The score was low and even. David managed to get a pass into the end-zone to the lofting hands of Absolon on their first turn with the ball. They scored first, which meant a strong likelihood they would win the game. The other team scored, neither making their field goal. *God, I just want to make another score...* The voice of Saltier and the offensive line coach took over his thoughts. Do not run with the ball.

The clock was running out, and it was third down with three yards to go for a first down. The three kings on his offensive line were amped. They were the only ones big enough to compete. The rest of the line was outweighed, but not outrun. That was one thing David could count on. *Like Coach Saltier said, they do what I tell them and they have speed.*

The ball snapped and David ran back within a collapsing pocket. Three linebackers pressured Absolon, making a bullet impossible. The pocket was collapsing to the right, making the free tight end inaccessible. *Not today, not now, no!* He screamed in his head louder than the fans. If David had been only three inches taller, he could connect with him, but the option was gone as fast as the thought occurred.

Time began to slow as he went over his options; then the line split opened like the Red Sea. Just to the right of the center, and flowing with the whole melee, a clean line and open space beckoned. The other team's defense poured all their effort into keeping David from running and Absolon from being available. Even a bomb dropped from the heavens was a lost option. In less than a wink, David bolted for the open turf and tried to block the coaches words. *Don't you ever run with the ball. They have killers out there down yourself in the pocket. NOT NOW A-HOLE!*

First down was five strides away. One, he was near the line. Two, he was over the line of scrimmage with only nine feet easily covered with three strides to go. Three, and the first down with a scolding from the coach for running with the ball was assured. Four, went into the ground. All the police and extra security had left out the possibility of a rodent making a home just past the 50-yard line.

Half of David's foot sank into its burrow and planted firmly. He stretched toward five, pulled his hip out through the socket and dislocated his knee. A lineman with his eyes on the prize of his life hit David at an angle chest-level high. This picked him straight up. Another lineman hit him from the opposite side. With David's leg locked straight, the blow snapped his femur. The other players fell onto him and each other, flexing David's knee the wrong way and hyper-flexing his back, and stopping all the pain below his mid-section.

The pile untangled, leaving David slumped over and face down. His foot remained in the hole, the obvious look of a leg broken in two places. One player grabbed his foot and pulled it out. Players on both sides tried to make sure he was okay. He heard the shouting for the players to move. Some said they'd heard snapping.

David's breathing was shallow and rapid, his mind reeling as he began to regain awareness. On his back, he saw faces from every direction. He was strapped and taped down to a board, helmet and all. Confusion reigned. He could hear the announcer talk about the uncomfortable silence. He drifted in and out of consciousness. He could not move, nor could he feel anything below his chest.

Three days later David roused in the hospital after the first round of surgeries. He tried to speak to someone he thought was a doctor. The man seemed like a real healer. "Am I dead? I don't feel hurt anymore." He tried to smile at the kindly presence. He felt the man tell him no. A gentle hand hovered over him. He felt the pressure of the bed against his back and the weight of a thin blanket. He felt so much better with him there. David hoped he would be back.

Was I floating away? Did he pull me back? God, was that your son? Could he please come back? Oh, how I wish I knew how to pray.

David fell back to sleep.

4

YOUR OWN PATH

A full week after his last major surgery David began to stir. He surveyed the long green curtains that surrounded him with foggy eyes. Directly over his bed, the drop ceiling was made of large, white tiles and light panels, not the metal bells with intense bulbs like in the operating room. He wondered where this was. There were not as much equipment surrounding him, and for once it was quiet.

For the first time in over a month, the amount of painkillers he was prescribed had been reduced. He could feel more of his body; hands were equally strong; left leg, foot and toes seemed about right to him except for some numbness. The lower right side of his back, through his crotch, down to his right foot were non-responsive. He knew they were there. He traced his free hand down his chest and over his crotch. The tight skin over well-defined muscles felt familiar to him. His body stopped sensing his hand's position as it traveled below his navel. As his fingers probed the area of his genitals, he felt no sensation. He did find, however, a long, thin tube protruding from the tip of his penis and the tape, which fastened it against him.

An IV tube was taped to his right hand. On the tip of his finger, a clip held something with a wire in place. He tried to see the path of tubes. He trailed the wires up and to the right; he saw that they were joined by even more coming out from his chest. Television screens monitored his heart rate, his breathing, and the distal oxygen sensor that came from his finger. In his drowsy stupor, he thought the machine was keeping him alive. A horror grew within him. He became overwhelmed by thoughts of never being able to play football or to run, and losing that which he felt defined himself as a man.

"So you're it, huh? The Robby Robot keeping me alive. I never asked for this, but I will stop it." He was still in enough of a stupor to make his attempts at unplugging himself feeble.

A petite, Asian woman walked in. "What you do? You, David, stop that now!" She grasped his left hand and tugged on his smock.

He turned to her lazily. "Not getting this right. Can you just unplug me? I want

25

to turn it off. That's all I really need."

"No, David. Why you say that? Such a good, young man. You can start everything again. There is lots of time for you to think what could be new and good for you. This is a great place. Listen to me, please."

Her name was Pech. Tiny, her shoulders just barely the height of the side of the bed. Her pretty, brown face wore a motherly countenance with warm assurance. David became transfixed on it as she told the story of escaping the Khmer Rouge and being the only immediate member of her family to make it out of Cambodia. She had considered herself lucky to be alive and fortunate that criminal thugs did not operate the overcrowded boat, which carried her to freedom.

As she continued to talk about the family who took her in and gave her a new life in this blessed country, David felt a new swell of emotion. An idea within took root. *To forge ahead and rise above this tragedy was also the way of a champion.* The sounds of familiar voices echoed in the hallway.

"Well, if you're gonna die, this is a hell of a place to let it happen. I mean, hey John, check the private room; someone is taking care of the little bastard now." Pech turned and locked eyes with Gahl, a sour look on her face as he walked in with John.

John cut in front and walked up to the bed. "I'm sorry ma'am. Let me apologize for my friend. We have all been together since childhood. I am John Kemp. This is Pastor Gahl."

Gahl bent down as much as his towering frame would allow. "Do excuse my salty language. It was only meant to give the meat slab,—I mean, our friend here— a bit of a stir." He had broad shoulders and a face to match, bright, white skin save for the ruddiness, and platinum hair like that of a horse's mane.

Pech let go of David's hand and faced John with a warm expression. "Oh, everybody know you, Mr. Kemp. You on the TV and cereal boxes. I am Pech. I take care of administration stuff. You and Dr. Gahl are on the contact list. Excuse me, Dr. Gahl. I can come back later." She picked up her attaché full of the casework she had for that day.

"Oh, let's allow the young ones to talk for a bit." Pastor Gahl and Pech went over by the door.

"Are you going to help us watch that young man, I hope?" Gahl asked pensively.

"Well sure, Dr. Gahl, but you are here now." She gripped her attaché case.

"To you, just Gahl. I can't stay. John has two Olympics to attend. I was hoping I could give you my direct number and receive status updates often." He calmly handed her his card.

"That would be very nice. I'd be happy to help, Gahl." She smiled.

Gahl returned to David's bedside.

"So, Red, when did we become a doctor?" David sounded perky.

"Boy, that story is longer than my..."

John cut Gahl off. "List of things to do today. David, we're here to make sure you don't beat up the physical therapist, and to have lunch with you out in the quad. Red thought it might be a good idea for you to see some sunshine." John spoke while stooping over the bed and pinching David on the cheek.

David's physical therapist Brian arrived. Once a champion downhill skier, he explained the physical therapy he would begin soon. John, Gahl, and David listened with rapt attention as Brian regaled them with his story of recovery after a nasty spill. He had been injured nearly beyond repair, so he empathized with his new patient, now a fallen athlete, too.

To his great relief, David learned the numbness and catheter were temporary. Once unplugged, an orderly helped him downstairs to an open lunchroom with view of a small indoor garden. The dining room was expansive. Green carpeting contrasted the oak furnishings. Windows three stories high reflected light between two buildings into an area two pick-up trucks wide. The fake waterfall fell into and flowed along a stucco-coated stream that ended up in a small pond. Careful observation revealed the landscaper's poor attempt at hiding the pond's plastic edges. The plants may have been real. The cheap goldfish certainly were, and they had plenty of algae to peck at.

"Wow, I have never seen nature faked so well," David cracked, propping himself up in his bed.

"Yeah, it's like being in a fishbowl with a view of another fishbowl. I just don't know if we're the fish or the cat," Gahl said.

"Perhaps we can enjoy the atrium." John said.

"It is really nice to see you two. John, did you make both U.S. teams now?"

"I did. Track and Bobsled."

Gaul poked John in the arm. "That's a fucker! What do they want with a skinny kid like you in a bobsled?"

John cocked up an eyebrow and sat tall with mocking sophistication. "It's quite simple, my dear man. I'm fast. My instructions are push hard, jump in, tuck down, hang on."

"What about all the screaming, 'Hey, this ain't natural, man!'" Still on drugs, David spoke loudly.

"David, did we finish our jello?" John sounded almost condescending.

Gahl smiled like a Cheshire cat. "So, the therapist says you'll be up and around soon, as soon as next semester. What are your plans or do you want to go on as a meat slab?"

"I really don't know. What do you do when it's all taken away?" David asked, his voice trailing off.

John looked at David and caught his eye before he spoke. "The field will call you one way or another. I know you, my brother. For you, it wasn't just some place to be or screw off. You made yourself into the player you are today. You can help others do the same. I think you will find it the most exhilarating experience of your life. I can't begin to tell you just how rewarding it is to hear someone say, 'You changed my life.' Every new dawn breaks for a reason. Trust me on this. Take it on when you are ready, just like that physical therapist did."

"I'm not you, John. No one is. I can't even go over this now." David put more jello into his mouth to try and ignore the conversation.

John came in close. "Not many people have your perspective. Just as the therapist lit a fire under you, you can inspire someone else to pull themselves out of a hole. Coming from you, there will be no doubt in your understanding and perseverance."

"I'll give it some serious thought, right after I can pee on my own again," David mumbled.

"How can I ask for more?" John appeared content to allow the conversation to end.

Gahl thanked God for John as the three of them went back up to David's room, where he would spend the next six weeks learning to stand up on his feet.

A new spring semester found the school's once greatest player making his way carefully down the long hallway. He was early to his next class. The rest of the students had not been let out yet. It was best, he thought, not to run into anyone as he hobbled along. His crutches were literal arm extensions. He felt ape-like using them. He waddled and wobbled one painful step after the other, trying not to fall. *It's a bitch to keep my backpack on.*

The concrete on the open part of the third level looked rather solid, he thought. Planting the crutch tips solidly made too much noise. The hallway's length seemed to grow in his mind as the mild tock-tock of the hard rubber tips broadcast his movements. The silent, solid hallway began to echo. Practicing one way and then another, he developed an Elephant's walk that allowed him to move along without making noise. It was kind of a rolling touch adding pressure to lift him just enough to keep his lower back from feeling too much pressure.

He had his classes carefully planned and spaced out. He could leave late from one class and arrive early to the next one so as not to be seen *crutching* around.

"There is my hero!" squealed the head cheerleader as she wrapped her arms around his neck for a bear hug.

So much for incognito, he thought. "What's with the business suit?"

"I was just giving a presentation on being your own positive role model. Now that's something you should start doing." She double-blinked her piercing, blue eyes.

She was Polish, beautiful, and funny. She had the kind of white skin that ignored the sun's efforts at tanning. The highlights in her naturally blonde hair were trendy, but not overdone and were well matched with her dark blazer open just enough to reveal a shiny, cobalt blue blouse, and closed just enough to emphasize the distance between her cleavage and the blazer lapels. A matching pencil skirt complimented the ensemble.

"How to get crushed in two easy lessons?" he asked.

"No. Let's not be a troll. When you figure out what your new life is going to be, the whole process will become an inspirational story for others. It really works, and it really helps people. It may be too soon, but I see you out there on the field as a coach. The players would really respect you. You could teach them from a player's perspective." She smiled.

He was not sure her positive tour-de-force was impenetrable. "Like learning body shop from a wrecked car?" David tried to act like he was late.

"That's the pain talking. You will know when the time is right. Just move toward that direction. Place one foot in front of the other. Don't rush. I'll be around." Her right hand cupped the left side of his face while she roughly kissed the other side.

She briskly walked away in heels that were professional yet sexy in the way that they accentuated her legs. He noticed just how good she filled out the skirt. What was that saying? Two cats fighting in a burlap bag? In this case, some kind of stretchy fabric that fit snugly yet still hid the panty lines if there were any.

He double-checked his mind's calendar for the date he would be able to return to complete and total function. The therapist said something about six months. *The sooner, the better,* his hormones barked loudly. The small pad over his penis meant to catch leaks barked back.

He arrived early to his Sociology class. Professor Englert was a world-class authority on Pacific Islander natives, and an insufferable football fan. He entered the small stadium style classroom with its wooden floors and fold-down seats. They were impossible with crutches for him to get in and out of without being awkward.

"David, you have to sit in front. It's the rules." A voice boomed from the opposite side of the room.

He hobbled his way toward the middle of the front row next to the stairs, took a seat, and found a way to prop his crutches up against the wood and over metal rail that lined both sides of the center aisle. It was glaringly obvious from the mismatched style that the railing was installed well after the room was finished. *Maybe front and center was a good hiding spot,* he thought wistfully.

The man behind the voice walked into the class from the side and down to the front row. A huge smile was plastered on his face like those you see in generic Christmas movies. "The state is exceedingly specific about the rules. You see, Mr. Dryer, it is much easier to rescue someone in your current condition from the front of the class. I am Professor Englert." He reached down and shook David's hand.

"Thank you, Professor Englert. I'll do my best not to cause problems." He gave the professor's hand a solid shake.

"Still strong and robust, I see. They snapped you like a carrot and twisted you up like a towel, but you're still fighting on. That's lion-hearted man!"

He was used to being a celebrity, but not in his current state. The professor's cheerfulness and enthusiasm brightened him up. "I guess that's what champions do. I don't know much else at this point."

"Now, that's what I like to hear! Mr. Dryer, in this coming semester we get to spend together, we will explore a whole world where men, just like you, get back up and stay up. In your reports I expect a first-hand account of crawling your way through the worst of times to living your dreams in the best of times. They won't need to be written if you care to do them verbally, and I know you can speak in front of a crowd." The professor even gestured finger quotes around the 'worst of times' reference.

David could not help taking an immediate liking to him.

"Most of the people in my course, David, are here because they have to be. I'd like to think that this course would help you see a part of yourself in others who have achieved great things. I know it sounds more like a history class, but that is the way I teach it. It's a beginning course. There is a bit of science, but keep in mind I'll always be available. I think you'll find as I did that sociology, which is really the literal study of others, is an encompassing technical art."

David shifted up in his seat, matching his growing mood. "You know, Professor, I've done a bit of that myself. I mean, you have to study the greats to become one yourself."

"That's exactly what I'm talking about, David. I am really excited about what you come away with in this course, and I sincerely look forward to your presentations. Do them your way. Yes, I think that'll be best."

As the classroom began to fill, so did David's mind. A thought began to overwhelm him. *You can change your mind. You can change your mind—if you want to.*

Since it was the first day of the semester, most of the classes were filled with outlines, calendars, required list of textbooks, and last-minute student additions into class in place of those who registered but did not attend.

The class finally ended. David sat patiently, waiting for everyone to leave. One student walked up, excited to see him and surprised he was back at it so quickly. Students began to form a short line in the middle stairway, waiting to say the same, wishing him the best, and appearing impressed and inspired.

Oh, that cheerleader had been right. Down to the bone she was right. Keeping her promise, she met him in the library often and accompanied him around campus for short, motivational talks. At times, he heard her sentiments echoed in conversations with other students.

As the semester wore on, he and the Professor formed an odd team. Troubled and troublesome students would come to the professors' offices, where David would either play the 'good cop' or the 'don't mess with me gangster.' He became a teacher's aide, and he was allowed to continue in the fashion that suited him.

In years to come, he would even assist with his vast knowledge in Pacific Islander studies. His juxtaposing stories with personal experience made the other professors howl with laughter when no one else was around. Sitting among them in their shared office, David savored the camaraderie.

He soon began to realize that teaching was not a well-respected profession. What a horrible waste of money, though, sending brats to a four-year daycare for babysitting; he being the biggest one of all.

Pech made sure his dorm room was clean and food vouchers updated. Occasionally, he treated her to movie nights by showing up to whatever was playing on campus and paying for popcorn. Two hundred bucks a month went far in nineteen eighty three.

The last week of the semester found David wondering what he would be doing the three weeks between semesters. With a sandalwood walking stick given to him to celebrate his new paid position, he left the professors' offices. The stick was almost as high as his shoulders. There was a flattened egg shape at the top of the stick that was met by a cone shape, allowing him to hold it with ease or rest both hands so as to keep weight off of his lower body. It was rare, created from a single piece of sandalwood, intricate designs carved into the upper portion its significance lost on a first semester sociology student.

A gentle breeze carried with it a familiar perfume that took hold of his mind and senses. Vivid memories from years of playing suddenly flashed in his mind like a loud movie. Many scenes fought to dominate his attention. Without thinking, he changed direction, walking past the door to his classroom to the hallway's edge, pressing his body into the corner. Three stories up, he could look out and see a part of the football field.

Truck sized mowers cut grass allowed to flourish for the last few months, finally erasing the trampling of cleats. His team had been inspired to go the distance. Their final victory meant an unusual punishment to the field as they practiced far into winter. Two men commandeered mowers large enough to cut the entire field in 20 minutes with precision. Razor sharp blades were set to a height the supervisor specified. He walked crosswise behind the machines' path to make sure trimming was to perfection. *God what devotion to cutting grass, I never knew.* David realized the field would never stop beckoning him.

It was arranged for David to return home for a few weeks. John paid for the trip by train, a deliberate move on his part to provide David with a change of scenery. John reminded David he would not be in his current situation if not for him, so the money could be taken as a loan if he deemed it necessary. It was.

As David put his few belongings together he thought about the long trip alone. Panic began to overcome him. His mind raced uncontrollably, and he broke out in a cold sweat. '*Not safe... not safe... not safe. SHUT IT!*' He tried to be the loudest voice in his head. '*The bus... the bus... leaving in 35 minutes. The train. Leaving by 11:30 a.m. Never late... never late... never late. THE FUCK DID I SAY!*' Some of the words growled out through clenched teeth.

He stood hunched over, resting on the sandalwood stick, staring at his large backpack. The backpack became his focal point. His safe place. *Fine. Whatever gets us out and back home, he mumbled to himself.*

Home would be wanting, not waiting.

5
HOME AGAIN

David was no longer a football star. He wondered if that was the reason his father stopped calling. He was hoping to at least have someone pick him up at the train station.

The restored depot was now a museum and not often used. There was a phone on the wall for stranded travelers. It had been installed decades ago; volunteers took turns answering it. Tonight's volunteer was Phil from the local gas station and repair shop, who picked him up.

David fumed as he waited. *I have gone from broken to useless. I got nothing but a wild ass mouth. God, at least let me get that degree. Please show me something about being useful.*

An old truck that seemed to have jumped right out of an advertising campaign for farm fresh produce pulled up. "Hey there! Heading into Leduc?"

Phil sat so high, he had to bend down a bit to look through the windshield. His long arms were bent back to hold the steering wheel. His blue eyes stood out with the help of sunbaked skin and dirty blonde hair.

"Oh, thanks. You seem familiar." David loaded into the classic 1948 Ford F-5 that was showroom clean and had a stake bed of oak.

"Yeah, Phil. I went to every one of your High School games. Really sorry about the last one. So what ya gonna do now, Dave? Bet ye'd make a smart coach." He kept his gaze out the windshield, the mid-western dark interrupted only by headlights quickly swallowed their incandescence.

"I keep hearing that. I have three and a half years of school first, then I can decide what to do with my broken down ass."

"Best get off that. Could be yer mostly broken down in the head."

"Sweet truck. Old." David fought off the encouragement with his poor attempt at changing the subject.

"Nineteen Forty-Eight. Had a tree growing right up through where my seat is. Went out the open window. Grew that way cause trees need light. Still have the

32

trunk all bent around tha' way it is, big zig on the wall of my shop, an' a picture of the F-5 here. Folks visitin' get a kick. I sell tourists some things hung near it. Leduc, a place to be. 'Member we called it 'lay duck,' the end of nowhere?"

Phil smiled in a way that surprised David. After all, who could stretch their mouth out that wide? "Nowhere sounds good now." Dave watched the bit of growing fields the kiss of light the truck's headlights allowed. There was no other besides the stars. In Los Angeles, everything remained lighted up all the time. That felt wrong, he thought.

It was a clear night, the stars so bright and clear. Outer space felt like the thing the world floated in. Stars in Los Angeles were on the screen or sidewalk. Here, they were three-dimensional. You knew you were a speck among them like David now wished he had remained.

"I'm no psychologist, but look, David. You were fascinating to watch. People like watching something special. Think of the tree that grew up here, where I sit now, and how lousy and rusty this truck was. Now, they both get used and are noticed and admired. Truck was so old and forgotten, the motor vehicles department didn't know it was still around. I'll see you at church. You wait and see if there isn't more for you. Just be who you were, who you still are. I like to fix things, make 'em nice, so they call me a mechanic. I know what I really am. A restorer. Find the real you." Phil's expression was warm.

David came home to an empty house. His father was gone, working the gas fields up North. A distant relative gave him a job. He had burnt out all other prospects. Everyone else knew better than to rely on him. David was grateful not to have to listen to his drunken rants. He ate canned and pre-packaged meals, watching TV for three days. That was enough. *Time to get out,* he thought.

It was a bright day with horsetail clouds floating free in the vast sky above. The entire town felt safe to him. It was liberating just to wander. He went toward the Hardware store past John's house.

"Hey, who got 'em a stick hea?" an old, dark woman said. She stood outside John's house.

"I'm David. I live a few doors down, ma'am?"

"Iada. Boy, what ya introducin' ya self fah? They nevah been so famous a Drya' descendant of Leduc from hea evah. Yeh gotta be tha moon to be bettah known for a state ah two 'way, mah boy. What tha hell ya doing up in they house all the time? I was about to get tha police ta check on ya?" She approached him and put her hand on his free arm.

"Eating out of cans." His gaze wandered away.

"If I catch ya ah heah ya doin' it again, Im'ma tell Gahl. He straighten ya out good. Food this way and they door is open. John want ya ta have some walking money. Please, no arguin'. Im'ma jest doin' as he says." She pulled out folded over bills from an ornate purse one would expect to be used in the evening.

"Oh, really? I'm doing fine." He shook his head.

"Nah, John insist. They pay a lot for his cereal box covah. He weep tellin' me how ya nevah go ta no university without him. Enjoy, lunch 'round 2:00 p.m. Now kiss this heah ol' lady and get off. John be back heah by 7:00 p.m."

He took the money, bent down a bit, leaned on his stick, and kissed her on the cheek. She went inside, cheerfully humming a tune from the roaring 20's.

David continued down the concrete sidewalk, crossed two streets going downhill, and ended up on the wood plank sidewalks that surrounded all of the buildings in the town's center. Poking around the hardware store, he stopped in front of a glass case that held a variety of items. There was a revolver with a white handgrip, some decals, old law enforcement badges, and a small, gold ring in need of a good cleaning atop an envelope. Had the ring not been so old, it probably would have sold some time ago.

"Lord, I have never seen such a fighter! David, you got brass ones, boy!" Maureen exclaimed. She was a fourth generation owner. Five Feet tall when she lied about it, and a face as wide and bright as the summer sky.

David turned and looked down toward the voice. "Well, hi, Maureen! What about brass?"

"Dense as a dried cow pie, but lion-hearted through and through!" She stood just tall enough to grab him above the belt line and squeeze gently, knowing how injured he was. "We were about to call the... here comes one now. What ya' got there, a little Bosche?!"

"Hello, Maureen. Mr. Dryer. Yes, this is my son, Burt. You know who this is?" he said, gesturing to David.

"Sure, David Dryer, the double D man, most biggest QB of all time, Daddy!" He was just knee high.

"Oh, you guys! It's just David now, really." He tried to deflect the attention.

"Well, that's my fault, David. We watched every game," Burt Sr. said.

"We're all getting' together at John's for dinner. We can go over who and what then!" Maureen cut off the fan talk. She still had an arm around him, like his mother might. She had been a distant cousin of his mother and the best of friends.

"It's good to see you both, and thank you, Burt." David extended his hand. The boy shook it hard with a big grin. His father took him to the part of the store that stocked boots.

"Maureen, Burt Sr. looked like he wanted to say or whine about something. You, keeper of all knowledge, better start talking..." David used his free arm and nearly picked her up while kissing her forehead.

"Make me talk! Fine, keep quiet then. You are home now. You have family here, some of blood but the better ones not. Learn to listen. You were funny on TV, but not now The answers you seek will come—answers just for you. Now kiss me and let me go."

He complied and let her get back to the shop. Walking past one of the big windows, he watched as Maureen found some boots for the boy. Their eyes met and he nodded towards Burt Sr, who appeared engrossed in his son's excitement about buying real cowboy boots. A ray of sun burst forth from a gap between the buildings, and he could see himself clearly in the window. The look of contentment staring back at him from his reflection infused him with the feeling that everything would be all right. He ambled, feeling a bit taller, gripping the walking stick a little bit lighter.

Phil's garage was to the left of where he was headed. "Thank Phil for the ride and see the stupid tree," he said aloud, checking around first. Crossing the road, he went around to the side that held the convenience mart. "Phil?" David called, looking around. He found the crooked trunk on the wall and the gaudy things on display nearby. The smell of gourmet coffee permeated the air, staving off the usual garage smells.

"There he is! Wow, what we got here is another celebrity visit!" Phil emerged with John's father.

"I'm telling you, that celebrity is my son. David, that is a fine stick you have. What do the carved designs mean?" John's father walked up to David with a smile.

"Hello, Dr. Kemp. Dinner at 7:00 p.m.?" David put a hand out. John's father pushed past the extended hand and embraced David.

"You are most brave as John always likes to say. You are a great son to have." Placing a hand on David's cheek, Dr. Kemp made sure they were looking directly into each other's faces.

"Father of my brother, I meant no disrespect."

"Listen to you two. David, glad we didn't have to send the deputy to your house. Hey, Mr. Kemp, Sr., gonna' tell him about the mega hurts?"

"Oh, my, Mr. Phil, any more formality from you, and I'll phone the newspapers. All of them."

"It's about that phone, David. Mr. Kemp, Sr. and Pastor Gahl put mega hurts in them. No more plugging the switchboard around. We just hand off the other end. No wires. Mr. Kemp, Sr. says there's going to be an inter-nets someday soon and this here is the beginning." Phil towered over both of them.

Looking up, David noticed nothing hung from the ceiling. Phil quickly shifted his eyes between the two.

"Electricity, running water, and cable just not good enough?" David smirked.

"My, we have poor foresight, David. The ancient libraries of Alexandria will soon be read by anyone anywhere they like. The whole point of university will be lost in a few decades."

"They got that sand valley where all this stuff is comin' out. Wozniak and a few other nerds kin make giant computers fit on a desk, David."

"My dearest friend, Silicone Valley and megahertz computers are already here with their mega bite memories... hey, let's get my son on his way. He has more walking to do." Mr. Kemp patted David on the back who was about halfway out the door.

"Woaaah, get out! Let me at some of you!!!" Jan bounced in accompanied by two other girls. Her reddish-brown hair would have fallen to her waist but for the gravity defying bounce that kept it aloft. Swaths of it whipped across David's face when she suddenly jerked to a stop before his feet.

"Little Jan Milnarcheck! Don't you know old people hate surprises!!!" David could not help being goofy.

"You're barely 21! Hugs!" She hugged him and buried her face against his chest. He placed a respectful hand near her shoulders and squeezed gently, discouraging her schoolgirl crush on him.

"Oh, my gosh! Where are you going? Want some help? Need to get something?" She beamed with enough radiance to light the room.

"Jan, Sh—."

"DAVID!" Both Phil and Mr. Kemp cried out in unison.

"You got some walking money. The girls could use some ice cream on such a warm day, David." The patting on his back was vigorous.

"What do you know about the walking money?" David looked back.

A hand strong enough to lift a small car engine and big enough to pick up a bowling ball without using any holes appeared in front of David's face. An index finger nearly touched David's nose and then pointed at the door. Phil let his hand relax and then proceeded with more pats on David's back. Out went David with three precocious teens anxious about starting high school. Jan trotted off ahead to open the door. The 'oh gollys' and 'goshes' could be heard over a half a block away.

"That'll get some youth back in his step. Can't count on it returning the swagger, but hey, there is time for that."

"You really are the best of friends, Mr. Tolson. I think the coffees are ready."

"Oh, who has to call the papers now! Hey, about the Sand Valley..."

David seemed to carry the stick more than it carried him. His stride lengthened, his steps a little more brisk. He was doing his best to get the whole ice cream ordeal over with as quickly as possible. After the ice cream was doled out, he would find some excuse to return home.

Jan was the ringleader. She bounced around in front, to the side, and around the back as the girls went through too many subjects for him to follow. They were loud enough for everyone in town to hear. He did not notice how their energy rubbed off on him. The four of them passed the store as Bosche Sr. and his son emerged.

"Oh gosh! Look at those boots! Woah, a real cowboy!!" The girls giggled.

Bosche Sr. let the girls fawn over Burt Jr., who smiled up at them. He stood very close to David. "I just wanted to say how nice it is to see you getting back on your feet again. I received a lot of phone calls. Well, Gahl will have something for us all on Sunday."

"I'll be there, and tonight, sans the parade, here." David's face belied his dry tone.

"Oh, unlucky you. Just humor us. I know how hard this is for you. Got enough money?"

"See you at dinner, Mr. Bosche." David bowed slightly as Burt Sr. turned back to rescue his son, who was starting to show the squealing coven his version of a clodding two-step.

"Well, I'll shit myself," David said quietly. Not that it mattered, no one would have heard him shouting over the ruckus the girls were making. He saw his reflection again. He was holding the stick, standing firm and erect with a broad smile.

The breeze carried a familiar fragrance. Grass. Someone was mowing the grass in the park a half-mile away. He looked back at the apparition in the window, pointed at it and said, "Coach, number one, never ever give up."

The silence in the air suddenly snapped him out of his focus. "Well, Mr. Number One, we're getting ice cream first!" Jan grabbed his right arm while the other girls stayed in front.

With the girls ahead of him, his embarrassment at being caught thinking aloud went unnoticed.

They all had their ice cream and the girls were talking like a single unit. "What will high school be like? What is it like to be a big star? Did you have a crush on Jan's mom?" The last question obviously flustered him.

The sage that was Jan's mother came out quickly in her daughter. "She was his mother's good friend, like family. David and I are like brother and sister. Sorry if I joke around too much. We talk way too much," she said cheerily

"That's fine, Jan. No sweat. Look, ladies, the thing about high school is the same as Junior High. It's just now you take the bus over the hills and there will be lots more students your age. I think more than a thousand." He smiled at them. Five years older, he felt almost fatherly.

They looked astounded at the idea of a thousand people, like when a big game happens or a rodeo.

He continued, holding up a hand like he was putting a stop to their anxiety. "You are still going to be great friends. There won't be any loneliness. You will always get the help you need, just don't be afraid to ask. I was a complete wreck. Now, I'm back in classes learning about the struggles of the ancient kings of the Pacific Rim. They lost everything, just like me. But they never lost who they were, kings, queens and princesses. So, to answer the other question, I was a big star, but not anymore. I get to find a whole 'nother way for myself now. I think it could be exciting. I don't know how it will turn out. I do know that I can put one foot in front of the other. Lately, that has meant a lot to me."

They had nothing more to say and it was about that time to leave. They went out into the summer sun and the sweeping view of the distant fields, which appeared to have no end.

Jan sidled up next to him. "I'm sooo glad I know you. Thanks for helping us out. See you Sunday!"

She ran off, giggling with her friends. Her long, thick hair with two bouncy waves caught sunlight with a toss to one side, her shiny river of hair released and caught it. He noticed the start of womanhood in her, a smaller version of her mother both in appearance and in heart. It was obvious she would become just as attractive.

The girls faded off into the distance, their laughter disappearing with them. Jan was beautiful, and it was okay to think of her that way. The longing to be youthful again, to start over and not have a back sewn together with metal, was powerful. He quickly buried the thought, taking deep breaths to push it down. He headed home, putting weight on the stick, happily looking forward to a nap and then dinner with John.

———

The fire alarm in David's head started to scream when a baby was handed to him. He and John sat on the couch together waiting for dinner. *They shit and spit up, and germs come out from all over!*

"David, she won't bite; does not have teeth yet! Hold her closer and up high on your chest to give her warmth."

"The warning would have been nice, John. I don't normally do these things."

"Closer, let her head rest on your shoulder. One hand here on her bottom. There, you're a natural. See, quiet."

"Oh-kay then. There's a good baby. Remember, only cough up on family."

"If she coughs up on you, then that's it, you're family." John looked around, beaming at everyone.

The large living room was full of people, who exploded in contagious laughter.

It is the summer of 1983 and John is qualifying for the United States Olympic team, David knows this and tries not to be awkward with John while keeping an eye on the baby and its possible sudden outflow. "So John, when is Oregon?"

"I have to leave tomorrow before noon, so breakfast and I'm gone. Sorry Dave, or does everyone have to call you Double D man?" John beamed at him.

"Ah, all of you least of all... Look, man, I'm good, I know the way through the train station and that place at Olive Era street for the cab. In fact someone told me they have a bus just for the University. I got a phone number to call, so all I have to do is show up and get there, easy. Now, this town needs someone to keep it on the map, as they say. So... why are you going to the snow? I forgot to ask," David trailed off.

"I have some speed that the US bobsled team says they can use."

"You're doing bobsled, after you swore never to get into anything like my old Radio Flyer again, you're doing Bobsled?" That made the room burst out in laughter. When the boys were about ten, the heroic David and his red wagon were often spotted breaking the speed limit. They zoomed past the corner café until one day when they were mercifully snagged by the freshly plowed soil of the adjacent farm fields.

"Wow, David, such fine memories you doth conjure. Yes, Bobsled. They give me a helmet." John made big nods and stared at the floor, allowing the rest of the room to finish howling with laughter.

David took a long look around and then at John, who stared at the floor and gently shook his head. "I'm going to do just fine, thank you for showing me how to get around, none of your lessons go to waste, my brother." David concentrated on the baby as John turned to look at him.

"Well, David, feel like home again?" When John's father spoke, the rest of the room fell silent. He sat close to Bosche, Sr., whose son sat near his feet. The large room was filled to capacity. Everyone sat close together. Sanguine faces turned in his direction and then back towards David.

"Yeah, Dr. Kemp. My dad is out in the fields now. I'm sure he would be here."

"That's good, David. You have more time for classes now. Please talk about university learning. The way it is now."

"Oh, I think video is really helping. There is a video for any subject now. When you go to the library, they have a computer behind the desk to direct you on where to find a book or a VHS. They say all of that will be on computers soon. I can't imagine such a thing, but that's what they say."

"Right, those are mechanical things, always changing. What are your specific studies now, and do go on about what you really like."

"Sociology, some English, some math. I would have to say Sociology, the study of peoples. My main professor, the one who helped me get a job on campus, teaches a lot about the Pacific Islands, how they were led, what happened to them post-World War II, how they reformed. Funny thing about people who refuse to give up who they are, they reconstitute almost back to what and who they were before. Television has changed some things for them. Modern aircrafts bring in visitors, or tourists, I should say. Far from the beach, off the beaten path, they still practice their customs and display their beliefs. It never stops. Even back at the beach, near the hotel, people can see everything if they knew what to look for."

"That is truly insightful, David. A gift you have in abundance. Insightfulness will truly help in all things as you become who you are meant to be." Dr. Kemp nodded slowly, giving his attention back to David so he could end the discussion.

"A baby holder?" David beamed at Dr. Kemp, patting the baby on the back. The room quickly filled with laughter, and then emptied for dinner.

Sunday morning could be easily identified in Leduc. Cars did not move. Cyclists began to arrive from neighboring towns and a city only 20 miles away. Every local walked that day unless they had to leave. Yard sales that would include BBQs were commonplace. Church was held in three 40-minute shifts, starting at about 9:00 a.m. David walked into one starting about 11:00 a.m. He parked himself in a rear pew, near the aisle.

Gahl stood behind the small lectern. "I thank the Lord today for the safe return of our son, David Dryer." Gahl pushed his arm out and with a flat hand gestured to where David sat.

David felt pushed into his seat from the sudden attention.

"Crushed down and back up. Sound familiar? It is the way of life for a champion...."

David's attention wandered, the eyes were taken off of him, some phrases got in and the rest he did not have the ears for. After the sermon he went outside. The sun shone bright and high, almost at peak as the church let out. In the back, some returned from earlier sermons for the social. A BBQ blazed. Among the loosened ties, beer, wine, and sodas were carried. David found Mrs. Milnarcheck and her carbon copy, Jan.

"David, I'm sorry we couldn't meet up sooner." Her smile was as warm as the day and bright as the sun. She wrapped her arms around him.

"Thank you, Mrs. Milnarcheck. Gosh, you two are twins! Wow, and you shop together too!" His playfulness got him a hug from Jan.

"Yes, these things happen, David. What did you think about the sermon? Feel anything special?"

"Well, lots of people have to get along. You know, they have things to get through like that Psalm guy he mentioned."

David looked so thoughtful, Jan burst out laughing.

"Well, I'll let you two talk. Be right back." Mrs. Milnarcheck entered the church, leaving the two alone. She found Gahl coming in from the back.

"I think he slept through the whole thing." Gahl shook his head.

"No, he just does not get information in that way," she said, holding her purse in front with both hands.

"What, the human way? Complete meathead. I worked on all that for a month. What a waste." Gahl threw up his hands as he looked out a window.

"The ideas must generate from within. He has to have them cued up inside first. Try to think of imprinting. Something will trigger him talking like, well one of those times he was in front of reporters or a crowd. He comes up with new combinations that fit the wild personality everyone seems to follow around. His mother and I used to laugh about that a lot." She kept her eyes on him.

He turned and looked back at the 5'8 professional looking teacher and quickly surmised a lesson was being delivered.

"Oh, my. Well, let's just see if certain things work the way I think they will. I have to look for someone. I thought I saw him earlier. Please ask everyone to gather near David."

"Gahl, that Cheshire cat look is the beginning of trouble. You and your schemes again…"

"Please, Martha. A smidgen of trust for little Ol' Gahl…"

She turned on sturdy heels without altering the suspicious look on her face and went outside.

Gahl went out a back door and caught Mac, a long-retired television writer who covered high school football for the papers.

"Wait, whoa whoa whoa, Mackie! Hold up, my man!" Gahl ran up and hunched down to get his face to the same level as the old man walking up the street.

"You never talk enough, do you!?" Mac did his best to straighten up. No jacket fit his curling over frame, so he just bought extra-large ones. He was smiling, always cheerful. He poked up his hat.

"I got a big one to ask ya. Look, David is here. Could you throw down an interview? Just ask him about some of the items we talked about in church today. You went to two sessions. So, did you get it?"

"I have no idea what is going on here. But, when I got up, I felt as if I had to be here today. I didn't even know David was in town. I don't want to bother him, but it sounds like an exclusive. You got a pass somewhere?" He beamed at Gahl while he gestured towards some of his pockets. The two looked like they were in a huddle.

Gahl took Mac through the church and tried to navigate the crowd. Three feet of thick auburn hair bounced around. It took a minute for him to recognize Jan as she approached folks and practically shoved them in David's direction.

"Eeehk-scuuse me, everyone! This is Mac or Mackie. David, remember him? The reporter?"

"Well, what the hell dragged you into church, McMac!?" A sudden outburst of laughter from the crowd fueled David. He forgot what it felt like.

"The best football player ever to come out of the nearest four states, son. I'll bet the pastor will have a chat with you about the mouth later." He was as loud as the group.

"Mine or yours! Hey, big Mac, want some ballet?" He shouted an old reference Mac had used.

"Hey, kid, the only thing dancing here is your mouth!" He waited until the crowd settled, and he would not have to shout just three feet away. "Now, I gotta say that so very few would venture forth from such a beating as you have had. What have you today to take around for the sake of others so afflicted? What about the sermon today really inspired you?" Gahl patted Mac on the back.

"Well, Pastor Gahl said that I was a son returning home. I look around, and it's like I never left. Sorry I missed John this morning, but I have a hard time getting up nowadays. But I do get up. If for no other reason than to say to that which would keep me down, 'I win and you lose.' One foot in front of the other makes for walking. I walk a road less traveled. There are those who have gone ahead. Those that follow are also followed. Life works that way, one step at a time." A short applause followed.

"Well, I can see that today had quite the impression. So many have been inspired and impressed by your skills. I expect you to become a coach, if for no other reason than the Tolson twins can play for you."

"Hey, is that right?" both boys said in unison.

"Well, even I have heard of the two of you. Yup, first year freshman punching the line and sacking quarterbacks together? I hear you two have the lowest run yardage ever." David looked them both over. They were enormous even by midwestern standards. Fast and smart. They won science fairs together, talked at the same time, and were as nice away from the field as they could be ferocious on it.

"We're going to play for you. You will coach, right? That university has an engineering program, a pool, and you can take the bus to the beach." They walked up, casting a shadow over David. Everyone burst out laughing.

David touched his shoulders with the boys' chests and barely poked his head out between them. "Yo, Dr. Gahl, do I have a choice here?"

Gahl studied his fingernails and said nothing. David stood erect, looking back and forth between the eager faces of the twins. "You two sweethearts have nothing to worry about." The small crowd roared with laughter.

The small party broke up, and David wandered off by himself. He went downhill towards the school, turned left, and thought about all that had happened. He kept his thoughts warm. There would be something to do, he thought.

Looking up into the distance, he noticed an old man struggling with what appeared to be a branch out of a bag.

"Hi. Let me help," he offered.

"What, you... David Dryer? What gets you here?"

David replied with his own question. "What's with that scraggle in the bag of—is that dirt?"

"Yes, it's a tree, and I want to plant it."

"Let me help. I've got all day."

They carried and hobbled and rested until they reached a small clearing in the park. The area showed a depression where another tree had been removed and the stump ground out. The grass had not taken over. The soil appeared loose. Digging by hand would achieve what needed to be done.

"It's a beech tree. They get really big, nice and slow. They got 'em 300 years old in some places, 120 feet or more of shade. This one here will only be 40 or so feet by the time you retire. Ready for shade in 20 years?"

"That's a long time. Hey, the blood on your hand is bleeding through the tape."

"So what. Good for the soil. Remove the bag, please, and just ease in the whole deal."

"Okay. Just cover it now?"

"Yeah, easy. Take care of it. It's not supposed to be here, but neither am I."

"Sounds like a good story. I got time."

"I don't. I was supposed to die a while back. Cancer's got me now. I can feel it eating away inside, day and night. I took off from the county hospital after getting back my clothes. They took my wallet, so I took their money out of a snack room. They can get change for the candy somewhere else... my wallet, if I knew where it was. I was not the best I could be for my family. I'm from the line of Leduc. You're the other, the Dryer branch."

David pulled out the rest of his cash. "Finish the story. Put this back in the snack room."

"Blessed! Finally! Hey, that's exactly the cost of the tree and bus fare. Look out there at all that farmland. Up here on the hill, looking over all the houses, that was ours. The families got along well. One of the Lundbergs, a mean, crappy one named Bob, talked everyone into going into a co-op. The co-op subdivided, and the ownership got blurred. He raised cash and began to drill for oil. There was no oil to be found, but plenty of natural gas. More subdividing, more loans, more bullshit. He keeps collecting payments and taking advantage of folks. We'll lose a third of everything. Let it go. Just keep the core of it all, the Dryer house and the fields you see out there. You will inherit a part of it all. Never let them go. Like this tree here, let it grow."

"Like that wacky tree in Phil's garage?" David questioned.

Water drops fell on the newly patted-down soil gently tilled over by the old man.

"I owe Phil, but not money. You tell him about this tree. Ask him to name it," the old man said solemnly.

"You tell him yourself. We are going there now. He is giving me a ride back to the station."

"I don't have your guts. Please help me. I'm not right. I'm through, David."

David's shadow loomed over the man watering the tree with blood, sweat, and tears. He reached down with the aid of his stick and grabbed the man's hand, pulling him up.

He left the man in the snack shop and went to get Phil. Phil wore a warm smile and managed to reduce his size as he got closer to the old man who, at this point, had run out of tears.

"I never gave you my name. Philippe, please..." the old man implored. Phil cut short his apology. "I should have made time to see you, Dad, despite what they told me. Can it be fair that we begin our journey together from here?" He hunched over to make eye contact.

"You mind picking me up at the house, Phil... Philippe?" David said, walking out and avoiding eye contact as he wiped his eyes on what he hoped were clean sleeves.

"Grab a bottled water, David, and I'll see you in about 40 minutes!"

Phil spoke only about the good things since the time the old man crashed the F5 and broke the family business. They both agreed that Philippe had made a good name of Tolson.

The two could be heard laughing all the way down the block. The old man had on a fresh shirt, new bandages, and had washed up. He had the new style water bottle with a pull top that allowed sips, but no drips. He had gone through most of it. David tossed his bag in the back of the truck and sat near the window. The sun had just dipped below the horizon.

Philippe began, "Daddy here says you guys planted a stolen tree in a spot where another one went bad!"

"Good times. Only the best!" David said as he began to laugh.

On the way to the station, David learned about the cousins scrapping for bigger shares, getting loans, and losing everything. Phil refused to allow the hospital to keep the old man. Dr. Gahl and Dr. Kemp helped in that regard.

They pulled up to the station. Philippe was about to turn off the motor.

David motioned for him to keep the motor running. "It's been really good. I really appreciate the ride and everything I learned, Mr. Leduc. I will watch over Philippe's boys when they get to college, if they get to mine, and I'm coaching." David made his way out of the truck.

The old man began to speak. "Don't look so far ahead. I got my son back. Learn everything you can, no matter what. It will all come around again. After your father passes, your inheritance is secure. He was never able to obtain any loans and refused any from Bob Lundberg, the one he is with now. That's the only smart thing, well, besides you. David, you'll find your stride. Philippe is a restorer. That's what I mean. Learn. Don't worry about four years from now. Hey, I got the twins to catch up with, too! Life's short, son!"

As Philippe and his dad disappeared into the night, David's thoughts began to fill him with warmth. *Did you answer that crappy prayer? I have a lot to be thankful for. Giving me time for that, right?* In answer to his questions, a warm breeze washed over him, carrying the smell of summer blooms. In the distance, he heard the train approaching.

During his last few weeks and final hours, Phil and his dad made sure the tree stayed put and remained healthy. In the end, Phil restored his step-father's soul.

6
THE FIELD CALLS

The sun had not yet cracked the horizon, but there was no more sleep to be had. David puttered around the seemingly empty campus. Before he could use his food voucher at the campus diner, he decided to wander in his overly worn tennis shoes. Not even a thorough cleaning could mask their wear and age.

He made it to the top of the quad between the administration building and library. Memories came rushing back of that fateful day with Absolon, the three kings, and most of the campus, and that unique individual.

Who was it? Oh yeah, Scratch! He smiled to himself. "Gotta find that guy and thank him." Along with the aroma of coffee, the sound of voices crept up behind him.

"Camel jockey! Sand nigger!" shouted a tall, pasty-looking boy who appeared to be drunk from an entire night of partying. The idiots who accompanied him joined in on his laughter. Their attention was focused on a small man behind the kiosk, the same kiosk which gave off the smell of coffee. The man said nothing as David approached.

"Go find trouble somewhere else, shithead." David sounded relaxed. He felt cool and calculating.

"Woah, hey this fuck and a stick, fuckstick!" The wobbly drunk gestured at David.

David made slow eye contact with the drunk's companions. "I would have to kick the shit out of all of you so the sober one could go back and warn others not to do this."

The two companions grabbed the obnoxious one and scurried off, his slurring voice fading as the boys moved off. David turned to the man at the kiosk and noticed a sign that read 'Farouk's' above the window.

"David, it's not much. But please, you have it." The man handed over what David recognized as a burrito.

"Oh hey, I got breakfast coming up." David smelled the fragrant package.

"Yes, cafeteria. Try this one and come by every day for more, please. Just don't

44

hold up my line with your flirting. Thank you. I do insist." The man was young, perhaps only five years older than David, but his countenance declared that he'd lived a lifetime.

David chewed the first bite. "Well, I gotta pay you for it somehow. It's really good! I know this is a burrito. They have them at 'Olive Vera' Street."

The man smiled to himself and nodded quickly. "Okay, David, pronunciation is not a forte for you. Just be here every morning and don't hold up the line, please. I would be most pleased. Oh, and please don't try to pay. Thank you."

"Hey, you're all right. I don't know what gives, but okay. Nice having someone around who wakes up as early as I do." David mentally catalogued the contents of the breakfast burrito. Eggs, bacon, hash browns, and cheese, "Really good, man. Thanks for keeping the heat out. Where you from, friend?"

The man looked up. "Beirut. You may be surprised to see a Christian man from the Middle East, but here I am and I'm staying. You're welcome. About the heat, David, I figure corn-feds are no fans of the peppers."

David smiled and chewed. He kept his walking stick tucked up under his upper arm. "So Farouk, is it?"

"Yes, Farouk. A troubled name like yours."

"Troubled?" David stuffed more burrito into his mouth, figuring a lesson was imminent which would give him time to chew properly.

"Mine, like yours, is a name of leadership. Here, I have everything I need for a living. I've met good Christians and Jews. Muslims, as well as my family, saved me. Although small, I work the way I do, because I do not enjoy someone telling me what to do. Until you are in charge, I hope you can learn not to be problematic. Go see what they have for you. Trust me, your experiences are valuable and your heart unstoppable. But it will break if you are shackled to someone who tells you what to do. Finish your food. Tell me tomorrow what you have learned. Oh, and don't block the line. Excuse me."

As Farouk finished, other students, having just stumbled out of dwindling parties and needing hangover food, lined up. At first, they wondered about David and what he was doing there. After catching an enticing whiff of the food, the crowd began to order. The line grew and Farouk motioned David to one side.

David finished his burrito in silence. He caught the scent of a distinctly familiar fragrance and quickly turned towards its direction. The smell of freshly mowed grass in preparation of the unrelenting trampling of cleats. Unmistakable. He felt drawn almost hypnotically to the source.

He followed a path between the buildings until the view of the field broke open as the last structures that make up the campus proper gave way to the largest open space for twenty miles. The sight loomed before him. How he'd never noticed it before, he did not know. When the smog blew in from Riverside, about 70 miles to the east, and the sun penetrated the haze, the sky looked like a movie still from Lawrence of Arabia it was an ominous shade of red, as if a raging fire advanced from distant farmlands.

He walked slowly to the practice field. He waited at the edge of it, out of sight of anyone who might arrive. Leaning on the walking stick as he absorbed the most pristine place available anywhere in Los Angeles, he surrendered his senses. Dew he could feel on his skin. Untrammeled grass reaching into the ground for the last moisture it would get today gave off an earthy perfume. He awakened to familiar sensations. The fragrances of summer, sweat, anxiety, and the sounds of clashing plastic worn by soon-to-be men intoxicated his senses.

"Passing turkeys and catching fancies there, Coach?" David's tone sounded flat as he approached the sidelines behind Head Coach Saltier.

"What's up, Useless? Nice stick." Saltier attempted to sound as dry as David.

"Your passing game is a nightmare. I need on-campus work, and food services won't accept me. I could help for real." He braced himself for Saltier's response by looking away, hunching down, and gripping his walking stick until his knuckles went white.

"I have an opening for towel boy as part of the equipment team. Sorry, David, that's what I got. We'll see what you learn. You can start whenever. Cool?" He stared down at David, who rose slowly and turned to face him.

"Who do I see, sir?" He started to turn toward the locker room, trying to hide the rush he felt.

"The guy you defended, Dr. Richman. The guy you said no one was supposed to call Quasi-Moto. Remember that fight I broke up? His real name is Richard. He calls himself Rich-man. No more fighting out of you. Not one more fucking brawl. Do what he says, when he says, how he says it. Coffee is free for the staff. Take him one, black. Have one yourself."

"Sir." David stood erect, looked him in the eyes, and then entered the locker room, feeling the quick pace he'd experienced back home treating the girls to ice cream.

He went into the locker room, passing players suiting up for practice and ignoring their attempts to speak with him. His nose led him to the coffee that was set up just outside the coaches' office. The home of the coaching staff was situated off to the right of a long hallway. The working desk of the head coach was occupied the furthest corner. The public office of the head coach was located in the administration building next to the dean's office near the center of campus.

Everything in the locker room was painted grey or a drab green. Although used in most of the buildings on campus, wood paneling was absent in the locker room. The area was neat and tidy, but drab. There were cages, lockers, showers, and painted-over concrete. It took him a few minutes to locate the office of Richard Melk, head equipment manager.

"Excuse me, Dr. Melk."

"Rich-man! You were told that! Sit, Double D man!" He grabbed his coffee with both hands.

David took a closer look at him. His hands were bent at the joints, fingers fattened as if stung by bees. Signs of extensive dental work hallmarked his smile, which began from the point of his chin. Wrinkles flowed up into his forehead like wind ripples across a pond. David could tell he smiled often.

Dr. Melk wore the dark blue hat and windbreaker of the staff which took care of the locker room equipment. He was hunched-over, sipping his coffee with the same excitement as a desert-crossing nomad devouring a fresh glass of water. Curious as to the big fuss over coffee, David took in his first sip that sparked a lifetime enjoyment. It was bitter cocoa like and warm. His nose opened up, his lungs took in air more easily. There was some chocolaty earthy thing about it. "Good."

Dr. Melk began to speak while adjusting his chair. "Good stuff. Thank you, David. I want to listen to you. Why are you here?" He glanced over and placed his feet on a pull-out drawer. The paint had long since worn off and the bare steel was polished right where the heels came to rest.

"I have to be here. I don't know what I can do, but the field won't leave me alone, sir."

"Rich-man, David! Rich-man! Keep going, please." His 60-year-old chair was constructed of oak; the screw that made it tall or short was bottomed-out. Rich-man did a hip shuffle, swirling the chair until one of the four wheels dipped into a chipped-out divot in the concrete floor and locking the chair into place.

"Well, Rich-man, it's like I can smell the grassy field from miles away. I can hear the equipment used to groom it. Then, there's the crowd. It won't leave me. It is my quiet place, despite the noise. What's that picture? It looks familiar. Below the... you're a MENSA?" David pointed to a wall covered in certificates and old photographs, sipped his coffee, and inhaled its fragrant aroma.

"Yes, David. I am a member of the roundtable society of high IQ yappers. I skipped out on being something special in mathematics back in the 60's, because someone lent me a camera with a long lens on it. Bam! Doctorate filed. I did sports reporting, fieldwork in 30 countries, any excuse to carry a camera. I learned to write well enough not to get fired. I don't like it, but hey, they made me add words to photos like this one of you." He pivoted, grabbed his coffee cup, swung around, gesturing to the large, grainy black and white photo showing the fierce eyes of David's face inside a football helmet.

"Wow, I looked pretty tweaked, and that guy rolling off my hip seems familiar and unhappy."

"You had just kneed him in the nuts and head-butted him for trying to tackle you for the fourth time. Your line had been punched through, so you baited them to come back and get it. After the third one was helped off the field, your side had the psychological advantage. Amazing you didn't get excused from the game. Now, tell me more about what that field and this game means to you." He pushed back thick glasses and sipped his coffee.

"I played decent and fair until those guys took cheap shots at me, punched me while I was down and swore they'd 'F' me over. That one spit in my face, and no one called it. So, I guess I went nuts on 'em. It's like family and war. You live like a king, you're mowed down like a pawn. I can help. I know the other side now. I can't learn it like you with a book, but show me and I'll get it." David held his cup and with his free hand, stirred the air in front of him.

"Let's start with uniform and place. Over there is an open locker with a lock and key inside. Behind me is the equipment room. For now, it's full of unused uniforms, pads, and other stuff you know. Find a jacket and hat like mine. The head coach likes us in slacks and dark shoes that can take a shine. We're not athletes and our job is important, so look and act that way. The players need to concentrate on the game. We do everything else." He smiled and retreated back into his coffee zen.

David took his cue and went to figure out what where everything was located. A large room with metal shelves held bags of folded jackets, boxes of hats and helmets, stacked shoulder pads. He found a jacket and hat in his size and returned wearing them.

"Okay, half-way there, Rich-man."

"Half-way, David?"

"Shoes and slacks."

"You remember what you're told."

"Works better that way. Reading is not easy. I finished about five books, though, even though I started out with about 20. I know John likes reading. So do you!" David brightened up at the thought of another window opening up for him into the world of thinking.

"I do. Go ahead and get around. Ask the players how things are fitting and just talk equipment. Anything you can't figure out, come to me. Go ahead, David. Off with you."

"That I can do. Thanks!" David turned on his over-worn tennis shoes and went into the locker room where some of the players tried to figure out pads and helmets.

"What's this water? What's the business man?!" Gordon was as large and dark as a person could be, David thought. He was one of the Three Kings, the most feared lineman in the league. The normal head is about ten pounds. Gordon's had to be fifty. Amazing that it came down to a small, pouty mouth and a lower lip that stuck out every time he was confused.

"Fishman, what's the wonder about?" David nicknamed him after a box of popular frozen cod sticks.

"Well, DAVID! What they got you doin' in that equipment hat?" Half-naked, he came up close and loomed over the former quarterback, looking as though he would pick him up like a newborn puppy.

"Easy there, Fishman! I got a lot of learning to do, and this is a great start. So, what's the worry?"

"Well, like usual, the helmet is way too small and the pads are gone. They have water balloons in here." His broad forehead crinkled in the center.

"Okay, they told me about these last year. They absorb shock far better and those are the large ones. Is this number on back the correct one for the opening?"

"Oh, yeah! I can't get it over, though." His large hand stirred the helmet's empty contents.

"Fine, just get your practice under-gear on, and I'll be right back. You know, all of you are now running late!" David shouted around to the rest of the players.

They stopped gawking. Sounds of rushed cleats, chatter, and metal doors swinging open and slamming shut suddenly reverberated in the locker room. It seemed louder than any train station.

"Rich-man, these pads..."

"Read the side of the boxes on this end." Richman barely flashed a warm smile in David's direction. His new equipment worker dashed into the room and scrambled to find the box and the smaller pads that would allow a basketball to fit into a pumpkin.

He scurried back in a shuffling limp towards the locker room past Richman, who only raised his eyebrow and the corners of his mouth at the sudden burst of energy.

David pulled out the pads that lined Gordon's helmet. "Gordon, put the helmet on. Forget the pads." Gordon did so as David picked through the box, tucking some of the pads into the wobbly helmet.

"Ah, that there is the one! David, I always said you's smarter than average!" Gordon put a hand on David's shoulder, covering most of it, along with part of his back.

"I'm glad were friends. Guys, you know the coach has been out there for a while already! Any other issues? Franco, those pads are too big. Give 'em here." The scurrying, box carrying, shoulder pad holding David went past Richman.

"This won't last, will it?" Saltier breezed in to hurry the players on and paused when he saw David running around hollering.

"I'll let you know. It will happen soon, I think. Now go on to your office. I'll see you for lunch."

"That's right. MENSA only." Saltier went to his office.

The former quarterback was a limping blur. A fire hydrant among the rhinos, grabbing poorly fitted items and replacing them with proper equipment. Richman reluctantly sent him off to class.

A sunrise in Los Angeles can be more beautiful than anywhere else in the world. This decade of 586 computers, MTV, AIDS, and Ronald Reagan began a campaign to rid cars of noticeable pollutants.

David stayed away from the fast-growing line of new customers. He already worked out a short speech about the events from the day before. Farouk listened while he kept busy.

Riverside was an hour and a half drive east of the campus. Smog from the previous day would return to the basin from there. It was standard for Southern California athletes to practice before it returned and made the air a choking hazard. The sky was dark red to azure. David walked toward the field, thinking about how it looked set against the amazing array of colors on the horizon. He contemplated how he might spend his first check to purchase some slacks and replace his worn out tennis shoes.

Walking onto the dew-covered field, he approached three players warming up. "Wow, you guys got my memo."

"It's all that AND a bag of chips, lil' man!" said one of the players who went by the name of Swanton. He was very tall for a player, even tall for a wide receiver. He also played basketball.

"Thanks. Okay, before they catch me doing this, let's think about balance and core. Remember what I told you yesterday about keeping your balance? Dancers practice vertical leaps. They go straight up, then down, landing on both feet equally. Keep everything tucked in, toss your arms up, keep them together, and bend one knee. Always look straight ahead. Do it gently. Never force it. You're trying to build muscle memory, not power. That'll come later. Do it all day in short bursts, concentrating on technique."

"Are we supposed to fag our way down the field there, Double D man?" Swanton, the new wide receiver, asked, expecting a big laugh.

"Football as we know it is about 90 years old. I'm giving you advice that started somewhere in 1490. Any good dancer is stronger than your chunky, fat fuckin' ass, and since you can't catch a ballerina to save a game, let alone your life, start leaping, homophobe." David had his stick gripped tight in the middle like he was about to swing it at someone.

―――

Watching him while hiding behind the stands, Coach Saltier turned to Richman. "I'll start the coffee. Let's roll before we're spotted." They went into the locker room past the open bleachers. The head coach kept his pace slow. Richman did his best not to hold him up.

―――

David showed up on time, thanks to the large clock on the wall outside on the score board.

"What kind of watch you got there, David?" Richman lowered himself onto his chair, pulling out his footrest.

"Rich-man. Good morning. Black, just the way you like it. And no, I have no watch." David handed him his coffee.

"Thank you. Open that little bag right there." Richman gestured towards a plain, small, brown bag on his desk.

"Oh. My name is on this. There's no note who from. How did this happen?" Looking into the bag, David's expression was all concentration and wonder. "There are certificates?" he asked, looking up in confusion.

"Yes, those will buy you shoes and slacks at the campus store. The watch was left behind, and it's been gone over. Go ahead, put it on. It's yours now. Today, leave early and buy the shoes and slacks. Right. Off with you and the inventory." He sipped the coffee, knowing their time together would soon end.

David turned once again into a blur, scurrying between the locker room and the storage shelves. He stole brief moments to admire his watch. 'Aviator' was printed on its face. It was self-winding and stainless steel. It's only flaw on the side, where it had been dropped from the bleachers. Sometime later, Dr. Richman would find out it was the only watch he'd ever owned.

―――

Six weeks later, David came into the locker room while the sun made its ascension into the morning sky. Only three weeks before the first game.

"Oh, my! Thank you for the coffee."

"As always, Rich-man! Hey, I noticed a new padlock at the bottom of my locker, and the door is open. Not that I ever use it, but..."

"Your new locker is across the hall towards the door. The same lock is on it. Inside you will find what you need in terms of a notebook, playbook, clipboard, and pens. You just need to get the hat and jacket turned in. Your last assignment with me is to get the coach's jacket in your size. You can find it yourself, I know." Richman sipped his coffee and smiled. It was not his usual, widespread grin. There was tightness about his lips and his brows furrowed slightly.

"To say it's been great won't cover what I received from you."

David stared into his cup and noticed the oil droplets glistening in the reflection from light of the hanging lamp. On the other side of the hall, the ambiance was better. There were no security wire panels and the walls were mostly white. It was adorned with wood trim and carpet, not steel cages and barred doors painted in dark green that seemed more like black in the dim lighting.

"Lots of personalities over there. Watch closely how Saltier handles them. He is direct, but never insulting. Do me proud and pay attention this season. You're getting the same pay so just learn to do the little things they ask of you. I got a new kid coming soon, so let's finish our coffee."

"Who paid for that stuff you gave me?"

"Ever see *It's A Wonderful Life?*"

"Always missed it somehow."

"Well, it's all in there. You just keep giving. Let the Lord worry about how you get shoes, slacks and tell the time." Richman rocked his hips. One of the four wheels in the old oak chair found the chip in the concrete, allowing him to safely lean back, feet on the paint-worn drawer. Because of his hunched-over spine, he was still bent forward.

"So there's a kid starting, eh? Is he a 20-year-old broken-down mule like me?" David took a long sip of his coffee, savoring their last sit-down together. He felt both excited and sad.

"He's 10 years old, name's Paolo. He came to my attention through MENSA. He is a rescue of sorts, already attending classes here. The kid is brilliant, but combative. He adores you, Double D man."

"I don't know anything about 10-year-old trouble. If he's any trouble, just let me help and I'll get with him." David locked eyes with Richman.

"You'll be his reward. Remember never to raise your voice with him. He's had a lifetime of that." Richman continued to sip his coffee. This time, his smile went from chin to forehead. The wrinkles turned into laugh lines.

7

PASSING LESSON

Privacy was a rare thing on this campus and David was grateful for it. After his time in the hospital, a cramped room had been found for him. He relished the second hand furniture that was better than back home. It was time to use some more certificates. The cracks had finally gone through his shoes and were starting to reveal his new socks on the sides of the toes. He clutched the now crinkly bag, only thinking of getting what he needed. He had three new shirts and pairs of socks he washed in the sink. The slacks lasted all week and were swapped out with shorts when he got back to his room. He thought about that bag holding the only riches in the world, afraid to spend them as if they would be the last time he could get clothes for the next few years. After Farouk's, he walked slowly to the campus store, wondering how bad the smog would get. It already hurt his lungs and bothered his eyes.

John caught up to David. "What are you doing, my brother?" John's smile could crack David's worst mood.

"I'm getting new shoes and being moved across the hall with a big promotion! Hey, what's this about a bobsled? What do you know about ice? I would have thought our wipe-out in the wagon would have knocked that right out of you." He felt taller and lighter with John around.

"Whoa with the energy! Good seeing you so spry! Yes, Bobsleigh not sled. They think my speed will help. The East Germans are dominating everything, so they thought I could chip down the time." John grabbed the door to the campus bookstore.

"Wow, John, good thing you got me started here. Thank God for that. I will be fine. Just don't get killed on that idiot ride." David pulled the certificates out of the bag. "John! I could buy the store!"

"Hey, my brother, don't ask where it all came from. Just remember to be good to your hometown. Now let's shop till you drop and then some! Back it up! DOUBLE D MAN is in the house!" Some employees appeared startled by John's sudden outburst. David relished his brother's one-armed hug and fist pump in the air.

Besides his one trip here, David had never shopped anywhere but yard sales and thrift stores. He received an employee discount, and a manager came around with more certificates for the campus store and other retailers. There was also one from Farouk: "To David, Double D man. No pay here ever. Don't block the line."

David burst out laughing, handing the certificate to John, who joined him. They laughed nearly to tears. For the first time since his mother's passing, someone measured David's feet and secured the correct measurements for his shirts, jacket, and pants.

Winter was cold for Bob Lundberg, Jr. His father's endless campaign was tight in this year of 'throw the rascals out.' It was true what the networks said. America was fed up with Tip O'Neill and the drunken, bickering congress. They just did not want their own bastards kicked to the curb.

It had been some years since David Dryer had ended Bob, Jr.'s hope for getting away from the cold that seemed to be the only thing in abundant supply. His mother constantly reminded him of his fortunate life, how his father provided everything, and how much smarter he was than everyone else. His father would have suggested the same had he been around.

Law school provided a welcomed relief, a near sanctuary for Bob. The law was absolute. Absolutely flexible, he discovered. Marliz, a lovely girl from New Mexico, had a smile as broad as her heart was warm. She was of mixed, dark-brown races. She was allowed to bring Bob to her home for the summer break. Bob was ensnared in a love that could easily erase any spite he had for not being able to continue his football career. For months, David Dryer never even crossed his mind. New Mexico and Marliz were beautiful. He saw himself with her and her family in a run-down office, providing nearly pro bono legal work. For once, life seemed like it would be happy.

At a fund-raising party for his father's never-ending congressional bid, someone found Bob and Marliz in a quiet corner, staring lovingly into each other's eyes, oblivious to the rest of the world. Word spread. Bob's mother set up an emergency meeting between father and son.

A few hours and some phone calls later, it ended. Marliz would be allowed to stay at the university and complete her education, provided Bob remained someone from her past. Bob, Jr. was swiftly set straight by his father. Bob, Jr. knew he was stuck between a rock and a hard place no wiggle room. No place for him to go. He needed his shitty parents and their wealth to complete college. His hate for David Dryer began to fester and grow. The constant plots for revenge drove him beyond his needed course of study. His parents took the credit for his graduating at the top of his class. He looked forward to the day they were both dead and buried.

The warmest thing in Sarajevo during the winter Olympics were the flash bulbs, thought John Kemp. He and another man from Africa were the only Blacks.

Skin-tight jumpers were not John's favorite. At least he looked every inch a man after all of his parts were stuffed into the form-fitting fabric.

John's thoughts became focused as he tuned out everything except what he'd been ordered to do by the coach. "Push hard, get in, shut up, and hang on!" The roar of the sleigh was barely muffled by the helmet. He could have screamed and the man in front of him would not have heard him. He wondered about the 'shut up' part a lot. The violent rides they endured did not even get them into the finals, let alone a chance at a medal in the Winter Games. Summer was coming, so was stardom. David was built for fame. John was not. He hated it.

"I don't need this Double D man cutting me off at the knees, Saltier!" The passing coach fumed in a closed session meeting with coach Saltier and David.

"What's wrong with him being out there before you feel like getting out of bed, Bert?" Saltier was direct, and as close to insulting as he got.

"Lil' fucker is trying to take my slot before I leave!" He turned to David. "At least let the body get cold!"

Before Saltier could cut in, David was in the man's face. "Man bitch! Since I started putting up with you, all of the players know you're a floater! A spinning floater! You only care about getting head coach somewhere, bitch!"

Saltier separated the two. "Bert, David is taking directives from me about morning sessions. It's good to get the heavy practice done before the smog rolls in. Your position here is safe. I know about your offers, and they are well deserved. Now, I want to talk to David alone."

Bert got up, shook his head, and sauntered off.

Saltier let the door close before he spoke. "Lazy fuck. I've been stuck with that wart for three years now. Smart in strategy, shitty in personality. You, David, need to pick up the strategy part. It has to go from something instinctive to something you can teach. The speech department has some classes that can help you. I've talked to Professor Englert, the Sociology Department head, and he thinks rather highly of the idea. He also told me you take things in by listening more than anything else. Now hear this, David. You cannot afford to let someone get your nuts up like that. Getting into a bitch-fight and scratching the way you did is not coaching. It's bashing. There is a point at which you may get stuck with someone you can't stand and that's just life. The fans and sponsors pay for everything you see, everything that surrounds us. The sponsors have a lot of sway, hence the wart. Pick at a wart, and it will get infected. I appreciate you standing your ground. You just work with Swanton, the up-and-coming wide receiver, and leave Absolon and the new QB to Bert."

"Yes, sir. I'm sorry. Your wife makes great cake. Please thank her for remembering my birthday." David got up, feeling his failure acutely. Everything Rich-man and John taught him seemed, for the moment, thrown into the fire. He felt speared in the gut as he shuffled towards the door.

Saltier was quick with a few more words. "David, your program has some very positive effects on the players. Stats are starting to reflect the same, and the people who matter are beginning to take notice. Make your amends and get that strategy converted from your heart into your head." In a rare moment, Saltier leaned back and smiled.

David turned enough to catch the head coach's smile. He nodded, smiled, and left quietly. He walked down the hall on his way to the library. Instinct told him to say something briefly to Bert. He took one step into the coaching staff's office. Old, yet clean, steel desks were lined up facing the windows. It allowed the coaches to be seen, and the players to be seen in the locker room.

"Sir." David waited for Bert and the other coaches to look in his direction. "I'm sorry for my behavior. It won't happen again." David stood and waited for whatever was to come.

Bert rolled his upper body in David's direction. "Okay, man. We're clear now." He went back to his paperwork. The other coaches waited for David to leave before they told Bert what they thought of him.

David walked out, grabbing his stick, feeling a few feet taller. That night, he put away his walking stick and made the decision never to use it again.

John left Sarajevo and the Winter Olympics behind early. In years to come, it would be discovered that drug-induced athletic performances left the United States, and the rest of the world, woefully behind in metals. Bright spots included perfect scores made by a British skating couple. John happily left behind so much cold. As the weeks of travel finally wound down to John's arrival at the campus, he found that it was somewhat like home for him, more so than Europe and less so than Leduc. The quiet, windy days he longed for were less than two years away. But first, the big ride of fame.

David waited for him in the great turnout where the buses, taxies, and limousines dropped off and picked up passengers. David assisted John with one of his bags, marveling at the little wheels attached to them. It took a moment for John to notice David no longer needed his walking stick.

"Getting so much better, my brother!"

"What, at coaching or getting along? It's been a few months. Did you hear about me and Bert?"

"The lazy, roly-poly? Nah, I'm seeing a man on his own feet!"

"Oh, the stick! Yeah. So I called Bert a spinning floater and a bitch."

John paused to laugh. He needed all the oxygen he could get. David's preoccupations were a never-ending source of amusement. "Yeah, okay, so that's at least what he is. So what's on your mind for real?"

David stared at the ground. "Well, this wide receiver, the one who starts next season after Absolon leaves, has this huge issue."

"He hates being gay?" John arched his eyebrows.

"Oh, I wondered about that. He called what I told him to do once, 'fagging down the field.' So is he gay for real?"

"Yes, my brother. No judgment being made. He's quite open about it, and a good man to boot. So, what about him has you vexed?"

"Vexed? John, I don't get vexed over guys." David looked right at him.

John stopped for more oxygen. He finally stopped laughing enough to talk. "Oh, my brother, I have missed the home we have, such that it is, where it is. Vexed is just stuck on something, like a problem you don't understand."

"Oooh, okay then. His behavior, more precisely, his dancing after receiving the ball has me vexed. It's not like he makes it to the end zone and does a spike or some kind of boogie-woogie or something he deserves to do. He runs like a ballerina after I taught him about core strength. He does it to tease me, but with the hands out the way he has them, well, they can get grabbed and he has never been downed by someone the size of say, Gordon." David mimicked with a free arm what Swanton had been doing.

"Wow, my man. You're going to have to get up close and personal with this one. He's a bit like you. Football is a sanctuary for him, as well. So, make it real. Tell him what happened to you. Like that physical therapist said, pass it on. I knew one day all that experience would come in handy."

"Okay, John, I get it. I got a plan already. Is there something you need before turning in?"

"Yes, a cheeseburger and fries. I had first class meals all month, but a cheeseburger and fries is something they don't have in the snooty world of high class."

"Right. Farouk's, best stuff there is. I can afford it. Just don't block the line, please."

John was almost laughed out at that point. He and David spent most of the evening together. John noticed how much his brother had grown, finally desiring the right things.

David woke up confused, not knowing why it was cold and dry. Where the hell was he? This morning, a Santa Ana wind was blowing. Called the devil winds, they were clean of smog but dusty of pollen and flotsam. His first stop was Farouk's. "Hey, man, what the hell is this? Two years I have been here with all weird weather. This is out there, man!" David broke out in a sneezing fit.

"Here, David, eat this and try to like it. The heat will help your sneezing and stuffiness. Hey…" He motioned for David to scoot over.

"Yeah, don't block the line." David took one medium-sized bite. The flavors were so familiar except there was a heat that started a bit on his tongue and went down his throat. He felt warmer. The taste was more robust, green. His nose began to feel warm and more open. Every bite made the pinch in his eyes lessen. "Wow!"

A petite girl at the window said, "I'll have what he's having."

At the field players were already warming up as David delivered coffee to Richman and Coach Saltier. He said nothing as his thoughts were using up every bit of brainpower he possessed.

"Odd." Coach Saltier said.

"Oooh, something's up. We better get under the bleachers for this one." Richman followed Coach Saltier as fast as he could go. The coach kept his pace slow. They ended up in their usual spot.

"Gordon," David called out.

"Yes, Mr. Coach, sir?"

"Look, man, I hate to ask." David looked around and got close. "You see Swanton how he likes to dance on his toes after he gets the ball?"

"Oh, yeah!" Gordon's lower lip stuck out. "He likes to do that to tease you for bringing ballet onto the field like you did." Gordon glanced in Swanton's direction.

"Yeah, you know, he has never played a game since high school, right? Someone like you has never handled him before, right?"

Gordon looked at David. "Yeah, man, he never got the business before. I mean, he was big in their small pond, but not here."

"Very good, Gordon. Hey, you don't mind me calling you Gordon, do you? I never asked, I'm a coach now, sort of, and well, do you?"

"Why? Shut up, Double D man! It's an honor to get a moniker from the man!" Gordon placed his hand on David's shoulder, covering it and most of his back.

"I'm glad were friends, Gordon. Could you just go and pick him up, bring him here, and keep him off the ground until I get through to him. No pain. I just want his attention."

Gordon's smile became bigger than ever. "Would you hold my helmet, Double D man?" Gordon handed the helmet to David, who took it with a smile.

Back under the bleachers, Coach Saltier did his best to see what was going on. "I hope a spanking isn't coming! That David will either put me in gold or irons!"

"Now now, he looked very thoughtful this morning. Let's just see how this turns out. Want the binoculars?" Richman nudged the coach.

"Without being able to hear? No. At least I can say I had nothing to do with this. Whatever."

With arms larger than most legs, Gordon picked up Swanton from behind and delivered the fearful player. He kept him suspended above the ground. He squeezed the air out of Swanton every time he said anything. Swanton quickly gave up.

"Thank you, Gordon. Could you turn him? I need to get close."

Gordon turned Swanton to the side like he would a loaf of bread.

"Hey there, Swanton. I got a feeling you want me to get to the point." David got up close enough to lick the tip of Swanton's nose through the face shield. He could saw Swanton trying to say yes.

"Okay, man, here it is. I hope you noticed that Gordon picked you up like a pair of wet socks." Swanton nodded. "So, here is the thing. You have probably guessed that it would be a real drag having someone like Gordon squeeze like he's wringing all of the water out of you." Swanton's looked horrified as the image filed his mind.

"So, my man, you don't want to do anything to get yourself tackled by someone like Gordon, right? Am I getting through to you, Swanton?" The terror on Swanton's now sweaty face assured David he was getting somewhere.

"Swanton, I can tell by the color your face is turning that you can picture a bad future, because you might not take my advice, advice I should have taken from other people. I would still be walking and my hip would still be made of bone had I just listened. You don't want to end up like me, right?" David heard a weak reply in the negative.

"Good man. Here is the deal. When you run on your toes, that's okay. You see, you're paying homage to that lesson I taught you about the ballet dancers. Here is the problem. You also stick your hands out like this." David made an exaggerated motion like a bird.

Under the bleachers, Richman started to laugh like never before. The coach caught on and began to laugh, too. David remained up in Swanton's face.

"You gotta admit, Coach, that boy has some style!" Richman said. "Let's leave before we're spotted."

David continued. "You see, man, anything you stick out is something to grab. I taught you core so you could get nice and tight when it gets crowded out there with little guys like Gordon. I taught you core strength and balance so you would be hard to grab, not so you could fly like a gooney bird down the field. So, are you going to do that anymore?" Swanton shook his head as much as he could.

"Very nice, Gordon. Please return Swanton to his feet." Gordon turned Swanton upright. "So, am I ever going to have to do this sort of thing again, or will I be heard the first time?"

"I got it, sir. Thank you. That was most instructive." Swanton caught his breath.

"All right, guys. Let's get back to conditioning." The players immediately did what David asked of them from that moment on. David gave Gordon back his helmet.

At the end of the day's fieldwork, David went back to Bert's desk and found him with charts and calculators. His steel desk matched the other coaches', and they were all in a line with each other. They shared a communal office with an expansive window that gave them a view of the locker room and part of the equipment room.

David came in with his coffee and sat in a green leather chair. With a large hump in both the seat and the back, it was the most comfortable chair he knew. It conformed to his back and helped push in his lumbar, which forced him to sit upright. He was determined to learn what he could from the round man.

Bert sat with organized papers filled with statistics that included large stacks of paper lightly marked with grids so he could sketch a graph by freehand for his overhead projector. David let the coffee's aroma drift into his nose after taking a slow sip from his mug. "So, Bert. I'm here to learn statistics, as much as you can stand to teach me." David knew his voice sounded timid.

Bert turned to him. "Okay, David. I can see that you're sincere about learning what I know. Unfortunately, you do not have the talent for math and numbers the way I do. Saltier's the same way. He's an artist like you. David, I need you to promise me something." Bert looked at David with a cocked brow.

"Yes, whatever you need or whatever it takes."

"Good. You must promise me that, in this discussion where I will be doing all of the talking, you will absolutely not take it personally. I need to teach you a lot, most of which you will not want to hear." Bert maintained what could be considered an upright position.

David could see that a valuable lesson would soon be handed down, and it wouldn't be in a manner he liked. He knew he needed to hear it. "Okay, I made a commitment to do whatever it takes, so I'm listening." David tried to conceal his fear by locking eyes with Bert and sipping his coffee.

Bert pulled a stack of papers until they were under his chin. "People often say there are two sides or ways of looking at everything. They say the truth is in the middle. Well, the truth is what it is. I am a left-brained type like Dr. Richman. People like us have to do the math for everything. The way you think is more sophisticated and complex, which allows you to figure out spatial and mechanical things faster. It also lends to a brand of stupidity that is most entertaining. You are not stupid, mind you, but your lack of impulse control nearly killed you. You and I love this game, but the difference is our approach. I tried screaming to get you to stop running with that ball. I have a pile of stats in front of me that say you made less than a 2% difference doing so. That means for every 100 yards you made passing or, God forbid, actually handing off the ball to a running back, you gained six feet, 5.3 to be exact. Not enough to tip the scales. It also put you in the hospital for a year and caused us to lose. That's not teamwork. There is no "I" in the word "team," you were all about yourself. When I thought you were going to die, I had the chance to unload on Richman and Saltier. I guess they still feel guilty about what happened. I made sure they understood what assholes they were. You didn't know any better and were rushed into the big leagues, in over your head, and it was too late to stop you or the machine that runs a place like this." Bert sat up quickly as if jolted by electricity.

David asked in an icy tone, "Was I laughed at?"

Bert took a long pause. "No, I never saw you as a clown, a magnificent waste perhaps, but never a clown. You refused to listen. What about now?" Bert looked like a man about to dodge a bullet.

David saw Bert's startled look and began to check his body for tension. He started from the bottom to the top the way his physical therapist and dance instructor taught him to do when they noticed the tension in him. His toes were flexed downward like an eagle holding prey. The hand not holding his coffee mug gripped the arms of the old oak chair where he sat, his knuckles deathly white. His upper body leaned forward slightly, his jaw taut. He took in a slow, deep breath and realized how his face made him look as if he were about to scream. "I'm sorry, Bert, for everything. I'm here to learn. You're right about getting upset."

Bert began to laugh. David was quick to follow. For the first time, the two shared a funny moment together. Two years of angst and unhealthy anger melted away in a fit of laughter normally reserved for those who survive a war or plane crash.

Bert held his smile and for once, David felt as if he were being treated like the quarterback David replaced. "You're going to learn more than I was ever able to teach Saltier! By the way, your first step into great coaching was getting through to Swanton! Gads, he was a pain!"

Bert handed David a short stack of stapled papers. David was familiar with some of the names contained in the papers. "Okay, David, it's late. Go over those, and tell me about everything on them. Read them yourself. I'll explain later when we can talk about the concepts of statistics. I hope you know I'll be learning from you, as well. So, don't get offended by anything I say or ask."

David nodded, got up and shook Bert's hand. "Speaking of late, I have not seen Paolo. I better go check on him. Thanks again for everything." David rushed out, feeling like he was on top of the world.

At the age of 11, Paolo had the size and countenance of someone older. He walked with dignity and a purposeful look to his face. David caught up to him as he crossed the quad. "Hey, man, going to class?"

Paolo was happily surprised. "Oh, no, today it's straight home. The bus is not for another two hours."

"Nice! Hey, had lunch?" David stood in front of this freight train of dignity.

"Well, no, I forgot it," Paolo said.

"Forget it then. Let's go. I know this great place. Farouk's!" David almost shoved the young man forward with his free hand.

David managed a burrito while the boy downed a double burger with fries, burrito, and two orders of taquitos. He was able to get David to try a taquito with guacamole. "You like this kind of food, Paolo?"

"Sure." Paolo stopped his conveyor of consumption and focused entirely on David.

"Oh, man, finish. I'll get you to the bus stop later. We can hang in the library after you're done."

David made sure Paolo had a library card and an open invitation to hang with him anytime. He had to explain what Farouk meant about sending David the bill later. He gave the boy vouchers for food that he could use anytime he was on campus. They were at the great turnout where buses, cars and limousines would pick up and drop off people. It was comfortable. The sun would not set for some time, so David worried less about the boy getting home to San Pedro where he lived. It took some prodding, but Paolo finally started to talk. "School is too easy for my age. I took all the advanced classes and now study here. My mother insisted I find some help with things, so Dr. Richman came to help. He got me here. So, do you belong to MENSA?" Paolo sounded so genuine, David barely contained his own laughter.

"I don't have your talent for learning, my man! Well, I have a talent. It seems complex, maybe entertaining? People like you are wonderful for people like me. I think, Paolo, that it takes all kinds. With an honest approach and positive outlook, anything can be accomplished. With teamwork, everything is possible. Do you like being part of our team?" David forgot what the question had been.

Paolo began to relax. "Well, I do. I may never be a great player like you. Maybe I'll get to learn coaching. It'll be nice. I like Dr. Richman. He is very smart and wise. I think you learn a lot from very little. I can learn much and still not know what to do."

David felt warmth. Instinct told him he did not need to answer a question, but address a feeling instead. "My man, at this point, just learning is enough. Very good people surround you. I'm glad we're friends." David grinned as he nudged the boy with his shoulder.

The bus pulled up on time. Paolo got in and sat in relaxed manner. He seemed happy and less stoic, thought David. He waved back at Paolo and looked forward to seeing him again the following week. *Purpose left with the bus. This is not lonely this is without reason.* The thoughts floated around as David lingered at the bus stop. He watched the sunset, wishing he had one of those cellular phones to make sure the boy arrived home safely.

8

FAME'S CRUCIBLE

John Kemp wanted to be famous and fawned over as much as any man wanted to be diagnosed with colon cancer. He missed the excited young man from Leduc and his fervor for a new day and adventurous discovery.

For a year now his normal routine of being entertained by his brother David's random thoughts was disrupted even worse than normal. The Mayor, reporters, President of the University, President of the United States, everyone, except David, was at his shoulder. David was made for this crap, not him. His thoughts wrapped themselves around the idea like an addict for a smoke. Law enforcement, along with the Secret Service, did their best to keep John in a protected bubble and yet allow him to feel as normal as possible. It was a daunting and difficult task. He stepped out of his dorm room to find a larger security detail posted than the previous day.

David pushed his way in as John pushed his way out. "Yes, good morning. I'm David. How nice to see you secret policemen of valor and regalia. Love the sunglasses. We're indoors now, don't you know?"

"Oh, my brother, how art thou?" John beamed. The halls of the dorm area were barely two men wide. Having them packed with nearly a dozen bodies was becoming insufferable. "For those of you not in law enforcement, I am not speaking to anyone in the dorms ever. Please scoot and don't come back here!"

John never got this angry, David thought. "We can skip Farouk's, John. It's probably more nuts in the quad." He walked up to John.

A slender, athletic man in a dark suit and a wire connected to his ear approached. "Sorry, sir. No reporters are here. These men are security and we also have two officers, Deputy Banks from the Los Angeles Sheriff's Department and Officer Sigman from the Los Angeles Police Department. I'm Agent Maltz. David, I am glad to meet you. I want the two of you to know that we're posted all over the campus. Athletes from other countries are already here, and the students are being very cooperative. So, about this Farouk's… if you like, we can give you a ride."

John looked at David and shook his head in disbelief. David spoke. "No need for wheels, my good spook. Follow us for the best burrito outside Olive Vera Street. You're buying. Just don't block the line."

John put a hand on David's shoulder as though he were blind. He was happy to be led out of his room by him. He missed him on the many occasions David was not able to keep him company. Agent Maltz followed, smiling with officers and security in tow. He and the seasoned officers would try to teach the fresh security officers to have a sense of humor later.

As usual, Farouk handed out burritos. The agent somehow got him to take some money. He waved a hand impatiently. David interpreted. "Oh, Agent Maltz, we can't block the line."

David waved him over to the side. They stood in a line nearly a foot away from the kiosk as patrons walked in and out. Agent Maltz was watchful, but also enjoying the novelty of the breakfast burrito. "Good idea, right!?" David said. He nodded and looked around.

A young girl with coffee in her hand approached John. She had unusually white skin, and long hair with purple-colored ends on one side and a buzzed scalp on the other. She had on torn, black clothing, dark make up, and a look on her face as though she were allowed to evaluate everything and everyone.

"Wow, John Kemp! So you're why the fuzz is all over the place? You should be protected. You're so nice."

David chimed in while John slowly chewed. "Got athletes from all over. We're part of the Olympic village! Neat, huh?"

"Yeah, football is brutal. Learn your lesson?" She didn't look in David's direction.

"Half your head's missing," David said dryly.

A familiar face joined them in conversation. "Shiz off tizzy mizzy! D-man's down with me." The girl took notice of the man's presence and strolled off.

David greeted the young man. "Scratch! Where ya' been!?"

"Just workin' to get better. Morning, Mr. Kemp."

"Scratch-man! How are you?"

He looked somewhat skeletal.

John managed to swallow the rest of his burrito. He noticed the application of heavy makeup, especially around Scratch's nose. It looked as though he were covering up what appeared to be some kind of large mole.

"I'm getting by."

David took a step toward him. "Hey, man, breakfast's on me. What do you want?"

"Too kind, too kind. Medicine is making breakfast hard to hold down. I might hit you up later. Anyway, I gotta jet. Nice seeing you guys." He attempted a weak smile, huddled into his hooded jacket, and walked towards the hospital located on campus.

"I hope he's all right. Looks like he has the flu," David said, watching Scratch leave.

"It's AIDS, David." John's tone was absent any condescension, yet it held a sad undercurrent.

David put his attention back on the burrito.

Agent Maltz stood to the left of John, David flanked the right. They were in a neat line off to the side of the kiosk. Small groups of security would walk up, and one person from each group would approach the agent. After a short conversation with Agent Maltz, the person would return to their group and leave as a unit. David observed this pattern several times.

"Agent Maltz, that's really interesting. You only need to talk to one person and the rest of them get it. How does that work?" David looked over the entire quad.

"We're just having small security briefings, David. Nothing major." Agent Maltz tried to finish his food.

John turned to him and spoke quietly. "David learns by listening. He picks up on things very quickly and can glean a lot from very little."

Agent Maltz nodded, finished his burrito, and said. "Well, David, to answer your question more fully, the teams that gather for a briefing have a lead. The lead listens to what I have to say like, 'go to another meeting' or 'take up a position somewhere', and they take their team off to where they need to be. I have general orders given to me by someone who knows me, my level of training and abilities. I pass on the same information, expecting my chain of command to filter down like it has been to me."

"So, chain of command. Is that what makes the teams work the way they're supposed to?"

"Yes. It's like your football team. You get orders from the coach, who takes them from the head coach and so on. Your head coach gets directives from the administration, which we hope follows rules. The whole mess comes down to something we have to do, each person being given a role. Chain of command is critical, constantly tested, and can get someone injured or killed if not followed."

"Sounds familiar." David finished his burrito.

For the rest of the summer John collected gold medals, endorsed clothing, appeared on cereal boxes, and attended talk shows. He was glad when it was all over.

John and David began their last year of college. For John, the happy routine of being shaken awake by David had returned. "Good morning, fastest man on the planet! Hey, convenient they brought the Olympics here. So, do you get free cereal for life? How about them shoes? Does Johnny Carson smell? I hear he smokes."

They stood in a spot off to the side of Farouk's kiosk to enjoy their food. Pech was picking up her order when David saw her. "Hey, Mr. Lightning, hold for a sec?" John held on to David's half eaten burrito.

"Hey, Pech! why so sad?" He hunched down trying to meet eyes.

"Oh, my son." She allowed him to embrace her with a vigorous one-handed back rub.

"Where are you going?"

"Oh, just work. Hey, after field practice, come see me in my office." She looked up with a tinge of sadness in her brown eyes.

David paused a moment. "Yes, of course, okay." He rubbed her back again and rejoined John.

"I hate not knowing what's going on. John, I know you tell me that mind reading is a bad deal, but I seem to be the last to know about anything."

John finished his food. "You're going to make new things happen, David. You always do. Let the things others have a talent for be for them. Don't sweat it. All will appear in good time, right?" John looked at him, waiting for a response.

"Yeah, man, will do, as always."

John knew the lesson was understood. He smiled and waited for David to finish his meal so that he wouldn't have to eat alone.

———

David and Bert spoke during a late morning scrimmage. Their new understanding came with a more relaxed body language. Bert glanced at his notes. "The defense is lacking today."

David responded quickly, "Yeah, the linebackers were up to something last night. I can see their normal read of the offense is lacking."

"All in their heads, David, not in their asses?"

"No, heads and asses have been swapped with those two. They're moving with the right speed, but they're getting started late and making dumb decisions. It's in the head. Their legs are fine."

"Well, my good man, you're right about the speed. Learn a way of counting ground covered with time, and you'll get the quick stats on how fast they're running. I'm convinced you're right about last night."

"So, they need to sober up! What now, replace them both?"

"No, it's a scrimmage so everyone, including us, gets to learn. Defensive coach might be going to a 3-4 or 3-3-5 formation. You and I are supposed to be doing offense."

The lesson from Agent Maltz took several laps around David's mind. "All right, Coach. Our quarterback is throwing like a slug. He has a great arm, but it's attached to mush. He needs to start launching that ball from further down."

Bert paused and smiled as though handing out a huge gift. "David, you're a coach, too. Never forget that. I told you, I'm here to learn from you, as well. Now, what about the mush? Tell me all about it."

The honest tone in Bert's voice made David stand up straight. "Well, my fellow coach, he is all upper body. When I threw, I started with my right big toe, bent myself like an archer's bow, and then snapped forward from my core. It's like my arm had very little to do with it. I know a dance instructor and tennis coach that can get him trained to throw bullets better than I ever could. I saw your statistics and compared them to my own. He has height, longer arms, and speed, but poor training despite his high dollar hometown."

"Started at your big toe?" Bert asked.

"Yes! Remember the time I had to take a few days off practice after the game that was all passing? My toe was bleeding, and I had blisters on others. I plant my foot and whip my whole body. Well, it's like the body is the handle and the arm is the whip."

"I'm going to let you do what you say. I'll check some stats after two weeks. You might be on to something. After all, it's 1983. Somewhere between Star Wars and the Ramones you're probably right."

David didn't respond. He stood with Bert the rest of the day and left the field elated he was now a coach. He was told he was. It was as if someone needed to say it.

After speaking with the quarterback, David noticed that Dr. Richman looked quite sad, staring at his desk. "Hey, Rich-man! What's up?"

"David, Pech is waiting for you at the hospital here on campus. Do you know how to find her office?"

"Oh, yeah. I told her I would come over. Okay, I'll go now." David took off towards Pech's office.

Pech had just put the telephone down when David came in. Although he normally greeted Pech like an excitable little puppy, he caught himself being more cautious. He still wondered about what was bothering her.

"David, it's Nguyen. He keeps talking about you and his football. Can you see him?" Her soft, brown eyes filled with tears as she looked into his. "Scratch, David. You sign his football."

"Scratch! Sure, let's go look. Good guy, really helped snap this campus back together after that big accident." He left with Pech.

They came to a wing of the hospital with temporary signs that said "AIDS Wing." Some signs displayed protocol, which meant nothing to David as he read them. They went into a large room with four beds all separated by green curtains. "Scratch man!" David said as quietly as he could.

"Double D man!" Scratch was barely able to respond.

David was shocked at the sight and the smell. It was a mixture of nail polish and the scent right after a janitor cleans up vomit in the bathroom. Noise was coming from the machines around Scratch and the others in the room. Seeing such a vibrant, young man looking as if he were shoved down a flight of stairs and half starved to death did not fit with the memory he had of the popular and intelligent man.

He looked over Scratch lying helpless in his bed and noticed every sore and protruding tube. The sounds of the machines became louder and the smell more intense. *Stop!* he screamed in his head. "Can we get you out, Scratch man?"

"Here to stay for good, my man. Hey, tell me what's going on with your coaching. I want to hear all about it!" For a moment, the spark and the fire for life that made him so popular seemed to dance behind his tortured face. David could see a bit of joy behind the yellow tinged eyes.

After a gentle pat on the back from Pech, David gave in to instinct and began to fill Scratch with stories of the past few months. Scratch learned that David no longer needed his stick. David invited Scratch to come watch his players. With Scratch hanging on to his every word, David forgot about the look and smell of the place and kept on with the excitement. He began to wrap up the conversation by expressing his gratitude at being called a coach when a familiar presence, the one he remembered when he was recovering, came up behind him. When David turned around, he saw no one.

There was a long annoying beep. Some nurses and a doctor rushed in. Pech pulled on his arm. In that moment, he felt the presence once again and thought he noticed what appeared to be an open window closing.

Pech held on to David's arm and gently led him back to her office.

Once they were in her office, Pech turned to David. "There were many times he had to know what was going on with the team and what the new coach was doing. Sometimes he had so many questions I had to ask Dr. Richman, who I made swear never to tell you. I'm so proud of you." She pulled out a football from a paper bag. It was slightly worn and had Sharpie signatures written all over it. David recognized Absolon's writing, as well as his own and that of the others.

"That's his, Pech. We can take it to him when he feels better. I would be glad to." He spoke towards the distance. He refused to accept the fact that Scratch was gone. He'd never watched anyone die before, so it just wasn't real to him.

"It yours now, David. You keep. Remember who is good and what you do. He confessed and made himself right in time. You help. Not understand, I know, but you help. Here, take bag, too."

He picked up the bag as though it were full of lead, gave Pech a hug, and left. By the time he got back to his dorm room, the reality that Scratch was dead ambushed him.

David put himself to bed five hours early. A quick change and he got into the small second hand bed. There was just enough room for him and the football. He rested a hand on it, feeling the beginning of the lacing with fingertips and the pointed end in his palm. Thoughts of that day in the quad and how the ball felt. How strong he used to be. Scratch working up the crowd, egging him and Absolon on. *Should I have held his hand this way, was he sad that no one touched him in his last days?* His question or prayer went out with some weight on his chest. He rolled the ball slightly back and forth with a delicate touch, just noticing that it was under inflated like no one was able to take care of it. Sleep may or may not come, he thought, but nothing else besides lying in bed made any sense to him. AIDS, once foreign, now became something he hated. It robbed him of friendship and cheated a most unique individual from a full life.

His eyes felt heavy as tears finally overwhelmed him. He drifted in and out of consciousness. He thought of John being the fastest man on earth and cried over the possibility of never being able to run again. At least David knew he was alive. Scratch taught him that. What to do with such a lesson? he wondered.

Okay, if for no other reason, good people like the game. I'll do my best with my part in the chain of command and not be a pain in anybody's ass again. No more. No more. At once he felt at ease, comforted by a peace that filled the room. Tranquility washed over him. David slept like a babe in the arms of an Angel.

School was out for good. A stinging dread took over David's whole body. It was a warm morning yet his legs were treading ice water. He stood at John's open door. "Hey, man, is that it? Going home with one bag? Looks more like a sack."

"Yes, my brother, this duffle bag contains everything. The rest of my stuff has already been shipped home." John looked into David's weary eyes.

"Well, can I get you something to eat first? Is there time?" David's voice sounded weak, as if he felt unwell.

John nodded and walked slowly with David to Farouk's. They ate in small bites and said nothing. They plodded silently to the great turn out and waited for the bus. The silence made David fidgety and forced him into making small talk.

"The free tennis shoes, do you get them in chunks or all at once? I mean, that would be a drag to have to pay for so much storage, not to mention the constant change of styles. I would ask for installments." His voice trailed off.

"My brother, I will miss you so. Check your answering machine like I showed you. We will play phone tag and set up times to talk. I have to go home. You have a new one here. Remember to come and visit your other home any time." John put his arm around David's shoulders.

They both waited in silence for the bus to arrive and then offered each other forced smiles. David lingered at the station for quite some time after John's bus departed. He eventually made his way back onto the campus, feeling alone and deserted despite the thousands of students still there.

———

Most of the hobble and odd gait in David's walk was gone. He was heading out of the administration building, having decided to hop on a bus, go down to the train station, and figure out the details of getting home from there. He still had one year of classes to go, having lost so much time recuperating, but a visit would be nice.

Running up behind the hunched-over David, Coach Saltier's voice invaded his muddled thoughts. "Hey, Moses, hold up!"

As David turned towards the familiar voice, he was taken by surprise at the thought of never seeing Coach Saltier again. "Are you running? How odd! Dang, is there a free hot dog somewhere?"

"Nice beginning to your relationship with your new boss. Burt's gone. He accepted an offer at another university. An emergency meeting is being held. We're thinking of promoting you to his slot to see what happens in pre-season. I can make up for any differences you may have in game experience, but you are extremely solid with the players and in your training. So, come with me to see the Dean and the President."

"Am I staying? Where will I stay? How am I going to live?"

"You're funny, David. You already get free food from Farouk's for life and there are plenty of on-campus apartments just for staff. Let's check it out."

A real job. David would make more in a year than his father ever did in five. He slept one more night in his dorm room, tossing and turning in fits of restlessness, daunted by the inevitable change, challenges, and different noises that awaited him.

Hey, we're trying to sleep here! David barked into the darkness. Several times during the night, he awoke in his familiar bed, the one he had gotten used to over the years. He found the football and rested his hand on it. *Some kids have teddy bears. I want to thank Scratch, no wait his real name was Nguyen, for helping me get here.* Once again, peaceful slumber took over and the warmth of his bed comforted him.

That night David realized Scratch made himself right with God. Pech's words finally registered. He knew John would be back home and he could visit him whenever he wanted. He also knew he would make football what it could be, the best place for the very best to excel.

In the morning, he brought only two bags into the small, one-bedroom apartment with a small kitchen, living room, and a bathroom bigger than any back home.

John felt Leduc an odd place without David Dryer and the noisy entertainment he was so natural at procuring. What a wonderful way to start a new life, never having to sleep on a train again, being pestered by reporters, or having to do another tedious photo shoot. The train stopped just after sunset. Still groggy, the world's fastest man was slow to get his bag, and even slower recognizing that half his hometown was waiting at the station.

"AaaaWWWWoooogah!" John's father was in the driver's seat of a 1930 Model A Tudor that had been in the family since it was built. Behind him, Phil drove his 1948 Dump truck with some kids sitting alongside him and a bunch of people piled into the back. The noise of the crowd reverberated in John's ear as the townspeople began to cheer in unison. The impromptu parade made up of two classic cars and some pick-up trucks went straight into town and towards John's new house. John contorted himself to fit into the passenger side while his father drove.

John's father laughed as the car puttered around. "They insisted, my son. I told everyone to stop this after today. There are so many questions. I'm so glad the Olympics are over, son!"

"Glad to be home, Dad. So this thing, did it ever get a makeover? I thought it sounded a little putt-putty. Does it still smoke?"

"Yes, but that's your concern now, son." They made it to the house. As they both got out and walked towards the door, John's father handed him the keys.

"Finally, a man of the family, a real man. So now the car can go to you. You can stop complaining about its workings, and so on, and spend your money on it, if you like. I did it 30 years ago, if I recall, working on the babbitting and such."

"It's in great hands, Father. Grateful hands indeed. See you at breakfast?" John wrapped his arm around his father, while firmly clutching the keys. "Oh, I should drive you home!"

"I can walk half a block. The car stays with you now. Sleep well, my son." He walked home with a smile bigger than John could ever remember.

John closed the door to his new house. It was as small and as tidy as most others. Tomorrow, he could look over his millions, make investments, take out some cash, and go over all of the other items like remodeling the house to his liking. He wondered about cable and perhaps a VCR when sleep finally claimed him.

———

Little Jan was not so little, John thought. She had that preoccupied look. "Hey, remember me?" John's infectious smile was broader than usual. He enjoyed the fresh air of Leduc that could be inhaled and exhaled without worrying about pollution first.

"Oh, you silly man!" She floated over to him about 10 feet, her feet seeming to never touch the ground. She engulfed him with a powerful hug before he could say anything else. "We were all ordered to leave you alone for a while. So, how are you? Getting used to Boringville?"

"I love Boringville! You'll know what I mean after some college. Hey, joining me for breakfast? David has such a wonderful new job now."

She cut him off, shaking her head with a glowing smile and started to walk away. "I'm meeting my fiancé. We're going to a new place over at the county mall. See you, John!" She walked away with a spring in her step, red-brown hair waving side-to-side.

"This way, little man." The voice of Gahl, the town pastor, chimed in. Being that much taller and wider, he practically blocked out the sun. John entered the Corner Café with him.

For John's first communal day back, the tables were arranged in a manner that could be enjoyed by many. Thankfully, there were no questions and plenty of happy faces. John knew the excitement was beginning to settle down, and that soon he could go back to being nearly anonymous.

John knew David could manage an answering machine. He left a message telling David to expect his call. In his usual, excitable manner, David was waiting for it, anticipation pent up for several days. "John, I'm going to be the passing coach! I have an apartment with a kitchen, and might have to take up cooking. I still get to use the library. They're going to have movies on tape! I'm thinking about getting a VCR. Do you have one yet? I hear they can record for hours and do stereo! I was told that one day a home theater would be normal. Farouk comes up with some outrageous stuff, huh? What's happening in town? Does Gahl still drink after church? What's Phil doing?"

John laughed to himself. He knew David would be fine. Sleep came early that night. It would still be a few more weeks until the time change and habits from life in Los Angeles would wear off.

9
A NEW LIFE

Five years later David sat in a familiar office unarmed with no one to help him. It was unprecedented to be promoted from passing coach in one year's time. Being a poor liar, David had no business being in the room.

Dr. Sirpouy, the President of the University, was a grand man in many ways. He, too, had accomplished much early in his life, and he loved football. He walked away from the game and into medicine late in the 1950's and retained his athletic physique. He was as gentle as a mountain of a man could be.

"Gentlemen, I know we are here to discuss, not negotiate, the contract for Mr. Dryer. I think what Head Coach Saltier had to say is relevant. If he says David is ready for assistant head coach, then I feel particularly comfortable with making that our offer." He closed his statement by leaning his large frame toward a thin, nervous man seated beside David. They sat at the end of a large, antique desk in an office filled with antiques and wood paneling, devoid of any technology, just as the President of the University liked it. Not even telephones were allowed.

A wiry, nasally man spoke in nervous, obnoxious tones. "Unacceptable! Five years as a passing coach!? Sirpouy, we go back, you and I. What am I supposed to take back to the other boosters? That this kid, not even Twenty-Five, is going to be the assistant head coach!? We can get decent ones for cheap! Shit, this is not some Podunk town! Someone with real talent could be brought in temporarily to allow David to season up a bit more. Am I really the only sensible man here!?"

Dr. Sirpouy inhaled slowly and sat up straight. "He took your personal choice for quarterback, a bad one, and had him winning games. The papers are touting David as the new 'wunderkind.' I know if we lose him now, it could be for good."

David sat hunched over. He was fond of Dr. Sirpouy and did his best to hold his mouth in check even though his fists were tight and breathing shallow. "That quarterback is a good man. He did everything I asked him to do and began to win. He had poor training, despite that high-dollar neighborhood he came from. I do have offers, but I want to stay here. If Saltier says I'm ready for the next job, then I believe that."

"And who the fuck asked you!?" the thin man demanded.

David turned to him and spoke in the deliberate, flat tone he used just before attacking. "Some of us have actual work to do. Dr. Sirpouy, I thought we could discuss building the line. The mid-western schools outplay the coastal schools because they have great lines. They obtain diamonds in the rough and work them up, like that quarterback I got up to speed. I would like to recruit locally."

"This is the kind of insolence I'm talking about! No one gets through to David Dryer! Oh, you're like Captain Kirk, the wonder-man, huh!? I have to say no, Sirpouy, another year at least." The man stormed out of the office without bothering to shut the door.

There was a long pause before Dr. Sirpouy spoke. David did his best to stay in his seat and keep his voice calm. He waited. He began to inhale, stretch out, uncurl his fists, and relax his face.

"People like him run the world. I run this University. The father of a son from the high-dollar neighborhood likes the idea of your promotion and believes you're right for the job. He has more sway with the other boosters than that 'man' who just left. Can I get two weeks to assemble and forward an offer to you, David?"

The confident yet warm tone in the President's voice was all David needed to hear. He knew he was being told the truth. "You have a way of convincing me. So that asshole, president of the boosters, is he just some mouth piece?"

"As you mentioned having work to do, so do the other boosters. That man has the time to come around and do the talking, as you say."

"I also said he was an asshole. You didn't miss that. Somehow, he also has a talent for finding the diamonds in the rough. Is there a path, a way we can get him to see that? He has the time, as you say, to find some real gems. Lineman, too. I wonder if he can be brought around like Bert?" David leaned forward, his voice thinning out from the stress of such a big idea, hoping he was somehow right.

Dr. Sirpouy's smile became more warm and broad. He gently pushed back his chair, stood, and came around the desk. David knew it was time to get up and did so, taking the President's outstretched hand.

"David, you are far more interesting to watch now than you ever were on the field. I don't know if I've managed to get through to you or if, perhaps, some experience has gone a long way with you. I like it, whatever it is. I'll convey what you've said. I think it'll have positive results. See you in two weeks?" He reached down to pat David's shoulder.

David noticed the good doctor was about Gordon's size. "I'm glad we're friends. See you in two."

Leaving the administration building, David stepped out into a day that was smoggy and sticky. The sun seemed to illuminate his ever-changing perception about life and people. Through the haze of brown, he could finally see a sliver of blue sky.

He walked to the edge of campus to the great turn out where the buses, limousines, and taxis paused to allow passengers in and out. It was the same spot where many times he waited for Paolo to come and go. Such a fine young man he was now. *Huge, but fine.* The thought made David smile. His mind began to race. *Get the lineman. Get off this campus and go to them. Stop the waiting and thinking and just go.* A chill and tightness gripped his chest. He walked in a cold sweat to Farouk's kiosk.

"My name is Michael, not asshole!" The wiry man from the office became visible in the shadows of the covered hallways.

"Dog dick, you're a real wipe. You're the kind of bullshit that greases the world, so what about it!"

The man stood for a minute, staring at David and sizing him up. "I'm wrong about you. I'm not paid to be wrong. You're going to be the next assistant head coach. I just got some phone calls and found a great lineman in Inglewood. It's rough there, but he's a great player and very good man. He has a 40 time that qualifies him for the track team, and it will take a lot of concrete to stop him. He can qualify for the basketball team, so footballs won't be going around or over him. Here's the name and address. Go see him today, if you can. I'll make sure he's covered. You know what I mean by covered?" With a greasy smile, he handed David an envelope.

David accepted the envelope as if from the mouth of a snake. He felt a wad of cash contained within, and then looked over the name, address, and telephone number written on the outside. "I shouldn't be calling you names."

"I deserve it. I, too, am sorry. You have a talent like no one has ever seen. I'm breaking some of my own rules. Seems like I'm looking into the eyes of destiny. I won't be forgetting the compliment any time soon. You are also a diamond in the rough. I am sincere when I tell you, to come to me for anything at all. You're the first person to recognize and acknowledge my talent and passion."

"Okay, Michael, but I won't take a bribe."

There was a smile on the man's face that struck David as genuine. "You don't know how a bank works? Well, I'm not a bank, but you need traveling money. That's to get you around, maybe buy the kid a pizza?"

David slouched over again, shooting a distrustful look at Michael.

"Don't look at me like that, David. It won't happen again, I promise." He nodded and grinned like people do at smart kids. "Oh, one more thing, he's surrounded by gangs who also want to recruit him. He's protecting his Grandmother, and I can't seem to get the police or anyone else to help. I don't mean to send you into the lion's den, David. I mean that. You're going to have to figure this one out." The man seemed lost in his thoughts, watching his own memories tell the story.

"Fine, okay, thank you. I'll work on it with your help." David noticed that Michael's intensity was body-wide, head to toe, like his.

Michael relaxed, straightened to his full height, and walked off with a spring to his step. David's mind tried to recall thousands of conversations with John and others from whom he sought advice. Before he put the brakes on his wayward mind and continued towards Farouk's, he allowed himself one more internal discussion. *Okay, so be honest without the hot-headedness. At least people will know where I'm coming from. Forthright kindness without the bullshit.*

A joyful Farouk darted about inside the small restaurant and retail store he'd built with his own hands. He set up the drawers, shelves, refrigerator, ice maker, Paninis, and hot plate inside the kiosk located on the sprawling campus. He finished giving lessons for the day.

"Okay, Jordan. I have a problem to take care of. You know what to do," Farouk said to the young teen. The excited girl continued to make a sandwich and was experienced enough to allow Farouk to spin, step, and get to the sink area where the coffee makers and blenders loomed overhead.

He filled a blender with ice and thick, chilled coffee with syrup. He let the blender whip everything together until only a slightly black, foamy mix remained. He poured the contents into two large cups, stepped out of the back of the kiosk, and meet David. "Over here, please."

"I know, man! How long do you think I need to learn things?" David mimicked with sarcasm.

Farouk refused to get caught up in David's skewering. "Drink some, we talk."

"Hey, you're not blocking your own line." David took the cup with a straw poking out from the lid. "Oh, nice, what are we doing? Hey, who is that?"

"Oh, I'm so fortunate, David. I'm to be married to her mother. So smart a lady, and a very good one at that. You see the daughter? Her mother is a woman with the same, if not unsurpassed, look. So very pretty!"

It was the first time David noticed that Farouk had dark gums. "Wow, big papa! So, a two for one. Done deal?"

"Oh you with your odd speaking. David, I met her mother and knew. I spoke to the pastor, then with her. She was so afraid I wouldn't like her. She does legal work and helps me with anything I want to do! Now, your problem. I have none. So tell me."

"One day, Farouk, I will understand how you know. But the thing is, I gotta get off this campus and go to a bad neighborhood. We have players around here that we can use, but I don't know why they won't come. A friend just told me there is someone from Inglewood High with size and speed like no one else. He won't leave his grandmother by herself. I have to get there."

"Tell me when you will be ready and Uncle Amat will pick you up and accompany you. That is, it. Enjoy this Frappuccino."

David drank with Farouk, showing him the outside of the envelope. Farouk nodded. They both finished their drinks, watching Jordan handle the kiosk without blocking the line.

He waited at the grand turn out. The tightness in his chest and cold sweat returned with a vengeance. David stood away from the curb, checking his Aviator watch and deciding to give the driver only so much more time before he retreated back into his campus apartment.

"Getting in please, Coach Dryer!" A bright smile greeted him from the inside of a cab. The man leaned over from the steering wheel and had the same dark gums like Farouk.

David complied, getting in on the rear passenger side. "Hi, Mr. Amat. I have to tell you; this is not the safest thing."

"Just Anwar for you, Coach Dryer! I know what we are doing and where to go."

David sat crouched, rubbing his cold, sweaty palms on his pants.

"Is the air conditioning too high? You seem cold."

"No, you brave and smart man. I have a condition. I will be fine as we get closer. Do I pay now or when we are all done, Amat?"

"You don't pay. Don't ask again."

David's mind was already reeling from his meeting with Michael. It went into overdrive, trying to spin every nuance, grabbing for some kind of answer. "Amat, I have the right and the power to find out and understand what the 'don't pay' thing is all about. I can get into trouble for taking free stuff, and I don't need it."

"A man in our family is one who stands strong against the bullies and bad people. You remember a particular bad boy, tall, yelling?"

"Yeah, he and his idiot friends. Never really saw them again except I heard the really tall, loud one just made All American in basketball."

"Yes. Farouk was about to leave the campus all together! This boy's father and friends are influential. You ended it, David, and restored Farouk's faith. I can't speak more about this, having said too much already. You just keep that under your hat, please."

"You got it, my man!" David looked over the changing landscape. It went from college clean to urban ugly in only minutes.

They came to a small pocket of south Los Angeles that was neat by comparison. The brake dust and urban flotsam blew in from just blocks away. David got out of the car and walked across the street towards the harsh faces that grabbed his attention. He approached who he thought might be the leader, a large young man wearing a white tank top. He wore a baseball hat with an emblem that was turned to one side, and had a comb stuck into the back of a large Afro.

"Hey, man, I need this one left alone. He has some real talent and can go places."

"And you are?" He gave David a look of contempt. He and the rest of his crew began to tense.

"Coach David Dryer." David motioned as if he were about to pull out guns.

"He's that wonder man!" said a tall young man, smiling and pointing at David. He and the others wore a similar style.

"Wonder why the fuck you're here, man!" The large one clearly ready to fight.

David spoke from instinct and didn't bother to look closely for the guns they were obviously carrying. "I'm here to give the kid across the street a real chance. I'm as willing to do what I have to as you are," David said, his tone flat.

After some jeering and loud laughter, one of the shorter, peaceful looking men spoke. When he did, the rest became quiet, obedient soldiers at attention. "That's Wunderkind," he said towards the tall, thin one. "Man, you're way out of the hood, Double D. As a respect, I'll keep an eye on his grandma. In return, you don't make noise as though you told me off. Clear?"

"Sounds good, you guys want money for pizza?" David pushed his hand into his pocket.

The small, quiet man laughed with the rest, shook his head, and waved his hand. The large man, now smiling, cast a shadow over David as he walked up to him. "The Double D man for real! Pleasure, bro!" He reached down, gripping him on the shoulder.

David took his outstretched hand. "I'm glad we're friends," David said with a smile.

The rest of the crew took turns with fist bumps, high-fives, and whatever suited them. David walked back across the street where he noticed Anwar gripping a large, silver revolver. "Easy, friend!" He spoke through the open window as he walked past the car.

"You have brass ones, Coach Dryer." Anwar kept the motor running and the air-conditioner blasting.

David was about to make his way to the house when an LAPD black and white on U-boat patrol pulled over to his side of the street and parked nose to nose with the taxi. Anwar gripped the wheel. He noticed the men across the street walk away. The officer spoke to David. "Sir, I have to ask what you're doing here."

"Oh, LAPD recruiting him, too?" David turned to the officer. "How about I guarantee getting him a degree first?"

The officer looked at Anwar, then back at David. His perplexed expression faded. "Double D man!" His grinned. "You got some balls being here, sir! Okay, Mr. Wunderkind, I'll be outside." The officer pulled a microphone from the middle of the dash near the floor and began to speak.

David knocked on the door. It slowly opened. A large, dark face became visible as a young man tucked his head under the top of the doorjamb. David looked up, leaning backwards when he spoke.

"Hello, I'm here to see Robert Calloway. I'm the new assistant football coach at what I hope will become your new favorite University. Would you like a free education and some pizzas?"

Behind him an old woman's voice spoke out with plenty of volume and energy. "Oh my, let him in, grandson! Hey, was you true about the pizzas? Boy here can eat!" David kept his eyes on the young man as he was let in. An ebony woman nearly as tall as the man approached David as he entered the room.

"Double D man coming to my house! Hey, wunderkind, I was thinking about you speaking at my church. Nobody, I mean ever, got up the way you did and made yourself into somebody. That is some real steel! Robert, did I not tell you how much better he looks in person than on TV!" She beamed at David. The young man also began to smile. A middle-aged woman and two older men came in and exchanged smiles with everyone in the room.

David's mind emptied itself of the endless thoughts that plagued him "This is my first time recruiting. Is it really going well?"

A short pause ended in laughter that shook the walls. Robert leaned over, putting an enormous hand on David's shoulder, nearly engulfing it. "I was told you would make it all okay!" He smiled and stood up straight.

"My grand uncles will fill me in on the details. I like basketball, but think playing for you would be just fine."

"I'm glad we're friends." David smiled back at Robert.

Soon thereafter, more family dropped in and convinced Robert that his grandmother would be left alone.

For David, the door to local talent was kicked wide open. Anwar was nearly pulled from his car by a few family members to join the party, which filled the house with people, laughter and food.

The house was adorned with sports memorabilia, plaques, and honors from the military and politicians. Robert's uncles were WWII veterans. Relatives from the LAPD and Sheriff's Department came and went. David learned about soul food. Any attempts made by him to pay were politely rejected. Robert's grandmother had been a champion tennis player, B movie actress in a couple of horror films, and had only recently lost her husband. Robert's mother had been a fashion model killed by her own drug habit.

The taxi left the house and headed back to the University. Anwar took a deep breath after loosening his belt. "I could be roasted myself. I'm so stuffed! David, what were those orange things like potato? My goodness, great stuff!"

"Sweet potatoes, Anwar. I know there's something like it called yams, but I get lost in the difference. Yeah, roasted for sure. I'm overstuffed. Can't thank you enough. Can you please take some money?"

"Only if you make me, Coach Dryer."

"Really, it would be insulting not to. Take it at least this one time for me. I will report to Farouk that all honor and good fortunes were maintained, my good man." David grinned as they drove back in the cool evening.

In his new apartment, David checked his answering machine. John had left a message. David looked at the time, added two hours, and knew it was okay to give him a call. "Johnnay! What the what, man!?"

"David, what have you been doing to pick up that new lingo?"

David could picture the wide smile on John's face. "Downtown! I met one of our new linemen. Grandmother was a champion tennis player, an actress. I met some Tuskegee airmen! So, what's this about your phone sound and megahertz?"

"Well, I got this cordless phone and it uses 900 megahertz to connect me to the base located in the kitchen. I can go down the block and still get calls. The machine is digital, just like yours, but the handset goes with me. Cool, huh?"

"Wow, slicker than quadrophonic in the car! Speaking of which, how is the A?"

"Ah, my dad gave me the car! Yes, starting next month, Phil is going to work on it. Oh, I forgot to tell you about 'not so little' Jan. She's getting married! Her fiancé is going into the Marine Corps."

There was a long pause. David's mind reeled at the idea he had been gone long enough for so much change. *Little Jan would go to a new life.* There was sadness about it, like death. He, too, remembered something he forgot. "Hey, John, Scratch passed away."

David looked up at a nearly empty bookshelf adorned with only the signed football. "I was there. It was the virus, like you said. I could just kill AIDS right now. I can't begin to tell you how helpless I feel."

John took a moment. "Being really great at something helps a lot of people. Phil is really good at restoration. I know my car is in good hands, and I'll be able to enjoy it for years to come. Just be the best you can possibly be. It will help. Scratch talked a lot about you and the team. It brought him joy like he provided for so many others. Like a big circle, when you follow your passion, your talent becomes the blessing you are meant to have and give to others."

"You're the blessing behind the blessings, John, my brother." David hunched over the answering machine.

"We all have a small yet significant part in the big picture, my brother. Okay, man, so what's happening? Did you get into it with someone today?" John inquired.

"Oh, you must know about Michael, the President of the boosters. Had to bitch slap him into reality. Found a good guy under the scales. Finally, someone in that league of want-to-bees came up with some line talent. Shit, they always want to pay for some star." David leaned back, seeing the files in his head as he spoke.

"Too close to tinsel town, my man! If they can't be stars themselves, they buy one. All that just to arrive at the party introducing the latest whoop-de-doo!" John ranted.

"Yeah, I got Mr. Whoop-de-doo today! I think I learned about the long term, though. I don't know how it all works, but for now I will just work at it," David replied.

"I'm going to sleep better now that I've heard that." The warmth in John's voice relaxed David.

They chatted a little while longer. David mentioned Farouk's impending marriage and his interesting uncle. John mentioned something about the old Walker House and how Gaul wanted to use it to help street people. They both slept well, knowing they were with each other despite the distance.

Far away in the northern Midwest, a cold-hearted son of avarice slept in a premium bed of a five-star hotel. It was the last night he would sleep alone. In the morning, he would be married to a woman who would fulfill his needs, according to his mother, and provide the right connections, according to his father. The money-seeking, power-hungry son of a congressman would use his parents in the same manner he would his soon-to-be bride, as simple tools. He would use them to get back the lands from the Leduc and Dryer side of the family. He was so hell-bent on it, his parents were merely a means to an end.

"David Dryer will come home to a renamed town." That thought allowed Bob Lundberg to smile. He smiled into the darkness, the only thing he was able to call it his own.

10
PROMOTION

David's twenty-seventh birthday was a few weeks away. Just in time to be lost in the rush to win the first games. He stood at the great turnout, which felt like a riverbank or the edge of the ocean. So many had entered David's life right here at curb side. Now, one would leave. Head Coach David Dryer stood with Craig Saltier, the man he replaced. Beyond the curb in his mind, wide-open waters brought fear. Going with the team, he could handle. He snapped himself out of his thoughts.

"Why the lack of parade? Oh, my, you're wearing shorts! Is that a scar or what?"

Saltier turned to the new head coach. "That scar had me in the hospital for a while. It's how I met Dr. Richman, an orderly at the time. He needed to work, because his rheumatoid arthritis cost him everything he could possibly earn unless he got healthcare. So, that's why with a genius IQ, the man handed out helmets and towels for us."

"The University took care of me, too. I don't know if I'm ready. When do you realize you're a grown up?" David stared out beyond the horizon.

"When you can play like a child, yet do what you did for Nguyen and Dr. Richman. You stayed with them until the end. That's grown-up stuff. Hey, you didn't spend a whole lot of time back home when your father died. I never brought this up. You were flown out there, took care of your business in three hours, and then flew back. I was wondering about it."

"To call my father an absentee asshole is disrespectful. So let's just say when I arrived, the ashes were already in the ground. In church, there was a line of people who walked by me, mumbling their condolences. Thank God, everyone left me alone about it. It's as if they knew the whole lousy story and went through some perfunctory task to call it done."

David nodded once at Craig and continued to stare out at the horizon. His gaze skimmed the roof tops of apartment complexes which lined every street around the University. He tried to imagine the place in Jurassic times with the tar pits and giant sloths, just as the museum depicted.

Craig's words invaded his thoughts. "The first rule of being a head coach is *you will fuck up*." Like he had so often in the past, Craig stood as tall as he could, leaning closely into David's field of vision. "Learn the difference between yours and someone else's. If it's yours, then say you're sorry and let them gas you out. It's their right. If it's theirs, be twice as gracious when they come to say sorry."

David thought a response would shorten the lecture. "I get it. Not the words I would have used, then again neither is that shirt, but I got it."

"David, at twenty-seven, you're the youngest to ever hold a position like this. You threw yourself into it entirely. Some men are able to accomplish the same, because there is no woman around to cause issues. Speaking of which, I like Dr. Tuttle, the woman you flirt with at the kiosk outside the science building. I'm surprised Farouk hasn't chopped your nuts off for cheating on him," Craig said with a grin. "My point is there's more to life, like compromise, that you don't know about. You learn by doing. Experience is the best teacher. Just promise me you'll have the guts to make a date with that woman. She won't wait around for you. And, for God's sake, get off this campus without the team sometime! It's not like it goes unnoticed."

"You know, if there were a parade for you, I wouldn't have to put up with this." David cracked a pained smile.

Craig paused for a minute, scanning the distance with David as they had so many times as the stood together on the side lines. "No one will miss you like me. You're a remarkable man. A real man, my son." Saltier blinked back the tears in his eyes.

David left him alone about it. He stood at the great turn out long after the taxi took Craig Saltier away. Eventually, he headed back into the busy campus. Many students walked about with parents, papers and maps in hand, looking a bit lost and bewildered. He helped out one of the students by pointing out his destination and thanking the parent for recognizing him. Suddenly, a crowd assembled.

A familiar, nervous voice seemed louder than the rest. Michael, President of the Boosters, swam his way through the crowd to David. "Okay, yes, we're so glad you're here. These people here will show the rest of you around. Thank you all very much. I know the coach appreciates your thoughts." Michael approached David.

"Okay, big man, now you know why there's delegation. I have the short list for you, the one that has your wants fulfilled. The first few pages are the ones open for recruitment. Next are the ones we're being pushed to go out and get. The last has a pair of running backs. We could have Paolo, but he's one more year away from being old enough, if he ends up here."

"Oh, Paolo is like my son. He will be here. He already graduated with an Economics Degree. I had to keep him busy somehow. Can't talk him out of playing ball with us here."

"Can't or won't talk him out of it?" The familiar greasiness in Michael's voice began to ooze out.

"You tell him he can't play here." His tone sounded playful.

Michael considered the possibility of telling someone four times the size of an average man that he could not come play ball where he wanted. "That really is a father's prerogative." He handed over the binder filled with names and statistics before he shuffled off.

The crowd remained, David's fun-loving personality took over. "Oh ye so weary from travel, tell me your tales of woe, and unto me shall fall such regard to the futures of all as warrants my attention!" The crowd went silent, Coach Dryer now the object of rapt attention.

"Now kids, who hasn't received dorm or class schedules? Raise ye hands if ye be pleasing." He closed one eye like a pirate. A sea of hands shot up.

"Ah, good fortune awaits as I, keeper of the secret path, can point ye to that yonder building." He pointed at the administration building.

"Tis the treasures ye seek! Off ye be wanderers from distant lands and be guided to your futures." Most of the crowd left except for a tired looking woman and a nondescript young man, the latter appearing as though he were cringing. David walked up to them.

"Hello, I'm Coach Dryer. Why the sad faces?" He gave both a warm smile.

The woman looked tired and exasperated. "My son was supposed to meet with the astronomy professors. They left a note saying they'd be out of town for two more days. There is nowhere my son can stay." She looked away.

Behind him a large yet soft voice interrupted. "Is that Piedmont?"

The scraggily boy looked over and made himself stand tall. "Wow, Paolo! Haven't seen you since MIT! This is my mom."

Paolo exchanged handshakes with everyone. "Yes, most good to see you again! T'ma, this is Piedmont, a prodigy astronomer. Younger than I and smarter!" Paolo had used the Tongan word for father.

Piedmont became animated. "Hey, I'm not the one graduating from MIT and looking forward to attending this University!"

"Only the best for my boy. Okay, you two look like you need some refreshments. I'll make sure your son gets his dorm opened up. Please, join me as we go to a faraway kiosk of delight. To Farouk's!" David waved his arm over his head as the rest followed.

They arrived at the kiosk. Inside, Jordan and a young boy mixed tuna salad. The coach spoke to her as he leaned down into the window. "Hey, who do we have here?"

She turned to him. "Oh, this is Max. Mom and dad are on vacation. I made them go, Coach! Here, try this."

She handed him a spoon-like fork and a pile of salad.

"Wow that's good! Okay, a round of sandwiches for my friends. Please, make mine just with the salad," David said.

"Oh, you're missing out! It's a whole experience with the other layers!"

"Now just a minute, little Miss Jordan. This sandwich thing I know about. Legally, two slices of bread with stuff in-between makes a sandwich. I'm just avoiding the ancillary distractions that'll keep me from having the good stuff between the covers. Deal?"

She looked at him with a curt smile. "No cheese, no lettuce, no tomato, no mustard, no mayo, no onions. Will that complete your order?" She cocked an eyebrow.

"Indubitably, milady! Oh, I'm buying for my friends here." He handed over a $50. She shook her head.

"Yeah, I know, but this is a party. Your father can give it back later." The look on her face compelled him to take back the money.

Everyone began to eat. Paolo's sandwich disappeared in two bites. Another appeared for him at the window. Again, swallowed up in two bites.

David went back to the kiosk and placed the $50 into the window under a saltshaker. He pointed at the large bowl of salad and made hand motions to spread it over more bread. Jordan nodded in agreement, glancing curiously at Paolo. David became quite tickled at the idea she was checking him out.

He was a sincerely good-looking young man. At seventeen, he was also an eating machine. At 6'5" and 250 lbs. of lean muscle, he was also still growing. The rest of the salad made five more sandwiches, which were placed in a box so they could be eaten while on the move.

The four of them helped Piedmont into his dorm and his grateful mother on her way home. Paolo tapped Piedmont on the shoulder. "Hey, man, I got access to the pool. Let's go!"

David gave Paolo some cash to get them set up with clothes at the campus store, as well as instructions to return the change when they finished swimming.

He was about to let the two go off by themselves so he could seek out Dr. Tuttle when a group of medical students came up the path. A welcomed and familiar smile beamed up at the coach, then at Paolo. The look of approval was obvious.

"Hello, Coach Dryer." The honey-laden voice of Ahnee was directed at David, but her eyes remained fixed on Paolo.

The long silence, the kind one experiences at church, made him fidgety. He turned to Paolo, who looked as though he were seeing the sunrise for the very first time. The sandwich consumption machine shut down immediately.

David looked back at Ahnee, then at Paolo, and then to Piedmont, who grinned wide. "Princess Ahnee, this is Piedmont and Paolo." He made a respectful hand gesture to both. Some of the other students looked surprised at what he had said.

"Me T'ma! Such formality!" Ahnee said.

"We're in public, please. You're getting your medical studies started early?" David inquired.

"Yes, I was accepted early. It's like going to MIT when you should be going to high school." She cast a smile at Paolo.

Piedmont broke into the loudest laugh. "Oh, sister, you got him good on that one! Oh man, Paolo, this is the royal girl I was telling you about! Her family put me up real nice at the islands. Got to eat with my hands and everything. Well, we're going to be doing some get-togethers, that's for sure! Okay, we're off swimming, so animate will ya, Big P?"

"Princess Ahnee," Paolo barely managed as he nodded in her direction.

She smiled and left with the rest of the medical students, who all appeared stunned to discover their new friend was royalty.

"Way to knock her out, Big P!" Piedmont bumped Paolo.

Paolo looked down at his amusing friend. "Well, what do you know about girls?"

"Woman, Big P, she is a real woman. At 6'2, she is a perfect fit for you. In the same smarts league, too. Can I add she's a hottie?" Being nearly a foot shorter, Piedmont got up in Paolo's face as much as he could.

David cut in. "Piedmont, let's watch how we refer to royalty. Now Paolo, your good enough for anybody, don't listen to anything different. She comes with some regulations you must follow. I can help later."

"Yes, T'ma, I understand. You see, Piedmont, Coach Dryer has a nice lady that he is late to go see. We need to leave." Paolo put an arm around Piedmont, directing him to the campus store.

Piedmont glanced back to the coach. "Whoa, Coach has a cookie! Wow, at your age?" His infectious smile made Paolo laugh.

"Why do you remind me of myself, Piedmont? Look, I have a lady that's the tops. She's very important to me, so we don't call a real woman a cookie. Now beat it, both of you. I'll see you at my place later."

The boys headed to the campus store while David made his way to the science building. His thoughts went into overdrive. *Okay, I got a son for all intents and purposes. No world to raise him in without a mother. It's possible Susan will ask why I waited so long. I could tell her I needed to get a real job before we went out or got married. This is a good deal, too. Dr. Tuttle is smart. I can just follow her lead everywhere and let the whole thing sort out as I go. Everyone else does it. I can, too.*

His mind continued to race. He could feel the tension building in his midsection as he approached Dr. Tuttle. "Doctor T! Sorry I'm late." He stopped within two steps of her.

"Oh, hey, Mr. Head Coach! Congratulations on the promotion. How do you feel about it?"

Her colleagues walked away, leaving them alone. "Well, like celebrating, with a special lady. What are you doing tomorrow? Want to just get out there and see what's new or go to a movie you haven't seen yet?"

"Oh, you're very sweet." She smiled in an awkward manner.

"Well, sure, you bring it out of me. So how would you like me to come get you? Do you want me to call sometime in the afternoon?"

"You're really very sweet for asking, but you should definitely ask someone special."

"I thought I was." David felt confused. "You don't want to go out?"

She paused for a moment before responding. "David, we're friends. You're married to this campus. Besides, I don't think it'll work. It was so very nice of you to ask."

"Okay, okay. Well, I know you have to go in now, so see you later."

She nodded in agreement.

He walked away, wandering towards the field. The tension in his gut found its way into his legs, making them feel like lead. It would give him some relief to pace the field and review his tactics, seeing himself as a player again, being able to run. He began to replay all of her facial expressions in his mind. The curt smiles, diverted eyes, awkward discomfort.

A familiar aroma caught his attention as he made his way to the off-season practice field. Fresh manure had been dusted all over it like dark brown snowfall. Any footprints he made on it now would keep the grass from being robust in those spots. Knowing it would take a year for the groundskeepers to repair the damage, David stopped in his tracks.

It would take decades to fix the damage inflicted upon his naive heart. *Oh God, what an idiot!* he thought. *What do I do now? How did I miss the signs? What went wrong?*

Standing on the edge of the field where side lines would later be chalked in, he scanned the field, imagined players on it, and remembered Swanton, Gordon, and Absolon. Saltier had been like a father to him, like the father he could be to Paolo. He may not possess the capacity to be a true father, but he could be a great coach. Plenty of time for that now. No one stood in his way. There would be no distractions.

The spring sun began to warm the air of the northern mid-west. In the hospital's private wing, a new life was held in the arms of Bob Lundberg. For a moment, all thoughts of his perfunctory wife, his hatred of David Dryer, his need to control the dynasty, and what the Leduc's and Dryers had taken from his family faded away as he stared into the adoring eyes of the infant so dependent on him. He drew the baby closer to his face, almost feeling his warmth through the blanket carefully wrapped around him. He was about to share the words in his heart with his precious son when his mother burst into the room.

"Okay, proud Dad, your father really needs you to finish the work you're doing on his campaign." Her cursory words, spoken with diet syrup in her voice, he simply filed away as one more thing to avoid.

He placed his son into his mother's arms without making eye contact. He consoled himself with the thought that everything would be fine once his parents were dead and he was in control.

Control over everything loomed as necessary in his mind. He wanted to spare the boy from becoming breeding stock for the dynasty. He would receive the charmed life Dryer could only wish for.

He turned over the boy for now, but walked away from redemption forever.

On campus Paolo and Piedmont came out of the pool area with brand new swim trunks, shirts, bags, and towels embossed with the University logo.

"You guys worn out?" David asked.

"Oh sure, had to show the island boy how to breast stroke. Gonna need it," Piedmont said, snapping his towel into Paolo's backside.

"Astro voyeur perv. You like the stuff then? You guys need food?" He let the boys walk in front of him as they made their way towards the dorms.

"Oh, I'm so full! I finished my sandwiches. Wow, Jordan can make good ones!"

Paolo stared into the distant horizon full of great food.

They dropped off a worn-out Piedmont at his dorm room and slowed their gait. "You're welcome to stay, if you like. You can call home," David offered.

"I have to be somewhere with my mother very early in the morning. There are no buses then. I should go." David nodded and headed toward the bus stop. Paolo seemed distant and in his own thoughts more than usual. "So, you know when a woman likes you, right?"

David almost choked. Paolo gave him a moment to recover. David turned to him. "Not everyone knows everything. More to the point, do I know everything about anything? The real truth is that each person, through their own experiences, learns life's many lessons. Give it time and be patient. You can always say no tomorrow." He sounded definitive, the way a drunk is sure of his logic.

They made it to the great turn out. Paolo knew something was wrong. He sensed that this man who was like a father to him was hurting. How he wished he studied more psychology. There was no math in that. Not real math, anyway. Only statistics.

As they stood there, he spoke the truth. "I'm so very glad that you help me. Oh, your change!"

"No, son, please keep it. I know there's more. I can read an ATM receipt." He patted Paolo on the shoulder.

"Did you buy those stocks and funds?" Paolo wondered.

"Oh yeah, I did. Micro something, Am Gen, Pfister, Pfizer? Please, you look at the list like you normally do when you stay over next time. The guys at the office are wondering where I get my info. How or when will I know how much it is all worth? I'm putting in like 80% of what I make in case things don't work out here. I noticed I don't spend much of the 20% that's left over."

"That's really overdoing it, but safe enough with the funds in proportion to the stocks." Paolo said with a confidence one has being able to pull up his own pants.

"Diversification! See, I learn, too!" He looked buoyed by the thought.

They waited together for Paolo's bus to arrive. As he was driven away, thoughts of being on campus full time came with warm feelings. He did not like seeing Coach Dryer look the way he did. My Jordan is a fine lady. Ahnee.... How does a girl her age become so lovely? Maybe he should get a cell phone...

Again, David waited alone after the bus departed. He paced the sidewalk and finally returned to his apartment. John had left him several messages. He played the last one. "Okay man, hey, it's too late for you to call back, but check in first thing so I know you're okay. Take care, my brother!"

He found solace in John's recorded voice. His thoughts began to stir. *I'm not alone, and there's plenty to do. It's too late. John isn't married. Guys can be single. What is that? Yeah, being a player or something like that! No need for distractions.*

David thought he felt some pain from his hip into his back. He checked his prescription and popped two pills.

"Take as needed. Better get more just in case." David popped another pill into his mouth, knowing it would allow him to sleep soundly.

11
PAOLO—A MAN CALLED SON

Finally, his son was with him full time. The crowd parted instinctively as Head Coach and his new defensive player, Paolo, made their way up an open hallway. The view on the right was of the quad, Farouk's kiosk, and the library. David was about to tell Paolo he just spotted someone when the clashing of something hard against metal caught his attention. He turned, expecting to see the young man walking alongside him. When he looked around completely, he saw Paolo holding his forehead.

"What in the world, son!" He was almost the first to reach him, but Ahnee was faster. She was practically a doctor so he allowed her take his third biggest player to the clinic while he inspected the pole for possible damage.

Finally, those two were going to spend some time together, he thought. David had many players left that needed help finding a tutor and proper mentor. No grades, no play. Paolo would never have that problem, not the man he called son.

––––––––

When news of his father's death reached Bob Lundberg, his first thought was *It's about time!* The late Congressman had been told to avoid the cold, but could not contain his urges. A young prostitute left him where he collapsed. An officer on patrol discovered the body hours later.

Bob set up a condominium for his mother and sold the family home. She was incompetent, his father had said when signing over the family trust to Bob in the event of his death. Bob gathered the money his father had left him in charge of and began to use it. He also claimed what was left of the political power to take over the gas fields in the northernmost part of the Dryer and Leduc territory. He had several influential people on the hook for setting up parties where power brokers could relax.

The contempt for his father grew stronger when he became the real power behind the scenes. Now, he could call on several congressman and a few senators whenever he wished, and they would all oblige him until they, too, died.

"That's right, ma'am. I'm Bob Lundberg. Tell the Senator that Miss Bambi has a problem that may go public if he doesn't return my call in 90 minutes. Another thing, don't you ever get bitchy with me again!" He slammed down the phone and didn't answer it for a week just to teach the sniveling submissive a lesson. Bob did possess some racy photographs. Since the Senator's re-election was not a problem, he was unstoppable. He could do almost anything, and it excited him to see just how far he could go.

———

Curiosity dragged David towards the clinic. It was located on the lower floor of the administration building, and had been since it was built. Blood tests could be taken, but nothing more invasive or technical. X-rays and MRI's had to be performed at the hospital across the campus. He found Paolo with Ahnee. They talked face to face, nearly kissing. He left them alone and went to his field office.

———

After four games, Paolo assumed the moniker, 'The Train.' David figured it was some stupid stuff Piedmont dreamed up. No matter. He sat with George, the Assistant Head Coach, in the formal lobby of the administration building, answering more and more insipid questions. To him, the reporters all seemed to be in collusion. They tried whatever they could to rile up the old preacher, poet of prognostication. It royally pissed him off.

"Well, Miss Tagamatsu, football, the American version, is a brutal cacophony with a core of ballet to it. When one is on the field and ninety-thousand people are screaming their guts out, you feel as though you're in the eye of the storm."

The reporter nodded and questioned further. "This is well-known that you employ different training techniques. Who's responsible for teaching the ballet you mentioned?"

David turned to Assistant Coach George Muntz. "George is quite accomplished at the matriculation process for unique training. George?"

Muntz, an all-star lineman during his heyday, tried not to look so surprised. "We have the cooperation from many staff members, who are already part of the accomplished and talented faculty of this University. Of course, Coach Dryer is uniquely qualified to speak on behalf of the unique training that goes on here."

"Thanks, wanker," David said under his breath.

"Coach Dryer!" A tall reporter accompanied by a video cameraman shouted. "It's been such a long time since you had a defensive lineman like Robert Calloway to work with. Paolo seems to be that kind of man, if not more. Could you tell us where The Train came from!?" His loud voice drowned out every other sound.

"San Pedro!" David shouted. He wanted to find Piedmont and wring his neck. Everyone in the room burst into laughter.

Three days later, a non-crucial game was being played. It was almost a two-hour bus ride, just short of requiring a flight. David paced the area behind the players that was in close proximity to the cheerleading squad gathered in front of the aged, creaking bleachers. This was an unimportant away game at a University barely qualified to compete in their league. A few fans sat in the stands. They were as quiet as the cheerleaders were unenthusiastic.

It was a winning game so far, before the half, although somewhat flat and boring. David was fuming. Paolo played as if he wanted to lose. The cheerleaders seemed uninspired, and the fans listless as though it was a hot afternoon instead of a chilly evening.

David stood looking through the gaps of the players towards a field that might as well be populated by Weebles, that silly-ass doll you can wobble, but not knock down. "Hey, George!" he shouted, fists clenched, jaw tight, brows furrowed, body hunched over like he was about to attack. The players in his line of sight towards Muntz parted.

"Yes, David?" Muntz responded wearily.

"Something wrong with the offensive line, like say, The Train!?"

The players between the coaches moved even further apart. "Seems a little flat, Coach." Muntz replied.

"Flat! Haul him in! Maybe flattening his ass with a boot will fix that!"

Muntz looked over at the other coaches, who also appeared surprised. He did as he was told, removing Paolo from the game.

Paolo and David went over to where the track began. "You're not here, Sole," David said in a special tone and using words befitting a father.

"Tam'a, my grandmother." Paolo shrank on his feet and nudged his facemask into the brim of David's up-tilted hat. They spoke like Samoan family in intimate form.

Paolo's grandmother was the only blood relative he knew that was safe. He'd often retreated into her little apartment when his Scottish mother and Samoan father argued during drunken rages. As a boy, he found himself the object of too many pointless fights.

David became enraged. His anger melted to just a growing lump in his throat. "Tu'u muamua le Atua I mea uma." David did his best with pronunciation of the proverb Paolo's grandmother loved, *When all comes down to nothing, God is up to something*. During the brief moments he spent with her, he would ask many questions befitting his study of Pacific Islanders. Often she would respond with the proverb: 'The person with burnt fingers asks for tongs.' He never understood it. Perhaps it was her way of making the questions stop. "Did she tell you to play?"

Paolo nodded. "Yes, as always."

"Sole, it's okay to let this game go. It's a nothing team. We can win without breaking a sweat. I can't have you getting hurt, because you're playing like a slug. Look, I can get you there on a special flight. Would that would be okay?"

"She would be angry if I left the game."

David's mind began to race once more. His son was hurting badly, and he needed to do something to keep him from getting hurt on the field. *Damn the game!* The screams between his ears were causing a headache. Something in the stands caught his attention.

There was a TV cameraman on each side, and near the end of the shabby stadium sat an old van with cables running to it. He felt warmth rise up within, the lump in his throat dissolving. "Does she still insist on taking that little TV with her everywhere?"

"Oh, that! Yes, my cousins made sure the hospital allowed it."

David got up on the tips of his toes to try and make eye level contact. He pointed to the TV cameraman in the stands. "We're being watched right now."

He began to nod with Paolo, who also noticed the other camera and van. "It's permission man, give her a good show. I will make sure we're there 30 minutes after the game. It will be good to see her again!"

Both nodded. Paolo stood up straight, went back to the side lines, and waited for the offense to finish. David turned to an aid and told him to arrange a special flight for after the game. He turned his attention past the listless cheerleaders and up towards the small crowd. He began to clench his fists and looked back at the cheerleaders with furrowed brows. "You girls think you can start a fire here?"

One of them turned and flipped up part of her skirt at him.

"Useless and sassy! Your dad know about that?" Two others did the same. He looked at the meagre group wearing his team's colors. "What the hell are you people doing?" His voice rang out around the decrepit stadium.

"Waiting for The Train, dumb-ass!" A brave alumna heckled while the crowed laughed. David began to unravel. The old preacher and previous star quarterback heckled back. "Oh and they speaketh a tawdry tone to the living dead and being dead themselves, they have no life for the living!" He raised both hands toward the crowd while walking towards them. The cheerleaders moved out of his way. "I call upon you dead spirits! Rise and be heard! Give no quarter to those we have travelled to defeat! Make yourselves heard! I call for... The Train!" He spun and pointed both hands toward the field.

In the stands behind him came a low rumble. "Paaaay-aaaaah-looo! Hit! Hit!" The crowd stomped their feet on the aging wood planks, causing the stands to shake.

The sound grew louder. "Paaay-aaaaah-loooo! Hit! Hit!" Eventually, the noise rose to the level of a steam train leaving the station. "Paaay-aaaaah-loooo! Hit! Hit!"

The cheerleaders lined up, mimicking a train with their body movements and pom-poms as the crowd became louder and more playful.

As the Head Coach neared the side lines, the defense began to line up. Noticeably larger than any other player, Paolo became infused by the energy and intensity of the crowd. The crisp air filled Paolo's chest, making him taller and wider. Bursts of steam could be seen coming from his face mask.

The spark David incited out of everyone had lit the fuel. In less than five seconds after the snap, Paolo had gone through the offensive line, taken the football from the quarterback, and ran it in for a touchdown.

Not long after the game ended. David and Paolo soon stood in the hospital with Paolo's grandmother. She had the chance to hear about Ahnee and Paolo's plans to work in finance. She declared David as his new father. Her word, in that regard, was final.

David did not sleep at all that night, feeling excited and being so proud. Paolo overslept, the professors forgave him for missing two classes the next day.

"You're just never going to die, are you!?" David joked with Professor Englert, his mentor and Pacific Islander studies aficionado. He gave the 70-year-old a very gentle hug and smiled into the cheerful face of his favorite professor.

"Oh, wait, you got problems there, little man!" He hugged David back.

David was impressed with the professor being so spry at his age. Englert tugged on David's arm and led him towards the office of the Social Sciences Professors. When they arrived, the room was filled with guests, the Chief of Police, President Sirpouy, Secret Service agents, and diplomats from the United States and Soma.

"Malo Talofa!" Englert said, motioning with his hands. "I present the father of Paolo, Head Coach, David Dryer." He moved out of the way to let David walk the only two steps available in the crowded office.

David looked around the room, smiling and nodding at familiar faces. "Malo Talofa. Malts! Man, don't you ever age!?"

The agent David befriended during the Olympic craziness on campus laughed along with the rest of the room.

"Coach Dryer, I am Ioelu. I represent the family of Ahnee." An average sized man by Samoan standards came forward. "I understand you are Paolo's declared father."

"Well, hell yes, man! Been working with my son more than 10 years now. He already graduated from MIT. We need him more than he needs us. May I add that he and Ahnee have a mutual thing going on? My Sole is good enough for anyone, royal or otherwise!" Englert backhanded him on the arm, trying to make him stop.

"Well, certainly! I came to see you about arrangements for a marriage, formally, of course, but later. I just wanted to know one thing now before we went somewhere more comfortable, no offense to the fine professors who call this office home."

"None taken! I'm sorry I didn't have the opportunity to brief the busy coach on the formalities we will conduct this evening. He is quite busy, indeed." He pinched David on one of his growing love handles.

David jumped at the rather merciless pinch. "Oh hey, my outburst, so sorry. Look, what's your pleasure? Did you have any questions?"

"My pleasure is we drop the formalities for now and go to this Farouk's. Agent Maltz won't quit talking about it." The room burst into laughter once more.

"Also, with the winning streak you are on, do you think you'll be going to the Rose Bowl? I like Pasadena, and that would make a fine reason to stay there. I would think your chances are very good with Paolo and the passing game you possess. Best in the league, I've always argued."

"My good man, it's my pleasure that you dine with me at a kiosk of great culinary delight! I'll be happy to discuss our team's talent in great detail. One and all come to Farouk's! Just remember, don't block the line!"

Farouk and Max had been forewarned about the crowd of visitors and prepared in advance fusion burritos of pork and fruit.

Ioelu was three bites into his burrito. "A true kiosk of delight, such an amazing meal! He must cater the wedding!"

After swallowing his food, David spoke. "Oh yeah, for real! Marriage. I didn't know about the marriage! Who knew?"

"Oh, my niece," said Ioelu, taking another bite.

"And your niece is?" David began to wonder why he'd been left out of the loop.

"Princess Ahnee. She knows. You had better tell Paolo." Ioelu looked at him with a tight smile while nodding his head.

"Well, sure, I think he'd like to know!" David was stunned. Once again, he received a backhand to his arm.

"He knows, David. Please give me time to explain after our lunch. Formalities don't start for another five hours. That's plenty of time. Let's just finish, please." Englert gave him a one-armed hug while eating another bite.

Professor Englert and President Sirpouy sat with David in his apartment. Englert was the first to speak. "Okay, look, they both made plans to get married. You would've learned about it if you'd gotten any of my emails. I just found out you haven't logged into a computer since you were shown what it looked like. All you have to do is act the part of the father, ignore Ahnee, and speak only to the diplomatic staff. Got it?"

"That's rough. I knew Ahnee before Paolo did. Don't you think that's rude, man? She's the village greeter and all that. What gives?"

Sirpouy cut in. "David, we all get it, so do the ambassadors. Paolo and Ahnee want a traditional marriage ceremony in honor of their island cultures. Therefore, we go along with it. It's the bride's day. We're making my offices available for the initial, formal introduction. Agent Maltz is doing what he can with security, given that word has gotten out and is spreading like wildfire."

"Word? That my son is getting married? What word? Who?" David looked perplexed.

"The entire campus, David. I think we'll be able to secure the administration building. Agent Maltz has escape plans in the works."

"Well shit, howdy! What else do I need to know?" David listened raptly as Englert went over the ceremony that had already been planned weeks prior.

A few hours later, David arrived at the administration building in a somewhat new suit. Although still deathly afraid of leaving the campus without his football team, his sincere embarrassment at never owning a suit forced him to visit the large men's section over at the thrift store across the street.

He found something that covered his body. He didn't even know what it was supposed to fit like. He observed that the shoulders did not bind, the sleeves came down to his hands, and the pants only required one cuff fold to work.

"Piedmont, you brat! Did you do anything at all?" He was nearly growling at the young man, who had recently filled out after weightlifting and eating protein for a year.

Piedmont hugged David, disarming him of any anger. "Wow, one day I'm going to take you in for something called tailoring. You look good, man. Don't sweat it. See all that?" He pointed to students scurrying around the edges of the quad, talking in small groups, pointing, nodding, and carrying instruments and tiki torches.

David looked up with an anxious expression. "Okay, man. Looks like you got my back on this one, perhaps for Paolo. I'll be very grateful if this turns out half as well as the gammara glomular thing that got you on TV and magazines."

"Father of my dearest friend, your knowledge of astronomy is obviously growing at a geometric rate." Piedmont hugged David again then sent him to the administration building.

David made it to the top of the stairs. For the first time, he noticed how winded the flight of stairs made him.

"Oh, what a nice color on you!" Ahnee was beaming at David as he came into the room, which was already packed with everyone he had seen before.

"Sorry, sweetheart, but I'm supposed to ignore you tonight."

Everyone in the room began to laugh. "After you bring in my husband to be." She smiled, and bent down to kiss him on the cheek. She spoke in her native tongue while standing close to David. The Samoans said something in unison and mimicked her hand motions.

Englert motioned for David to come over to him. "Paolo is on the other side of the building. Nice suit. Now go get him, bring him in, and introduce him to the ambassador the way I showed you. Go on." He gave David a gentle nudge. David noticed his eyes were bright and cheerful.

David walked out of the office and down the hall. *Was there a fire?* he wondered.

Coming out from the building and looking out onto the campus, he saw his son, Piedmont, and at least 200 students holding tiki torches. David did his best to fight off the tears. He turned around, knowing the two men would follow him. Excited voices and the shuffling of feet could be heard behind him. The flames on the torch tops appeared bent as students ran around to the other side of the building.

David walked into the office with Paolo and Piedmont following closely. They wore matching suits. David's was made of herringbone with blue threads throughout. His cobalt colored tie matched his suit, as well as his eyes. Lucky for him the white shirt was clean and pressed right off the rack. He was pleasantly surprised to find himself nearly matching Ioelu. He performed his greeting only to Ioelu, who responded in kind.

Paolo and Ahnee were allowed to be alone together in the next room, which was spacious enough for several dozen people. The room was altered only by the change in carpet and seating arrangements. It had been part of the official lobby to the administration building's official offices where David was sometimes made to perform his official duties.

He was not fond of the place until now. He noticed the walls had been cleared of the idiot posters meant to motivate students into greatness. The trophy case was covered with a curtain made out of some kind of finely woven, dried, grass or leaf.

David cast his gaze upon the enraptured pair. He never heard his son speak so passionately. Ahnee was radiant, laughing at something Paolo said. He looked back at Ioelu, then at the loving couple, and finally the rest of the room. David realized he and Ioelu were standing alone, apart from everyone else. No one seemed bothered by the moment. David completely forgot everything else he was supposed to do. "So, how long do we let them do that?"

"Oh, they will have a lifetime filled with such moments. What are you thinking?" Ioelu said.

"Let's all go for a walk out in the quad." David looked at Maltz, and motioned that they were about to go outside. Maltz nodded and spoke into his sleeve, grateful that Piedmont was able to help him coordinate with the students and ensure a safe zone.

Once they gathered the soon-to-be married couple and ushered them towards the door, Ioelu and David stood unified. They received hugs from both Paolo and Ahnee, who David was now allowed to acknowledge as a future daughter.

Paolo and Ahnee were the first to make it through the massive double doors of the administration building, which were being held open by a young man on each side. The deafening screams from the students crowding the quad were quickly replaced by the sound of drums.

There were torches everywhere. Ahnee almost fell over from laughter. There was an ecstatic and joyous look in her eyes when she smiled at David and Ioelu. Paolo held her arm as she navigated the steps leading down towards the quad. Temporary shallow pools with small floating candles dancing along the surface decorated the center of the quad.

"Kettle drums in place of Lali, neat!" said Ioelu.

"This is amazing!" David replied. "Right over there, Absolon and I started a game of catch. We were fill-in replacements for the starting line-up that happened to be in the same car wreck. A great man helped bring this school together. I'll miss him forever, I think."

"That is a wonderful story, and the best one to pass on to the rest of the family when you come to the islands," Ioelu said, looking at David.

The parade marched around the quad. David kept his fear of traveling to himself and did his best to enjoy the cacophony of noise and excitement. The fanfare made sense because it was for his son and soon-to-be daughter. It was a very long night. David went off to bed after Ioelu mentioned he looked rather tired and that it was okay to let the young people carry on.

John Kemp left one message on the answering machine, once again apologizing for not being there. He had a sick father to attend to.

David vowed to put every bit of focus and practice into being the proper father at his son's wedding. So many details of the wedding made no sense to him, especially considering the mix of traditions by Paolo and Ahnee, both from different races and Christian faiths.

Pain refused to leave David in peace. Thoughts began to fill his mind to the point of bursting, but immediately subsided once he popped some pills 'as needed.'

Thank God for coffee. David thought about how much nicer it would have been if John had been able to attend the wedding.

My son married before me, David mused. *Oh well, I made that decision.*

12

HOME CALLS

Twelve years later Head Coach Dryer lay atop his bed, waiting to see how much pain he would wake up to. He had a difficult time getting out of bed. His thoughts turned to the empty space that grew, a deep hole that would not refill, an echo from home spoke again.

Every lesson between the goal posts had been learned, retaught, and relearned. He had no idea what could be left for a forty year old single man, in a campus apartment with no skills beyond his perception and mouth. He could not cook, clean, or drive a car. He had no wife and had not tried to date a woman in the last ten years. He even gave away the dog the President of the University had given to him. Every day he woke to the same muddled thoughts.

In the last two years, prescription pills helped with the pain. One doctor told him he did not need them. He just found another one who sympathized with him. He became good at that. There was always a new one.

He took a few right away, showered, and checked to see if more pills might be needed. Ingrid was coming over. What was she, eight? Her little brother, little P they called him, was adopted by Ahnee, now a top pediatric surgeon. His son had done well with that one! They would arrive soon, meeting up at Farouk's so Ingrid and little P could run around. They were such great kids. *I really should get a dog for them to play with when they are here and perhaps visit at their home only fifteen minutes away.* His mind filled with visions of returning to his mid-western home in Leduc for a short stay.

Paolo was trying to keep up with Ingrid while holding little P. Ahnee was at his side. Ingrid spotted David with his coffee cup. She dashed up and stopped just short of trying to tackle him. She had been told that he was older and could not take such abuse anymore.

"What was all that about a crisis, son?" David took a long sip of coffee.

"Lots of bad financing. It's all over T'ma!" Paolo let down little P.

Ahnee bent down and hugged David. He accepted it, having overcome his

95

reluctance to display affection to her some time ago. "He means everywhere, not that the world is going to end."

"Yeah, man, please, if you're going to be all over TV, could you take some speech lessons?" David smiled for the first time in a month.

Paolo bent down and hugged David. "Everyone else knows what I'm saying."

"You have to come swimming, Uncle D!" Ingrid held little P's hands like they might dance. It was to keep him from falling over.

"Oh, I'm going to!" David bent down and took Ingrid's hands. She made little P wrap an arm around her back.

The four of them went for a walk around the quad, which was filled with the perfume of spring blossoms. *Why can't I leave?* David wondered, hanging his head low.

———

Full grown idiots, Bob Lundberg thought as he stood in the permanently hard mud of the gas fields. One of the wells was coming on line. He needed many more. He'd garnered the power he desired, but not enough cash flow.

"You've been here for years, boy. It's just pluming. I got the first one right after seeing one done. It's a wonder you didn't get that Tolson boy killed. Idiot, without the other we would be done!" The fog and the mud absorbed most of the volume.

The young man shrank.

Bob walked away to answer his phone. "Yes, start the foreclosures. Send Iada the notice to pay up or quit. No, I don't think she reads. There are buyers in South America. Sell the machinery there, take the cash and run it through Belize. It's all a write-off on this end." He began to pace, shaking his head violently. "Do what you're told and let me do the thinking. Yes, there is enough to have you arrested, too!" He closed the phone, put it in his pocket, and climbed into a fully furnished pickup truck.

———

Pech, David's adopted campus mother, sat in a cubicle with a computer and a few files. She maintained a desk and a private space away from the spacious office designed for her official title. She liked the quiet anonymity of the cubicle located just off the beaten path.

The computer had cross-referenced prescriptions on pills going back two decades for patients with the similar names, D. Dryer, H.C. Dryer, and more just like it. Fear gripped her midsection. She realized David was taking known liver killers. No one had ever bothered to order a blood test. She made an urgent phone call.

After a short while, she heard her name and a commotion about the location of her office. She approached the door as the president of the university and boosters were discussing the situation in loud voices with an attorney. "This has to be buried now! I knew him before you replaced Sirpouy, Mr. Johnson! If the doctors didn't order him to take a blood test, then it's their fault!" Michael had aged, but remained quite spry for a man in his 70's.

"This disclosure is poorly timed. We can't put him through rehab and continue recruiting. Players will sign on because they want to play for him. What if he's not ready by pre-season training?" the president asked. Both he and Michael looked at the lawyer for some sort of answer.

Pech was half the size of everyone else until conviction added about two feet. "My office, now! You, too, slick lawyer with tie!"

"Miss Nguyen, I appreciate your concern over David. I understand he is like a son to you. We are all interested in doing what's best for him," Johnson said while taking a seat.

She came around to her side of the unused, oversized desk. She hopped up onto her chair, her feet dangling behind the spacious expanse of oak.

"I read your letter, Miss Nguyen. You make several assertions. For one, without a blood test, we don't really know that his liver is seriously damaged. We need professional opinions to evaluate if this is an emergency or if some urgent action needs to be taken. I would suggest we find his doctor and consult with…"

She cut him off. "You suck, lawyer! Johnson, Sirpouy was real doctor. He would not even let the weasel in here. This my son! He not like adopted or just friend. He my son. You suck, Johnson! Now, I make call to home, Gaul, town pastor, and he get Dr. Fisher, real Doctor. He say even if only half pills are taken, it wonder he walking around. David got big friends. I tell them, too. I tell his lawyer! What you got, Michael?" She shot a withering look between the two she'd just skewered and then locked eyes with Michael.

Michael sat hunched over, his eyes staring deep into the ground. He raised his head and eyes, conviction contorting his face. "I am truly sorry, Pech. I will make sure these two are sorry, too. David is going home for a regular visit, maybe leaving tonight. I will make sure funds are available for any recovery he needs. Such things are covered in every contract for any University employee. I will keep it all off the record. He will be in good hands with Dr. Fisher. Better to lose this season than to kiss off the next ten. Okay, we're gone. Get up, you two." He stood slowly, as though pain suddenly removed the spring from his step.

"I don't think we've fully discussed what the ramifications are here!" Johnson said, standing quickly. The lawyer did the same, mimicking his facial expressions so that they looked like twins.

Michael imitated David's voice, the one he used just before striking. "Get out right now, or I withdraw my offer and this goes public."

They complied and left, shaking their heads. Both realized the money had just had the last word.

"What the matter with you?" Pech asked, smiling at Michael.

"I never told him how much purpose he gave me. David's sheer force of will against all that ADD and whatever else that sports psyche told us. It's amazing that so many like him quit early and fall apart. I wish he'd gotten married and smoothed over those rough edges. I hope he makes it back."

Pech walked up to Michael as he talked and wrapped her arms around him. "He is a good man, my son. Gaul tells me he has new help, Paul, like his own son, Special Forces, wanted to follow his dad." She looked at him with a smile, eyes brimming with tears. After taking a walk together, they ended up at Farouk's.

In his plush leather appointed pick-up truck, Bob Lundberg finally made his way through the fog and permanent mud of the gas fields. Noise from the caked-on soil splattering on the inside fenders as it flung off the all-weather, all-surface tires quickly subsided as he reached highway speed. He would drive the rest of the day and half the night to the halfway point near home. In a quaint hotel, he would have one of the local girls service him while his truck was washed of the soot, mud, and grease that was in every crevice and on the floor mats. He was about to relax when the mayor of Leduc called him. The steering wheel had a button for answering. "Yes, Mr. Mayor?" Bob said in a greasy tone.

"Hey, I have a meeting and need to know where we are with the Walker House." The mayor's voice sounded rough. He was a huge man, a former professional center for several football teams. He was more round than anything else.

"I had your reward faxed over to your personal line, not the office as you requested. The Walker House, according to the records I sent, was abandoned, willed to a dead relative of mine and donated the way you instructed. So, enjoy it, won't you?" Something about legal rip-offs tickled Bob like the teen prostitute he would be seeing.

"Oh, I know something about paperwork. Good job. It took a while, but it's more than I asked. I spread the word. David will be here soon. I don't know when exactly, but he's out now."

The mayor hung up without saying goodbye. Bob drove on, feeling confident about two things. His sons were as stupid as they could be vicious, and he was finally in control. They had a talent for making things look like accidents, like the time David's father was killed. He was a doper, too. Bob thought it might be nice to drive into Leduc and see if David Dryer would be feeling the pain. He smirked at the possibility.

At the church located in the middle of Leduc, Gahl stormed in off the sidewalk past his protégé, Paul, and poked John Kemp in the arm. John and Paul had been talking amicably in the church office about David coming home. Paul was excited to meet the famous coach, son of Leduc, and lifelong friend of John. He really is the brother of John, Paul reminded himself.

John went over to the visibly upset Gahl, who was already halfway done with one of his 40 oz. bottles of homemade beer. "Want one?" he offered without looking up. He knew it would be turned down.

"What's got you wound up now?" John sounded calm.

"It's David. Paul, get the fuck in here!" He took a long drink and stared at the floor. John moved his chair closer to him.

The 150-year-old plank wood floors broadcast Paul's steps as he came in through the front doors. He was a lean 220 lbs., standing at 6'. His neck muscles flexed whenever he looked around. He had been in the Special Forces just like Gaul.

"No more Mayberry for you! The Mayor just told me the Dryers no longer own the Walker House. So, no halfway house for the runaways." Gaul took another drink.

"I have a say in that, like I said. What else, my man?" John leaned towards him.

"David's been popping pills like candy. They say he could die. I already told Dr. Fisher, and he confirmed with Pech the amount he's been taking from the hospital. He would be dead already if he'd taken them all." He shook his head.

"Fuck that guy!" Gaul put down his beer and gripped his hands together. With eyes cast downward, John did the same.

Paul stood over them. "Did Dr. Fisher recommend a program? A huge University like that can afford the really successful ones."

Gaul looked up slowly, pain and anger etched into his face. "You're the program, my son. Sorry, but you're on active duty. Some guy forwarded a lot of money to the clinic with orders that no names be used. Dr. Fisher says he will be available 24-7. We have ways of making it all confidential. It's David. I helped raise him, now he's like his dad."

"When will he be here?" Paul asked.

"Late tomorrow morning. He left a message. He's taking the late afternoon train from Los Angeles," John said without looking up.

"The first three days are the most dangerous. When he gets here, I will need John to take away all of his pills, all of them. I will stay with him the entire time," Paul said with authority.

"What if he gets violent? His father was a classic drunk, Paul. I mean no distrust of your abilities," John offered.

"After the first night, there will be no worries," Paul said.

David wandered around the campus, up and down stairs, and in and out of empty hallways where he looked over portions of the campus. He saw Dr. Tuttle walking out of the science building, holding hands with a man while chatting excitedly. He thought about seeing what Professor Piedmont had to show him. He liked the photos of distant star systems and tried to pay attention and learn how they were made. He saw the professor coming out of the building with his wife, holding an infant. "Piedmont, what gives? Hello, Jordan."

"Just in time to introduce little J girl to Uncle D man!" Piedmont said with pride as he handed the swaddled infant to David.

This time, the germ alarms did not go off. David looked into the face of the child that had taken Piedmont from goof to father. "How are you, precious little Jordan?"

He held her for a while, enjoying the cooing and smiling. He felt the wonder of new life and felt a surge of regret regarding his own.

"Coach Dryer, you're something with children!" Jordan said with a grin.

"Your father isn't here, Jordan. You can call me David. Man, he was hard to convince that Piedmont was a perfect choice. Finally settled that over the ooh zoo. The Lord let me live, so never again."

They started to laugh. "It's Ouzo, David. Yes, that was a special occasion. I understand you've been having add shots in your coffee ever since!" Jordan said with an arm around her husband and a hand on the arm holding her daughter.

"They tell me the next morning I was found yelling at a diving board." David looked at the little tranquil face and then the couple.

"What a wonder. So did little J get your hubby to stop looking at the big bang?" He winked at Piedmont, who joined his wife in laughter.

"Oh, father of my dearest friend! What an uncle you're going to be. Please don't buy her stuff we can't afford! Okay? Deal?" He winked and accepted the baby back from David.

They parted after a group hug. David mindlessly headed for Farouk's.

"Oh yes, he called me names! I would not repeat them around you!" Michael said, having an animated conversation with Pech as David approached.

They both tried to suppress their laughter as he walked up. "Oh jeez, old stories! Well, the both of you are the best. I hope it works out," he said with a grin.

Farouk poked him in the back with a bag. "For the train, my friend. My uncle is already waiting."

"Wow man! Okay, please let him know I just have to grab one bag then I'll blast right to him. Thanks for everything! Hey, little Jordan is a complete peach. You're a lucky grandfather, my friend!" David held one arm open as he spoke. Farouk allowed a quick hug.

David waved goodbye and started towards his dorm. Pech walked up to him. "Be right back, Michael." She put her index finger up, and he responded with a smile and wave.

"David, you call me okay? Just let me know how you're doing, please." Her eyes were wide with alarm.

He placed an arm around her. It was hard to read her face. Maybe he would figure it out later, he thought. "Okay, sure. Hey, he's the marrying type, so no fooling around, all right?"

"You bad boy! What business you have?" She laughed and accepted a quick back rub.

"He was faithful to his wife till the end. I don't know a better man. Go enjoy." He let her go and walked to his apartment to grab his bag. As he cleared the quad, he heard the familiar sound of laughter floating in the air. More laughter came from the quad as Piedmont and Jordan rounded the corner with the baby. They joined Pech and Michael. From the supposed to be empty dorms, students emerged and congregated around the source of laughter.

David's thoughts formed around his day. Piedmont was a great man and would be as great a father as he made Farouk believe. He was also a popular professor who organized stargazing parties in buses meant for the football team. David felt some heaviness in his legs, as well as his heart. It was never easy leaving the campus, or Leduc, once there.

––––––

The rocking of the train normally bored him to sleep. In a private room and with all the amenities one could ask for, he kept his clothes on while stretched out on the bed.

What could possibly be wrong with him? he wondered. No wife, no family, not even a car. He seemed to be watching life pass him by as if he were a bystander on the sidelines. The sidelines made sense. He knew what the game was all about. That was easy. Football was easy. At least, now it was. Was there something else? Paolo and Piedmont looked so goofily happy. It was like they were really living. What the hell were they doing hanging around this old lump? *Oh, the pain.* It shot up from his foot strong and hard. *Okay, three pills, that's what it needs. Let's give it a few minutes.* He wondered if it was just his mind. It didn't matter. He waited long enough and took some more. *There. No more thoughts. Good.* He swiftly drifted to sleep.

13

FLYING ON THE GROUND

Danielle stood on the grass just past the black top on the western end of the school. An exact replica of her mother in appearance with her alabaster skin, and straight dark hair, the tiny nine year old possessed a talent for art that her classmates failed to appreciate. She waited with her head tilted downward, not seeing her favorite clouds, the small poufy ones that peppered the mid-western sky. They looked as though they came from a mold and were evenly distributed to decorate the serene blue sky.

A long shadow fell over her. Her lower lip protruded. "I'm too dumb for school."

"I know many different ways of being smart. Yours will take time to develop, Danielle. Please give yourself time," John said, unable to look into her face.

Danielle drooped over more. "Do we have to go in now?"

John waited a moment. "Not until you are good and ready. Danielle, did you notice this is your favorite kind of day?"

She looked up. "Yeah, cookie cutter-like, poufy cloud day."

Never rush a child unless you want them to learn tah be rushy-rushy. He heard Iada's voice and waited, watching the expanse of grass roll off into the endless horizon of farmlands stretching west. "There's something interesting about the clouds I think only you will be able to see with me. Maybe you could tell some friends and share how you see things."

"What do you mean, Mr. Kemp?" She lifted her head in excitement, looking at the distant sky.

"Have you ever noticed the clouds are all the same? Like from cookie cutters, as you like to say."

"Yes, that's why I like them so much!" She gushed.

"Good, Danielle. Did you know that they are all the same height off the ground?"

She shook her head. "No, they're not. Mom told me not to argue so much, but the clouds furthest away are closer to the ground, Mr. Kemp. See, they're almost touching out there." Her tone of voice sounded authoritative.

"That's a great observation! I can assure you that clouds of the same size are all at the same height off the ground. Now tell me, if that's true, then why can we see the sides of the clouds a little farther away and the tops of the clouds furthest away?"

"We would have to be higher than they are!" She squealed at the thought.

"We are, Danielle. We are. It's because the earth is a globe, and that makes the ground slope down as we look far away." He let that soak in. "You are always on top of the world no matter where you go. You can see it now. You can tell your friends."

She was focused into infinity of the distant horizon. She held her arms out to the side and splayed her fingers. "It's like we're flying on the ground!" She began to flap her arms.

The idea shook John like when David would come up with some insight. Like they were plugged into ultimate truth and could only parse out shards of understanding to mere mortals. *Amazing, thank you for her and all the good that grows around me...*

Jan Milnarcheck stood under a covered hallway where she could view the black top and expansive grass field. In the distance she caught John and Danielle flapping like birds together. She thought about the goodness of John and how Leduc was such an ideal place to raise a child. That seemed to be enough to live a happy life. She needed to tell John the train was coming. Since he was infamous for leaving his cell phone at home, Gaul sent her a text and asked her to send John go to the church. David was on that train. He never married, either. *Was he like John?* she wondered.

She knew he'd had girlfriends in college. John mentioned something about a woman who broke his heart and kept him from ever trying again. John was a wonderful man. He had looks, charm, and manners. She checked her suit.

It was suggested she start going to the Country Kick and similar places. Maureen was the only one bold enough to tell her she was much too young not to get remarried. Why did David always stir up so many thoughts? *I should be over him by now.*

John would either bring Danielle back to class or walk her home. He always knew what was best. It took a while longer, but they finally stopped flapping. John brought Danielle back.

"Everything okay, Danielle?" Jan asked.

"I'm fine. Do we have to go inside now?" she asked in a worried voice.

"I know you've been through a lot. You can either walk home with Mr. Kemp or return to your classroom. Mrs. Emmert is there. She'll be teaching art for the rest of the day." Jan bent down slightly, looking directly at Danielle.

"Oh, I've got something to show now! Flying on the ground! Great stuff with poufy clouds the playground, the sky, and Mr. Kemp. That's a lot of stuff!" She dashed off to class.

"You're a blessing, John," she said.

"Every blessing returned ten times over, the ones that don't bite you in the ass," he said like a naughty boy.

"Rash! Jonathan, please, let Gaul say such things."

"I'm just saying. David's going to be here later this morning. Paul and I will bring him to the Corner Café. Can you drop by?"

"Are you trying to set us up again? What did you mean, Mr. 'I got three cereal boxes framed, what do you got'?" She clasped her hands in front of her as she confronted the suddenly turned ten-year-old John. *God help us, David brings up soo much energy.*

"Oooh, fangs and claws! Look, I'm not saying, I'm just saying. We're all such old friends. I thought it might help."

Jan read the emotions etched on his face, which also showed signs of his lack of decent sleep.

"Well, I can say hello. It's just when he comes home, everybody mobs him. Then he just leaves. I'll say hello and be perfunctory to the drifting whirlwind that is David Dryer. Oh, no wait, Head Coach David Dryer, youngest, winningest coach ever!" She enjoyed another opportunity to engage in a wise-ass fight with John.

John's expression turned glum. His lack of sleep became even more apparent. "He will be here for a while this time, maybe for good. Don't know."

"You're scaring me, John. What did he do now?" She stood up straight.

"I can't say much. Please, just join us for lunch. You won't have to say anything. We can talk later." He looked at her with pleading eyes.

She had never seen John look like that. "No problem. I'll be there."

John walked into the church near the lectern and went straight to the office. Paul was speaking with parents and some children in the hall.

"You're on time. Where the ffff? Paul! We're ready for you!" Gaul's voice could be heard out in the street.

"I have lunch planned at the Corner Café with Jan. I think that will help in two directions. Did you almost cuss?" John asked.

"Fuck, no. Not too loud, anyway. Paul has me on some kick. Look, this is nasty business. Paul!"

The one hundred-fifty-year-old floor broadcast footsteps, some moving away and one set coming towards Gaul and John. Paul sauntered in. "Almost? You just did. You fat wailer just cool out. Hello, Mr. Kemp. How much time do we have?" He stood at attention.

"We have about 45 minutes. John says lunch is planned. That's good. Dr. Fisher is on standby. I am, as well. Look, is it really too hard for you two to carry your cell phones? I know this is Mayberry and nothing happens in 'Ole Leduc', but for fuck sake, can we just hook up this one time?" Gaul's face reddened as he shook his head of platinum hair.

Paul turned to John. "He means it this time."

"The only man that ever put me on my ass more than once was that boy's father." Gaul sounded reflective.

"Call it a day, Big Papa." John's word was final.

He and Paul walked to John's house to pick up his cell phone, then headed for the station in the Model A. Paul grinned.

"Okay, what's with the grin?"

"I like the old car. It's also nice to have something real to do. Not since the Special Forces, nor my time with Nash, have I felt something important was being done by me. I know everyone thinks God's work is never done, but I haven't done major things, John. Nash did important things. This is nice."

"It's nice pinning down an addict until he stops barfing?" John asked without looking over at him.

"It would be really nice to get Gaul to stop cussing. Don't worry about David. Just take away all of the pills. In a few hours, he'll have a tough time walking around. I won't have to pin him down."

They arrived at the train station. Paul looked around. "There's nothing like this place anywhere in the world."

After fifteen minutes, they heard the train. John sat on the bench and observed Paul, who stood his ground like a statue. Paul, at six feet tall, was shorter than John, but taller than David. John remembered Gaul sharing stories of Paul's early life, how he'd been wounded by gunfire at the age of 10. Gaul visited him in the hospital to make sure he was going to be okay. His mother was one of Gaul's rescue efforts. He made sure the gangsters, who thought Paul belonged to them, did not return unless it was by way of ambulance. He was an interesting mix, John thought. He had some Native American blood, along with a few others. He was dark and broad, but not fat. It was obvious Paul enjoyed working out. Troublemakers would occasionally find out he was well trained in martial arts.

Other people got off the train with David. He shook hands and thanked people. "Your son will do just fine. Hey, is that little Paul? You're a grown up!" David walked over to him and gave him a one-armed hug.

John embraced David, suddenly feeling the exhaustion of staying up most nights. "My brother, we have to do lunch, with Jan no less."

"Sure thing, man! Can we drop off my stuff first?" He hugged John with both arms.

"Cool, the Corner Café awaits!" John tried to sound enthusiastic.

At the threadbare house, John and Paul listened to every move David made while upstairs. Bedroom door open, bathroom door open, toilet, sink.

"Got all that?" Paul asked, looking at John.

"Yep, narrows it down. Do you think he took any?" John said, glancing up the stairs.

"No, he loaded up on the train. I could see it in his gait and the look in his eyes."

David descended the stairs, looking ebullient and beaming at them both. "You heard, my brother! The Corner Café awaits! C'mon, little Paul. When did you grow up? Do you shave now? Did you really keep firing for three hours after being hit in Afghanistan? I didn't know they let your kind into Special Forces."

Paul and John began to laugh.

Jan waited for them near the front door. Large picture windows allowed her to see them emerge from David's house. She checked her reflection in the window, front and side view. Her clothes were prim, which accented her beauty. Jan, however, felt the outfit made her look dowdy.

"Oh, stop it!" David bellowed while entering the cafe. "Did you grow up too, little Jan? You are just 100% woman! Hey, lunch is on me. May I, lady of the herringbone suit?" David tossed his head back, looking at her with mocking sophistication, and holding out his arm for her to claim.

"Oh, yeah? Who will hold you up, man of a thousand quips and barbs?" She took his arm and joined in their laughter.

David prattled quickly through the stories of Piedmont's new baby and Paolo's little boy P. Sleep began to take over as he started talking about the upcoming season and the tiresome problems of recruiting.

Paul, who would have normally been enraptured, sat with a pleasant look on his face. "Looks like we need to get you home, Mr. Dryer." He said.

"Yeah, no kidding. I might ask about retirement. I'll call Paolo about it. Jan, that business suit does not hide the fine lady you are. I don't know what else to say. Thanks for coming. I hope we see you more." He looked like he would fall asleep in front of everyone.

John couldn't recall a time he saw Jan glow the way she did just now. He and Paul walked David home.

John excused himself after they entered the kitchen and headed upstairs.

Paul became animated. "So, five freeway series games in a row! I just found out you're still one of the youngest coaches in the league!" He sat at the table, looking towards the end and hoping David would sit there.

"Good morning, Paul!" David sat down at the end of the dinner table he never used. "It's been hard. The players that come along tell me the same thing. They want to play for me. I still don't get it. There is still that wacky connection even after 25 years. I'm so tired. I know it's early, but I want to sleep. Can I see you guys for dinner? Thanks again for keeping this empty place clean."

"Always a pleasure, Mr. Dryer." Paul kept track of John's movements upstairs and felt relaxed knowing he had covered everything.

"Hey, is the big man tired?" John asked as he rejoined them, nodding at Paul over David's head as he came around.

"Yes, I am, my brother. Paul, just call me David. I am pleased to talk football any time. You're welcome to use the house whenever you like. I'll drop a line to John a little later. We can do dinner. Please let Jan know. I was just too tired and don't remember her saying much." David slowly climbed the stairs.

They heard the bedroom door close and the bed creak from as David settled into it. "Not too observant that David." Paul looked at John's bulging pant pockets.

John looked down. "Well, I don't normally steal." He looked up into the laughing face of Paul, who struggled not to make too much noise.

"Okay, well, you get a pass on this one," he said quietly.

John left as Paul sat at the table and prayed. He set his troubles adrift and waited. He pulled out his smartphone and sent a text to Dr. Fisher. "Rooster in the coop."

Dr. Fisher replied. "Standing by OAO."

Dr. Fisher, Paul, Gaul, Daniel, Phil, and some others were part of the loosely organized members of the town corps. They got town stuff done behind the scenes. He signed off with the customary OAO, meaning over and out.

Although it was only 4:00 p.m. in Leduc, it was time for dinner in Los Angeles. Paul heard David moving about upstairs. After more shuffling and some muffled swearing, David came downstairs to find Paul sitting where he'd left him a few hours earlier.

David looked like he had not slept in a week. He walked around as though stepping on nails. "Oh, hey, is it time to eat?"

"Sure, if you think so. Would you like to go now?"

"Yes, but I'm missing some things. I'm just so confused. My bag is missing some stuff."

"If you're talking about the pills, they're gone."

"Shit, Paul. What do you know about any pills?" David looked irritated.

"They're going to kill you and you don't need them."

David furrowed his brows and looked as though his thoughts were running like heavy syrup. He gripped the back of the nearest kitchen chair and leaned forward. "If I don't need them, why do the doctors keep prescribing them, Paul? How do you think they'll feel if you interfere with their job?"

"The doctors at the University have been informed and you've been red-flagged. You will not be able to go back and get more pills. Besides, you don't need them."

"Well, that's just fucking great, Paul! What, did you just make this up and convince everyone? Is this what everyone is concerned about? I feel as though I'm walking on broken glass, Paul! Do you have any idea of the constant pain!?"

"Yes, I've been shot twice. That's why I retired and went into the seminary. I consulted your University doctors, and Dr. Fisher is on standby. I've been helping addicts stay clean and sober for three years. You're not the worst case. You don't require hospitalization. I can be here the entire time. I don't mind."

"So the plan is we wait this thing out, and you keep me as a prisoner in my own home until I recover. That sound about right?" David looked anguished.

"You can tell me to leave any time. You can leave here and go to the county or back to the University. You just won't be able to obtain any more prescriptions. You're red-flagged. There aren't any dealers in town, and you don't drive. Besides, I'm here until you ask me to leave. By tomorrow morning, you'll want some company. You won't be abandoned, and you won't be left alone unless you ask to be. I can't force you to do anything," Paul said, his tone flat, matter of fact.

"You stole from me!"

"John took your pills. Good Samaritan laws kick in. You lied to the doctors, so the whole 'who said what' and 'who did what' is a legal wash."

David looked incredulous. "My brother, John, knows about this?"

"Very few people know. Dr. Fisher, Gaul, John, and I are the only ones in town who know. Unless you decide to talk, no one else will find out. No fathers, mothers, cousins, nor anyone else knows what's going on here. It's just you and me. Nothing you say or do will be shared by me with anyone, not Gaul or John. Only Dr. Fisher will be apprised of your ongoing physical condition. When you're ready, he'll come by. It would be wise to have some blood drawn to make sure you're not damaged internally." Paul kept his hands crossed in front of him.

David looked as though he just witnessed something terrible. He released his grip on the chair. "Die? Am I going to die? What? Why? I'm not a bad person."

"No, you're not a bad person, David. This happens to a lot of people. Please feel free to get some rest. That's orange juice. Please drink the whole bottle before going back to bed. We can also grab some dinner if you prefer. I'm here to help you, but I can't make you do anything you don't want to. It wouldn't take long if you allowed Dr. Fisher to take a sample."

David picked up the medium-sized bottle and drank it all without taking a breath. "Yeah, do that while I'm sleeping. I'm going to think about it, Paul. You can use the couch thing over there in that room." David's words trailed off. He trudged upstairs like a man climbing a steep, muddy mountain.

After about a half hour, Paul sent a text to Dr. Fisher. "The rooster has crowed."

"Coming to the hen house, OAO," Dr. Fisher replied.

Dr. Fisher took the blood sample from David, who lay passed out atop his bed. He had a messenger waiting at the clinic, and the county hospital lab had already received the funds to run the sample as soon as it came in. "Money buys a lot of convenience, Paul. David looks fine. Get some rest. Let me know if he starts to shake or convulse. Otherwise, you know what to do." Dr. Fisher smiled warmly and left.

Paul stretched out on the couch, replaying part of the conversation he'd had with David. He wondered if celebrities were talked to that way and whether or not it mattered. In the big scheme of things, it didn't. As he became more relaxed, his thoughts drifted to Nash, the man who'd taught him everything he would ever need to know about addicts.

———

Nash

Paul saw him in his dreams. He was the old-looking man, sitting on a park bench. He had been an addict most of his life, and at fifty, he looked more like seventy-five. The bench was located at the far end of the park under some trees. The park was near West Los Angeles, a full forty-minute bus ride from the place the man called home.

Home contained the smell of freshly washed urine, vomit, and clothes worn for months by wanderers of the streets. It had an upstairs area where he could sleep if he chose to without being surrounded by the addicts. He saved it for those whose recovery needed the feeling of accomplishment.

Paul sat next to the man attracted by the joy he exuded.

"Good afternoon, I'm Nash."

"Hello, Nash, I'm Paul. I'm in a seminary. I couldn't help but notice how happy you are, enjoying this bright wonderful day."

"Yes, I'm blessed to be here. The clean grass, flowers, the scent of ladies' perfume."

It took Paul a moment to locate everything the man described, and just a little while longer to notice the smells. He noticed that Nash had on old clothes, oversized for his bony frame. He also noticed a bible that looked like it, too, had been discarded and then resurrected by its new owner.

"I would like some of that," Paul said.

"Some of that what, Paul?" Nash asked.

"Some wise words about how I haven't wasted two years in school with more to endure."

"I'm always surprised by the Lord's blessings. I can help you appreciate everything you have. I run a recovery center and have a bus schedule with me to help you get there."

"You're a good man, Nash. That's obvious. I have a car and would be happy to drive you," Paul said warmly.

"Oh, my. A car might make me miss an opportunity. I was going to the mall today, but was drawn here to my favorite spot. I don't know if I was directed here or if the open space and laughing children were just what I needed. Here's a card one of my friends makes for me. It has the address and telephone number of the center printed on it. You'll come when you're ready. I get up before the sun."

Paul drove to the center the very next morning. The smell of disinfectant and institutional cleaning supplies hinted to what he might find inside. The field hospital where he was stabilized after being shot had the same smell.

Nash prepared food while the volunteers cleaned up. Nash staffed the place by himself until, as Paul soon discovered, some of the addicts recovered enough to help. Paul took out the trash, which contained clothes so over-worn that skin had come off with them while they were being removed. He had experience with bodies left in the desert heat until they were blackened and bloated. This seemed worse somehow.

He washed his hands and lower arms. The kitchen was tidy and had plenty of cookware. It was also filled with name brand foods. "Nash, I hate to ask, but how do you afford all of this nice stuff?" Paul pointed to shelves full of just add water, bake or boil, and microwave items.

"You can help me clip coupons later. It's all free, Paul. Even the owner of this building lends me the space for free. He tells me that developing it would cost more than what he gets for writing it off as charity. One of the ladies, who drops off her newspapers with coupons inside, told her companion she thought I used them for cleaning or toilet paper!" Nash laughed as he checked a pot with simmering minute rice and some other items.

Paul noticed the large stack of newly emptied boxes in an open plastic trashcan. "Do you want all of that out, too?" he asked, pointing to the stack of boxes.

"Sure, but there's a man who comes to pick up the leftover paper and cardboard. He makes money from the leftovers. I have leftovers, Paul! Imagine. If you open your heart, you'll witness many blessings. There are too many to count, and what would be the point in counting when they are like the grains of sand on an endless beach?"

Suddenly, the smell from the pot overpowered all others. Paul found what he was missing.

Two years of working at the center, two days a week, had transformed him. He became an honor roll student. He learned the techniques of coupon clipping, finding deals, and accepting every blessing offered.

Professors let him teach classes, taking front row seats when he spoke. Gaul would arrive the following week to watch Paul graduate. He would also learn about Nash and his ability to sustain such a center.

Paul never felt more alive. He would treat Nash to an unlimited taxi pass and gift cards for a haircut and a new suit that would fit him properly. He could not wait to invite him to his graduation. He would keep his speech a surprise.

He came up to the center, but was forced to park half a block away. The police had the building surrounded, and he could see the residents being taken out of the front door and lined up like cattle along the sidewalk. Some looked as though the sun would burn them up the way they hid their faces.

At the yellow police tape, Paul spoke to an officer, who summoned another. He escorted Paul to an alley just behind the center. Just beyond a detective, he could see Nash, half-naked and laying mostly upright. He was in a fetal position. Someone had taken his shirt.

"Do you know about the body, sir?" the detective asked.

Paul informed the detective about the victim. He stood rigid as if ready to fight, hands at his sides, and stared straight ahead at Nash.

The coroner finished his examination and commented it appeared to be from natural causes. The coroner and his driver wrapped Nash in a clean, white sheet.

The detective apologized and excused himself. Paul saw him stand, facing straight ahead towards the driver, who was about to push the gurney into the van. Other detectives and officers lined up in the same manner. The driver glanced over at Paul, as if waiting for someone or something. Paul recognized the military-style honor and joined them. Nash was respectfully loaded into the van. Once the van pulled away, the lines slowly dispersed.

"I can get the residents taken care of Detective," Paul offered.

"I'm sorry, sir, but the place is condemned. The fire department has been given orders by the County Health Department to seal it. As skilled as Nash was at carving out a piece of heaven in this bit of hell, there's no way anyone will be going back inside. The power is being cut now."

Paul exchanged polite words with the detective, who then told him, as he had done many times before, it was time to wake up.

David's couch was more comfortable than an Afghanistan field. The dream did not happen often. When it did, however, he was reminded to be grateful for just being able to wake up. He rolled over, pushed up to his feet, and went into the kitchen. He found David seated at the head of the table, looking like he just lost a 12-round boxing match.

"The couch folds out into a bed. It's really easy." David's weak smile barely reached his tired, pleading eyes.

Paul knew he would to make it.

14
SOBER?

"You're among the living, Mr. Dryer," Paul said, coming to the table and sitting down.

"Is this what you call it?" David questioned. The sun was coming up. In the dining room, David's only view was of the front door. He acted as though what little light might find its way into the house would incinerate him.

He looked at the band-aid on his arm where Dr. Fisher had taken a blood sample. "It's better that way. How much or how long will this take... I mean hurt, Paul?"

"Oh, wait!" Paul went to the kitchen and opened up a cooler on the counter.

It was next to a space where a refrigerator belonged. *If I'm going to stay here, got to get a fridge. Look at this shit-sty. What if Jan sees it?*

Paul came back with another bottle of orange juice and some pills. "Here, down this whole thing. These are to help for the next two weeks."

"Enough pills, Paul. Never again." He opened the bottle and took two swallows.

"Okay, take the brown, solid one. It has vitamins and minerals. Forget the capsule."

David complied and finished half the orange juice.

Paul placed half a sandwich in front of him.

"So that's considered a breakfast of champions now?" David inquired.

"For now, the main thing is time. It'll help, but not much. Still, your appetite won't return for a while. Recovery will take time. There's no way to get around it. You seem to be a fighter. That's good." Paul ate the other half of the peanut butter and jelly sandwich.

David took slow, deliberate bites, sips of juice, and the vitamin pill. "We just wait? I can't believe you're going to hang out here the entire time. What happens now?"

"This is day one. By day three, I'll know whether or not you're strong enough to go out and have some real food. Skipping the capsules means it'll hit hard today

111

or tonight. I won't leave you. Like I said, anything that happens here stays between you and I. Only Dr. Fisher knows about how you are doing physically. Everything else stays between us. John will never know unless you tell him."

"By day three, can I get an add-shot?" David asked.

"Is that something Dr. Fisher should know about?" Paul picked up the sandwich wrappers.

"Now, Paul, let's not be dim. I'm usually the dumb one. You're going to tell me that an add-shot is some foreign concept in Leduc?"

"I regularly travel from the big city to here. I've been dealing with drug counseling and recovery for a while. This add-shot is a new thing. Is that something you did in Los Angeles?"

David stared at Paul for a long minute. "I believe such things started in Seattle. It's espresso added to coffee. It's like you can skip the paddles, pour it into a dead man, and up he shall spring into life immortal." He turned up his hands as though tossing the idea to Paul.

"Well, I'm sure the corner café has that add-shot or can figure one out. You will earn one! Did not know you were in Seattle?"

"No, I'm in Leduc, the place to be. If the only thing I do for the rest of my life is to make add-shots available to the whole Midwest, then that is my new mission." David cracked a smile and let his gaze fall to the table.

"Run yourself through the shower before you fall asleep again. You'll thank me later." Paul threw the wrappings in the trash.

In a big city to the north Bob Lundberg waited for a VIP. "I better avoid making this a habit," he muttered, lying to himself again. He took two more pills with a beer. He waited in the stateroom of his corner hotel suite. It was bigger than most houses with a full working kitchen and adjacent bar. He had two young girls waiting for whomever they were supposed to entertain.

The senator finally arrived without staff, as advised. "I assume you're Bob Lundberg." He approached Bob, keeping his hands at his sides.

"I am, and I have this place, plus whatever you please. There's a lot more on standby, just tell me what you like." Bob lowered his outstretched hand.

"I like business. That wasn't some empty campaign slogan. You say that there's a fast track to getting my people employed. That's what I'm interested in." He looked at the girls at the bar like they were unwanted cars.

"Okay, business then. What you have is land rich for what's underneath. I don't care about ownership, just some cash flow. Punching a hole is expensive. I've technology that can do it without any environmental issues. Your people will make six figures a year for blue-collar work. What I need from you is to clear all rights of way, use eminent domain or whatever politics you have, but get me access to the spots on the map I sent to your office. Keep the protesters out and the media back. Your landowners get lease money after a time. Your people get paid right away. I, of course, am ready to make generous campaign contributions through a network so the money is quite clean. The only thing I can't do is hand you the plan on paper. That's why your predecessor and fellow party members encouraged you to see me personally."

"My predecessor was excused for ethical violations that I helped investigate. I was informed about you. You were the power behind the man, your father. The world has changed in the last 20 years. Your name is popping up on blogs and search engines, Bob. You're worth more as a dried-up trophy head on my wall than any connection or contribution. The people that owed you down to the mat are gone. They've died or left office. You might as well enjoy the room and the girls. They're of no use to me. Oh, those fellow party members? They're on their way out, too. I was just curious to see you and your reaction to the news that your reign had come to an end. The secretary you used profanities with last week was my wife." The senator finished, and strode out of the suite.

Bob walked to the bar.

"Well, what kind of party are we going to have, big man?" the girl asked, trying to be cute.

"You girls are done. I paid in advance." He fished around for some ice to go with his drink.

"What about our tip?" she demanded.

"Here's a tip. You're a fucking whore. Go fuck a couple of times before you go back to the barn! Double dip or double DP, but get the fuck out!" He pointed a shaking hand at the door. They left quickly.

His thoughts refocused on what needed to happen. He silently vowed to control those places on the map. Who owned them outright? Tolson's brother was with Iada. She was certainly a part of it. First, find out about David Dryer. Was he back in Leduc to stay? Bob poured whiskey over three cubes of ice and to the rim of the tall glass. *Stupid ass Senator*, Bob thought. *Those girls were top-shelf.* He would have had them himself, if only he didn't have that problem. *Wonder if the pills did that?* Time to call his sons, have them visit Leduc, and get some ground intel. He looked out of tall windows in the room that overlooked the city. He saw the reflection of a sickly old man staring back at him.

Paul waited in the living room on its remaining chair, reading his texts. *Paul, the tests are really good. His cholesterol is a bit high, but you can exercise that down. There's no liver damage or anything else. Is he taking the prescription? O.*

No, he's the bull-headed fighter you said he was. I just got another sandwich and bottle of OJ into him. He's back in bed. I think this will be the worst, O.

Okay, will sneak over @ 02:00. OAO.

Roger that. OAO. Paul put down his cell phone and lofted his thoughts to God, thanking Him for everything and asking for His guidance. A few hours later, the churning came. Still three hours until Dr. Fisher would arrive. He heard David writhing and muttering into the darkness. Paul suddenly wished the bull-headed coach had taken the capsules. He wondered if he should follow the advice of Nash. *Just let the addict sweat it out and go through the horror only a mind can imagine.* He sat down, closed his eyes, and listened for anything more serious. It would be a long night for David.

David found himself on a football field. It was longer and wider than it was supposed to be. The goal posts on both ends swayed in a breeze he could not feel or hear. There was some color, there was some movement, and the ground had something crawling under the grass that felt like nails under his naked feet. Paolo was screaming at one end of it. He wanted to come onto the field, but was horrified.

David bolted towards him. His teenage legs were back. He felt the rush of the wind on his face. The wind carried the smell of the room that Scratch died in. Suddenly face down, the crawly things under the grass suddenly began to pop up. They were small faces with empty eyes. They tried to bite him. He tried to get up, but the faces bit down on his hands. He looked back, propping himself up. The ground began to pull him in by his foot. He jerked hard and his leg came out, leaving the foot behind. He heard the crunching of it being devoured.

He tried to walk towards Paolo, but he was gone. The field turned into water. He began to drown. In went his other foot. He sank to his knees. Young Jan stood on the sidelines. She laughed with friends and then walked away. He struggled to breathe. Pills emerged from his skin and fell to the ground like seeds. The faces began to eat them as they fell. They asked him to join in.

He felt a fire rise from within. It exploded out from where the pills had been and began to burn down the field. The goal posts blazed, the grass withered, and only the baked solid earth remained.

"I will not!" He awoke to see Dr. Fisher and Paul standing by his sweat-soaked bed.

"That's the worst of it, David," Paul said.

"You're going to make it." Dr. Fisher touched his forehead.

"So this is Paul's plan? Let me sweat it out and almost die?"

"You're going to be fine. The blood tests I took confirm the same."

"I just want an add-shot," David groused.

"Is that from Los Angeles, this add-shot?" Dr. Fisher asked.

"It's from Seattle," Paul jumped in.

"David is from Leduc," Dr. Fisher said dryly.

"You're on my list, Doctor. It's okay. It's a good thing," David said, trying to get up.

Paul helped him. "Good, man. Okay, straight to the shower."

David showered while Paul and Dr. Fisher changed the bedding.

David came back out. "My pee is really yellow and stinks."

"Yes, that's dehydration. Come downstairs. Let's get a bottle of orange juice and a bottle of water in you before you sleep again."

David drank the liquids. "How close was I?" he asked Dr. Fisher.

"Well, obviously, you didn't take anywhere near what you could have or for as long. I know about chronic pain. There are people who have to manage it. They're monitored constantly. I would say that another six months at the level you had in your system would have caused some real stress. If you were a drinker, that would really have ruined you."

"I drank once. Oooh zoo. They said I was found yelling at a diving board the next morning. My poor son's best friend, Piedmont, needed help. Well, that's why I don't drink anymore. The nightmares were about as bad as this last one. Am I going to have anymore?"

"Hard to tell. Paul actually knows more about this than I do. This is the non-clinical way of getting someone cleaned up, so to speak. You're a remarkable man, David. I've never seen anyone go through so much and still want to fight another day." Dr. Fisher shook his head in amazement.

"David, I can say that it's going to be much easier now. You might still dream vividly, but let it all go. You've a lot of letting go to do. I agree with Dr. Fisher. You're a remarkable fighter, and I think you'll find a new outlook when you go back. It's one day at a time from here on out," Paul assured him.

"Well, thank you both. I don't know what else to say. Paul, I hope you finally learned how to open up the couch into a bed," David said.

"Special Forces here didn't know how to operate a folding bed?" Dr. Fisher joked.

"Caught him sleeping on it yesterday." David smiled.

Dr. Fisher began to tell them some stories. David learned how Paul was rescued by Gaul. Paul learned about the feud between David's family and the ones up north, as well as how the whole town was glad it was all over by the time David went to college.

A while later, David needed to rest. He told the other two to do the same. Dr. Fisher went home.

David found himself on the sidelines again. He was being carried off his feet. He heard a song, the angel song from his mother. She said nothing, yet he heard everything he needed to know. He saw his life.

Looking out at the burned-over field and the sun caked dirt where grass once thrived, along with chalk lines now blackened, he saw himself on the 50-yard line. His young self looked back. He walked over to where he stood. His younger self removed his helmet. How young he had been. It was odd. His younger self looked youthful, but wisdom etched his face, the brash smile replaced by aged knowledge.

"Thank you for everything," his younger self said. "Time for new fields."

The ground beneath his feet changed into fresh growth. Furrows replaced the burnt chalk lines, and the stench in the air turned to the perfume of spring as the sound of birds awakened David. His watch said ten. "Coach's clothing are all I have. Pretty sad, man," David said, slowly hobbling on legs that felt every bit of pain he'd previously managed to mask with pills.

"Ffff, I was expecting you to be up and around tomorrow!"

"Paul, did we almost cuss? Do I need to call Gaul? Shower, son! I'm calling John. We're going to the Corner Café and get this add-shot thing started, okay?" He stood there as though weights sat upon his shoulders.

Paul showered while David telephoned John.

The trio arrived at the Corner Café. They found Gaul seated at a table, looking as though he'd just received the worst news of his life. "Big red, why the funk, man?" David asked, hobbling up to him.

"Oh, hey." Gaul responded, not looking up. "The mayor told me the Walker

House is a done deal. I can't get the county to even let me lease some space. No recovery center outside the city."

"What can we start you all off with?" a waitress asked.

The others asked for drinks. "I would like a large coffee with an espresso added to it, please," David said hesitantly, as though it might be illegal.

"Okay, I'll get the add-shot with the others and I'll be back." She walked away.

John and Paul burst out laughing. David looked like he'd just discovered Christmas.

John was the first to speak. "Oh my brother, that was good. So, how about some clothes, man?"

"How about a refrigerator, man? My house looks abandoned. Know anybody who can help get it all fixed up? I mean, I think the last makeover was in the 70's." David shook his head, going over the mental catalogue of outdated everything.

"Yes. Paul here, along with his sidekick, Deputy Bosche, is quite handy. I just throw money at them and everything happens."

David got his coffee and savored its aroma. The Corner Café had purchased its blend from Africa and Sumatra. He recognized the vanilla overtones followed by a chocolate trail. Farouk was a very good teacher. He sipped repeatedly until half of it was gone.

After the group ordered their food, David turned to Paul. "Well, we're going to have to spend some money then. Gaul, what's all this dragging you down? I thought the Walker House had something to do with my inheritance? I don't get the issue."

"Well, I know you've been busy, as well as the others. Turns out it's something with unpaid taxes. I can't afford the lawyer it would take. Hey, we can go over all this later, my man. I'm really glad you're home, and hope you visit more often." Gaul tried to concentrate on his meal.

"I have one day at a time to get through for a bit. I know everyone knows what I mean. Well, good to be home. I have to call my son later. Don't worry about the Walker House. If you need it, then I will get it for you." David took a long draw of his coffee.

"Oh, yeah, Bill the mayor was a center for a few pro teams. Should go talk to him. Hey Paul, how long does it take to make over a house? What about a home theater? Do kitchens take a long time? It would be nice to ditch that crappy dining room, too. I hear you can get a whole home theater with surround sound just like at the movies! Hey, that brings up popcorn makers and so on. Gaul, do you think I could pay Paul here to help me shop? I have no idea about what goes into a kitchen. I had one back at the University, but who needs one with Farouk around."

"No more coffee." Gaul reached for David's cup. He barked and jumped out of his seat when David applied a generous amount of pinch to his side.

"Keep your fucking hands off of my coffee! I swim five times a week and toss weights around. I may have had a problem, but I can take care of you."

John put a hand on Paul's shoulder and patted a bit. Paul leaned back and closed his mouth, then looked at John's face. John looked away. "How about two deep breaths, one each, and then we get back to eating?" John spoke quietly and with enough gravity to make everyone follow his guidance.

David suddenly became sullen and hunched over. "That was wrong. I know how wrong I am. I'm sorry, Pastor Gaul. Paul will help me, he will."

Gaul also looked sullen. He raised his head to look at David and the group. "I was a bit rash, David. Please, let's get back to breakfast."

David nodded slowly, straightened up, and finished eating with everyone else.

A state away, a world away in a place time was told to leave alone, Iada began to stir within a mansion made out of logs that sat near an old, slow river's edge. It had been hand-built a generation ago by a man not allowed to own or run it. He was large, black, and could play as dumb and innocent as necessary. John Kemp's great-uncle Wellington made sure of some things before he passed away when John was a boy. He made sure John's father was accepted by the family and that Iada would have the mansion and lands he purchased with the help of those who looked White. He recruited Jews and Armenians to pose as the first purchasers before they deeded the land over to him. He made quick cash taking dives in prize fights sponsored by the Mafia. He leased land to others for farming. He was as smart and kind as he was big.

There was a voice within a mist that floated along the tops of the trees which surrounded the cleared acre in the front of the log mansion. Wellington had built the mansion and rented it out to businessmen looking for fishing and hunting adventures. The voice became louder within the mansion busy with orphaned children eating lunch.

"Yes, Lord. Yes, Lord. I will call right away! Josephine, can you get your cousin, John Kemp, on the phone for me?" She spoke in an accent representative of New York and the Louisiana Bayou. A pretty, young girl quickly handed her a phone. "Yes, hello, John? I'm impressed that David will stay."

John had just gotten back from the Corner Café and was loading clothes into the dryer. "Aunty Iada, I just said he talked about Jan being grown up and some other things. We just had breakfast and…"

Iada cut him off. "I was having a premonition about it. Lord tells me as a woman what you don't ever get as a man. My son, your brother is home to stay. You wait until he starts to fix that house or even talks about it, and you'll know."

"Iada, as connected to the Lord as we all know you are, however could you have known?"

"Bosche sent Josephine a text saying as much. He's gonna help Paul."

John kept his mouth away from the phone while he laughed as quietly as possible. "Okay, the truth always helps, my lovely aunt."

"The truth is he would be dead if not for you. He'll tell you. You'll know he's there to stay after that. You tell me when, I'll come. We'll get this family all straightened out. I don't like what Bob's doing. I don't like that he's got Tolson's brother up in the gas fields. I don't like the Lands Sakes Company. David needs to fight to keep his own. If he's the fighter you say, then we have the soldier we need." She said the last part with a strain in her voice.

"Fighter? Paul says he's been walking around after not taking any drugs to help him ease down. He ate well. Hey, do you know what an add-shot is?"

The conversation ended playfully.

———

John finished folding the laundry and walked over to David's house. He went upstairs to put away the small assortment of Coach's clothing, walking past David and Paul who sat talking in the kitchen. He came back to join them mid-conversation.

"So what kind of makeover are you going to do, and will you be getting your own laundry machines?" John asked, stepping into the threadbare kitchen.

"Well, as soon as I get more strength. Paul says that Bosche can come over in a couple of days, take measurements, and make suggestions. John, I think it would be nice to get something to wear besides coach clothes. Paul's already taking care of a lot of things. Can you help? I don't have a car."

"No problem. I'll come get you tomorrow after you call. Still getting up before the sun, my brother?"

"Not lately! How long has it been?"

"Just a couple of days." John smiled approvingly.

"Seems like a lifetime. Everything seems like a lifetime. How old are we, John, 47?"

"Yes, give or take a day. The two of us were born in the same week, Paul."

"That must've made gift-giving easy!" Paul said.

David began to smile. "After my mother passed, the only people who remembered my birthday or did anything about it were the Kemps. So, John is my brother in so many ways."

"You're a good brother to have. You look really beat, man."

"I'm feeling all those years now. It's all catching up. I'm so tired." They let David go upstairs.

"Is that normal?" John worried.

"No, it's not. I promised, no details about what happens here. He's every bit the fighter you said." Paul sounded kind.

"Well, I hope he stays. A real war is coming. An ugly family feud that everyone let go of until now." John stared at the floor as spoke. He looked at Paul with an approving smile as he stood and left.

"I can only resist so much. Please be kind to me as I rest." David spoke a prayer into the dim light of his bedroom. He fell asleep in the late afternoon and did not wake until just before the sun came up.

His dreams took him around Leduc and the farm fields. He saw himself and John playing as kids. Phil was giving them water and a lesson about dehydration. His stepfather was a happy apparition sitting behind him as Phil patted the boys' backs as they left. He found himself alone, floating upright as though walking, but was being carried through fields of low-growing vegetables.

He saw Jan from behind as she looked at a scarecrow that was talking. She turned to him with a horrified look on her face and tried to say something. David knew what she meant and floated past her towards the scarecrow.

The old man on weathered beams of crossed wood spoke with rotted teeth and eyes pecked out by crows. "You're going to leave!" It hissed at him.

"I am not! Get off there and make me!" David said in that tone he used when he was about to get physical.

As always, the cheerful sound of birds told David that dawn was arriving in Leduc. Fourteen hours after he went to sleep, David awoke to a new day and a new life.

15

ON YOUR FEET

"Scarecrow can kiss my ass!" David barked, knowing he was beginning to wake.

The sound and feel of Leduc was so unique, it was easy for him to recognize he was there as opposed to the many other places he traveled. It was always difficult for him to figure out where he was in a hotel. The high price and oversized beds did nothing to alleviate the disorientation. He would wake up so often, knowing only that he was not at the University or in Leduc.

He thought it was funny that he always deduced he wasn't in Leduc first. He rolled over, swung his feet over the side, and pushed himself up into a seated position. He paused, wondering how much it would hurt this time.

In the last four days, he had not taken a single pain pill. *Put one foot down, then the other.* He stood up on feet and legs that felt stiff, but not stabbing. He stretched his hands up and out. No shooting pain from the toes or that feeling like his feet were going to collapse. Just to see if he'd beaten Paul awake, he threw on his coach's windbreaker. It went down just enough to cover his underwear.

"I'm glad John brought over some stuff yesterday. You're not going out like that," Paul said as David walked into the dining room.

"There are many who wish they had this very windbreaker!" David tossed his head back in regal fashion and pulled up the jacket enough to expose his underwear.

"Only in Los Angeles," Paul said, smirking and pointing to a bag on the table. "Let's get those on. We're going for a walk or jog, depending."

"What? Paul, I swim. The running thing was over for me twenty-five years ago."

"I know, but we're not going to do it until it hurts, just enough for an assessment. I want to see if there are any problems. Dr. Fisher will get a report. You're going to have a bit of OJ, warm up, jog if you can, then breakfast."

"Fffff! Yes, mother." David spun on his feet, taking the bag upstairs. After a quick shower, he opened the bag and found a running suit, new socks, and shoes. He heard Paul showering while he dressed, and waited for him downstairs while having his prescription of OJ and a vitamin pill.

"Look at you! Okay, let's get going." Paul led the way out the door.

Just outside, Gaul and John waited in similar outfits. The sun had now lit up the sky, but had not yet risen high enough for direct sunlight to hit the small town or distant fields.

They walked down Main Street, passed the Corner Café, and made a left onto Cause Way. The slopes on the hillside still had spring grass on them. In the distance, the slope faded down and one could see a bit of the highway that ran North to South on the Eastern outskirts of town.

As they headed downhill on Cause Way, David noticed the bus stop where he, John, and Pete used to wait for a ride to school. It had a new bench with a cover and a signpost with bus numbers on it. He thought about how the buses would come in off the highway, then make a right turn on Starling, another right on Cause Way, and stop at the corner of Business Route. *First Street and Cause Way were the only ways in and out of town.* He thought himself weird to be having such random thoughts over a new bus stop.

"I would like to learn to be more calm," he said.

"You were doing so well!" Gaul bent over in laughter. John and Paul tried not to join in.

Even David realized that was the only thing said since leaving the house on a perfectly quiet morning in Leduc. The realization of it made him join Gaul. They all laughed until it hurt.

They made a left on Starling. John began to pull ahead in a jog. David passed Paul to keep up. Paul poked at Gaul, who was falling behind him. John jogged a bit faster. They jogged past Jan's house and were coming up on the school.

David tried to run a bit more, but the stiffness in his lower body warned him against it. John slowed to a walk. Just as the group cleared the school, David managed to catch up. "So there it is, the Walker House."

John stopped at the corner of First and Starling. "Yes, part of your inheritance. Gaul and Paul had such wonderful plans for it. Kind of like what my Aunt Iada does with the old resort my Uncle Wellington built. A big change of scenery really helps people who actually want out and are willing to put in the effort. Otherwise, some of the temptations that caused their misery are just too close. Well, it was a great idea."

"I don't mind if they have it," David said still a little out of breath.

"I'll have to check on back taxes or whatever," John said, turning to him.

"I have some help to ask for. My son knows what to do with such matters, either personally or with some help from Ralph and Cathy, that dynamic duo you see on TV. I keep seeing their names on things from the Island Chain Investment group, the company my son owns. They're pretty sharp," David said, looking past John to the house.

"The best things never change, my brother. You're one of them."

"You know the Dynamic Duo?" Paul asked incredulously.

"I never met them. I just recognize their names on my paperwork. I haven't brought up my inheritance, though. I'd better do so," David said, looking back at Paul and Gaul.

"I keep forgetting who you are, David. Well, time for breakfast. I think David and I would like to zip out to the city. Who wants to come?" Paul said, counting four hands.

They came up on Jan's house as she emerged in sweats to grab her paper. "Good morning, trouble-makers."

They all responded in kind. David approached her. "We're off to breakfast. I know this great place around the corner. It's on me!"

"I'm grading papers before class, but am free for supper. Can I meet you there at 6:00 p.m.?"

"At least, I'll be there. It's still on me. Till then." He bowed and twirled his hand in front of him like a sultan. She smiled, twirling the paper in front of her and mimicking him in kind.

The foursome continued on. No one spoke until they sat down for breakfast. "Well, that was a smidge brassy, but smooth anyway. Four days in town and the chaloob has a date!" Gaul said.

"Oh, come on, Gaul. Jan? We're all friends! Geez, give a man a chance to recover already," David said.

"Is that you, Coach Dryer? How about your usual, if you promise to handle it this time?" The waitress set the table off with laughter.

"I promise. Oh, and I'm ready for some real food, chicken fried steak with scrapings' sauce!" he said, becoming animated.

The waitress paused and looked over. "John, that is?"

"Oh, pardon my brother's vernacular, he means gravy, and he promises not to explain what inspired the scrapings' sauce reference."

"That reference would be the floor of a particular eatery whose very name cannot be mentioned in such polite company!" David said, pounding the table lightly.

"Hey, big man, you promised!" she said. "Okay John, Paul, and Gaul, I got you covered too. Hey, John, who is Jan all excited about?"

"I wouldn't know!" he said, squinting his eyes and pursing his lips.

"Oh, okay, I'll be right back." The waitress left quickly.

Gaul looked at David, who turned sullen. "Cheer up, man. You're rich!"

"Well, one can be rich in many different ways." David stared at the table.

"You've got a nice date tonight and you're going to act like this? Shake, awake son! Life's going well!" Gaul put an arm around David.

"I don't think it's a good idea. Jan's into someone else. I shouldn't be rocking any boat." David stared into the distance.

Gaul looked incredulous. Before Paul could stop him, Gaul shouted, "Where's Maureen when I need her? Dense as a fucking dried cow pie!"

"Outstanding work there, Pastor Gaul," Paul said as if he'd just tasted cow manure.

"We're all going to breathe deep on three. One, two, three." John drew in a deep breath. The rest followed. "It would be very rude for you to break a date with Jan, David. One way or another, you can at least learn about what she likes."

"Vodka with crème soda," the waitress said. "Okay, fellas, what will it be, and who wants scrapings' sauce?"

Gaul burst out laughing while pointing at Paul across the table. Paul did his best not to laugh, staring down with all his might. "Oh, man," John let out slowly and began to laugh too.

David looked around at the red faces. Some of the other patrons in the restaurant were starting to laugh, too. The cogs in his brain began to turn and smoke. His face reflected his mind's churning as he tried to put everything in order. When he pieced enough together, the possibility began to make him feel light and warm. "I heard you," David said, giving his order. The others followed suit once they calmed down enough.

Bob Lundberg, Jr. continued to walk down Business Route through town. His father had told him where David Dryer lived, and he wanted to arrive in an indirect fashion as though sauntering around town. At least no one knew him. That was good.

He hated Leduc. The only good thing about it had been David's father, who purchased the best weed and was liberal with it. He, in turn, would be liberal with the pay. It was a rip-off, of course, paying him with two other names. His father was in the rip-off business, so why not practice a little.

He made a right to travel uphill on Cause Way. He smelled the coffee, bacon, and pancakes. At least he was away from his asshole dad and idiot brother. His brother was only good for keeping a lie straight. It was an accident when David's father died. Bob, Jr. acted like they set it up. It was the one time his father was truly delighted with him. It was more a screw up, he thought. The gas wells had needed more expertise than his father had been willing to pay for.

He made a right turn on Main. David and his group were just making their way out of the restaurant, chuckling. "Mr. Dryer!"

David turned with a smile on his face and reached out a hand. "Hello!"

Bob, Jr. took it, shaking vigorously. "I had the pleasure of working with your father. He never stopped going on about his big boy! I don't mean to crash your party. I'll be in town for a while, please let me buy you a beer or something later?"

"Well, coffee is more my style," David said.

"My friends call me Sam! Sorry, I'm not used to meeting a celebrity! Hey, here's my number. You can reach me at any time. I'm stuck here for a week doing county paperwork, so any break would be welcomed." He nodded and smiled, letting the rest of the group break off as he turned into the Corner Café.

They walked away. Bob, Jr. could see the house David and the brown man went into by looking at their reflections in the large café windows. His father obsessively sent texts while drunk, so they were hard to read. He sent one back. *I met him. He thinks I'm Sam. I have the setup. Cool out.*

The setup was a camera in his pick-up that he could monitor with a cell phone. He parked the truck so he could watch the Corner Café and David's house.

David was back in his coach clothes. "Okay, I'm going to replace these today!

Where first, Paul?" he yelled upstairs.

"We're going to be picked up at the clinic. Let's go see Dr. Fisher," Paul said, walking to the door.

David reluctantly followed him down the block and over onto Business Route to the clinic. No one waited since it was not yet open. Dr. Fisher yelled out to them from the back of the clinic.

"Is it time for a sample?" David asked like a cranky 10-year-old.

"No, in a few weeks. Paul's been observing you, so have a seat. Let's get the shoes off. Paul?"

"Yes on the short leg and pronation. He described tarsal pain, so maybe bursitis?"

"Let's see." Dr. Fisher grabbed both of David's feet and squeezed hard in some places. David reacted to some of them. He then had David lie down and pull up his legs. After a few more tests, he made some notes.

"Okay, the problem is the back, and it's aggravated by severe arches in the feet and one leg being shorter than the other by half an inch at the tibia. Paul, you know where to get the inserts. Here are my notes."

Outside, John sat in a passenger van, Gaul riding shotgun. The door slid open and David followed Paul inside.

"And we're going where?" John asked, looking up into the rearview mirror.

"Your favorite shoe place, my man!" Paul said in an excited tone.

"Road trip!" David shouted. He watched Leduc disappear and saw the big city ahead in the distance. The last time he drove into town was with his mother. It always felt safe with her. They made him feel safe, as well. He wondered when he would be able to make the trip on his own.

Idiot actually did it right, Bob, Jr. thought to himself as his brother Harry drove up in a rental car.

"I scored. We can get wasted hard in about an hour." He drove them out of town.

"Good man. It may take longer than that. All this stupid shit has to work." Bob, Jr. looked at his smartphone's screen.

"Yes, there's the Corner Café and the talkative waitress who thinks I'm interested. That blue shit to the right is David Dryer's crib. Gotta love technology, man!" He smiled sardonically, looking forward to becoming numb as soon as they returned to the hotel in the county mall.

"So, you just gonna shout out when and I run the fucker over?" Harry asked.

"No, don't be a dumbass. We just collect information. Killing him would be a very high profile deal. Dad gets to deal with it. Don't listen to him when he's fucked up. Not that he's ever sober anymore. You and I are taking over soon, so don't get anxious." He continued watching his phone as his brother drove along, feeling on top of the world.

"Hey, have some lunch. They'll be ready in an hour," the store employee said, taking David's shoe choices with him.

"This place is all high tech with its twenty-thousand dollar computer. That's fast!" David said, looking around.

"At four hundred a pair, they damn well better be quick. Are you hungry yet, or do we go for some threads, my man!" John was excited.

"I'm hungry again, but let's see about some clothes in case they need time, too." David walked out into the huge mall.

The others followed. David tried to sort out the noise of the children screeching their shoes, yelling, and the different music styles coming out of different stores. There was no gridiron to stare at and clear his head. Everything seemed to crash in on him at once. He took in a deep breath and realized that just walking was beginning to hurt. John put an arm around him and pointed to a men's clothing store. The cacophony stopped its piercing intrusion as he sat down. He looked thankful and absorbed the quiet. John talked to the staff. Soon, David removed his polo shirt and tried on button downs, jackets, and pants.

A salesman put color swatches on his shoulder. David reacted like a man trapped in a dentist's chair. John told him it was normal. After a while, the patient salesman, with the help of the others, got him into a wardrobe of blue and light brown. Once they finished, David took home two bags of new clothes with more to be delivered later.

"Hey, shoes are ready!" David hobbled a bit as they all returned to where his custom orthotics were being made.

After some instruction, he put on the new tennis shoes with the inserts. David walked twice as fast as before. The group did a lap around the mall while David excitedly peered into each restaurant. They went back to a place with a jungle theme. "I would like monkey ribs and some sloth filets, please," David said as calmly as he could.

"Do you carry genuine tree sloth or is it farm raised?" Gaul said.

"Oh, I hate that. Ask for real tree sloth and you get that light pink colored sloth. No, mine has to be actual jungle caught sloth, or I'll just have a burger," John said, putting down his menu and joining the other two in staring at the waiter.

The waiter took his time, waiting for Paul and trying to act like this was new.

A short minute later, Paul, who looked like he wanted to stay above the jokes, began to order. "The python plate looks really nice. Do you recommend poached or grilled?" He looked up at the waiter with a neutral expression.

"Poached, sir, and may I say, good choice?" he said, holding up his order pad.

"I will take the number eight, salad, no onions," Paul said, putting on a regal air.

The rest ordered the same way. David became drowsy on the way home. Paul assured him that the clothes would be fine for his date. He tried to nap, wondering what to say and how to act. Forty-five minutes later, he woke up with two hours to spare. "Paolo!" He remembered to call his son.

"T'ma! What has you calling me so late?"

"It's 5:00 p.m., son. Oh, I'm in Leduc now. That's right, I never call you after dinner. Anyway, my son, I have to talk or would rather like to talk about retirement. So, who do I contact?"

"I will be there tomorrow." Paolo's low, gentle voice contained finality.

"Son, I know you're the big man. Someone else handles my money. Please, I can call someone in the morning."

"T'ma, I handle your money. No one else. The short answer is yes, provided you don't spend more than a million dollars a week."

"Very good, son! I like this joking out of you. Did Ahnee take you to comedy classes?"

Paolo took a minute to stop laughing. "No, T'ma. I'm going to be in that area anyway, so see you around 10:00 a.m.?"

"I know that tone of voice. It means you're serious. Okay, son, where do I meet you? I have to arrange a ride."

"I'll have you picked up at your house. I'm so excited about this! Okay, does that convenience you?"

"Over the top, my son, over the top." He said their customary goodbye, showered, then went downstairs to see who was talking to Paul.

"What the hell!? Is that little Bosche? Gads, man!" David hugged the civilian dressed Deputy.

"Well, sir, it's so very good to see you! So what's going on?"

"Well, this isn't some TV episode from the 70's I want to live in. I mean, look around this shack! Paul showed me some magazines. I picked out something I thought was neat, but you guys figure something out. Like John says, I just throw the money."

16
CONFESSION

As David sat on the edge of the foldout bed he had grown up with, he suddenly regretted that Paul didn't have anything better than a 40-year-old mattress to sleep on.

It was the fourth night and the pain grabbed him hard. He needed painkillers, but he knew he could never touch them again. Paul sat with him. David had never known such a struggle, and he was sorely unprepared.

"I lied, Paul. I lied to me. I lied to my players. I told growing men they could do anything they needed to do without steroids or drugs. They didn't know how wiped I was. What am I supposed to do? I was talking to Jan and thought I was about to pass out!"

Paul put his head down and tried to hide a smile. "Well, David, it could just be infatuation or worse!" He turned to David, who began to lighten up.

David looked at him with a smile and felt a little better. Perhaps it wasn't an episode, he thought. "What's worse than an infat-ee-ation?"

Paul laughed. "Dun dun dah dah, dun dun dah dah, dun dun dah dah dun dah dah dun dah dah." He sang while patting David on the back.

The tune of the wedding song finally soaked in, and David joined Paul in laughter. "Oh, man, am I as dense as a cow pie." He shook his head.

"My man, if I may say it like John, we will go over everything starting tomorrow. I'll always be available. It's what I do. We need to get you a cell phone so you never have to worry."

"Okay, Paul. I noticed something strange. A brand new pick-up truck has been parked in the street across from the Corner Café. No one knows whose it is. Do you mind taking a look?"

Paul stood before David finished his sentence. "Sure, come on."

They went out the front door together. The truck was in view immediately. Paul's sudden actions worried David. He had been in Special Forces, and like Gaul, was into electronic field surveillance. The stories all sounded like something out of a James Bond movie or a high-tech thriller novel.

He followed Paul's lead as they passed the truck and went down Cause Way. Paul looked ahead, and he made a left on Business Route. "Let's keep walking like we're going out for a stroll." Without looking over, Paul pulled out his cell phone.

"Hey, big papa, someone parked a bug across the street from David's house. It's the silver pick-up, brand new. We're walking to the church and will see you there. Okay, fine. I hope you have some results by the time we get there." Paul walked faster.

The small level of danger lit a fire under David's feet. They made their way through the church to the exit near the back. They heard Gaul swearing under his breath. He was twisting a pole and pulling on two lines that ran up and down like those you see on a flagpole. He looked over to a laptop, which was connected to a box with a wire that ran up to the top, there was an antennae pointed sideways with small, solid wires coming off the sides.

"Paul, did I not say to lube this shit up? What's with Mr. Pick-Up Truck that I have to halt my imbibing midstream? Hello, David."

"If you quit guzzling, you could lose some lard," David said, his tone flat.

Gaul looked at him. "So what set off your radar on this one?" he asked Paul.

"Dumbass left a blinking LED on his center console bright as a road flare. I saw it from across the street. Camera head is about the size of a lipstick tube. What's worse are the loose wires coming from the cigarette lighter and running under the passenger seat. I don't know who supplied the goods, but they definitely have a first-rate chaloob doing the fieldwork. So, I figure the camera is on a cell freak and being viewed remotely."

Gaul worked the pole and the lines in smaller movements. "They're not even encrypted."

David looked at the laptop and saw a green, grainy view of his house and the Corner Café. "This looks like it's from some submarine movie. Here's the periscope. That's just evil. Paul, did you say dumbass?"

Gaul barked. "No one's perfect. Fuck! Okay, Paul, I'll spool this, but I won't have the whole story until late tomorrow."

"Fine. We can do a little more investigation before doing anything. Wonder if we can just ask Bosche to pull that truck away?" Paul looked at the screen.

"That would ruin the counter intelligence. Chaloob or not, someone wants to know when David is coming and going, and probably who he's spending time with."

"Then he knows I left with Jan. Who does things like this? I've been taped on the field. We do cryptic hand signals so no one can read my lips. We've got to tell Jan!"

"Easy, David. I'm sorry. I know this seems like a lot. Look, they're just starting to gather information. You noticed the pick-up today?"

"Yes, and I'm failing to see why we should let that thing stay there. It's dangerous!"

Paul stood in his line of sight. "Okay, I get the danger. We want to find out who's doing this, right?"

"Sure, find the owner of the pick-up and beat the shit out of them!"

"If the suspect is just some field guy, and I'm thinking this isn't a bright fellow, then we ruin our chances of finding out why he put the truck out there."

"I'm struggling, but listening." David clenched his jaw.

"Good. Gaul is recording everything coming off that device, the one making the picture. He'll be able to find out where it's being uploaded, but not now. It takes more expertise than we have now. So leave things alone for at least 24 hours?" Paul held out his hands towards David.

David nodded. They decided to leave. Gaul found his beer and looked at the screen once more before going out into the back.

First thing in the morning, Deputy Bosche rode through town in his Sheriff's cruiser. He paused in front of the pick-up parked across the Corner Café long enough to memorize the license plate, and headed to the school. He was asked to secure the field and move everyone off of it so that a helicopter could land.

Good thing it's Saturday, he thought. It was the only day of the week it was clear. Tomorrow, cyclists would lounge on it before heading back to the city and distant suburbs. He ran the plate number. Since it came up as a rental and not a stolen vehicle, nothing could be done about it until an official complaint was made.

He heard the helicopter in the distance about the same time a large, black SUV rolled up on him. The driver got out and introduced himself. They waited together on the black top as the large, executive helicopter circled twice overhead and then settled down in the center of the field.

The helicopter's blades came to a complete stop before the back door opened and Paolo emerged. He walked up to Bosche. "Deputy Bosche! How nice to finally meet you." He reached down to shake his hand.

"Sir, the pleasure is all mine! Your contribution to the center and the school was unexpected. I hope you enjoyed the pictures."

"Oh, my wife adores the little ones. I'm ready to come down and speak at the high school towards the beginning of the season. That new charity foundation, Flying on the Ground, looks very promising. I believe it's the one you and Gaul helped to organize. Well, the efficiency of his other organization is impressive. I know more will be coming once I get the word out." He shook hands with Bosche again and greeted the driver. The pilot and an aide put two large cases in the truck before taking off.

The aide, platinum blonde, five feet tall, and extremely fit, approached Bosche.

"Hi, I'm Cathy. Paolo is really impressed with what you and the other men are doing, Deputy." She extended her hand, and he shook it.

He noticed her strength, but also how thoroughly feminine she looked and smelled. "Call me Burt! I only wear this thing on duty. So you're the Dynamic Duo, you and Ralph? How did that come about?"

"Well, Ralph and I met in high school. We were in the same math program."

The black SUV pulled up to David's house. Paul saw who it was and rushed over to the stairs. "Hey, get going! Your son's here!"

David descended the stairs on sore legs. "Man, stop with the yelling! When do the effin' withdrawals... son!"

"T'ma! Do you need cash?" Behind Paolo, the driver hauled in the cases one at a time.

"Oh gosh, no. Son, how are you? Have you met Paul?" David motioned for him to sit down.

Paolo shook Paul's hand. "You're the one working with Gaul. I'm so very impressed with both of you. I assure you that more funds will begin to pour in as soon as I recommend you both to friends."

"Wow, I'm speechless. Okay, how about I leave you two alone? The driver and I will get a table at the café." Paul looked like he'd just discovered Santa is real.

"An add-shot sounds great. Okay, we'll catch up," David said.

"Still with those add-shots? Hold on, let me show you what I brought you," Paolo said, putting a large case on the table. It was made out of solid black plastic with rounded edges and two front clasps. He released the clasps and opened the lid.

"Here's a laptop that contains all of your financial information. It's secure and will automatically connect you to the Internet. These are various passwords, and what they are used for." He handed David two cards with the same printed information on them.

"This is a smartphone. It does almost everything a laptop does." He handed David the phone and showed him how to use it.

"This is a list of people to call. I'm on the list. Find my picture and press. Easy." He went over the details of David's accounts.

"When you say five hundred million, what does that mean exactly?" David looked at Paolo with wide eyes.

"It means you never spent any money. Millions of dollars a year compounded over twenty adds up very quickly," Paolo said in a patient tone.

"I can retire? Is that what you're saying? What was that you said about not spending more than a million dollars a week?" David asked.

"I've had to put some of my clients on an allowance, because they'll do that very thing. They'll earn more money in five years than they'll ever need to live comfortably and travel the world forever. Still, they buy personalized jets and mansions for every day of the week and that begins to add up. They do the opposite of what you've done. I'll help, as always. I personally keep track of you."

Showing David one of the contacts in his phone, Paolo continued, "This person will provide you with transportation or anything else you need. Just give her a call. She knows about you." He let David reclaim the phone.

"I saw a really nice kitchen in a magazine. It cost eighty thousand. You're saying don't spend much more than ten times that a week and I'll be fine?" David looked at Paolo with pursed lips and furrowed brows like he was trying to figure something out.

"Oh, I wish my kitchen were that cheap!" Paolo laughed and shook his head.

"Okay, T'ma, these new cards are for you. They'll be attached to an account in which money will be deposited on an ongoing basis. You can spend it comfortably.

Call me if you need to make bigger transactions. There's a checkbook, as well."

"Okay, I'll go custom," David said, looking around the 1970's styled room. "Son, I'm not going back to the University. I've things to tell you, but not now. If it still pleases you, I'd be happy to come to your house and visit with everyone. Is that okay?"

Paolo paused and nodded. He smiled with relief and his eyes became cheerful. After showing David how to use his new cards, one Titanium credit card and the other a debit card, they walked over to the Corner Café.

They drove back to the school after lunch. Paolo introduced David to Cathy, who was still chatting with Burt. "Cathy, this is David Dryer."

"Coach Dryer! Wow, the real man in person!" She shook his hand.

"No more. Thank you, but no more," David said with some hurt.

"Cathy will handle everything. Oh, I forgot, the other case contains a printer with instructions on how to set it up. There are also gifts for your birthday. Please hold off until October to open them? There's a way for you to shoot video of yourself opening the gifts so that the kids can watch. I'll help you with that later." Paolo left with Cathy.

David watched the helicopter disappear into the distance. He felt such a burden being lifted from his shoulders. The twisting anxiety disappeared from his midsection and all at once, it became hard to stand. A voice interrupted his thoughts. "Sir? Mr. Dryer? Would you like to leave now?"

David turned to look at the driver. "I'm going to walk now. Thanks, anyway." He walked through the school and headed for home.

David felt like he was gliding more than walking. Something about saying the truth and feeling it lightened his mood. The day seemed brighter, the fragrance of flowers suddenly became like an intoxicating perfume, and Jan was better looking than ever. He came to a sudden stop when he heard the laughter.

"You, sir, will walk off the face of the earth moving like that!"

David turned to find Jan staring at him from her small front yard behind the hip high picket fence. "Oh, you're the flowers! I should have known." He felt his face turn bright pink.

"Didn't mean to startle you. You looked so deep in happy thoughts. Can I get you some water or something?"

"Sure." He followed her inside. Her floor plan resembled his. If you opened the front door, you could see the stairs going up on the far side of the dining room, which was also an extension of the kitchen. Located to the right was a living room with contemporary furniture in it.

On the wall of the living room was a large screen with tall speakers attached to the sides and one directly below. A large, black box sat on the floor. Behind him, there were three more speakers on the wall and another box with an antenna and some lights. He sat on the couch facing the screen when suddenly he leapt up and spun around to see what was behind him.

"David! What's the matter?" Jan asked, holding the remote.

"What in the world!?" David said, looking like he just saw a ghost.

"I was just putting something on for you. Sorry, I guess the volume was turned up."

"That's okay, but why is the sound behind me? Is that quadrophonic?"

Jan explained surround sound which David did his best to understand. "Okay, tell you what, how about a movie here tonight? We'll just have a pleasant time. Is that a smart phone?" She looked at his breast pocket.

"You know about these? I can give you a call! I just need to read how you make a picture that calls someone."

She helped him with the contact list, took a photo of herself, and added her information. "Look, you can even set an alarm for a particular date and time to remind you to call me or to do something. Would you like to see that?"

"There's lots of time, sure." He nervously handed back the phone and noticed how strong yet soft her hands were.

She smiled like a nurse with a patient. She set the alarm to remind him to call her at 5:00 p.m. He did his best to hear what she was saying, but he got lost in the details of her face. He could watch it forever. He strained over every movement and expression, trying to see how she felt. Was she just being nice? They chatted about the town, who was doing what, and then suddenly it was over. "So I'll hear from you at five. Okay, David?"

"Oh, I can guarantee that, Jan." He felt off-balanced as he left.

He walked to the outskirts of town, trying to burn off the energy he suddenly felt. He went up Cause Way and then up the hill until he spotted the Corner Café. He noticed that the pick-up still sat there.

Before he could think, he reacted. Reaching down, he picked up a rock from the side of the road, rotated his upper body, and threw it with a snap of his hand. As expected, it went through the windshield and cracked the back window. He continued up the hill and waited in front of the Corner Café.

He waited over thirty minutes. He finally saw a car driving south on First Street. He could tell that two young men were in the front seat. The car continued on its way. After fifteen minutes passed, he saw Sam walking up the opposite side of the road, staring at the sidewalk, hands jammed into the pockets of his windbreaker. That's odd, David thought. It was a rather warm day.

When Sam got closer to the truck, he looked up at it then across the street. He suddenly stopped and froze. After a pause, he walked across the street towards David. "Sir, how are you?"

"Much better, Sam. How are you?"

"You hungry? Do I get to treat now?" he asked with a smile.

"Sure, let's go." David noticed the strain on Sam's face. They went into the café.

Gaul watched Paul, who was looking out of the crack in the curtains of David's front window. "What in the clusterfuck is going on, Paul?"

"You tell me, fat boy!" Paul turned around to a red-faced Gaul.

"You said he was going to lick this problem. That's the old school David ramming his fucking head into things again! Shit all mighty! Needs replacement therapy, my ass!!! He needs a proper ass-kicking!"

"Or perhaps he needs a good fight. Didn't you suggest the very same thing?" Paul stood his ground.

In the café, the two sat down and ordered. "Taking a break from that county paperwork?" David noticed Sam's facial movements and his generalized squirming. Typical of the heavy drug users he'd been forced to excuse from the football team.

"Yeah, it's nice to get out for a bite to eat," Sam said, trying to appear relaxed.

David knew the restaurants were better at the mall near City Hall. Being in the same spacious parking lot as the Country Kick made it practical for them to stay open late.

"You sure like walking. How do you get around in town?"

"Oh, there's people coming and going, buses when they run, or taxis. The hotel can arrange anything! Yeah, it's nice to be here." Bob, Jr. said. He felt confident David believed him.

"Cool, man. So, did my father ever bore you with stories of my coaching?"

Sam sat straight up and put on a confident smile. "No, man! He was all about you and your coaching and the players you got to work with. All those games you won. He never stopped talking about it."

"My father was grateful for Bob Lundberg giving him a job when no one else would hire him."

"Oh, my—boss, Mr. Lundberg, was glad to have such a hard worker. He was smart and could take care of everything. They were really great with each other. Hey, enough out of me. What do you plan to do now? You think you're going to go back soon?" Sam asked, finally looking at David.

"I'm staying. I've a lot of family business to take care of. Apparently, my inheritance may have been stolen. I should've been paying attention to the people who were running the estate," David said in that menacing, flat tone he used before attacking.

After saying their goodbyes, David returned home to find an astonished Gaul and mischievous Paul. Gaul walked up to him. "So this is your idea of counter-intelligence!? What school did we attend? Impulse U?"

Gaul suddenly found his great head perched atop an index finger. David thrust Gaul's lower jaw upward and pushed hard. Gaul had been leaning forward, so he was caught off guard and now resting on it as though his great head was on a spike.

David held him up a moment more and turned to Paul. "That idiot is Bob Lundberg's son. I'd bet the other is close by. They're driving around in that four-door rental I saw. I bet they're meeting on Business Route near the General Store and that damn chaloob will get in and out of here. He'll probably send a tow truck from the county side later."

Paul turned to Gaul, proud of what David had uncovered. "Well, does that confirm your results?"

Gaul stretched his jaw. "No. The server recording the signal scrubbed the client destination. Without the help from the National Security Agency, it'll take a few weeks to find out."

David stretched one hand in front of the other. "Okay, the way I see it, Gaul can zip on down to see Maureen at the General Store and work up some more intel. I have movie night with Jan, so if no one minds, I'll take a repose." David strode through the dining room and up the stairs.

"Repose? Since when does coach boy do a repose?" Gaul looked incredulous.

"You're looking for a four-door rental car with an idiot behind the wheel and Sam, who's really Bob Lundberg's idiot son," Paul said, patting Gaul on the head and pinching his cheek.

He was just in time he thought. The alarm on his smartphone had gone off. He called Jan to confirm their plans. She assured him she had everything they needed. He just needed to show up.

The sun, still an hour from setting was becoming directional, glowing on everything with a western face. He could see a few clouds and the yellow beams on glass panes. The trees in the park above town appeared taller and more colorful. "Thank you for everything, and please remind me to take prayer lessons soon," David said quietly, looking up at the heavens.

His route took him to the outskirts of town, south on Cause Way, where the pick-up had been parked. It had been removed in the hours since he'd thrown the rock through its windshield. He knew that no one would be calling the cops about it. Only one person cared, and the chicken shit wouldn't make that call.

Crapzilla! I said 'chickenshit' right after praying. Good one. His mind reeled from a flurry of thoughts. *Darn, I should get a card!* He walked down Business Route to the General Store and found Maureen. "Hey, Aunty! I need to pick up a card. Do you have any of those?"

"Only the one that just came in!" said Maureen, who stood less than five feet tall and had a sunbaked personality to go with her happily weathered face.

"Perfect! I like that. Something new. Just what I need," David said, looking around. A small, golden ring on a shabby, brown envelope in the glass case in front of him caught his attention. He noticed it didn't have a price tag. It was placed between two matching ivory handled revolvers. A blue rock sat just below the revolvers with the words, *turn me over* written on it. If one glanced inside the glass case quickly, the whole arrangement appeared to be in a heart shape.

"Dense as a dried cow-pie. Look yonder, David!" She pointed to a spinning rack loaded with cards for every occasion.

He spent some time turning the rack, picking out cards, and not liking any. He felt someone behind him. Turning, he looked down to see Maureen, who held a small bouquet of flowers wrapped simply with paper.

"Just take these, my boy!" She smiled warmly, her eyes twinkling with hope for him.

"That's perfect, Aunty! How much?"

"I'll put it on the bill." She handed him the bundle.

"Let's close that register with a bit of cash. How much?"

"Eight bucks!" She spoke loud enough to be heard across town.

"Sure, eight, but is that price arbitrary?"

"Arbrit-tarry? No they're from a bush not some tree, David."

"Dense as a cow-pie." He kissed her on the cheek, nudging her at the same time, making her take a step in order to maintain balance. He handed her a ten and bolted out the door.

Later that night at Jan's house, he learned about home theater, popcorn makers, and something called chill-axin.

17
THE FIRST SUNDAY

"I promise in the new kitchen you can have a coffee maker, but for now you need to shake it loose and get off too church." Paul said to a stunned David.

David stood in his t-shirt and underwear. "An add-shot is all I ask. Just a quick one."

"You have 15 minutes to get yourself into a pew. Good thing it's a five minute walk."

David took that as his final word and went to take a quick shower. They walked into the church together. Paul went ahead to the front. David noticed the filled church had one seat and it was beside Jan. He kept walking towards the front. John turned and shook his head and pointed to the rear. David looked back. Maureen was giving him small hand gestures in Jan's direction. Jan looked as though she were trying to be patient with a silly boy.

The church bell rang, startling David. Muffled laughter broke out as he walked back towards Jan. When he got closer to her, she stood with the rest of the church as Gaul took his place at the lectern. She helped him find his way through the songs and prayers. The Bible with its numbers and semicolons completely vexed him.

When it was over, she touched his shoulder. "Add-shot?" He nodded and they headed quickly to the café.

"I know what you need. Hello, Jan!" the waitress said, leaving the two alone.

"Wow, David, you're becoming popular all over again," Jan said with a smile.

"The crowds are smaller. I liked the movies last night. Paul says we can get a popcorn maker and coffee maker in the new kitchen. I wonder how that will turn out." David looked in Jan's direction, but he peered past her into infinity.

"Ah, coffee is here. So, David, why the rock through the truck window?"

He took his first long sip of coffee. "Parking violation."

"Okay, I guess you still have the rocket arm." Jan sipped her water.

"Gun, they called it a gun," he said, smiling at her with a Cheshire cat grin. "Talk flows around this town as fast as I hoped." He turned a bit serious. "I just want you to be safe. You see anyone weird approaching, bolt. Let me know about it right away, all right?"

"Sure I will. Have you picked out any specific kitchen design?" she asked, blinking quickly and shaking her head a bit.

"No. I have no idea of where to start, either. You've got good ideas, Jan. I could pay you to help me out. It'd be no problem at all. I already have Bosche and Paul ready to put it all in. They're going to start a tear-up next week." He downed more coffee.

"Tear-out? I'd be happy to help. Maureen carries a lot of design magazines in the General Store. We can go make some tear sheets after brunch."

"Okay, so it's a tear-out, then measurements, tear sheets, then decide what can go in?" He nodded.

"David, what other than being a coach have you done?"

A cold sharp spike went up through his midsection; David drew in a slow deep breath through his nose hoping to hide his face on top of the mug. "Well, Jan, it's all encompassing. Many specialties are needed and you're surrounded by people who want to try something new, and you can't just start a new hobby whenever you like, so I am here now and trying to make things work."

"Well, it's better to pick a look. Then the kitchen, dining room, and even the living room can match." She looked at him as though trying to pass the idea from her head into his.

"I like the Jetsons and the sleek wood. Can we do that?"

"You like mid-century modern."

"No, not antique stuff, just the modern, but with the wood too. I like those sleek leather couches, too."

"Danish mid-century modern, that's what it's called." She nodded in approval.

"I knew you were an expert."

"I read."

"There are many things I like about you," David said, beaming at her. He didn't care about the hot flushing he felt in his face. They ordered their meals and laughed together like they had the previous night.

Danielle looked up, her big brown eyes bright and her curly, shoulder-length hair bouncing. She brought her face as close to Maureen as she could get it. "Why did you bring out the old ring, Aunty?"

"Time for it to be used, Danielle. Didn't take long for the first bite, either. Oh, here they come," she said as Jan and David arrived.

"Hi, Aunty. We need to tear it up. Do you have any mid-century Danish modern?" David tried to sound like an expert.

Maureen stared at him as though she'd just stepped in wet cow crap.

"We would like to buy some home improvement and design magazines," Jan clarified, trying not to laugh.

The two walked over to the magazine racks, passing the glass case. David's attention strayed to the ring and the guns until he could no longer turn his head.

He noticed a group of two hundred cyclists passing outside the picture windows that ran the length of the store. They rode within inches of each other at a pace faster than most cars went through town. The cacophony of mechanical noises, heavy breathing, and the whoosh of air felt exiting. "When did all this start up?" He pointed out the windows as another group flew past.

"A few years ago. They take over the town on Sundays. Gaul has been holding church from sunrise to just past sunset for quite some time now. About 10:00 a.m. to 3:00 p.m., they come in from the city and the new housing developments to the East. Some of my neighbors hold Sunday BBQ's just to make some money. It works. They pack the café and the ice cream shop. Look at these and pick out the ones you like." She pointed to the home décor section of the magazines.

David became dizzy by so many choices. "I'll just buy them all. You said we could tear them up, right?"

"Sure, let's get a notebook and some tape and knock together the designs you really like."

"Where would you like to go and do this?" he asked.

"Anywhere you'd like. You might want to do this at your house, choosing stuff as you look around."

"Your place is better. I don't have a fridge."

"My pleasure."

At Jan's place, they placed all the magazines on her kitchen table. She went to retrieve scissors as David received a call from Paolo. "Son, what's going on?"

"T'ma, you asked me about the Walker House and why you're not inheriting it. Well, Cathy has a report. I'd like to bring it to you."

The cold spike shot up again. David fought it, forcing himself to say something he had always wanted to. "I'm coming to you, son, as soon as you'd like to have me."

"Any time will work. With the children home, it'll be fun!"

"So, tomorrow then?"

There was a pause as Paolo talked away from the phone. David recognized Ingrid yelling somewhere in the house. "Oh, you've made a lot of people happy today! You're going to get another phone call in a minute from a woman who lives in the city near you. She'll take care of all of the arrangements to get you here."

"You're the best, son! I'm looking forward to seeing you!" He hung up with Paolo. A warm sensation overtook him head to toe. He felt terrified and excited. He received another phone call as Jan arranged the magazines. He took the call and confirmed his willingness to leave town by 5:00 a.m.

"What? You're leaving?" Jan looked hurt.

David took a moment to process her expression and could not figure out why she reacted in such a way. "Maybe for a few days. My son says he knows about my inheritance. Don't say anything, but I think Gaul and Paul should have that Walker House. That would be a great place for what they do." He paused further, not sure how she would react. He felt heat in his cheeks. "Jan, I'm not going back to football. I just don't want that life anymore. I've done enough. It's time for something else. I like being home, in this one. I've got more than enough to retire. I don't know what you think of that."

She looked shocked and a little embarrassed. "I like you being home."

He suddenly felt giddy. They returned to the chatty laughter. They used scissors to set aside anything that caught David's eye. They gleefully made a mess, which Jan would clean up later.

———

At a cheap hotel north of Leduc, Bob Lundberg put his two sons in a room not fit for his dogs.

"They saw the camera, fool!" He stood over both boys, who sat on the edge of the bed.

"David probably figured out you're not Sam, either." He looked around the room with its single bed and cheap television that was unnecessarily anchored to the rarely occupied dresser. The room was meant for hourly customers.

"At least you know he's home and looks as though he's going to stay. I got it. He's got a thing for Jan. I can use that later. For now, he has Paul and Gaul around him all the time. That ass-wipe made his money and now he wants the inheritance, too. No, that's the last thing he'll get. The two of you will be heading southeast by about one hundred fifty miles from Leduc. There's an orphanage run by an old woman named Iada. She's related to John Kemp and is somehow related, or at least financially related, to the Leducs, who are cousins to the Dryers. Lay as low as possible. Be there as concerned former co-workers of Tolson. Specifically, I want you to be able to kidnap Josephine and bring her to the gas field office at a moment's notice. There are a lot of sly, off-the-record dealings going on. Leave when you're sober." Bob walked out, without a backward glance at either of his sons.

———

Like children creating a new kind of Christmas, they tore, cut, and properly assembled the pages in a notebook. David looked like a man chewing on something bitter. "One more time, but slowly, Jan. This thing is five thousand dollars, but you can't pull a bed out of it? What kind of couch costs that much and just functions as a couch?"

Jan wore that vexed look again, like what you do when a kitten craps on something. "Would it be a problem for us to just go to the county mall so you can see it for yourself?"

He agreed and did his best not to reveal the rising anxiety of leaving familiar territory. The tension in his body hit hard, but he did not let it overwhelm him. The car was familiar. "Jan, was this your mom's California car?"

"Yes, David, good memory. The Monza with the big V8 and wussy carburetor, as Pete says."

"No one could forget this interior. All white and that stereo with the big knob."

She grinned. "Yes, a super tuner almost behind you between the seats."

He was almost feeling calm about the short drive by the time they arrived when Jan mentioned something about locating the car after they parked it. She asked him to remember "J7."

David looked around nervously several times before they stepped into the elevator. He finally understood all of the jokes people made about going to one of the big football games. Finding their car in an ocean of similar metal and paint jobs finally impressed him. At least the Monza looked odd with its white top and sky blue paint. He screamed within his own head to *knock it off and enjoy*. A surge of playfulness infused him. He began to skip as they walked along, looking at Jan and trying to get her to join him.

"No more add-shots!" She laughed and skipped along with him. "Okay, this is a furniture store with some of the stuff we saw in the tear sheets. Let's go look at the couch over there and you'll see what I mean about it converting into a bed with a button stretching out and not up and out."

They walked into the store and a salesman approached. "What may I help the happy couple with?" He smiled at them.

"Well, sir," David said, trying to appear sophisticated. "We are Danish mid-century moderns, and I'm liking this couch that folds into a bed. I'd like to see how it functions before I make my decision."

"Very well, observe." The pushed a button on the side, and it stretched out flat.

David looked as though he'd just discovered Mars. He tried it several times, explained the design of the house, and left with Jan taking the man's business card. "You know, for fifteen-hundred, that's really something. So what does the five-thousand dollar couch do that the other one doesn't?" he asked.

Jan took her time explaining. They went to three additional stores to look at kitchen and bathroom décor. They ended the trip with an early dinner at a popular hamburger stand.

David said nothing all the way home. Jan dropped him off at his house. "I can call you after 4:00 p.m. Tomorrow," he said.

"I would like that." She nodded and drove off.

David felt a presence and turned around. John stood in front of his house. David approached him. "What's going on, John?"

"I need to get you a driver's license."

"I don't have anywhere to go."

"Jan drives you to the mall. How much longer in high school are you going to stay, buckaroo?"

"Fff, what? High school? Let's go in." He followed John into the house. They sat in a living room. "Why so anxious to have me drive?"

"It's a bit ghetto when only the lady owns a car, my brother." John looked at David in the way he always did when delivering an important message. It was a forced smile, a *get with the program* sort of expression.

David could tell he wouldn't win this discussion. John would not allow complacency. "If I get a license, I will need a car."

"Just like a grown up!" John said, loudly.

"J7." David looked down, unaware he'd spoken aloud.

"J7? Explain."

"I met a lot of people who came to our games. A lot of them wondered how they would find their cars. Well, Jan parked in row J, space no. 7. Man, I'm beat.

Did you know they have a couch that automatically folds down into a bed then back up again into a couch? I'm not very grown-up am I, John?"

John's face suddenly wore the look of someone who realized they might have gone too far. "I'm sorry, my brother. Grown-up is not the right way to say it. You've done the right thing, lived a good life, and have been a very strong man. I just want to see you get out there and live. Before you go back, let's do some things to get you more involved in life. Maybe you can make a life with Jan. I'm sure she'd like that. I don't mean to rush anything along. I know the recruiting season is about to begin."

David looked serious. "You saved my life; you, that fat loudmouth Gaul, and especially Paul. No one ever had a better brother than you. I'm home. The field gave me everything it could and I, in turn, gave it everything I had. It's time for this new field of life. No goal posts, no markings. I may be scared shitless about going to the mall, but that'll be my problem. I'm flying out of here at five a.m. I have to be at the Municipal Airport by four forty five a.m. I'm going to see Paolo. I made the arrangements before I even thought about it. I enjoy that about being impulsive. It's gotten me to do something that fear previously kept me from." David nodded and smiled.

John took a while to respond. "So we can work on your driver's license when you get back?"

David roared with laughter. John joined him. They laughed till their sides hurt.

"The only thing you got is that crappy A thing. What is that?"

"Oh, you crapzilla! I told you it's a 1930 Ford Model A Tudor. Yes, you're going to learn to drive in it once you pass the written test."

"You used to run faster than that thing!"

"Nah, just seemed that way!"

"By the way, what was with you and that bobsled? It's not like you spent a lot of time doing it, but you never went back."

"Talk about scared shitless. I took my coach's advice. Push hard, get in, tuck down, and hang on. I wouldn't get up until it came to a complete stop."

David paused a moment. "Don't get up until you make a complete stop. I've rammed my head into a lot of walls. I've never tried ramming it into the *don't leave the safe place* one. Push hard, get in, tuck down, and hang on? Is that it?"

"Yes, my brother, that's it."

"Then that's what I'll do. Good thing we're dumping the goal posts, for a while anyway. I have no idea what this new field is or how far it goes. At least I can hang on until it comes to a complete stop."

"Well, that's just life," John said.

David looked like he accidentally swallowed poop. "That's it? People just hang on? What was all that in church this morning about a great plan and finding your place in it?"

"Wow, you actually listened! Sorry, man, that came out wrong. Look, you have something special to give. It's not a job or position in life. It's more like what you are, a fighter. You can be a fighter for good or for bad. Being a fighter for selfish reasons means you're not in the great plan that God has set out for everyone. You also have to choose to follow it. That's a lot to go over later. You look like you need some rest. I'll bring you to the airport tomorrow morning."

David nodded. His feet and legs felt tired, but not sore. He went through the dining room and gave Paul a quick itinerary of his plans over the next few days.

Morning was about to start as David got up before the alarm. The smell of coffee and bread filled the air. He came downstairs and saw some small appliances on the kitchen counter he had not noticed the night before. Paul was sliding eggs from a small non-stick pan onto one of three plates. Toast popped up out of a new machine as John stepped into the kitchen. It was only 4:30 a.m., time enough for breakfast.

"I understand you're staying?" Paul asked in David's direction.

"Yes. Oh, I'll be right back!" David put his coffee down and bolted upstairs. He came down with the notebook he and Jan had made the day before. "Look here, Paul." David handed the notebook to Paul opened to the kitchen section. "I got this jones for Danish mid-century modern. When we're done, I don't want to see so much as an electrical socket leftover. Forget the money, let's get a crew together and punch this out," he said with an excited look. He forked up some eggs and bit into his toast.

"Nice stuff. Thank John here for the toaster, coffee maker, and pans."

"Fank you, Jawn," David said, his mouth full.

"Weecomb, Daby," John replied also with a stuffed mouth.

"You boois ah gweat!" Paul said, joining in.

David enjoyed two cups of coffee and some hearty laughs. He put together an overnight bag and John drove him to the airport in the 1930 Ford Model A just as the sun started to make an appearance in the east. They drove towards it, going past the county municipal buildings, high school, and mall.

The Municipal Airport was new to David. A short chain link fence surrounded the parking lot, a man in uniform on its edge waving at them. They parked as close as they could and John walked with him to the small gate that had no lock. The man in uniform turned out to be the pilot, and he escorted David to the airplane.

David could see John in the parking lot as the small powerful jet took off. He could see the rising sun on the back edge of the wings, which also reflected the cobalt blue of the sky. So often he and John would talk about the sunrise. "God, show me my place. I'd like to know Your plan," David prayed. The anxiety of traveling away from his safe place quickly faded.

"Mr. Dryer, we have coffee with an add-shot and a breakfast burrito waiting for you," the pleasant and professional flight attendant told him.

"Oh man, my friends are taking care of me again." All of his fears washed away. And for the first time he enjoyed flying.

After the jet disappeared, John stayed a while longer, enjoying the scene as the sun came up with its warm glow, kissing the eastern face of buildings and trees. He thought it neat that this particular dawn represented the start of David's new life. As he stood in the crisp, morning air, he felt warmed. There was a slight soreness in his mid-section. He thought perhaps it might be the coffee.

18

PRODIGAL FATHER

The rising sun made the back edge of the executive jet's wings a bright orange. The tops of the wings, cobalt in color, reflected the new day's emerging blue. Somehow, the wings reminded David of swords.

The night before his trip, he'd tossed and turned. He fell asleep on the plane before his burrito and coffee were served.

Two hours later he awoke alone and felt immediately confused. Alarms in his head clanged, and he began to breathe heavily. The smell of coffee assailed him and a pleasant voice penetrated his escalating panic.

"Sir, everything kept just fine. Are you ready for some breakfast?" The stewardess made eye contact as she spoke.

He took a long, slow breath, and for once felt silly getting worked up about waking up in a strange place. "Absolutely. How much longer?" He accepted the coffee and acknowledged the burrito in front of him.

She smiled. "About ninety minutes. There is a bathroom at the rear of the aircraft, and we have a kit with a toothbrush and floss."

He began to drink the coffee and noticed how quickly the sun kept up. It was a 150 miles an hour faster than they were going. His destination would set him off by two hours. He knew that much. David was not going to make any effort to acclimate to the time change since he did not plan on being there long enough.

Compared to the airfield he departed from, the Santa Monica Airport was packed. It was the same size, just a lot busier. He took a short walk from the jet to a waiting helicopter that would take him to Paolo in only ten minutes.

The helicopter rose above the airfield. He saw the ocean to his left and the mountains coming up fast. It looked like they would fly right into them. As the density of houses began to taper off, the winding roads made their way around one large, flat spot created atop a ridge's crest. Although not visible from up high, it became the largest feature in the area as soon as they got closer. More than two entire football fields could have been built on it.

A huge mansion the size of half a playing field came into view. David had only heard of such homes. The roof of the house had castle-like peaks and was covered in dark blue slate. The property grounds appeared manicured to perfection. He spotted the pool as they began to hover between the mansion and mountainside.

"Okay, sir. This is a hot landing. The blades will still be going, so exit the way I instructed you. Paolo will be standing in the spot I want you to immediately walk towards. I have a card I would like you to give to his wife. She saved the baby of a friend. Is that okay?"

"Beyond okay, my man!"

The executive helicopter landed in what David thought was a rather tight space. He took the card and fist bumped the pilot. Paolo stepped outside as the engine wound down. David grabbed his bag and walked straight to Paolo, who escorted him into a small waiting room.

When Paolo closed the heavy outer door, David noticed that the landing spot was surrounded by short wrought iron fencing. Paolo turned a handle on the wall down to the position that read 'closed' in large, block letters. At that moment, the noise from the helicopter became louder. David could hear the blades taking bigger bites of air. The sound of its departure was the cue for Paolo to raise the handle and open the door into the rest of the house.

"Oh, man, look out!" Little Ingrid ran up and grabbed David around the waist, almost knocking him over.

"Oh, no. Ingrid, please!" Paolo nearly shouted as David picked her up.

"You're getting to be a big girl! Mwa!" David kissed her cheek then noticed someone at his leg. He looked down into the warm, brown eyes of P. He was called 'little P' after his father. David crouched down and placed an arm around him while Ingrid clung to him.

"My little man, how are you?"

He mimicked his sister by wrapping both of his little arms around David as far as they could go and bumping his head into David's side.

"Now that the helicopter is gone, the pool is open." The honey sweet voice of Ahnee could be heard all over the house. The children rushed out of the sliding door and across the patio.

"I have that effect on children," David said he watched the kids.

Thunderous laughter broke out behind him. Paolo's laughter could fill the entire house.

"Oh T'ma, you're more fun than a pool!" Ahnee joined in.

David straightened up and realized he wore a dejected look. A man who appeared to be in Paolo's employ took his bag as Ahnee showed him the way outside. She walked past a round, wrought iron table and matching chairs. Two people sat at the table, and David recognized them at once. The Dynamic Duo stood and shook his hand.

David sat in a chair next to Paolo. Both of them enjoyed a great view of the pool. David counted three adults and nine children in total.

"This is neat. I've never seen both of you together."

Paolo shifted his chair up. He wore a Hawaiian shirt, sandals, shorts and a face that reflected joy and concern. Cathy and Ralph were in business attire. "T'ma, we looked into your inheritance and the Walker House. There's much more to do. It seems the Land Sakes Company has been acting as an umbrella to numerous micro corporations, which are defaulting on loans that have usury rates. I think Ralph and Cathy can bring you up to speed with what they have learned."

Ralph put his coffee down. "The investigators keep coming back with the name, Lundberg. I don't know what mechanism is being used here, but I smell a brand new Enron. Mr. Dryer, your inheritance was managed by a loose group of people, most of whom are gone now."

David took one of the cookies in front of him as the information began to process.

Ralph continued. "A garage owner in Leduc and an Iada, who seems to be related to Mr. Kemp, had legal control of everything. It was all undisputed until 10 years ago. It appears they signed over vast amounts of land in terms of leasing with options to buy. Cathy's been paying attention to the government's involvement." He picked up a butter cookie.

David said nothing.

Cathy turned to him. "The Mayor of Leduc has legal control of the Walker House. How he came into possession of it can be unveiled, of course. The same trail I followed went back to an Lundberg. He is the son of a late congressman. There are many cases where a rightful owner has control of something and gives it up, because they can't afford an attorney or taxes and they're afraid of going to court. They get scared to take on the city. They call it 'throwing paper at someone.' Cities like to engage in such practices to take over vacant lots that have no known owners. It's far less restricted than eminent domain and very quick once done."

David put both of his lightly clenched hands on the table.

Cathy pursed her lips like she might smile, but did not. "At some point, the micro corporations Ralph is combing through and the government paper trail are going to collide. I just don't know how or when. I know we can't stay here and have proxies take care of it. This is vast, spanning three states, and thousands of people are involved."

David sipped water. "The Walker House is not some empty lot." He stared at the table, his fists now tightly clenched. "It's a house as big as this one, overlooking endless farmlands." His gaze came up. He opened his right hand, palm up, and made a sweeping gesture to encompass the lawn and pool as if addressing a full stadium. "Pete, the garage owner, had a father-in-law... he told me not to worry about it all. I see I've been negligent." His hand came down with his gaze. He stared at the table, both hands relaxing. "I really want that house to go to Gaul and Paul so they can help single mothers stay off the streets. I can afford to buy it back and give it to them. I'll find out when I get home. This Lundberg you mentioned, that's Bob Lundberg, my distant cousin. Not a good person. If it comes down to it, I would like to know what it'd take to buy a controlling interest in Land Sakes Company."

Paolo leaned forward. "Land Sakes is a publicly traded company. It would barely take $200 million to buy more than 70%, if it comes to that, but is that what you want?"

Ralph's eyebrows arched over the rim of his glasses. "Wait a minute here. What would be left of your current assets? I understand there was some severance after the University, but how do we justify doing that?"

"Oh, bright boy, do you know what's going on here?" Cathy managed to sit an inch higher.

Ralph wore a contemptuous smile. "Just lay it out already and quit with the dramatics."

David looked up to watch them banter back and forth.

Cathy leaned in like she wanted to close the distance before smacking Ralph. Gesturing towards David, she expounded. "The man here left the University with a package topping six hundred twenty five million." She sat back taller in her chair. "I don't know about your version of significant, but I think the frugal coach can live on at least 1/10 of that."

Paolo's head mimicked David's, moving back and forth from Cathy to Ralph, almost like a tennis match. David noticed Paolo was enjoying himself.

Ralph leaned back as though dealing with an impetuous child. "We're still talking thirty percent going into what may be a difficult venture both financially and emotionally. We don't always let clients handle their cash."

Paolo smiled. "Too late. The keys were handed over."

Ralph slowly turned to Paolo, who said, "My father is quite a fighter. Have I not told you this yet?" Paolo turned up his hand in Ralph's direction.

Ralph took a deep breath. "Okay, so to proceed with our client, the plan is a hostile takeover, digging up all the dirt after?"

David sprang up in his chair. "Yes! Do that, Ralph! I can go in and fire all of the bad employees then."

Ralph nodded and then looked at Cathy. "So, he says to do this. What if it's all hot air, and he's bought pennies for a dollar."

Cathy looked at Ralph. "Hard to be a plaintiff as a third party. The alternative is to gather up every person who obtained a loan for less than one hundred thousand, which could possibly be thousands of plaintiffs, and then involve them in the lawsuit. I don't see this as a simple one-issue class action suit, either. This could involve billions of dollars. We can't get federal help until a jurisdictional institution like a bank becomes involved." Cathy paused. "There was foreign money involved. I know a fresh kid at the State Department who can smell the blood if I show him which ocean to swim in."

"Those are great reasons!" David shouted.

The rumble from Paolo's chuckling ended the conversation. "I believe we have two people who need to be on television in Los Angeles."

The driveway gate opened and a black SUV, the type David had seen in Leduc, drove up to the helicopter pad. Ralph and Cathy left. David felt so much better.

Staff began to move things from the kitchen onto the lawn. A huge picnic without a table was being set up. There were piles of food in large bowls. Paolo turned to him. "Well, how about a nice bit of lunch?" He smiled bigger than David could ever remember.

Still seated, David saw that they were alone in that moment. "I had a problem, son. Paul and Gaul saved my life. I've lied and been dishonest. I was scared to leave my home, the campus, and Leduc. I don't know why, but not anymore. Never again." Tears threatened to spill from his eyes. His hands were turned palms up. "You've invited me so often. I missed Ingrid and P growing up. Can I come here to open up my gifts?"

Paolo rested one hand atop of his father's. They both sat a while longer and spoke quietly. Paolo waved away anyone who came too close to the patio. He waited until David cooled his face with ice water and felt ready to join the picnic.

The children did not bother to dry off. Ingrid brought P over to sit next to David, who had Paolo to his right. Ahnee emerged from the house, took her place beside her husband, and performed a short ceremonial greeting and prayer.

Her arm movements were as graceful as her voice was lovely, David thought. The place was serene. The grass edges rolled off and an expansive view could be seen from most areas on the property. The ocean was on the right, urban sprawl in the center, and a narrow view of Los Angeles on the left.

A long pause was observed. David felt a nudge and looked over towards Ingrid, who leaned over P. "You're supposed to have the first bite and really like it," she whispered.

David complied. There were small bowls of poi, shredded pork, and cut vegetables placed in front of him. The lack of silverware or chopsticks meant eating with the fingers or the sticks of carrots and celery.

He used two fingers in the pork dish and tucked the food into his mouth. He obviously misjudged the amount and had little room to chew. Children began to laugh. He crossed his eyes, puffed out his cheeks, and nodded his head, making sure to look at everyone, including his son and his wife, who were trying to sit properly and laugh at the same time.

It took some time for the children to settle down and eat. Ahnee took long looks between her husband and the man he considered his true father. She kissed Paolo playfully on the cheek and smiled at David. "What do you think of the luau, David?"

"As lovely as you have always been, Ahnee. I see Ingrid is also an emerging lady of honor." He looked over at the girl.

Ingrid flushed, stood quickly, and kissed David on the cheek. Little P tried to do the same. David bent down to assist him.

"You are a most honored guest, true grandfather." Ingrid made arm and hand gestures in a quick sweep, just as her mother had done earlier. She quickly returned to her normal self. "Oh, wait till your birthday! Remember, we get to watch you on the computer."

"Your father says I can come here and open them. How would you and P like that?" David asked shyly.

P made a happy cooing sound while leaning over onto David's knee. P sat cross-legged, but tried to sit up higher as he looked into David's face.

"Thank you, P. I'm sure I'll like what you got me."

P smiled his big, brown eyes filled with happiness. When he returned to his food, he leaned against David's leg as he ate.

"Just like his dad. You know, Ahnee, as a teen, if I could get Paolo to say more than, 'that is good' or 'that is not good,' it was really something! One time, he expanded the conversation to, 'my, that was more than adequate.' I mean, really. MENSA at ten! A whole universe going on between those ears, and it took an entire box of sandwiches to crack the code!"

Paolo almost fell over laughing before David could finish. Little P imitated his dad and Ahnee playfully tried to keep her husband from stretching out on the warm grass.

Dessert was accompanied by a dance from Ahnee and Ingrid. It became obvious to David that neither Paolo nor Ahnee would allow their children to ever feel alone.

At the end of the dance, the staff reappeared and began to clear the lawn while the children retreated into the house. Paolo bent down and made a swing with his hands. P climbed into it, and they followed everyone inside. Ahnee approached David.

"Next time, Paolo says we're going to have dinner and a proper show with fire!"

"I've never felt more like a member of a family in my life, Ahnee. I sure would love to look around. You busy?"

She took him to the southern part of the expansive yard that was occupied by a garden of herbs and dwarf citrus trees, the highest of which only reached his shoulder. Ahnee walked with stateliness, matching her pace to David's.

"I don't know that I've ever seen my husband so happy." She smiled at him.

"I feel the same. That sandwich thing was true, but the day he started blabbing was after your first date. Man, could he go on and on! It was like he'd been repressed or something," David said, looking off towards the Pacific Ocean.

She smiled and appeared to be blushing. "The stories he would tell of you on that field. Lighting up an entire stadium, turning Swanton over and getting into his helmet to make a point! He is Paolo until he needs to get across to someone who won't listen, and then he becomes you! He emulates you like a proud son does his father."

Her words made David feel warm inside. His emotions swirled around and through him, and he tried to manage them. "Like P tries to emulate his father? I've had a kind of illness, Ahnee. I passed on many invitations, but no more. If it's still open any time, let's have more get-togethers?"

"Father, nothing would make us happier. Please tell me what you would like to do this evening?"

"Movie night!" David perked up. "Jan says I need to see 'It's A Wonderful Life'. If you don't have it, I think I can go get it. It has to be somewhere within twenty miles. I have a smartphone that can help."

"Wow. That's my husband's favorite movie! We have it."

"Awesome. I was wondering about P. He doesn't talk much for his age. Is that from the trauma of his mother leaving him?"

"There were drugs in his system. It was fate how Paolo was visiting me in the hospital when he saw him. We wanted him for our own right on the spot. Some children are slower. With Ingrid keeping him close and his father's doting, I think he'll do well. Let's not forget his grandfather! You almost made him talk."

"The funny thing is, I think I know what he meant. Where did Ingrid get her name?"

"Ingrid was a nurse who retired to the islands. She was very wise. I always wanted to hang around and learn what she was doing with the patients. One day, she said I was a healer and more than smart enough to be a doctor. My uncle heard about her words and sent me to medical school. That is how I met you and then my husband."

They walked and talked a little while longer. David was surprised at the number of questions Ahnee had to ask. David realized he had kicked down an old door never to be closed again.

The sun began to set in Leduc. Gaul worked on a new mini contraption that made his beer. *Such a joy.* He began to think as he looked over the carefully constructed coils of tubing and connections that took care of every brewing step besides dumping in the ingredients. Heavy footsteps encroached on his quiet moment.

Jan came up behind him. "All right, jar head, what is it now!"

It was supposed to be a quiet night. Gaul turned to her slowly. "It's Monday, love. What could be wrong?"

"If he's staying, then why the leaving?" she shouted.

Gaul was grateful the church was empty. He also wondered about the hormone rage at this time in her life.

"Okay, join me." He handed her one of the 40 oz. bottles of potent malt liquor. They went out the back door.

Like a parched desert wanderer, she tilted up the bottle and brought it down with a hollow popping sound. "So, is he staying? Am I wasting my life here or what?"

"Jan, he took one look at you and that was it. Fff, don't be so impatient with the little man. Gads, girl, he asked you to pick out curtains."

"Not that you care, but we've had several get-togethers and it's always just a hand shake. A bit more would get some connection going for me, brother!" The bottle went up and down again, the echo of popping only heard in a receding tide of beer. Soon, it was empty.

"Look, I'm going to tell you something, but you have to shut up about it." Gaul gestured with an open hand toward her.

"Fine. Great. Fine. Lay it out."

"Lack of intimacy, he has it really bad, along with some agoraphobia. It isn't constant, but does happen often. It might have been trained out of him early, but we know about his upbringing. Paul with his psychology rag has him pegged."

She took a long pause. "So what does it for him intimately?" she demanded.

"Gaul, who the…" Paul walked up.

"All right, psycho man. We gotta get this David thing figured out!" Jan exclaimed.

Gaul looked up at a slightly stunned Paul. "I don't know if she's had too much or not enough. Jan, which is it?" Gaul asked, rising to his feet.

"Let's all have another round." Paul reached for a chair.

Gaul went over to the racks of alcohol he had been hoarding for the Monks' Oktoberfest, a holiday of his own design. He knew he would be able to replace what they drank by that time. His footsteps trailed off and another set walked up.

"John, what has you stopping by?" Paul was relieved he showed up.

"Well, with David gone, I thought it might be safe to sample the Monks' Oktoberfest batch."

"Yep, heard you!" Gaul shouted from inside. "Someone call Fisher!"

Less than a minute after the phone call, Dr. Fisher arrived through the gate between his backyard and the church grounds. Gaul returned with four bottles. He held them up in Dr. Fisher's direction and received a nod of approval. Gaul went back inside for one more.

"Step it up, Padre!" Jan yelled as though attempting to be heard over loud music.

Paul looked at her, then at Dr. Fisher. "Well, what do you think. Doc?"

Dr. Fisher looked at her, down at the deck, the empty bottle, and back up at Paul. "I think aversion therapy is great."

Paul turned away and tried his best not to laugh out loud. It did not work. John joined in. Gaul returned and handed Paul three bottles. He gave Jan a bottle, bent down, and placed an arm around her. "It's your night, my dearest."

"I think we're riding the line on the potency here, Gaul." Dr. Fisher peered into his bottle after a quick swig.

"Did anyone want me any other way?" Gaul asked.

The first round of raucous laughing and ribald humor began in earnest.

19
HOME BREW

"Oooh deh."

The voice sounded familiar. David awakened in an unfamiliar place. He didn't panic. His mind did not race. He raised his head to see beyond his chest and encountered the big, brown, curious eyes of P. He cooed again and glanced in the direction of some unfolding activity.

"So, what do you think? Should we go join in?" David asked.

P smiled wide and made the cooing sound. The patter of fast-moving feet burst into the sunroom, which was now dark.

"Oh my P, here you are!" Ingrid approached them. "He never wanders off! We're having movie night, so we get to have dinner on the fly. You'll see dad make real popcorn!" She tugged on David's arm.

David got up from the low couch. He checked his watch, hoping it wasn't really 8:00 p.m. He remembered the two-hour difference and suddenly what his friends were doing back home in Leduc.

"Oh, Gaul, I wouldn't dream of you changing!" Jan took a quick swig from her bottle. "You know, it just pains me that David has been away forever, and it's like he hasn't done anything. He has no idea."

John nodded, facing her and the group. "Well, the campus took care of everything. Someone always told him when and where to go. You might think he had it made. He also never had anything of his own. He took his first big failure at life too seriously." John took a swig of beer. "He's the kind of guy who can't remember the day of the week, but he'll remember what someone likes or hates or the taste or smell of something no matter how much time passes. He's all right-brained, that fellow."

Jan looked introspective. "So, on the charts of intimacy, five being tops, I'm getting two and so far that's good."

Dr. Fisher nudged Paul and whispered, "Did anyone call Maureen? I don't think this is man's territory."

Paul suddenly perked up. He went to Gaul and asked what the four stooges were going to do with a frustrated and inebriated Jan. Gaul suggested a call to Maureen. After a short talk, he stepped off the porch and fired up the grill.

"Good idea. Paul, I think the fridge is bare. Anyone still sober enough to get me to the county side for groceries?" Gaul asked, looking around.

"Nah, Maureen is bringing sausage and beans. A man's meal!" Paul shouted from just ten feet away.

"Now we're stepping up!" Jan held up her bottle.

Maureen arrived with a bag containing canned beans, tortillas, and packaged sausages. The boys cooked the beans in the cans and managed not to burn anything. They gathered far enough away to allow the girls some private space. For once, Maureen answered all of Jan's questions without quips or sayings. She talked to her the way Jan needed, and she listened when Jan wanted to speak.

Jan's thoughts became somber. Before she left, Gaul listened to her as Maureen had. The fire inside of her cooled off and some answers were certain. David was staying. He wanted her. It was neither her fault nor his. She could be patient and enjoy watching the boy unfold into a man.

Paolo was doing the one thing he relished and that he was actually good at in the kitchen: Popcorn. He used a lobster pot nearly as big as Ingrid. He measured with precision the amount of kernels and oil it would take to fill three quarters up. He watched his son, daughter, and David play on the floor with P's favorite toy, a collection of colorful, plastic snap-together shapes that P would assemble with profound speed, precision and accuracy. He possessed the gift of being able to recreate exact replicas of buildings or objects he saw.

David sat cross-legged, looking over what was in front of them. P handed him one of three identical pieces of the collection. He gave Ingrid one of the others, then held his piece over his creation, moving it around as though he held an airplane.

"Oh boy, P, are we flying!" David mimicked his movements.

Ingrid held onto hers. "He puts things together really fast. I always know what they are, but not this time." She watched her little brother and the stacks of blocks in the middle.

"I've seen this. Ingrid, can I have those magazines?" David pointed at the coffee table. Ingrid handed him the short stack. David quickly looked them over and found what he wanted. He flipped through one particular magazine, stopped, and turned the page to Ingrid so that she could see P's creation. Her eyes became wide like saucers, looking at the picture, then down at little P as David turned the magazine layout towards him.

"Wow, little brother, this is a great one!"

David showed the opened magazine to Ahnee as she walked into the kitchen.

He then pointed to what was on the floor. She poked Paolo's arm, gesturing to the trio on the floor.

"Is this what you're making P? This city of the future?" The image depicted a futuristic city with flying cars, blue skies, and happy people being transported on conveyor belt sidewalks.

His oversized head bowed down and then came up to face Ingrid. His eyes welled with tears and his neck showed strain as though he was about to yell something. "Hey-een!" he shrieked.

David jumped, a bit startled by the sudden noise.

Paolo's eyes looked like they might burn holes in the air. He stopped making popcorn and slid an arm around his wife, who also looked pleasantly shocked.

"Good one, P. Hey, who's that over there?" David leaned over and looked at his parents.

P looked over and without much effort said. "Pah-eeh! Mah-ee!" He turned back to his car and began to fly it around.

Ingrid leaned toward P and kissed his head. "Who's playing with us?" she asked, looking into his eyes.

"Pah-Dayer!" He went back to his car and raised it up to meet Ingrid's. "Eep eep!" he said and started to fly away.

David turned to Paolo and Ahnee, who both looked about ready to weep. "You know, he may never stop talking now."

He picked up his car and flew around towards Ingrid. "Eep eep! Hi, Ingrid."

He flew over to P. "Eep eep, P!" P startled him a second time when he squealed with laughter.

For some time, they flew cars and said hello, imagining how wonderful the future could be.

Later during the movie, David sat on the floor with his back to the couch. Paolo took up one end while his wife leaned against him. David's drawn up knees supported Ingrid, while P leaned against hers.

Ahnee looked up at her husband's tranquil, sleeping face and then at the man on the floor, who today had finally become a real grandfather. She thought how cute it was, him watching the movie so intently with Ingrid while P slept like his father.

High above West Los Angeles, Ralph and Cathy looked over the same information. Some of it was hearsay, the kind they could not use in court, but enough to get what they needed for prosecution. Ralph turned to her. "Looks like dear old Bob is a classic control freak. This is way too much for one chucklehead to juggle."

"One die-hard plaintiff and a court date will collapse this whole house of cards. That's it. You owe your wife a call, and I'm outta here." Cathy slapped him on the shoulder and left.

Ralph shut down the computer and closed up the file, locking it away in a safe. His disposition became lighter just thinking about the video chat he would soon have with the whole family. He often thought how his plain looks had no business being on television. He and Cathy were such opposites. Maybe that's why they were popular.

Fresh news off the presses this once: Cathy liked a man.

Once again, David woke up without wondering about his location. He knew it felt familiar, but no flood of thoughts assailed him. He went down to the kitchen, which was staffed by two people preparing breakfast. Someone must have heard him coming and brought out the espresso machine to make him an add-shot.

"Wow, who said something?" he asked one of the staff.

"Who do you think, granddad?" Paolo managed to sneak up with P shadowing him.

He put his arms around the big man for a quick hug and bent down to pick up the little one.

"How are you doing today?" he asked, lifting little P up to face him.

P placed his head on David's shoulder and hugged his neck. "Fine, fine, fine!" he squealed.

Paolo laughed and David turned so they could look up at him. "So, this grandfather thing. I'm thinking I get to do all of the spoiling and doting while you do all of the work, okay?" He leaned into the big man.

Paolo put his arm around David. "Okay, sounds good. Let me show you where the diapers are."

They went outside and had breakfast together. P sat on David's lap while Paolo helped feed him. "Oh, Ahnee was sorry about not being able to have breakfast with us. The hospital called."

"Not to worry, son. I promised her I would be back often. Let's see what I can do to make you sick of me."

"Won't happen," Paolo assured him as he dispensed financial advice.

"I'm going to try, anyway," David said. He finished his breakfast one-handed, keeping an arm wrapped around P.

For the first time, he considered the flight home just another normal thing. David felt none of his previous anxiety. He watched the western desert give way to the fertile mid-west. Sleep came quickly. He dreamed of a city with flying cars, clean buildings, fresh air, and happy people. He dreamed of a future in which P could talk.

David awoke without a thought as to place but time. *Will Jan give me time, can I ask her to wait, be patient?* He floated his thoughts upward. The plane came to a stop. He got out with his bag. As he came down from the plane, he looked around and tried to spot the Model A. Jan shouted at him from the gate.

"Hey, girl!" He threw an arm around her and kissed her on the cheek.

She responded by wrapping her arms around him and giving him a quick kiss to the lips. "It's okay to do that now, my man."

He responded with both arms and a longer kiss, and held her for a short while. They pulled back and smiled at each other. "So, my lady, what happened to John? What's going on in this new hometown of mine?"

"Home brew and other things. You might want to stay at John's for a while."

"Do I get to see why?" He looked surprised.

"Of course, you do!" She drove him into town.

David shuffled in his seat trying to be lower in the car. The roof was just touching his hair. "Hey Jan, this was your Mom's car. Mooza or something?"

She smiled. "Monza, David. Dad bought it in California near South Gate just outside Los Angeles International Airport and drove it home."

It almost smelled like her and coconut oil like they used for tanning. "Yeah, white interior and roof with sky blue paint. It had air conditioning. The first like it I had heard of."

Jan nodded. "Dad thought it was cool with its big V8 just like the Corvette, but in a lady car. She never allowed him to pull the engine, get rid of the smog stuff and supe-it-up."

David remembered a story from Phil. "Like it's a cam and two barrels away from actually going fast."

Jan took a minute to respond. "You have an interesting memory, David." They parked in front of John's house. A large dumpster sat in front of David's, the kind he saw on the back of big rigs.

They walked inside and saw four men covered in white dust. For once, John almost looked like everybody else. David burst out laughing. It took him a while to settle down.

"Hey, John, now that half my house is missing, can I stay at yours?"

"Of course, my brother! How was the trip? Paolo?" John asked.

"Wow, man, this is something else! So the whole kitchen's gone. Cool. What's all this white and grey stuff, Bosche?" David could not contain his excitement.

Bosche began to explain about the dry wall, new wiring, and plumbing. David interrupted with an invitation to treat everyone to dinner four doors down the street. Bosche continued about the renovation.

"We're lucky school is out for the summer. The bin will get swapped out twice more. The high school boys looking for work were really grateful. It'll take three more days of tear out. Did you want us to keep anything? Bed? Couch?" Bosche trailed off.

"No. My mother always wanted to make the place over. I remember that and am able to put away any poor feelings I have. So, what is it called when you take things all the way back to the wall?"

"Sometimes it's called 'ripping it to the studs.' It isn't needed anywhere else except the bathroom, if you want that made over."

"I want everything done, top to bottom, walls, floors, roof, home theater…"

"Hey, Bosche, if daddy fat bucks here has the green, we could make the living room larger, put in triple pane windows, and sound dampening drywall and insulation," Paul said.

"Paul, with the mouth load, what does all that mean?" David looked around.

"You can get your surround sound up really loud and the neighbors won't hear a thing." Paul gestured with sweeping arm movements, as though to gin up the crowd.

David saw the excitement in everyone's dust-covered faces. "Let's do that!"

The boys did their best to dust off, and then they all headed to the café. They looked like a motley crew, David and Jan their ringleaders.

"Well, I said get a crew and punch this out. I didn't think I'd see John looking like Jack Frost, though," David said, avoiding eye contact.

"Tomorrow, after the run, you can help rip up the living room." John's flat tone set off Gaul.

"He'll hurt someone. Shit, just let us do it." Gaul smirked.

"Now, boys, let's all play nice," Jan said, looking around.

David paused for a moment. "I like being home. I think it's a good idea to make that house mine. Having friends with me is the best idea." He went back to eating his meal.

He rode with Jan to her house. She parked her car, and he kissed her goodnight. "Because it's allowed now," he whispered bashfully.

It was calm and quiet as he walked up Cause Way. His thoughts began to churn things over and over again.

The truck was gone. He walked past his house and the lights were out. How strange, he thought. It was the oldest looking house in the neighborhood and the least maintained. He wondered if that was some sort of message. He looked skyward.

All of the homes were built off of the same train of boxcars that brought wood all the way from Arcata, California. Every single house was a kit. After her husband died, the woman after whom Walker House was named built the entire town.

Immediate relatives could have a house with five others rented out. It was a cooperative. Everything worked out fine until greed came into the picture, lawsuits were filed, and families split apart.

The whole town had been built within a year's time by a small mass of workers who came from the town where Iada lived.

"Uncle Wellington!" David exclaimed as he stood in front of his house and cried as quietly as he could. "Oh, Mother, what a trail of crumbs you left me, but that's all you could afford."

He walked into John's house and quietly made his way past Paul, who slept soundly. David rinsed off his face and then lay down to allow his thoughts to drift.

Reaching a bit of an epiphany, he smiled to himself as he looked towards the sky once more. *I get answers when I listen, don't I?*

20
RUNNING

"First thing means first thing. Come on, John, this is embarrassing." David was up before everyone.

He waited outside for Paul and John to clean up. Gaul, clad in a brand new running suit, said, "We're going to be last."

"For now, compete for yourself; conquer only your doubt, Gaul. That's the lesson this really teaches."

"Well, listen to Mr. Coach here. Tell me, will you be this perky later?"

"No, this will take a month to get used to, at least. Later, I'll be as perky as you'll be mouthy," David said, smirking at Gaul.

Paul and John stepped outside and led the group along Main Street past the Corner Cafe to Cause Way, going left and downhill past Starling, and then out of town. They half-walked, half-jogged the upper most dirt roads that overlooked the fields and separated them from the highway. The hills above town kept the highway hidden as they jogged northward. Soon, the path and the highway began to converge until it loomed above them by about the height of a one-story house.

The lesser paths perpendicular to the one they ran on were one half mile apart, making it easy to know how many it took to run one mile. They kept a good jog going. Gaul started panting about a mile in. Paul turned back with him. David continued with John, west about a mile and then back to town.

"Let's warm down from here," John suggested.

"Okay. It doesn't hurt. This orthotic business is like having new feet," David remarked.

"How does everything else feel?"

"Well, the hip, knee, and back are all doing well. I can't believe the hospital didn't think to check my feet. Ever since, I can stand and walk around without any pain."

They made it to Main Street and encountered Jan. "Can I get you boys' breakfast?"

David kissed her quick. "I should be buying."

"No room for your wallet." She arched up an eyebrow, then led them both into the Café.

David glanced at John with a curious expression, but decided not to ask.

"Work clothes. I don't have any work clothes. Do you, John?"

"I have some older stuff I use."

"Okay, after this, we get my wallet and I'll get us something from Maureen's shop. What about a hard hat?"

"Oh, how adorable. John, get him a headlamp, too," Jan said without looking at them.

"David, I think some clothes for the job and gloves will do. Paul and Bosche have all the tools."

Jan promised to bring lunch later.

David decided to make sure he and John wound up with matching outfits. "I was thinking about bread crumb trails, John."

"Do go on."

"My house, yours, and Jan's are all the same. They were all built with redwood from Arcata, California, brought here on a single long train with all the major beams pre-cut to order. This whole neighborhood was the pre-fab of its day. Mother told me Wellington had a lot to do with it. What do you know about that, John?" David began to put on a work boot as he spoke.

"Yes, Main Street was supposed to be named after him, but it wasn't politically acceptable. A very long time ago a young woman rescued the grandfather of Iada's husband in the woods. He was from the north, a blonde man, we think a Lundberg." John stopped and gawked at the box Maureen positioned on the floor in front of him. She dashed off before John could ask about it.

"Yes, John, you need a pair, too. Please, it's on me." David continued with his other boot, placing his special insole.

"You kill me, David. Anyway, story goes that Iada's husband took the advice of a precocious, large, and very intelligent teen and headed off to the same city the blonde man came from to look for a wife. He found Iada in a coffee shop. She worked as a cocktail waitress at night, obtained stock advice in the morning, and had friends invest for her before she went to bed at noon. He fell in love with her on the spot. I understand he tried to teach her to read. She was the one who taught Wellington how to use proxies to buy things like property. So, that is how the Kemps own a share in the lands that surround us. I just don't know what or how much, but the Walker House is part of it."

"Those are the bread crumbs I'm talking about. I've been told this will take a while, but the Dynamic Duo will be working on the Walker House and some other inheritance stuff. Whatever they find, I'll make sure you get yours. I have to find that rotund, useless door stop of a mayor and get Main Street renamed, among other things." David paused for a bit and leaned closer to John. "I really like the idea that we could be blood relatives. Your family ignored my dad and kept me fed in so many ways." His voice trailed off. He pulled back to hide the rush of emotion.

"I am so happy you're home for good, my brother." John went back to his boots.

They went to David's childhood home. Thoughts flooded his mind, the warmth of his mother and the bitterness of his father. The place would be his now. "Paul, what do you have for ripping the walls?"

The four teens that came along to help laughed with the rest. Paul gave David a long bar with a curve and flat-forked spots on the ends. With the furniture already gone, Paul gave him quick instructions on what to do with the bar and then showed him how to use the dust mask.

David punched a hole, worked in the curved part, and wrenched off some of the lath and plaster. Large chunks fell onto the drop cloth covered floor. He started in the middle, up near the top, and then down. A few hours later, the walls and ceiling in the living room were down to the studs. It felt neutral. *That's what we're doing. Getting back to just neutral. Even.*

Two weeks later, a morning pattern developed. David ran alongside John, and Gaul had jogged four miles plus penalty laps around town for cussing. Paul suddenly found himself laboring to keep up, astonished at how fast David had come up to speed.

"I don't get it. Aside from being an athlete at the same time as John, how have you managed to get up to speed so quickly?" Paul said, looking stressed.

"I swam five days a week. I took dancing lessons, too. They were free, and it was nice to be with people," David said, his respiration unlabored.

With winter just was three months away, Bob Lundberg knew he needed to strike soon and hard as he loomed over his sons, who lounged on a dirty couch in the field office.

"This is very simple. You boys will end up with nothing if you're not absolutely sure. When it's time, you have to make the trip down and be back with Josephine in three days. You know the back way in and out?"

The boys nodded.

Bob continued, "No one will be able to follow you through that thicket. Stay put here. I've an intelligent man to talk to." He walked outside to meet with Tolson. "Hey, my man. Didn't mean to keep you waiting."

"Bob, you're family. Your sons are idiots. Don't let them near the rigs anymore. Hire good people like I told you, where I told you to get them."

Bob was not a small man, but he was half the size of Tolson. Most people were. "I've gotten the word out. I understand there are many applicants. I would really like you to stay, and I'll certainly pay extra."

"That's another thing. Most of what I get out of you is stock in some companies that don't do well. I don't see their names on any exchange, and I'm going to have that checked into. You promised me money for my inventions, and it's been too long for that. I've got to go. I'll be back in three weeks. Whatever you do, get good field people and don't bother me with any emergencies. I won't be running back here."

Tolson got into his truck and drove off into the mid-day mist across packed mud. His diesel pick-up had enough fuel to make the two-day trip straight to Iada's without refueling. He would sleep in the truck along the way to see his twin.

This could fall apart faster than he could take. Bob stood for some time, clenching his jaw and fists as he cursed his stupid sons.

The paint was dry, the roof was done, and it was time to furnish. The spring in David was nearly unbearable. He tried to stay back with Paul and Gaul, but they waved off David and John. They went down Cause Way and crossed Starling. John sounded labored as he struggled to keep up. David, who had lost a lot of weight, ate less the more he lost.

"Hey, what are you? Jonathan Livingston Seagull?" John shouted over to him.

The thought of wearing John out became a charge of electricity that shot straight to David's feet. He took off, skipping the turn they normally used and adding two miles to their six-mile run. He laughed, knowing John labored to keep up. His dreams were coming true. The crisp, clean air burned his throat. His shoes kicked up dust clouds, leaving a trail in his wake. He turned the corner to head back into town, aware that John wouldn't just let him win.

John found his second wind, something he had not used in 20 years. He threw down more energy into every stride. They ran side by side up Cause Way, past Jan who stood in her front yard. She looked incredulous, barely waiving at them.

They came to the corner of First, still sprinting, and went left uphill. John fell behind. Hills were David's specialty. Just past Phil's station, David came to a quick stop, allowing John catch up. Both were winded and happy.

"Hey, we better warm down. Don't you think?" David said as though it were an original idea.

John could only nod.

"The roof is done, the paint is dry, and the floors are in, John. I have a house. Time for stuff, bro!" David grinned. He hopped and skipped and could not be contained.

John smirked, shaking his head as they walked to the Café.

David bounced inside and kissed Jan. "Hello, my girl. We're going somewhere right after breakfast. I'm taking you into the big city. We're going to outfit the house and have it all delivered."

Jan turned to John as they sat down. "Has he had any coffee yet?"

John turned to her, looking dejected. "I'm so glad it's Saturday. You get to supervise him now."

After breakfast, David inspected his house. The floors were of pristine, wide plank hardwood. Bosche was a genius with his table saw and wood selection. The poor patchwork his father had done was gone.

He felt the presence of his mother. This would have made her happy. If she were smiling down upon him, he would make it a proper home with a wife. He caught himself and almost fell over at the thought.

He showered and changed at John's house and then made a call to the woman Paolo had recommended many months ago. An hour later, a polished black SUV showed up.

Jan was surprised to come out and find only the SUV in front of her house. David came out still extremely amped.

"Okay, girl, leave the small stuff behind. We're shopping till we drop and then shopping some more!"

Without saying a word, she climbed into the SUV.

"Thirsty?" David said, opening a small door panel in front of them and revealing a variety of drinks.

"On the road? I don't think that's a good idea, but maybe after we stop."

"No road. It's always a good idea to drink something just before going up. The air is dry past a few 1,000 feet." He handed her a fizzy water drink like his.

"This thing flies?"

"No, that does." David pointed at a helicopter as they drove up to the same gate John had dropped him off when he went to Palo's.

Jan finished her water and looked worried. David held her hand and smiled, waiting until her pulse slowed and she smiled back.

He walked with her, holding her hand and explaining what to do with the seat belt. The helicopter warmed up and Jan began to look worried again. David looped an arm around her and held her even closer.

"I've done this a lot, Jan. Just enjoy the view. Have you ever seen the town from above?"

"I've never been in a helicopter before. David, this is how I lost my husband."

David had a difficult time processing her comment, but he trusted his emotions. "Fly with me, Jan. Fly away with me."

He twisted their interlocked hands a little. She looked at him with worry and adoration, nodding slightly. David pushed a button. "Hey, man, can we circle the town? We want to see it all from the air."

The pilot nodded with a smile. The helicopter gently lifted up, tilted forward, and ascended. It only took a few seconds before the helicopter hovered over the hills that guarded the town from highway noise. They flew over and around the town.

"The school!" Jan exclaimed. "The café, church, store. Hey, Phil is outside looking up at us." She waved at him. They circled around once more. Jan turned to David. "Where are we going?"

David hit the button again. "Okay, man, thanks." The pilot nodded and they headed towards the city.

In a few minutes, they began circling above buildings. Jan looked excited as she gazed out the window, her eyes and focus seemed to be all over. They landed on one of the larger buildings and waited for the helicopter to wind down to a stop. As they made their way outside, a professional looking woman walked up to them.

"Hello, Mr. Dryer and Ms. Milnarcheck. I'm Suchi, and I'll be taking care of you today."

"What do we need?" Jan appeared puzzled.

FLYING ON THE GROUND

They went inside and rode an elevator down from the roof. When it stopped, they stepped into an expansive room where six people waited in two groups.

"Jan, we need manicures, pedicures, massages, and new clothes. After we're done, we get to shop for the house. After that's finished, we can pick up our new outfits and head off to the club. Do I have that right, Suchi?"

"Perfect, sir. Can I suggest we measure first?"

"Indu-b-idah-bly, Jan?" David made an exaggerated hand and arm gesture towards the staff that brought them to separate rooms.

With their measurements taken, and hands and feet done, it was time for lunch. Suchi took them to a restaurant with a skyline view. They both ate light entrées and salads. Suchi then escorted the couple downstairs to a waiting limousine.

"Kind of fancy for just going to the mall, David," Jan said with a smile, finally putting things into perspective.

"It'll never be too good for you, kid!" David fired back.

Suchi led them through the mall and into a shop with open offices in back. David scanned all of the appliances, not really knowing what they were used for. Suchi introduced them both to a man behind one of the desks, mentioning something about Bosche. Jan began to wonder about the tear sheets when suddenly the man brought out the very book David had given to Bosche earlier in the day.

"Well, that thing has gotten around," Jan said, surprised to see it.

"Oh, yes, I know Bosche. He's worked on some really interesting projects," said the man behind the desk.

"He's got a twenty thousand dollar table saw." David said matter-of-factly. He tried to keep his patience in check while they went over what seemed like exhaustive details. Kitchen cabinets, thanks to Bosche, were easy to figure since he had already sent the measurements. The salesman was able to work up a model of the kitchen on his computer. That alone made him dizzy. When it was finally over, two hours later, he felt like he had just been thrown down a flight of stairs. Jan finally let him know it was done.

"All right, sir. That just about covers everything. You are free to go now." The man smiled.

David shot up from his seat, shook the hand of the salesman, and practically yanked Jan out of her chair. Suchi resumed her role as their guide.

The staff was entertained by David's stories of hardheaded players and behind the scene antics. He had been informed that Jan would need more time, so he thought it his responsibility to entertain the crowd.

Jan stood in front of three mirrors, having a hard time believing her reflection. She was suddenly grateful for joining on some of the runs with Paul and Gaul, along with her swimming. The dress plunged politely in the front and complimented her figure from the knees up.

"Suchi, we're going dancing. Did anyone know that?" Jan became concerned.

"Go on and try it," Suchi said with a smile.

Jan walked in a circle, spun around, and noticed the dress hugged and moved with her. "I'm convinced. What a great color! It's like black and something else."

"Yes, the black has a cream tone in it. You'll find that all of the clothes we're sending you will match your color palate," Suchi said, gesturing to one of the women. "This is from someone very special. Please, put them on."

Jan lifted a cobalt black pearl necklace out of the leather bound bi-fold as though it were a baby. They started out the size of grapes in the center and then whittled down to half that size on each end. They matched her dress, which matched her skin, which in turn matched her hair. She looked at herself in the mirror, not minding her red-brown hair and how it made her hazel eyes stand out. She always thought it a mistake, the greenish center fanning out into a hazel brown on the edges. Now it made sense, but the cost of it all. "I'm glad these are just costume jewelry," she said sounding meek.

"It takes thousands of dives to gather enough black pearls to find a string like this that matches and has a variance in shape ranging from large to small. They came from Tonga and the surrounding islands, and they are a gift. It's called costume jewelry because it matches your outfit. I must speak for the staff here and say it is a very nice combination."

"Paolo." Jan blushed.

"He said you were smarter than average and... well, just a moment."

Jan turned around to see Suchi make a hand gesture towards David's fitting room. She stood in a neat line with the rest of the staff. The quick footsteps of fresh shoes on carpet grabbed her attention and she looked towards the opened door between the two rooms.

"Oh brother, we're going to have to scuff these up. I'm sliding around." Bounding in was a fit and freshened David in a black suit that matched her dress. He wore patent leather shoes. He looked up at Jan and tried to stop, but slid along the carpet, spinning halfway around like he was on ice. "Sorry, Suchi. Where are you hiding, Jan? I thought this was the room." A burst of laughter broke out. Suchi touched his shoulder and guided him to face Jan who stood on a pedestal in front of three mirrors. David took nearly a minute looking at her.

He felt a gentle nudge on his back and walked to the platform. He drew as close as he could get without stepping up to her. How funny, Jan thought, his face turned from incredulous to one of seeing a long lost friend. It looked like he was allowed to breathe. He held out his hand to help her down, and she gently pulled him up.

They shared a gentle kiss. The room erupted in cheers and laughter. She turned to find Suchi and her staff looking at them with elation. David held Jan close as Suchi approached the pedestal.

"Magnificent! Are you both ready?" Suchi asked.

David turned to Jan. "Oh, yeah," they said together.

They went downstairs into the same turn out where they were picked up before. Jan stopped them suddenly. "What is that!?" A car nearly as long as a bus, shiny black and chrome with sweeping fenders and polished fabric on the roof was where the truck was, a driver held open the back door.

"This is a 1932 Lincoln. I was being a bit sneaky when I made you look through a book of interesting cars. They were all limousines."

The driver helped them into the back. The car quietly growled as they made their way around the half circle. They drove to the middle of the city. There was a large, flashing sign that read, 'Club'. It was surrounded by lights, which illuminated the entire street in front of it. A line had formed outside by a crowd waiting to get in.

David and Jan had no idea that most of the people would wait for hours. The driver parked the car. Two large men in overcoats and matching caps came out and opened the car door. Shouts and flashes of light assailed them blinding them temporarily.

"Coach, what are your big picks for the year? What about a big offer for the pro team?"

David walked quickly with Jan into the club's decadent interior. A man in a suit approached them, escorting them to a table overlooking the dance floor.

The carpets were red with flowery details. Sweeping brass banisters separated rows of tables on curves that came away from the dance floor like an amphitheater, each row higher than the other. A large band situated above the dance floor played classic tunes from the 30's in front of a giant pearl clamshell.

"Okay kid, let's cut this up." David pulled Jan from the table after they ordered something to drink.

He pulled her close and she followed. She had no idea he could dance. They danced, nibbled their food, and sipped on their drinks for a few minutes between sets.

It was a long, slow song, and Jan rested against David. She felt tension rise within him.

"I love you, Jan, I just plain love you," he burst out.

She stood on tiptoe and whispered the same into his ear. He'd put every ounce of himself into being her man. She knew that now. David conducted a short conversation with the driver, and they took the Lincoln all the way home. The smell of the city abated, to be eclipsed by the sweet fragrance of home.

21

A FABULOUS LIFE

"Hey, man, Jan loved this car. Can I call you directly for future dates?" David asked from the back seat.

"Now that's an honor, Coach! Call any old time, even for a breakfast run somewhere or maybe a nice trip to the track. Do you like horse racing?" the driver asked, pulling up in front of John's house.

"Cool, hold up. I'll take a picture then put in your phone number." David stepped out of the vehicle.

He stood across the street to admire the car that had given them the ride of their lives. It was the longest and largest car he had ever been in. He looked over the elegant, sweeping lines, which curved upward from the front end, dipped down towards the front doors, and flowed upward again near the back doors and rear bumper. The chrome details were understated. He thought the headlamps looked big and somewhat cartoon-like. He took a photo, added the owner's information into his address book, and then watched him drive away.

He felt tired, yet elated; a kind of tired one experiences from being at the fair all day. Reluctantly, he went inside. Suddenly, loneliness washed over him even though Jan was only a few minutes away.

I can do something about that, he thought. *I could ask Paul about this one! To think, at my age!*

"Well then, how did it go? What did you kids do all day?" The questions came rapidly and loudly from the bothersome four. Paul, Gaul, Dr. Fisher, and John waited in anticipation inside the living room with eager looks on their faces.

"Am I on probation? What's this, curfew?" David looked back at the smiling faces.

"Easy, my brother. We're wrapping up movie night and just anxious to hear about the details from the helicopter. Phil says "hi" by the way. What exactly was that block-long car you just stepped out from?" John asked.

"That was a 1932 Ford. I forget the rest, but what a smooth ride! Jan had never been in a helicopter before and was really nervous about it. We had a concierge named Suchi, who took care of everything. We went to a nightclub where Jan discovered my proficiency in classical and ballroom dancing."

The other men laughed and nodded approval. "My wife has been wanting to try it," Dr. Fisher said, beaming. "There is a new doctor beginning her residency. I believe John knows her. Her mother was one of Gaul's 'best ever' rescues. Maybe I can get her to come out."

"It's on me, Dr. Fisher! Car and everything."

"We could just take that thing to church and then breakfast somewhere," Paul said.

"The owner said it was cool. He also mentioned something about horse racing. Oh well, I have to shower. Peace out, y'all!" David took off.

———

John watched David bound up the stairs. He suddenly felt warm, and the growing pain in his midsection took a break. He wanted to say something, but Gaul spoke first.

"So, Paul, we hear the chimes of midnight, but how about the gong of wedding bells?"

"In time, Gaul. I think very soon. Peace out, y'all! Hey, all the stuff comes in Thursday, so David can move back into his house without me. I'm thinking he can call if need be." Paul glanced at the pile of folded sheets and blankets.

They stood silently for a while until John spoke. "Finally, it's a fabulous life for my brother. Finally."

"I wonder how he'll adjust to a new house and surroundings. Could that trigger a relapse?" Dr. Fisher asked.

"So far he's done the right thing when the pain hit, which was twice in the first three weeks. Running replaced his need. Jan is a great focus for him, too. Better to fight for a normal relationship than some big deal like the inheritance. I believe the suddenness of living alone will stir the right pot within," Paul said.

All felt a warm glow within as they went to bed.

David's thoughts swirled happily as he tried to sleep. *Okay, Paul said he would help me, so what do I need now?* He waited patiently for a response. *Cooking. I need learn how to cook, because that's part and parcel of living in a house. I better learn how to cook. The school provides cooking classes. I can visit the school and see about volunteering. Tomorrow, the church will be hosting a BBQ. I can attend, help Jan, and start to cook.* David turned onto his side. *I hope I don't make hell out of the hamburgers.* He paused. *Good one, David. You just said hell right in the middle of pseudo praying. You know what I mean, right?* Waiting for a response, he fell asleep, at peace and understanding what it felt like to receive an answer to his prayers.

———

"Step, step, step, tink, thump. Gurgle, tink, thump. Dribble, murmur, step, step, step, bang, scoop, tok, tok, murmur." The sound of the coffee maker and the aroma finally relaxed Paul. Conversely, David banging around the kitchen worried him. Time to get up and see about this new enthusiasm.

"Good morning to you, my good fellow. Coffee will be ready soon." David stood tall and proud like someone who had just shot huge game on a hunting expedition.

Paul looked around. It appeared David might have gotten it right. "Okay, you're feeling good. On Thursday, all the stuff you ordered is being delivered. It's amazing how fast cabinets can be made. Bosche tells me robots take care of it now. It'll just take hours to hang them into place. How do you feel about moving into your new pad?"

"I'll ask you the same when you and Gaul occupy the Walker House." The coffee machine beeped. David poured a cup for Paul and handed it to him. "You guys are funny. Might as well discuss the elephant in the room. I told Jan I love her, and she said she feels the same about me. I need to learn how to cook. Do you feel like staying with me a while longer?"

"Not that I enjoy sleeping anywhere near Gaul, but you're going to have to get comfortable in your own skin, the one you're growing into."

David looked injured. He took a deep breath. "I cannot thank you enough for what you have done for me."

Paul watched him for a while. He could see David was taking it hard, but slowly resolving the issue.

"Like I said about phone calls, twenty-four seven still holds for life. I think on Friday we should practice preparing lunch and supper. On Saturday, you can prepare supper for Jan and follow it up with a movie night."

"On Thursday, I can visit the school and help make lunch for the kids! That's great practice," David said with excitement.

"Thursday is cabinet day. Furniture and kitchen appliances start coming in on Tuesday, and maybe the home theater system."

"Life used to be so much easier! Okay, Paul. It sounds fine. Maybe a lesson this afternoon?" David poured coffee for them both.

"I'll think about it. Hey, Gaul is having some special people over to hang out. You should do so, as well. I promise it won't run too late."

David raised his mug and clinked it against Paul's. "Partners in crime. I'm down with that!"

They continued to drink their coffee and chat about furnishings and cooking. Paul was impressed by how much David could learn just by observation with an ear or an eye. He hadn't taught him to use the coffee maker.

David walked over to Jan's house to escort her to church. "Remember, we're actually going to pay attention to what Gaul has to say today," Jan said, swinging his hand.

David did his best to listen and remember just the theme. Find your passion and your purpose will follow. *What purpose was there in wanting to get into a big fight?* he wondered. *That's how you became John's friend.* He began to reminisce. Some assholes in school were teasing John about refusing to shower with the others.

Good one, David. He smiled to himself. *You just said asshole on the church grounds. Oh, well, only God heard me. I'll ask Paul later if he understands such things.*

People lined up to attend the next gathering. Some parishioners from the first service worked in the kitchen while others began to set up tables and chairs. David did his best to follow Paul's instructions. He had never seen how the contraption folded out from under the table and locked into place or how the stack of chairs became upright when lined up.

The second service had just ended. John returned after changing at home and waited outside for Gaul.

"Mr. Kemp, I fly on the ground too! Daddy, it's him!" shouted a young girl.

John felt stunned. A large, fit looking man dressed in military attire walked up to him, extending his hand. "Hello, Mr. Kemp. I'm so very glad to meet you. My daughter learned how to handle bullies in her school through the advice on your website."

His wife joined in, shaking John's hand and introducing her family.

"Wow, this is something! I don't get to meet celebrities often," he said, looking bashful.

"He's cool, daddy! I learned I could see things in a different way. I have a gift!" The little girl ran off into the backyard to join the other kids.

John kept calm. "Well, I haven't been a celebrity for quite some time. If I can help in any way, I'm happy to do so."

"It's been a while since you were on a cereal box!" the man said.

John smiled, thanking the man for his service and politely nodded while the man's wife helped him find a place to sit. John set out to find Gaul. He located him, along with Daniel, in the church office.

"I need to know why I'm suddenly famous against my wishes, Pastor Gaul."

"You're going to love the new one! I met a new friend. Gotta jet, Mr. Kemp!" Daniel rushed over, hugged John, and dashed out the door to find the girl who had introduced her father only moments before.

Gaul did some quick mouse and keyboard work then turned with a Cheshire grin towards John. "Now, John, no one can make you famous."

"Six months after the Olympics I sat in here with you, sobbing over my elation that it was all over! Why? What is it now?" John hovered over him as though lecturing a 10-year-old.

Gaul stood and dashed off to the kitchen. "Sit down and take a look. That's an order!"

John sat and perused the website. The graphic on the first page was a hand drawn picture, which appeared to be a drawn over photograph. There was a link for discussions, contacts, best of, and featured quotes. He saw himself, his words, his sayings, and his life thread throughout the website. The familiar sound of heavy footsteps alerted him to Gaul's return. He placed a beer in front of him.

"Shit, Gaul, I did all this?" He turned to look at him while taking a healthy swig.

"May I remind you that today is Sunday?" Gaul looked mischievous while tilting his bottle towards John's. They clinked their bottles together.

"I didn't mean for this to take off as much as it did. Next thing I knew, I was selling advertising space and recruiting monitors to keep the creeps out. I really should've said something, son. Really."

Halfway through their beers, John looked over some of the sayings, as well as Daniel's amazing artwork. Gaul sat with him.

"I just didn't want to do anything outside of Leduc ever again. Retirement meant no more glare from the unforgiving limelight and phony get-togethers with now dead politicians and their edifice trails. I feel invaded and dissected all over again."

"The way you live and who you are is a calling, John. Would you hang up on God?" Gaul asked.

John continued to browse the website while they finished their beers. He cracked a wry smile. "You organize a single parade, and I'll smack you in the ass in front of everyone."

"One more beer?"

"Yup."

Gaul ran off back into the kitchen and spent another hour with John. He kept quiet and listened.

———

A shadow with platinum hair fell on David as he finished taping down the last plastic tablecloth. He looked up. "Hi. Am I doing this wrong, too?"

"Oh, Coach Dryer! How wonderful to finally meet you. I'm Anna Tolson, Jack's wife. He and his brother played for you."

David thought she was as large as she was beautiful. It wasn't an obese large, but the kind one gets from working on a farm. She was nearly Tolson's height, 6'5. Her voice was mousy, but her handshake quite authoritative. "I'm happy to meet you. Is Jack nearby?"

"He'll be here. I gave him a break from church. He drove straight from the gas fields to Iada's house to visit his brother and then returned home. I thought it would be nice to let him sleep in and join everyone tonight. He works so hard, but I have doubts about this Bob Lundberg he works with."

"I can address that. Look, make sure he stays here for a few days. I have people who need to speak with him."

She looked close to tears. "I'm sure he will. He says he won't miss the boys' first week at football summer camp."

"Boys?" David asked.

"Oh yes, twins run in the family," she said cheerfully.

"Big ones?" David inquired.

"They're going to start their freshman year. Jack says they are to play only for you!" She nodded her approval.

"Anna, I won't be coaching anymore. I don't want you to worry about anything. Trust me on this one. You're family, Anna. I will explain later," David said with outstretched hands.

She quickly clenched him to her generous bosom. "I'm so glad you're here. I don't know what else to say!"

"I'm glad we're friends," David replied.

She released him, embraced him again with one arm, and turned to face Jan. "This here is a keeper!" She squeezed David forcefully, nearly causing him to lose his balance.

"Well, keeper, we need some grub for the BBQ. Gaul has money in the office. Here's a list." Jan did her best not to laugh.

"I need a license and a pick-up truck," David said mournfully.

"Jack can get you to the market. Wait here and I'll find him." Jan marveled at how fast such a big woman could move as Anna quickly left the backyard.

"David, is there a reason people just act upon any suggestion you make?"

"I'm a natural?"

"Natural what?"

"Leader guy?"

"You're a natural born leader. Is that what it is?"

"That's what I'm told, Jan." He began to look thoughtful as he wrapped his arms around her, bringing their noses close together. "I could use some help figuring it out. This is a new life for me. Do you like sharing it with me?" He kissed her ever so gently.

She kissed him back enthusiastically. "I do. So help me God, I do."

They lost themselves in a passionate embrace. Shutting out the rest of the world, they did not hear what sounded like a bus park itself in front of the church.

Heavy footsteps approached. They paused for a moment, watching the Tolson's make their way towards them.

"Well, it's true! Hello, Coach. What are you and Jan doing over here?" He encircled them with his massive arms before they could respond.

"I'm glad we're friends," Jan gasped.

"You see? Helicopters, limousines, and the like, just like I told you!" Anna gushed.

Jack released them. "So, what's this run we have to do?"

"Well, Jack, I'd like a ride to pick up some groceries. Here's a list. Jan, does this say for how many?" David asked.

"About 150. Get some cash from Gaul, and I'll see you when you get back." She quickly kissed him.

"Okay, but I'll cover this one. Let's roll, Jack!"

They made it to a large, dark grey pick-up that took up nearly two parking spaces.

Off to the side, a man sat upon on a three-wheeled bicycle. David noticed he had an aluminum leg just below one knee. "Hello, Coach Dryer. Are you going to be here tonight?"

"I sure will." David reached down to shake the man's hand.

He then climbed into the biggest truck he had ever seen. It was a quad cab with an extended bed and a raised four-wheel drive suspension. The turbo wound up as the truck began to move. David was impressed at how quickly it got up to speed when they hit the highway.

"At this size, is it still considered a pick-up or something else?" David asked.

Jack burst out laughing. "What else could you call it? Sometimes, I need to pull a heavy trailer now and again. Before I forget, Pete's father-in-law left something for you, so go on and see him when you have the chance." Jack kept his eyes on the road.

They parked outside of the large grocery story and went inside. David looked at his grocery list, nervously glanced around the market, stared back at his list, and hesitantly scanned the aisles.

"Not a place you're used to? This is a great store and has almost everything. Let's take a walk around so you can see where everything is located, pick out what we need, and check it off the list." Jack sounded reassuring.

Relieved by the simple plan, David listened to Jack explain the signs at the start and end of each aisle that hung from the ceiling. He described how produce was at one end and the Bakery and Deli at the other and how meat was located on the back wall. He discussed how each aisle specialized in packaged foods or household items, and how there were two rows of freezers with ice cream and frozen dinners.

"My wife does not like me walking up and down the aisles. She says, 'If it's not worth making, it's not worth eating.'"

"Is that why you both look fit?" David asked, turning to him.

"Listen to you!" Jack grinned.

"We're both going to need carts." They grabbed shopping carts and headed for produce.

"So, how's life been treating you?"

"It's been good, Coach. Anna is very smart, and still big enough to make the boys respect her. Part of my deal with Bob Lundberg and the Land Sakes Company was for 20 of the 50-acre parcels they own. Odd thing, though, it was part of a swap for patents my brother and I owned. I received a 'pay up or quit' notice. I'm looking to hire a lawyer to get that fixed. The land is mine! Anna worked it herself." Jack looked visibly upset.

David stopped and turned around.

"Bread crumbs," he said to Jack.

"We forgot bread crumbs?"

"Jack, I have great lawyers. Can you trust me long enough for them to talk to you?" David smiled at Jack.

"If you can fix what's going on, I won't be able to contain my happiness. What about the bread crumbs?" Jack asked.

"Go ahead, get happy. You and I are going to see Pete tomorrow. My mother laid down a trail of bread crumbs that make their way into Pete's garage." David began to toss ears of corn into his cart, along with five sacks of potatoes. "Don't be surprised if you find out we're cousins, my man."

"My wife said that all Leducs, Dryers, and Lundbergs are related; they came out here, we went over there. A lot of back and forth happened. Of course, Jan's mother was an import, but what a fine family member she became, anyway."

"Thanks for letting me know." David felt relieved.

"Sure seems like a lot. Does the list have briquettes on it?" Jack asked.

"No. It has sausages, hot dogs, hamburgers, and buns for both," David answered.

"Candy apples?"

"If Jack wants candy apples, then candy apples it is," David joked.

Jack laughed and topped off David's entire cart with packages of candy apples. They paid for their loads and nearly filled up more than half the bed of the truck. Other workers from the store cleared off half a pallet of briquettes, brought them out and helped load it in.

Jack revved up the engine and headed for home. David thought the truck sounded like a train.

"Hey, Coach, did you ever pay a bill like that before?" He laughed a little at his own joke.

"I've never been grocery shopping before. I quit coaching, Jack. You can just call me David from here on out. I'm home for good."

Jack nodded and smiled. "Being a coach is something that never leaves you. You can be born a coach or molded into one like yourself. My wife told me 'the coach' personality will always dominate, but I know better. You're looking for something or someone to show you where the next game will be. You're home now. Give it time."

His words made David feel at peace.

David allowed the evening to wear on, helping a little here and there, but doing his best to stay out of the center of everything. Jan asked him to swing by her place when he was finished with the guys, but not before 8:00 p.m. Evening finally settled in as the last of the tables and chairs were put away.

"David, I'd like you to meet the Veteran Riders. We're hosting them tonight. I'm looking forward to hearing some stories. Craig, why don't you start us off?" Gaul prompted.

The man with the aluminum leg stood up. "Well, I finally get the chance to thank Coach Dryer for inspiring me and my buddies while we were pinned down in Afghanistan. He once said, 'Getting to the goal lacks meaning without knowing why you got there. A fighter only knows how to get there, but a man of faith understands the meaning will come later.' We listened to you over the radio. Your team was down 30 points before half time in a game where the chance of victory was slim to none. I don't know what you said to your boys during half time, but I'm sure they felt as dead as we did that day. I can stand here and admit that. What an amazing thing to feel so inspired." Craig sat back down.

David looked around and saw commiseration on the faces of the others. How odd that he had forgotten what he'd said until now. The hours passed and one lesson began to sink in.

I can have faith and trust that the reason will manifest itself. I fight, that's what I do, he affirmed.

"Been kind of quiet, Tolson. Share anything you like," Gaul said.

"I like having David back in town. It's awesome he wants to retire with us. I went with him on his first supermarket run tonight. The boy learns quickly!" He laughed heartily at his own joke. The others got caught up in it, as well.

"Does my brother, David, have anything he'd like to say?" John asked.

"Well, I had no idea what my life had become until now. What you men have done is beyond me. To say I brought meaning to your life brings meaning and purpose to mine. We were buying stuff and Jack said…"

"Please don't buy anymore!" Jack laughed even harder and everyone else joined.

After they settled down, David spoke. "Sorry about the leftovers. I'm glad there was room in the fridges and people were able to take some home. I've been saved from myself because of the very people around me. I don't know what else to say but thank you. I didn't realize how wonderful my life truly was until now. I don't know what else to do but to keep on keeping on like the man said." He bowed his head.

"Jan's waiting. You could go do that," John teased, causing another outbreak of laughter.

David felt energized. He offered his goodbye before rushing off. He heard their laughter as he made his way to Jan's house. He arrived just past 8:00 p.m. The smell of freshly made popcorn filled the house.

"Did you think about what movie you wanted to see? I picked out some and put them in that pile on the coffee table," Jan said from the kitchen.

He picked up the stack and sat down on the couch, recognizing the titles of movies he'd previously mentioned to her. "You've got to be kidding! We have to watch this one. It's my favorite!"

She returned to the living room, and they shared a tender kiss. He handed her the movie, 'Donovan's Reef', which she happily inserted into the player. Throughout the film, they laughed and made hula-like gestures every time the Hawaiian music played.

After a long while, Jan fell asleep against his shoulder. David leaned back and admired her beautiful face in peaceful slumber, allowing him the contentedness to drift off into sleep.

22
BREAD CRUMBS

No running today, David decided as he slowly began to stir. Jan's head rested in his lap. She did not see the entire movie, but he didn't mind. She needed to rest. Always up before the sun, he knew Jan loved to sleep in.

He sat quietly, allowing his mind wander. Elaborate dreams began to manifest in his thoughts. He envisioned the structure of his day; bread crumbs, Phil, Paolo, and the dynamic duo.

An hour passed. Jan began to move. David wondered if he'd awakened her. He stroked the side of her head ever so gently. She began to rouse.

"It's early enough to have breakfast at the Corner Café," he whispered.

She nodded and raised herself slowly.

"Go on ahead. I'll meet you there."

David stood, stretched, and walked out the door into the fall air. He took a slow, methodical walk. He knew Phil might be up with ready-made coffee in his shop, but he wanted to take Jack there as he'd promised. His thoughts came in fast and hard. *Do it now! Just get it over with!* he thought. *I run the show. Shut it!* David screamed in his head. Going uphill on Cause Way and looking down Business Route, he could see Phil's garage. A large pick-up like the one Jack Tolson drove sat parked out front. He knew Jack did not park there, but the truck looked similar. *Perhaps I should wash my face and brush my teeth first,* he thought as he made his way to John's house.

As he approached the house, he heard a lot of rustling and muffled voices. He opened the door and was greeted by a half dozen inquisitive faces. The usual suspects, along with several bike riders, stood in the living room with arms crossed some with cracked smiles.

"So, me laddie, where ya been all night?"

"Where ya sent me last night, ye blarney boy," David teased John. He waited for the laughter in the room to die down. "Okay, everyone, breakfast is on me. Let me get washed up first, and I'll meet you all there."

After freshening up, David waited outside of John's house to watch for Jan. The rest of the men got ready. From where he stood, he had a clear view of the Corner Café and part of Cause Way. He waved at Gaul, who stood out front looking irritated.

He saw the front windows of the General Store between some of the houses. He noticed Jan walking past the store windows and then he caught a glimpse of something menacing in its reflection. Across the street from the General Store, a scarecrow of a man watched Jan.

David bolted across the street. The sound of skidding cars and blaring horns brought all of the men out of the house. Gaul ran down Cause Way. He and David converged upon Bob Lundberg.

"Who the hell are you?" David demanded in a flat tone.

The man turned to him. "David Dryer!" Bob extended his hand.

David paused a moment, then he hesitantly offered his own. The shake was firm and surprising. Bob although the same age, looked nearly 30 years older than David.

"Okay, Bob, what brings you to town?"

Gaul shook his head in an exaggerated fashion.

David quickly glanced in the same direction, but could not make out what was causing Gaul's excitement.

Twin barrels of Damascus steel decorated with ornate carvings slowly lowered. Maureen unloaded the Remington 1889 side-by-side shotgun she'd had fixed on Bob Lundberg.

Jan heeded the advice from a hand signal and kept right on walking. David avoided acknowledging her presence.

"Isn't that your lady, David? It's kind of rude to ignore her." Bob revealed poorly kept teeth behind his greasy smile.

"Why are you here, Bob?"

The sound of dozens of feet pounding the pavement surrounded them. John and the rest of the men flanked David on both sides.

"Hey, I was just waiting for the state office to open up and figured I might as well try and see Tolson. Just enjoying a leisurely stroll," Bob said, leaning back slightly with an upturned chin.

Everyone felt something heavy moving along the wood planks. Jack Tolson's footsteps divided the crowd as he made his way through the small group.

"Lundberg, what are you doing here?" Jack asked.

"Jack! Just the man I'm looking for. Look, man, I can pay whatever you want." Bob turned around.

David noticed Anna had joined Jan. The two disappeared from sight.

"I told you no, and I mean that. Now, I asked why you were here. You know where I live, and it's four blocks away." Tolson got up in Bob's face, looking as though he might pile drive him into the ground.

Maureen continued to observe the scene through her opera glasses. She had her shotgun cracked open and ready to have the shells placed back inside. She text messaged Dr. Fisher.

"Get the gauze ready, Doc. Biggest ruckus since Big Jake is brewing five doors down from the clinic. OAO"

Bob looked as though he might begin to shake.

"Jack, I didn't want to wake you. I was just walking around, passing time."

"Pass it somewhere else, Bob. I've given 'shoot to kill' orders if your idiot sons come anywhere near my farm. I don't know who sent the 'pay up or quit' paperwork, but it's my land now."

The phone in David's pocket began to blow up. Jan was trying to reach him. Without taking his eyes off of Bob, he answered his phone.

"David, knock that shit off and come to breakfast," Jan said.

"I guess Bob will be moving along," David said flatly. He pushed Bob with his shoulder as he walked past him and put a hand on Jack's arm to turn him around.

The crowd walked quietly to the Corner Café, Jack the only one without a smirk on his face.

Dr. Fisher text messaged Maureen. "Okay, I can get there in a minute. OAO."

She replied, "Dag blast it, all broken-up without so much as a single punch thrown! See you before you check in. Like that new girl ya got. OAO."

Table space had been made for the small crowd. Jan and Anna waited together. Anna looked at Jack, her eyes filled with sorrow and worry.

Jan looked like she wanted to hit someone and waited for everyone to sit down. "If anything ever happens near the children, you boys will find out the meaning of hell on earth," she said before sipping her coffee.

David placed a hand on her knee, squeezing slowly and progressively harder until she turned to him with a puzzled look. "I love you, girl. Good morning." He kissed her gently and kept his nose close to hers.

"You should have seen him! He had that scarecrow nervous and ready to back down. Damn, haven't seen anything like it! Hey, David, you know your life story would make a great novel!" Craig exclaimed.

David's face was still close to Jan's. "Don't ever ask me not to worry about you. It's not going to happen." He locked eyes with her.

She kissed the end of his nose. "Wow Davey, you're going to be in a novel."

He released her knee. "Craig, it's no life like the brave one you've lived."

Craig became lively and animated, and could be heard throughout the entire café. "It was like the old west. 'What the hell ya doin here, Bob?' Almost like he had a gun on him. Hey, you do have a gun? Yeah that arm of yours! Oh, that's going into the novel! Hey, Jack, is that what he was like on the field? Was he all cool and like, 'I'm going to eat your heart out if you don't pack up and leave'?"

Tolson began to chuckle. With his tummy against the table, it began to shake. His booming laughter bounced off the walls.

Jan rescued her coffee cup from the earthquake that shimmied the napkin holder and other table settings. She tilted her head in David's direction. He held her hand under the table. He knew it would be okay. They would talk about it later.

John, Paul, and Gaul remained silent.

After some assurance that Jan would be watched over, David went with Jack to Pete's garage. "You're going to be the first one in a novel from Leduc, David."

"That can't be real. Thanks for dropping 'coach' from my name. It feels more like home that way."

"Sure. I hope that lawyer can help. You know, your life would be a great book. Don't let being from here change that. You could write it yourself with some help. Jan could do that," Jack said.

"I'm not a writer, thank goodness." David shook his head.

"Just connect your mouth and your fingers, and let it fly!" Jack's laugh was deafening.

They walked into Phil's lobby, which still displayed the half tree on one wall and various trinkets for sale. Some of them looked as though they were left over from 30 years ago. Pete came in from the garage. The noise from the air tools lessened greatly when he closed the door.

"Jack, I see you brought David."

"Hello, Pete. Things sure are getting exciting around here. David and I almost had to wipe down the boardwalk with Bob."

"He might deserve it. Well, Coach, or is it anymore?" Pete stopped in front of David and looked down.

"I'm home to stay. It's great to see you again. My house is being remodeled, and I want you and the whole family over for the party." David smiled up at Phil.

"I like that idea, cousin. My father-in-law wanted you to have this when I determined you were home for good." Phil handed him a leather-bound notebook.

David took the book without opening it. "I'll get some help with this. So, Phil, what do you know?"

"Well, I know about Big Jake and Wellington and how they built this town. Jake was a huge man like Wellington. They both liked to play fight and roughhouse. The General Store used to be a bar, that's why it looks the way it does. The ice-cream parlor was a barbershop," Pete began.

"They made a lot of money together. Big Jake helped Wellington buy land and conduct business. Wellington was African-American and Creole, I think, and was related to Iada. He used to prizefight and did some booze running during prohibition. They both are related to John Kemp through his mother." Pete paused to let the information sink in.

"Jake's great granddaughter is Maureen. She is the second to last direct descendant of the inheritance that has to do with the farmlands and the Walker House. Her father was my stepdad, the man you helped plant a tree. I made my own way, David. I don't want anything to do with what's going on. I own what I have with no debate. I grew up around all the hate your dad and my stepdad were embroiled in and don't need it. It would make a lot of people happy to have this business settled once and for all. Maybe that book will tell you what you need to know. It would take an awful fight to get it all back."

Jack suddenly stood up straight and turned to Phil. "Oh, we have a fighter! You should've seen him with that awful Bob Lundberg."

David cut him off. "We need to go see Cousin Maureen, my plus-sized friend."

David reached out and hugged Phil. "I hope you act the family you are. I'm so very glad to be home."

Phil began to tear up a little. "You saved me and my stepdad in a lot of ways. I can see there's a lot of fight left in you. That's a good thing. The fight to mold yourself into who you really are is a big one. I will always be around for that."

David departed with Jack in tow. He walked straight over to the General Store and hoped he would stop being emotional by the time he reached it.

"Maureen!" David yelled.

"What are you starting a ruckus over now?" she asked, standing directly behind him.

David whirled around. "How do you do that?"

"What's up, defender of the realm? Need something special for the lady?"

"Sure. Before I grill you about some history, why not? What is it?"

She walked behind the counter and pointed to the ring on the shabby brown envelope surrounded by two guns.

"The ring or the guns?" David grinned.

"There's being as dense as a dried cow pie and then being one, David."

"Okay, I get it." David turned, having noticed an odd display of old Jonnas, a shirt, a hat, and boots. It looked like an invisible man was leaning up against the wall.

"What is that?" David asked, pointing to the display.

"It's a keepsake. Tourists like it. They can spot it from the sidewalk and sometimes come in for a closer look. That's how I sometimes get them to buy something," Maureen said, looking proud of her marketing efforts.

"Whoever wore it was more than half the size of Jack, who is about half the size bigger than me. My boy, Paolo is that big. I thought he was more of a genetic freak, but I guess I was wrong. Was it actually meant for someone to wear?" David turned back to her.

As he looked over the outfit, a warm fondness overcame him.

"Big Jake ordered that and a few others that I still have packed up," Maureen explained, breaking into his thoughts.

Jack smacked a stunned David on the shoulder. "That's a huge pile of bread crumbs, David."

David took a long, slow breath as if to fill his mind with needed oxygen. "Maureen, I'm having an exclusive party at my house on Saturday. I need you to come over and tell us all about Big Jake. Do you think you could? And please tell me what you know about the ring, and maybe I can I put it on reserve."

"I don't have reserve service, but I'll save it for you. The ring was actually supposed to go to your mother. Her grandmother held off passing it down over two generations because of the husbands. They came from up north and were part of the family that settled in the area. Your mother understood that, but something about your dad held her madly in love, anyway. The story began with a man who migrated from the same place your father grew up."

"You mean like what the Dryers kept split from the Lundbergs?" Jack inquired.

"That's right. Why do you know about that?" Maureen turned to Jack.

"Anna, she's researched the family tree and says the same things about the northern people, that there is some connection from the south. She thought Iada might know. John's parents knew."

"That's why I'm having the party. Please continue." David patted Jack on the arm and looked at Maureen.

"The ring is at least a hundred fifty years old or more. It was made on the east coast. A man who migrated with other immigrants from Sweden or Norway purchased some land in the northern area. There was a fiancé waiting for him once he established a home and a life for himself. As soon as he was able, he went to obtain the ring. By that time, however, he was delayed about two months. Presuming he was dead, the woman married into the Lundbergs. Feeling despondent he took one horse, packed up all of his belongings, and headed south." David and Jack listened raptly. "I assume he worked the land as a woodsman since farming was out of the question. Before Iada was born, a widowed woman sent the ring with an accompanying letter that explained it belonged to its rightful heirs and would bring the wearer the harmony and love she experienced. My grandfather, Big Jake, knew the entire story, but he never wrote it down."

As though possessed, the leather-bound notebook twitched in David's nervous hand. "Can you be there Saturday night?" he asked Maureen, his tone serious.

"Of course. I'll see you then." She walked off to the shoe area of the store.

"Let's go find John, Jack." They walked swiftly out the door.

John Kemp opened his front door to what looked to him like Tweedledee and Tweedledum. David and Jack stood there like enthusiastic salesmen anxious to make their pitches. John noticed the old, leather-bound book in David's twitching hand, and he wondered what the excitement could possibly be this early in the morning that couldn't wait till later.

Something strange and uncomfortable bothered his mid-section like it had a few days earlier. He could use it as an excuse to push whatever this was past lunch or just get it over with. "As if you're not allowed inside." John opened the door wide, and they followed him into the kitchen. Coffee was disbursed.

David began to speak at a rapid, but lucid pace. He handed over the notebook after explaining its origin and possible contents.

"We might be closer to being brothers than just in affection, John." David tossed out his comment with a dash of hope.

"My wife, Anna, can attest to much of what you just heard, John. She's got all that family lineage stuff down solid. It's her hobby," David's former all-star lineman said.

"John, I figure we could throw a party at the house on Saturday, invite everyone and hash out who knows what," David said.

John's eyes grew big over what he was reading in the book. "I just got a call. We can start the upstairs today. The cabinets are a day early. It's amazing what robots can do! Bosche is going to be there in a few minutes. I'm going to call Iada. She can be here Saturday. Finish your coffee, boys. It's going to get busy!" John said, putting down the notebook.

"I'll have to call Jan, cancel our date, and ask for her help," David said, taking a sip from his mug.

There was an uncomfortable, long pause, which was gently broken by John. "Did you make solid plans with Jan?"

"Well, as solid as usual. I come up with an idea, and she agrees to it. What the hell is the matter with you two?"

Jack spoke first. "A gentle hand in all things makes a man in the marriage, David."

"I ate what?" David asked.

"He's trying to say that you need a steady hand on the tiller to gently guide the boat, David," John offered.

"John, it's really up to him to figure it out for himself. I think we're overstepping a boundary here." Jack looked past David as he said it.

"You mean let David just get burned and figure it out?" John began to calculate lost time, relapse.

"Both of them. How much can or should we be around for every little compromise?"

"I'm right here, Jack," David said.

Jack put an arm around David and drew him close, almost lifting him off his feet.

"Jack has been married for quite some time. He's the wisest counsel in the room. I'm going to defer this one to his better judgment and meet you both over at David's house," John announced.

The flurry of things to accomplish at David's house became a blur that had morning turning to afternoon before anyone realized it. Jan arrived with bags of sandwiches, chips, and sodas. As everyone ate, David turned to her.

"Hey, this is really nice. We're going to be ahead of schedule. There's a lot to do tonight. I was hoping for a late get-together. Do you think we could reschedule our plans tonight for Friday, instead? I believe we'll be done by then."

There was a long pause. John managed to herd everyone else out into the backyard. Jan finally lifted her face to meet David's.

"Why don't we just chuck the whole week? That should keep you free and clear to take care of whatever you need to!" There was a hurt and a bit of fire in her eyes that David had never witnessed before.

In a flash, David's mind replayed everything Jack had said. "I just thought it'd be nice to get this finished for us, Jan."

"It's your house, David. Enjoy it anyway you like. I was just making a lunch delivery to come see you. Thanks for letting me know how the week is going to go." She got up abruptly and left.

David watched her until she was within sight of Maureen and the General Store. He did his best not to allow his flummoxed feelings to impact him negatively. He groped for Paul's inspiring words, but could not find any. His mind raced until his head hurt.

The floor broadcast heavy steps that came up behind him while he stared out his front door. Arms bigger than most legs wrapped gently around his upper back and turned him towards the backyard.

"We need help digging and raking. It's best you know how to take care of a lawn and plants," Jack said matter-of-factly.

David did his best to allow his natural ability to hyper-focus keep him on task. His gaze never wandered twenty feet beyond him. He rarely looked up except to thank the young men who came over to help. Each waited to shake his hand. He was the first celebrity they had met.

He left messages for Jan to call him back, and he thought about going over to her place and knocking on her door. The strange emptiness he felt was more painful than anything he had ever experienced.

After returning emails from Ingrid and Paolo, he lay awake on John's couch, listening to the owls in the park above town. They were talking to their newborn, teaching them to fly.

He finally sent Jan a text message. "Fly with me, my sweet. I reach out my hand to you. Take it when you are ready. Fly with me, Jan. I'm waiting for you." He drifted off to sleep, hoping Jan would come to him tomorrow.

23
NOT THAT BAD

David dozed. His space on the couch felt familiar. The ceiling seemed equally familiar. The moving sounds of Leduc reassured him. He held the button on the smart phone until it came to life and placed it into his shirt pocket. He continued with his routine of placing his folded blanket with the others. Today, his sat on top.

His phone chimed, indicating a message. He poured a cup of coffee and helped himself to some leftover food in a covered pan. After placing his dishes in the sink, he checked his message.

"I'm trying," Jan had replied at 3:00 in the morning.

David realized she had been up half the night, as well. The thought that he was not available when the text was sent caused a tension in his chest and mid-section. Should he text her back? He wondered if she'd texted him deliberately while he slept. He found his running shoes and headed out. He turned down Cause Way and was about to head out towards the fields. The group had already completed a lap. He caught up to John, who looked exhausted.

"Whoa, brother. What gives?" He jogged, but John slowed to a walk.

"I don't know. Need a tune up, I guess. I'll see Dr. Fisher about it later today. I bet I'll get another R&R order," John said, avoiding David's gaze.

"C'mon, Davey!" Gaul taunted, poking David in the butt and running towards the Walker House.

John looked at him and nodded. "Go teach that mouth a lesson, please. He kicked everyone's ass this morning."

David smirked and ran off after Gaul. He passed Jan's house.

"Good morning, love!" He yelled at Jan's front door and took off after Gaul. He caught him before he could turn uphill.

"Is this a warm-up?" he asked Gaul.

"Go bite, kiddo, special forces training kicking in!" Gaul bolted ahead uphill.

The competitive spark lighted, David shadowed him through town and into the fields. He could tell Gaul was out of gas as they made their way back. He sprinted ahead and stopped at the first corner in town, jumping up and down as though he were boxing.

"Oh, man, what happened?" he shouted in Gaul's direction.

"You stupid kid. Let me catch my breath!" Gaul teased between gasps. "Look, you have to be careful about changing plans on Jan. There's some real underlying trauma going on. I don't know how else to explain it. Right after she lost her husband, having missed his last phone call, she's been a freak about time, keeping appointments, and so on. It's an obsessive-compulsive thing, but with deep pain as well. Any time you need us, Paul and I will be here for you." Gaul patted David's arm and walked off.

David slowly made his way down the street to Jan's front door. He felt confused and upset. As he knocked on her door, he felt guild for causing her anxiety. He shouted out her name when she didn't answer the door.

"What do you want?" asked a voice out of nowhere.

David looked around first. Jan stood on Maureen's porch.

"I want to see you, love. What are you doing?"

"Come over here, you jack-in-ape!" Maureen yelled from inside the house loud enough for the whole neighborhood to hear.

David walked over and entered the house as Maureen emerged from her kitchen.

"Look, you two, there will be plenty of time for both of you to figure the other out. No one else is going to do it for you. My dearly departed and I worked out just fine, despite the fact that he wanted children. We had a lot of fun in the trying, and then just in each other's company. Don't let it come to blows. David, missy here will do her best not to nag you to that point."

"He broke a date to play with the boys!" Jan said, crossing her arms.

"I came up with an alternative plan, Jan! You have to be reasonable."

"Both of you shut it! I've got to open the store now. Go on and get a walk in before you say any more. You've both been coddled way too much. David, as a coach you did little to nothing for yourself. I applaud you for trying. It's about time life kicked you in the ass. Jan, I love you, but dammit! You could have offered to hang out with him and the boys. You know you're welcome to any time. You won't get any more hand-holding from me. Get out and make up proper." Maureen closed the door after nudging them both outside.

They began to walk towards the school and the Walker House. David kept quiet. Jan slowed her pace.

"Should we walk the other way around towards the park?" he asked.

She nodded and they turned together. She reached for his hand and gripped it. "Fly with you?" She looked at him with tender eyes.

He turned to her with reciprocal tenderness. He nodded and held out his other arm like the wing of an airplane. She joined him. They continued down the block with outstretched arms, smiling the entire way.

Somewhere deep in the woods, thin clouds kissed the tops of the trees surrounding the open space of a grand cabin. Inside, children took their dishes to a counter that extended just beyond the kitchen where a teenager received and washed them.

Iada prayed aloud as she made her way to the kitchen for another cup of coffee and a biscuit.

"I've heard you, Lord, and I will make my way to Leduc tomorrow." She stepped into the kitchen and was handed the coffee and biscuit without prompting. "You're all such a blessing. I'm so sorry that y'all are leaving for the University, but that's what you wanted and have earned. I supposed someone told my Josephine that I'm wanting to see her?" she asked the other teens as they prepared lunch for the 100 or so children who were always around.

"Yes, Iada. The word went out, and then so did you. I'm glad you have habits I can rely on," Josephine said, strolling in.

She was 21 years old and nearly as dark in complexion as Iada. Her face was angular and sleek-looking. She communicated warmth and competence with ease, and she walked with poise.

"Oh, my baby! Speaking of which, the Tolson boy brought us a fish and left you a carving. He's so grateful for the sleeping bag you gave him. I want us to drive off to Leduc right away to see your Uncle John and that David Dryer. Going to want to be there by late Friday for a big get-together being held on Saturday. Please ask for a car to get there and stop over one night at a place nearby so we can arrive easily. I know it's a nine-hour drive, so let's try for seven and have a nice stay. No bed bugs." Iada took a bite of her biscuit.

Walking up to Josephine, a young man held up a trout longer than his forearm. "Oh look, we can invite some friends over for that!" She smiled at the young man. "There was a time he helped me catch one just like it and held on to me to keep it from pulling me into the river." Her eyes twinkled with the memory.

"He your protector. That's a sure thing. Funny, he didn't get sad when you went off to University. No, he told me in the only way he could that you would do well and to calm down about it. His brother brought the boys over and he talked about you being like his daughter." Iada beamed at Josephine.

"I'll call Uncle Wilks and take care of the hotel." Josephine left quickly.

"Hey, girl." David turned to Jan. "Why don't you come and work with us?"

"I don't have work clothes." She looked off into the distance.

David dragged her off to the General Store. "I can fix that. No concierge needed."

Maureen looked ready to throw them out. David explained the reason for their visit. She took care of them in short order and quickly shooed them out. "Jan, I'll keep your other clothes at my house. Come by and get them later."

They returned to the house, navigating a path around large boxes placed on the front lawn labeled with letters, numbers, and up arrows.

Bosche approached them. "Hello, Jan. Glad you're here. David, we're ready to start putting up cabinets. The boys have the bathroom stuff upstairs. You can go up and help hold the cabinet while we screw it into place. It'll be good practice for the kitchen. Jan, in the living room, the only things to hang are the big screen and some small speakers. The rest is decorator ready."

David turned and kissed Jan before she could say anything. "Well, love, see you when I get out of the bathroom." He headed upstairs.

David did his best to pay attention to the method of holding up the cabinet while Bosche screwed it into the wall. His thoughts remained with Jan and how she looked in Jonnas and a plaid shirt. She was a country girl if there ever was one, but she also possessed sophistication and poise. Then, there was that wall. "Bosche, how patient do I have to be?" he asked, hiding what was really on his mind.

"You hold the box, screw it down tight, and she's all yours to do as you please." He faced the cabinet, and it made his voice echo.

"I'm going to conversation school one day," David said, his mind suddenly clear.

"Goodness, David. I would think you could teach classes on speaking."

"I just failed. It's hard to explain. I'm glad for the rail pieces or whatever the hell they're called. All I have to do is make sure this doesn't slide."

"French cleats, my man, almost don't need anyone's assistance. They're easy to make on the table saw. You just place her on top, slide her around until you have her where you want her, and then screw away."

David looked over at one of the young men helping with the house project. "Glad to know these cabinets with the French rails have a feminine tense associated with them. I went to college. I know about French stuff." The young man nodded with a smile.

The day wore on, Paul and Bosche providing instructions for mounting, hooking up the sink, and placing wires for the living room speakers.

Anna delivered lunch a little later than usual.

Maureen greeted her and Jack. "Hi, cousins! I just had a tiff with the both of them. They seem to want to do all of the hard work first."

"Anna, I forgot to tell you. David broke a date with Jan yesterday. They have just gotten around to talking." Jack waved at Gaul as he entered the house.

"Yikes! Well, how much does he really know?" Anna asked.

Maureen cut in. "None of that matters. Look, let's stay out of it. Let them come near to blows if need be, but by all means they have to work this out or we'll all be involved till kingdom come."

Jack and Anna nodded in agreement.

Someone suggested David take Jan out to the new back porch complete with the new furniture Jan had picked out. It rested on new paving stones butted up against freshly laid grass. They began to eat quietly.

"This backyard never looked so fabulous. My dad always had piles of junk. My mom never came out here. One day, I cleaned it up and we enjoyed it together.

My dad was furious over it. He said I 'fucked up his whole plan.'"

"Well, I can understand not wanting to have things moved around without being told, David."

"I was 12 years old, Jan!"

"You like disturbing things and people. That's the coach in you. I thought you were retired!" She left quickly through the back gate.

How often will this happen? Can I have an answer sooner than later? David finished his food and rejoined the construction crew. He could tell everyone was trying to leave him alone.

Bosche put up the French cleats and David hung the cabinets on them. His mind wandered constantly on what he had said and how he had said it. After a few hours, he took a short break and went out into the backyard to pick up wrappers from the table. He noticed Jan only took a few bites.

He sent her a text. *I want you to sleep well. Please, let's take this a bit more slowly. Fly with me?*

She replied. *9:00 p.m.?*

Sounds great, love.

He went back to work. The tension in his gut began to dissipate.

———

John's appointment at the clinic finally arrived. A young woman, the daughter of one of Gaul's street rescues, was drawing blood and taking notes.

"Margaret, are you a full blown doctor now?" John asked.

"Sure am!" she replied with a smile. "I completed the program early. Ahnee asked me to stay at Children's Hospital, but I wanted to be home for a while. Dr. Fisher is letting me intern with him. I'm getting paid and everything I do adds towards my residency. I've been apprised of your condition, John, so there's no need to go over a lot of details. Have you ever had an MRI before?"

"No, I haven't. What is it for?" John asked.

"Well, in your case there could be a hernia or a few other things most men would never get. So, I want to rule out most of them. At your age with the additional parts you carry inside, I think it best to make sure things are in the proper place. No strain at all. This is an order for an MRI with contrast. You'll have to drink special orange-flavored goo over a 24-hour period. No eating. This will be a complete scan that I hope is just a base line." She handed him a large manila envelope.

"Hernia? No, I don't have that kind of muscle pop. Just this dull ache deep inside," John said, patting his mid-section.

"Hernia can mean any organ poking where it doesn't belong. You could also have some inflammation that would be unique to your condition. I want to get the complete picture."

John grinned. "Could I be pregnant?"

"No, my father of mirth and merriment. I just want to see completely. It's never been done and should be for someone carrying around extra parts." She leaned over and gave him a hug.

John walked home slowly, hoping 50 was not going to feel much worse. She was right. He thought perhaps he should wear something supportive with all of his running around.

David thanked everyone and handed out $20 dollar bills to the young men, even though Bosche was paying them. His bathroom and bedroom were ready. He walked over to John's house to retrieve his bags.

"John, my brother, I'm moving out."

John smiled, slightly pained. "Well, my brother, I'll only miss you two doors away." He hugged David and stood back, keeping hands on his shoulders. "You're ready. Please don't let Jan slip through your fingers. You can figure everything out later. Please marry that girl."

David's face wore the day's efforts, which were mostly emotional. He felt it from head to toe. "Okay, my brother. I'm working on it." He left for his empty house decorated with brand new furniture. The smell of drying glue and fresh cabinets lightened his mood as he made his way upstairs. He took his time getting ready. He had two hours to himself before he left for Jan's house.

Maureen sat with Gaul in the park which overlooked the entire town.

"How funny we are. You give me shit about raising someone and yet neither of us have any children. Well, I know you being married over me. Jan found a happy place here in Leduc. So did I. I never cried so hard in my life until her husband died."

"You really help people with boundary issues. Okay, so David never got out much and was coddled too often. But look at the man he became. How fun for us to watch him finally mature." She took a swig of her beer.

"So much change in such a small place. Listen, the owls are talking. Look, there goes David. Do you think he can coach himself now?"

"I do. I believe you can retire now. We all adore Paul. He's one stout son of a gun!"

"Wonder if they'll push me out," Gaul pondered.

"No, that church is owned by us. You'll stay on in the expanding category of CEO or some nonsense like that. The Walker House will become what you want it to be."

"Are you ready to retire?" he asked.

"I am. Jan is a fine replacement or successor, if you will. David will bring together the family fortunes when he's ready. Defending Jan the way he does, I can tell Bob Lundberg will be no match for him. Iada doesn't know that yet, but she's aware of everything else. Hey, when can we sell this beer?"

"When I make CEO."

"Well shit, then talk to Paul tomorrow."

"Language, girl!" He and Maureen laughed long and hard as they watched the moon-glow spill across the fields.

He knocked on the door softly, and then knocked again. He looked over at Maureen's front door to see if it would open and Jan would pop out. He lifted his hand to knock again just as the door opened. Jan stood there in an old pair of sweatpants. Even without make-up on her face, she looked as fresh and as clean as a mid-western day. David stood there silently, taking in her loveliness under the soft glow of the moon.

"Are you going to hit me?" She teased with a smile that brought about the delicate dimples on both the sides of her mouth.

David paused then realized he had been standing there with closed fists.

"I think the new rule should be that we stop arguing after 8:00 p.m." He relaxed his hands and brought them into resting position.

She nodded and stepped back to push open the door. "We can always tell each other to go to hell the next day."

All of their pain converted into laughter and happy memories of the silly things they shared in random ways well into the early morning hours.

24
SUMMATION

After only a few hours of restful sleep, David found himself waking up to unfamiliar surroundings and smells as though he awoke in a department store. But this was his new room. The sounds of Leduc were comforting and familiar. The easy to read clock reminded him it was time for a run.

He was able to find everything quickly now that it was organized. He had more clothing choices than ever before, not just clean or dirty. The smell of the new furniture and cabinets remained dominant when he walked downstairs. The rush of fresh air almost sent him into shock when he opened his front door.

"Well, good morning, man of the world," John said.

David gave John the once over. "Can't go this morning?"

"No, going across the hill today. I need some big tests. I hope to see you for lunch. Enjoy the run. Paul is waiting for you down on Cause Way at the corner of Starling. Go kick some ass!" John gave David's arm a pat.

David jogged slowly at first. His thoughts seemed to run faster than him. That all changed when he saw Gaul shadowboxing and making gestures in his direction.

"The fat Ffff." He laughed to himself, quickening his pace past Gaul, Paul, and Bosche.

"Ffff, boys, got some pepper under those shoes today!" Gaul hollered loud enough to be heard across town.

David taunted them, allowing them to get close only to sprint away. He turned around more than once to make sure no one dropped dead. He continued all the way into town.

They jogged along Starling past the backside of the General Store. Jan came outside in the same pair of sweatpants she'd worn the night before.

"Well, my man, showing them how it's done?" she called out to David.

"Oh, my darling of Starling. Please entreat us with your divine presence at the cafe of wonder." He slowed his pace.

"I shalt entreaty thee indeedy, oh man of ye new manor." She bowed and performed a twirling motion with one hand.

David and the others did the same as they continued on to the cafe. They heard Maureen as they made their way down the block.

"What in the cracker box was all that?"

David reached the Corner Café and found Jan waiting for him. He sat close to her on a bench that could accommodate five more with a long table in front that could be made longer. The plastic wood veneer of the table was well kept for being sixty years old.

David took his time, carefully looking over the menu.

Jan broke into his thoughts. "What's on that mind of yours?" she asked, caressing the side of his head right above his ear.

"Everything and nothing." He turned to kiss her lightly on the lips. "Things really do change. So much remained the same for me for so long. I come home to retire and now all this shit starts up. I'm going to go find the Mayor today. He's been hiding." He looked deep into his coffee.

Jan hugged his arm and smiled.

Jack Tolson sauntered into the cafe. The soft thumping vibration of the floor announced his entrance. Anna and their twin boys followed close behind.

"There he is! Boys, we're on our best behavior now. We have adult things to talk about, okay?" He looked behind him at the happy, agreeable twins. They greeted everyone and found seats across from David and Jan at the far end.

Gaul, Paul, and Bosche walked in together just as a black SUV pulled up out front. David knew instantly it was Ralph and Cathy.

"Oh, they're here! Hey, can we get the Dynamic Duo over here by Jack?" David asked, gesturing at the threesome.

Bosche spun around like a trout being snagged on a fishing line. He was out the door, assisting Cathy before David could lower his arm.

"Wow, David, it's like you have the force or something," Jan joked.

"He has the bug, too!" Anna said, causing her husband to laugh out loud.

David could not see what Anna was saying in silence to Jan. She had managed to block his view of her lips and could tell she was mouthing something. She appeared as excited as a kid climbing onto a roller coaster for the first time.

Bosche carried two large, black leather cases, the type that holds files in the upright position. He and Cathy chatted excitedly.

"Okay, then. Jack, meet Cathy and Ralph. They have a load of information for us."

They greeted one another as Bosche sat beside Jack and Cathy next to David. She took one of the briefcases and folded down one side. A computer screen and keyboard appeared. She turned it around so everyone on either side could see. The mouse and keyboard were wireless.

"So, Grandpa Dryer, how ya been?" Cathy smiled at him.

"This is Cathy. She and Ralph are lawyers who work for Paolo. Despite their TV appearances, they're extremely qualified attorneys. I hope you found the copies we sent to you were in order, and that they assisted you in some manner."

David's tone sounded sober and final.

"Yes, I did. May I say that Anna is a remarkable investigator?" She looked to Anna, who appeared startled. Cathy continued. "What we have here is something called 'throwing paper'. It's a cheap trick used by attorneys to see if anyone has the backbone to stand up for him or herself. Some call these nasty grams. In your case, the letters were generated from a form, boilerplate document if you will, and were probably widely distributed. I have copies of what was sent out to potential plaintiffs." She displayed colored maps on the screen.

"This map shows the location of potential plaintiffs. It's based on the holdings of the Land Sakes Company."

"It surrounds the town and goes half-way into the next state," Jan noted.

"Where are we?" David asked.

Cathy moved the mouse to place the curser closer to the top of the screen. "We are here, sitting together in the middle of this spot where there is no indicated color."

Cathy explained what they were attempting to do. Anna mentioned she'd put out the word for people to show up today and bring their letters and any other papers. As she spoke, pick-up trucks began to fill the streets outside.

"We better hurry up and finish," Anna said.

They all ordered and ate quickly.

"Jack and I know we own our property, the county says so. I'm not that worried about it. What about my neighbors? Who financed them? What will happen to them?" she asked.

"Depends on things like usury rates on the loans and any form of intimidation. I'm pretty sure we'll have a hard time making Land Sakes Company just go away. Paolo allowed David to buy the controlling interests in it. Paolo will arrive tomorrow," Cathy said between hurried bites.

David glanced at Jan, who looked horrified.

"Love, what's wrong?"

"You're involved!" she hissed, her fear now focused on him.

"You knew that. It's all about the Walker House and so on." The expression on his face revealed his confused emotions.

She pointed at the monitor. "That is a whole damned state, David! You never said you were trying to rescue a whole state!"

He held her hand, refusing to allow her to pull away from him. "Easy. I didn't know all of this was happening. I have very powerful friends whom I trust with my life. You're looking at a game plan. I don't think we need to travel anywhere," he said as several more people entered the cafe.

A couple walked in. The woman carried an infant, and the man held a binder and several large manila envelopes.

"Inga! Over here, sweetie," Anna called out to them.

"Right here, Inga. It'd be a pleasure," David said with a broad smile.

"Don't let him scare you, Inga. Hello, Jim! David can manage. John taught him," Jack said, reaching out to help.

Swathed in blankets, the baby was gently passed across the table to David who cradled her close. The baby looked content and drifted off to sleep. David shifted nearer to Jan to be closer to her. He felt her start to relax. When he looked at her, he could see a mixture of joy and pain cross her face.

"You're always my first worry, love."

She leaned against him, began to get teary-eyed, and hid her face against his shoulder.

"What a great dad. Lots of practice, Mr. Dryer?" Inga asked.

"I was taught by great people. It's nice to meet you and your family. You're in good hands. These aren't just attractive faces you see on the television."

Everyone listened to Cathy.

Jim asked, "Are you saying this pay or quit notice might be fake? I know we've paid the bills. The balloon payment makes no sense, and it was not part of the original agreement."

"It could be hidden in some fine print, but it isn't in the contract you signed. At least you have a case against the balloon payment, insofar as the usury rates that are specific to the area the contract was signed in. More research needs to be done." Cathy closed her briefcase.

"For now, the bottom line is whether or not Land Sakes Company is legitimate. Paolo says it is, but there are irregularities. He'll clarify tomorrow. They bought your contract, but they may have funded the smaller corporation in the first place. Allowing the smaller company to go bankrupt, buying the assets for pennies on the dollar, then calling in all of the loans is not even close to legal. The problem will come from how aggressively the Land Sakes Company wants to fight everyone."

"We would be flat out broke if they foreclose, ma'am," Jim said in a mild tone.

"They won't foreclose," David said calmly.

"That's quite a statement, Mr. Dryer. I want to believe it. We're talking about a corporation. I don't want to lose our farm." Inga looked even more forlorn.

Jan raised her head from David's shoulder. "Inga, Jim, David will fight for you. Trust me. He's a fighter. This I know. He's got his armor on and his army behind him. Please, don't worry about it anymore."

Jim sat up straight and smiled across the table. Inga looked as though she didn't know whether to laugh or cry.

David shifted his gaze from Jan to the hopeful couple.

"That, and I bought the controlling interests in Land Sakes Company a while back. I'm going to find out how they managed to rip me off, too. I'm going to find who was responsible and deduct some lifespan, at the very least." David kissed the baby on the head as she stirred.

The table began to shake again. Jack covered his mouth with his hand, trying to muffle his laughter. Jan hugged David's arm and kissed his cheek. Cathy and Ralph began to greet the flow of incoming plaintiffs.

Jan and David walked Inga and Jim to their truck. They exchanged phone numbers. As the family drove away, David turned to Jan. She looked up at him. "This will have an ending, right?" she asked.

He held her close and began to move, swaying to music unheard, wrapping an arm around her waist, taking her hand in his, and holding it up like in the Club.

"No, it won't. Fly with me. Fight with me. Love me as I will always love you," he whispered, continuing to hold her close until she relaxed.

She rested her head against his chest. "Would you also like me to coach you, Coach?"

He stopped and leaned back to look into her eyes. "Sure, what you got, girl?"

She took a step back and reached into her purse.

"These!" she exclaimed, handing him a stack of flash cards for his driving test.

He quickly looked over the cards and burst out laughing when he figured out what they were.

"Oh, baby, you're the cutest thing. Just remember, every day ends on a good note, my love." He leaned down and gently kissed her.

She returned his kiss with fervent ardor, caressing him possessively and kissing him aggressively. She released him abruptly and dashed across the street to catch up with Anna.

David walked home on wobbly legs.

In a small, sterile room, John placed his belongings into a locker. He thought the whole security thing was silly since the key they gave him could not go through the MRI.

The technician positioned him and tucked pads into any open space between him and the curved bed. It was very comfortable at first, but being stuffed into place for an extended period of time made him fidgety.

It took almost an hour. Although muffled by earplugs, the noise kept startling him awake. Finally, it ended. The technician, who had been jovial when he arrived, seemed suddenly more business-like. John hoped his attitude before his MRI was used to help him calm down.

"John, it was a pleasure to meet you. Truly. What you've done with that website is fantastic. Thanks to you, I try and fly on the ground every day. The doctor will receive the results today." The technician smiled at him, his expression pained. Unlike before.

John thanked him and went home, hoping to enjoy a nice lunch that would clear the orange goop out of his system.

David looked over the flash cards. Some held words of encouragement. He kept those in a separate stack and retrieved the cards he knew well. If he recognized the card and could answer quickly then that card was put aside. *Yes, I know that one. Good. Away you go.* It took two hours for him to be able to leave half of the stack at home.

John called to inform him he was ready for a hearty lunch. David walked over to the café and saw a long line of people waiting to get inside. People were carrying folders and manila envelopes. A waitress saw David and motioned him inside.

"Hey, it's rude to ignore the lady."

David spun around to face John. "You goof! Let's go."

He ordered a soup and kept going through his cards. Lunch arrived and David was more than halfway through the remaining stack, having put more into his shirt pocket.

"What are we doing, Davey?" John asked between bites of his pastrami sandwich.

"The race is won with every step taken." David put down the cards and turned to John.

"Nice. Where is that from?" John spooned a bit of soup.

"I got these cards from Jan. They contain the whole DMV deal. I have all the lights, turn lanes, hand signals, and so on down pat. Alcohol to driving ratio is a bit weird. Stopping distance makes sense except for the math. She also added some inspirational phrases like the one I just repeated and, if you think you will succeed or fail, you are right."

John paused for a moment and stared at his food. "Letting someone into your life is hard, David. So far, you've been buddied up. I know things between us are as tight as they come. I've seen that women are quite different. Anyway, Jan is really helpful to you so go easy on letting her in, my man. It'll be worth it. I know that much." John went back to what was left of his sandwich.

"I'm going to do the right thing. Don't worry." David finished his soup.

David sent out texts to the usual suspects. A small group would gather at David's house to help him, John, and Jan break in the new living room.

Evening finally got the crowd to taper off at the Corner Café.

"Someone needs to send Maureen and Phil big fat thank you notes for coming over with boxes." Cathy glanced at a pile of boxes chest high and five steps wide stacked against the wall.

"One of the guys in the back has a hand cart. We can stack these in David's garage. Speaking of which, he paid for a high-speed photo copier, which is being delivered by tomorrow and set up by a professional." Bosche said that last part as if insulted.

"I'm sure you could have handled it without an issue, but we need you with us." She grinned, wiggling in her seat to sit up straight.

Bosche turned red at her display.

Ralph acted as if he heard and saw nothing.

"Okay, one last thing. Can you get her out of here?" He looked at Bosche.

Bosche nodded and helped the young man stack the boxes on the cart.

"It's a good thing there's only a few more weeks of school left. We can get one of the high school kids to make copies and another to help with mailing and so on."

"I'll make sure to pay everyone, of course." Jan accompanied Bosche and the young man.

Ralph text messaged his wife to expect a phone call. It was close to bedtime in the high desert of California and his thoughts turned to the past and of home. It was about 15 years ago when a funny, brown, Armenian man discovered his talent for math. He was a member of the High Desert Math Club when the man arrived at his house located on the bluffs above Lake Los Angeles.

It was a neat and tidy home. Although older cars and trucks were parked on the streets, they were not run down like in other neighborhoods. They were kept in good condition, especially the 1948 Ford F truck that had a dumper on it. His father used it for construction and hauling.

The Armenian man told his parents that the local schools were no place for their only son. He recommended sending him to Claremont located just over the mountains. Ralph had never traveled outside of the area he grew up in and loved.

The desert was as beautiful as it was harsh. Only special people, real people, understood that. His wife reminded him of the desert. She was as simple as he was, but truly lovely if you knew what to look for. Her smile was like the sunrise; bright and full of hope. Her embrace was like the sunset, warm and relaxing.

He met Cathy while attending the exclusively Caucasian high school. He walked the campus with dignity, dressed in his second-hand clothes. Working with his father made him strong. Bullies left him alone. Sometimes he spent too much time alone.

One day, he waited with other students in the Advanced Academic Center. The Cal-Tech professor was running late, causing most of the students to become antsy. His name tag read, 'AAC Member Ralph'. Cathy's read, 'AAC Member Lundquist'. She was being teased by some of the boys. One of them was on the basketball team.

"Miss Lundquist, they're not going to stop until you say something." Cathy turned to him. Her deep blue eyes blazed fire. Ralph stepped back.

She looked like someone trying to figure out a huge problem. Suddenly in a voice Ralph had only heard on loud constructions sites, she addressed her tormentors. "Self-adulating, troglodytes of low achievement, the bunch of you! You scuzzy pimple pickers bring the 'un' to cool!" The windows rattled and the boys moved away from her. Ralph made a friend for life.

His wife always made sure Cathy had a place to go for the holidays. He received a text from Maria, called home, and listened to the stories of his eldest son, daughter, and little boy. He was grateful David had invited him to stay at his house while he was in town.

By the time David walked Jan home, the moon settled into its position in the western sky. Its soft glow kissed the dew-covered plants in the fields.

"Let's sleep, for real." He nuzzled her nose.

She tensed a bit. "David, let's work on piecing together complete thoughts," she said, gently kissing him.

He hesitated. "Oh jeez, Jan. I mean, let me see you to the door. Sorry. I want us both to get in a full night's sleep."

She laughed. "I think you're right, my man of virtue and valor." They kissed tenderly.

David walked home as if floating on clouds, and listened to the Owls trying to teach their young. There was a slight chill in the air, but David barely noticed as he was warmed by thoughts of Paolo's impending arrival.

He knew in his heart that everything would be fine with Jan. Like most nights in Leduc, he fell asleep feeling happy and content.

25
GATHERINGS

The polished black armored Rolls Royce Phantom silently approached the great cabin. The spectacular sunrise was reflected on its exterior. Some of the orphaned children stood on the wrap-around porch to have a look.

Josephine came out to greet the driver, followed by two teens who placed luggage into the trunk.

Iada could be heard praying aloud. "Lord, I know I'm supposed to be moving. Thank you, darlings, for the coffee and biscuit," she said, leaving the kitchen and crossing into the open area where hungry children occupied tables at various intervals throughout the day.

"What is that thing out there? I said a car, Josephine, not a polished bus. Why they flags, girl?" she asked, walking through the huge double doors that had greeted guests over 90 years ago.

"I know. Have a talk with your nephew about that. Everything's loaded. We can go." Josephine wore business casual attire.

Iada wore semi-formal evening apparel. Between the hat, pearls, and dress, it was hard to pin down the era. The ensemble would have allowed her entrance to every high society party from 1920 through the 1950's.

She had a brief conversation about the car driven by her nephew and owner of the service. Neither one backed down in the affectionate fight. She accepted a warm embrace, a kiss on the cheek, and let him handle the door. She finally took her seat as Josephine opened a polished knurl wood cover, revealing a screen for computer or television use.

The DVD began to play when she turned on the console. There was also a generous supply of requested sour mash, ice, and short tumblers. The familiar title sequence to the classic cartoon overtook over the ambience of the polished wood, chrome, and leather interior.

"Oh, my. You got my rabbit Bugs Bunny on there. Oh, Josephine, this is a wonder. I'm in a seat more comfortable than my bed. You have my sour mash in here, too?" She accepted a glass.

"It's all taken care of, he said. He drives you, period. You're to be chauffeured in the best car he has, period. He handles the hotel arrangements, period. Only the best hotels, period," Josephine recalled aloud as she opened her laptop.

"This needs more, period." Iada held out her empty glass as she laughed.

"Hey, easy. It's a long trip." Josephine poured her a refill.

"More. You have a young, steady hand, girl. Hey, I get car sick, so this here is good for my health. Thank you." Iada went back to her cartoon and not so lady-like sips of her sour mash.

Josephine checked for the controls of the seats that would later recline into more of a bed when the time arrived. Afterwards, she checked the inventory, returned Cathy's email, and sent an email to John.

The brilliant rays of the sun colored the wings of the business jet made to accommodate its only passenger. The oversized furniture was custom made for Paolo. The jet came in for a final approach, nearing the town and tipping a little to one side so he could get a better view.

It would be the first time he stayed at the house of the man he called father, and he looked forward to it with great excitement. As the plane descended, he saw the SUV waiting to pick him up once they landed.

It felt like Christmas somehow. David sprang out of bed. The smell of freshly brewed coffee permeated throughout the entire house. *Thank you, God, for that machine.*

The constant smell of glue was starting to irritate him. His thoughts were enthusiastic, but organized as he went through the routine of dressing and stretching. While waiting for everyone out on the front porch, he went over his DMV flash cards. Ralph brought David a cup of coffee and helped test him. *Wow, I got it. Don't need these anymore.* He could hear Paul and Gaul walking down the street from church. Cathy emerged from John's house. Bosche drove up the street in his pick-up truck followed by a black SUV that David recognized from the last time he and Jan had their big date.

After the vehicles parked in front of the house, Paolo jumped out and embraced David. "How nice this all looks, T'ma!" he said, looking around the property.

"Let's get your stuff inside, son. You made it just in time." David helped with his luggage.

Paolo looked as though he were being mobbed by short people while enthusiastically greeting everyone.

The entire group decided to go for a run around town and into the fields as the sun began to peek over the horizon. The heavy thud of Paolo's feet joined the chorus of foot sounds.

David turned around to look at Bosche and Cathy, wondering what the hell was so interesting they couldn't stop chattering as though the other were hard of hearing. Paolo tapped him on the arm. David looked up at his wide, perceptive grin and thought it best to leave it alone. Nearing the end of their three and half mile run, they slowed their pace in front of Phil's garage. More cars than usual were driving into town.

"Anyone for a second lap?" David asked.

"I need it," Ralph said.

No one said a word as they breezed past John's house and out of town.

"I feel like I've invited trouble into Leduc. Jan's right. I should shut the hell up and retire," David said, becoming pensive.

"Breather!" Gaul demanded.

The group stopped before heading downhill, which would have led them out of the fields. The morning was crisp, the air fresh. They were able to admire the breathtaking view of the fields.

"David." Gaul broke the peaceful silence. "The trouble has always been here. Look, it's in your nature to get deeply involved with an issue at hand. After this blows over, and I believe it will, you can find something else to busy yourself with. I'm learning a lot from the little tykes at the church day care." He looked at Paolo. "I know what you mean about retiring. We never truly retire. I teach. I nurture. I've transformed from being a warrior. You, too, will find something. Let your talents come to the surface."

"Funny that a preacher should mention it. David used to preach about football and contests. I have news about that talent," Paolo said, smiling first at David then at the crowd.

The crowd held their breath.

"Son, go ahead, we're right here," David encouraged.

"Land Sakes Company is publicly traded. It isn't widespread news, but it isn't a well-kept secret either that David now owns a controlling interest. Because of this, Ralph and Cathy have sent a letter demanding a shareholders meeting. Land Sakes Company has never done this, and it's against the SEC rules," Paolo finished with obvious excitement.

"Good thing, son. What is an SEC?"

"SEC stands for the Security and Exchange Commission, which regulates stock trading. We found a senator and others who wish to attend. David could stand before them and demand answers. We could provide the questions."

"A big, fat showdown with Bob Lundberg. The final showdown. He'd be gone for good?" David asked Paolo.

"Legally, yes. You would gain control of the Land Sakes Company, and we would settle with all of the plaintiffs."

"I hope this doesn't mean I have to kick people off their land, their farms, their fields of hope and dreams, like the family we met yesterday." David was appalled at the idea.

"People accepted bad loans, T'ma. They knew, or should have known, the consequences. I know you'll try and help those who wish to stay. First and foremost, we have to see what's going on cash flow wise, and take an inventory before any decisions can be made. I think everyone would agree they're better off with you than Bob Lundberg." Paolo looked around at the faces in the crowd.

"I agree, David. There's nothing wrong with settling the books, or whatever is going on, if you're fair about it. Too many people follow up with dumb after being stupid. That's how we end up with ex-wives and daughters on the streets. Please don't get me started. We better head back. The little ones will be at the church in another 90 minutes." Gaul sprinted off.

They cruised at an easy pace into town, skipping the lap around First Street and heading straight for the Corner Café. Pick-up trucks were everywhere. David noticed a lot of them were brand new and had extra doors on them like Jack's.

"Hey, everybody, go inside. I'm going to grab my wallet." David jogged a few doors down to his house. When he returned, he noted the cars were parked all over town, even in front of his house.

A burly man with questionable hygiene stepped into his on the sidewalk. "Scuse me, but is this where that Dynamic Duo is?" He brought his face close to David's.

"Back up," David said.

The man complied.

"Yes, they're meeting potential plaintiffs for a class action lawsuit with regards to the Land Sakes Company. Just stand in line and you'll be able to register with them today," David said, trying to sound professional.

"Well, I don't need any classy action or whatever you call it. I know a lawyer who says…" He stopped mid-sentence and went to his truck to calm one of his children. He returned to speak with David. "This lawyer says maybe something's bad with the loan, but I don't care. I just want out. I hope I can leave with what I have here and just go."

David had second thoughts about the man. He looked at the new truck with its expensive interior like all the rest. There were covered belongings loaded onto the bed of the truck and an exasperated mother seated in the cab.

"I'm David Dryer. I bought the Land Sakes Company, and I am going to straighten it all out. I think you can get out with what you have. I'd like to see you get out as well, but on better terms."

"The coach! Sir, I would like that a whole lot. The land is dry. Nothing they said worked. I showed up with nothing and can leave this way. That's good." The man smiled and returned to his truck.

Breakfast went by quickly. John sat quietly, picking at his soup. David couldn't handle his silence.

"Hey, I got this test all done and figured out. Ralph tested me this morning. Jan made me flash cards. Do you think we can take the test today?"

John lifted his head and turned to David. "Yes, let's do that. We can take the driving test tomorrow since you're such a fast learner."

David stared at John, pausing much longer than usual. Jan stroked his back.

"You'll be fine. Thank you, John. Did you want to borrow my car?" she asked, stroking the back of David's neck.

John smiled. "Thank you, but no. I think he should learn on the old girl."

"I thought you were trying to help," Paolo said to John.

The occupants at the table burst into laughter. David felt flustered, then cross. "I think the honor of learning how to drive in the old girl is something special. Okay, my brother, you're on. Thank you." David looked around to let everyone know he was just fine with John's decision.

Jan squeezed his upper thigh until he laughed.

David let Bosche and Ralph shower first. They had been at the Café all day, dealing with plaintiffs. He showed some of the students, who had shown up to build his new home, the location of the copier. He was grateful one of them knew what to do with the machine that took up a car space. He heard an 'AaaWwwOOOga' from the street and knew it was time to go.

John waited for him in the single tone Grey Lady, the 1930 Ford Model A Tudor his father had given him. They drove away from town into the warmth of the sun.

"I never thought I'd leave the noise behind... the noise from my home town," John said loud enough to be heard over the wind.

"People think I'm making all this noise, don't they, John? I'm done with the bullshit, brother. Lay it all out," David urged.

John nodded slowly. "Yeah, they do and it's about time too. The murmurs and whispers are above ground now. Get this over with David. Settle the whole mess. It's better that way. Make way for Jan. Clear out the dead."

"Ever get the feeling you're being used, John?" David asked, looking out at the horizon.

"Yes. I let them use me for three years. I returned home without a care in the world except what the hell was the matter with some child," John reflected.

"Before I bitch about what I got myself involved in, I want to know how much of a child people really think I am. I know I'm not smart like most in the way others are able to figure life out. I also know I'm lucky I've been surrounded by amazing people. I just want to know how much of a joke I really am. Seriously, I want to know what it is that's lacking inside of me that others find so entertaining, John."

John turned off the car after parking at the county office buildings and turned towards David. "I've seen my share of losers. You're no loser, David. Yes, your lack of connection to common sense is comical. So what. You obtained a college education with your ears, eyes, and heart. You passed tests like everyone else and maintained excellent grades. Someone had to leap out in front. You did, and you became one of the winningest coaches of all time. I've never known anyone else who could boast of such accomplishment." John turned away, and then looked at David with tears in his eyes and a pained expression. "I was being tormented and you put an end to it. For no reason other than you are who God made you, a genuine man from the very start. Without you, I wouldn't have a brother. Take some credit, David! A real man accepts help. I did, and you helped me to live." John bowed his head.

David's flushed while his eyes held tears. "I hoped to come home and finally grow up."

"You've been a grown up for quite some time now. Believe me, you're ready." John stepped out of the car. David followed.

As they approached the building, two ladies already in line near the entrance greeted them.

"Mr. Kemp. Mr. Dryer." The tall one extended her hand.

John shook the lady's hand. David followed suit. The tall one was named Elsa and the slightly shorter one, Jonna.

"I wondered if you were home for good, Mr. Dryer?" Elsa asked.

"Please, just call me David. Yes, I'm retired and here to get my driver's license."

Both ladies smiled. "Well, we understand there are attorneys in town working on a case involving the Land Sakes Company," Elsa offered.

John cut in. "Yes. Cathy and Ralph, the Dynamic Duo from TV, are at the Corner Café talking to potential plaintiffs. There's an entire operation in charge of copying and scanning located in David's garage."

The ladies looked at each other. Jonna nodded.

"We'll come over this afternoon. If they're in the process of discovery, I feel it is our duty to be there to offer assistance," Elsa said as they made their way into the building.

"Damn! What in the providence of the equinoxial shizzle was that?" David asked incredulously.

John doubled over from laughing so hard. He ushered David through the double doors once he regained his composure.

Bob Lundberg sat in his chair like a boy awaiting the principle in his office. On the other side of the expansive, antique, baroque desk sat an aged lawyer in a green, high-backed, leather chair. The lawyer had been listening to the young man who had been whispering into his ear. He finally waved the young man away.

"Bob, I knew your father well. It has been wonderful to see you grow up. The problem we're dealing with here is the demand letter. You can hold a shareholders meeting and be the chief executive officer of the company. I've suggested a meeting in one week. That should suffice. Answer any questions. You don't have to change policy or do much beyond just answering the questions in any manner you see fit." The lawyer stood. "It was nice to see you, Bob. My staff will make arrangements and see you well." He nodded.

Bob stood. He had been there for over an hour. He felt like he was talking to Lincoln. The statue, anyway. He followed the young man out of the office.

"How close to dead is he?" he asked, speaking softly into the young man's ear.

The young man turned around and fixed Bob with an icy stare. "Follow exactly what we tell you to do down to the letter. The demand in question didn't come from some hack, as you so naively assume. You've been insistent, Mr. Lundberg so this meeting was arranged. Mr. Sven has been homebound for years. It's my opinion we should drop you as a client, but I'm not being considered in this manner. The best you can hope for is not being sent to prison. You'll lose control of Land Sakes Company, possibly to David Dryer, and I can't stop that. Go on home. We'll have someone come out and prepare you. Do everything they tell you and how they tell you to do it." He waved his arm in the direction of the door, and Bob walked out.

David came out with papers and a positive attitude. John patted him on the back and got into the passenger side of the car.

"What's this?" David asked, appearing confused.

"You are now allowed to drive with me or another licensed driver in the car." John wiggled the keys so David could see them.

David made his way to the driver's side. He got in one leg at a time, which somehow was more difficult on this side. John explained the controls to David, and he had David mimic double clutching.

"Now start it," John said after showing him once.

David turned the key, opened the fuel valve, pushed up the timing leaver, and pulled down the accelerator. He pushed a button on the floor, which made the car turn over and sputter to life. As it came alive, he pulled down the timing leaver and allowed the car to idle. He looked over at John with wonderment.

"Like I showed you, clutch in, then move the stick up and left." John smiled.

He noticed David was a quick learner. If he could see it, then he could do it. "You're catching on faster than I did, David." After about an hour and a quick trip down the highway, John told him to return to town. Because the brakes were not modern, he made David travel down First Street in low gear, riding the engine until they reached Starling. David drove fluidly, obeying every command.

John reached over as they approached Jan's house.

"AaaaaWwwoooOOOOgah!" The sound of his horn caused David to jump out of his seat.

"Relax, man. You have the feel for her. She's not going to change, so just take it easy and cruise." John had on a parade worthy smile. They drove throughout town, finally parked the car in John's garage. "As time goes on, it'll begin to feel like second nature."

David stepped out without a word. He looked completely exhausted. John gave him a one-armed hug and asked him to meet up for lunch later in the day.

David decided to wander towards the General Store. He passed the line of people in front of the Corner Café, saying hello and shaking the hands of those who recognized him. Paolo approached him from behind.

"This is going quite well. There are plaintiffs telling other plaintiffs what to do and most are bringing in paperwork for their neighbors," Paolo said, joining David in his walk. "What seems to have gotten you down, T'ma?"

David looked up. "Nothing, my man! I just drove for the very first time and am exhausted. I just needed to walk it off. Please don't let me keep you from anything."

"Not at all. Cathy and Ralph now have back up. This business at the Café will end tomorrow. I'm going to walk this off, too."

David put an arm around his back and gave him a hug. They went down

Cause Way and made a left onto Business Route. David wasn't sure where he wanted to go.

"Hey, we could peruse the General Store. You should meet Maureen." They continued along the wood sidewalks. Paolo nodded. As they moved along, David glanced over to the ice cream parlor. Gaul was in attendance with some of his daycare kids, along with the Mayor and two other men.

"Son, go on ahead. I need a minute." He crossed the street and went inside.

Gaul did his best to teach the little ones manners. Some of them came from broken homes. David walked in and made a beeline towards the Mayor.

"Mr. Mayor. Afternoon, gentleman." David stood as though bracing for a windstorm.

"Just Brian, unless you would like me to refer to you as Mr. Dryer," the Mayor said.

"No, David is fine. Brian, I want to talk about the Walker House. It's my inheritance, but I find it's going to be converted into a bed and breakfast or some such nonsense. I don't know how that happened, but I do know it's got your name written all over it. I want it to be given to Gaul and Paul for their halfway home project." He tried to maintain his cool.

One of the men leaned forward as though he were going to speak. Brian raised his hands towards them, one in each direction. Something in his body shifted, causing him to look up. He wore a veiled smile.

"You were gone for 25 years. In your absence, dead assets appeared all over the place. Now you come home and wish to unravel all of my hard work? Work that people have a vested interest in? Sorry, David. I think life has passed you by on this one."

"How would you like not to be Mayor anymore?" David asked in a lethal tone of voice.

The Mayor said nothing. His companions looked as though they'd been slapped. David turned on his heel and walked out.

Gaul was grateful David's anger was not directed at him. He noted that the Mayor flushed, just like the two flustered fools accompanying him. He turned his attention back to the tykes, and he happily taught them how to retrieve the last of the ice cream from a cone by sucking it out of the bottom. Gaul smiled to himself. *Good thing Paul was not around to bear witness.*

26
ALL IN

David stormed across the street and strode into the General Store. He saw Maureen behind the glass counter and felt as though something was missing. He turned around and noticed that Big Jake was no longer hanging from the ceiling.

"Something has a spur in your tuchus, David. What now?" Maureen shouted.

"I think the Mayor needs to be shot. How did he ever get hold of the Walker House?" David asked, shaking his head.

A familiar voice replied from the dressing room. "He doesn't own it, David. Please cool down."

David recognized Paolo's voice and looked towards the dressing area. He glanced at Maureen, who suddenly wore a Cheshire cat smile.

"Sure, son. So how do you explain this one? I'm just all out of ideas here."

A gentle thumping and jingle broadcast Paolo's approach. He sauntered up, wearing the missing suit.

"You own the Land Sakes Company. It owns the Walker House, which was financed to the Mayor in the same manner as the farms. Wait until he finds out he owes more than it's worth," Paolo said with a smile that overpowered his face.

Warmth began to rise inside of David. His face turned slightly red as he looked at Maureen. "What have you done to my son?"

"Why don't you just haul him outta here?" She tried to hide her blush.

"Son." David gave Paolo a complete once over. "Wow, what a spitting image. Let's roll."

Paolo followed David out.

David could definitely feel and hear Paolo's footsteps. The jangle of spurs immediately followed the clunking and thumping of the boots. David noticed Paolo's game face in the reflection of the ice cream parlor's window. It was the one he used on the field. Sudden elation made David feel giddy. He shot a withering gaze at the Mayor, who looked stunned at the sight of Paolo.

They walked to the Corner Café. Paolo sat on the bench near the door and pulled a smartphone from his shirt pocket. He leaned back, stretched out his legs, and propped his feet up on the spurs that found crevices to rest in.

"I got some help from Jan. Hope you don't mind. Can you call her? I think it best for the two of you to have lunch out of town." Paolo looked around as he made a call.

David complied. Jan informed him she was in his garage and would meet him in the dining room. He walked in and had a seat in front of his long, dark table that still reeked of newness. In front of him was a stack of flash cards. He began to look them over them and ruminate over their contents.

"I'm calling for a vote of... geez, what does that mean?" His thoughts turned to mud.

"Hello, love." Jan bent down to kiss David. "Good thing you found those. Let's go." He got up and followed her out without asking questions.

As they stepped onto the sidewalk, he recognized two familiar faces.

"Hello, Elsa and Jonna. This is my girlfriend, Jan."

They exchanged handshakes and pleasantries. Jan saw they were pulling short stacks of boxes.

"You look like you're moving somewhere" Jan asked.

Elsa smiled. Jonna nodded. "We have materials for the Dynamic Duo. David, you may be interested in these."

"Woah! Those are government boxes! Sure, let's..."

"We were just leaving. It was nice meeting you both. Go ahead in. I know you're expected." Jan smiled, pulling on David's arm.

She came very close to yelling at him as they walked to her house and got into her car. She did not speak until they got onto the highway.

"David, you're explosive. It will be useful when the time comes. I have to talk to you about strategy."

David listened begrudgingly as she gave him a rather long speech about what he was supposed to do and when. "So, I'm an end run? A kind of October surprise?" he clarified.

"You're the spear tip. I really want this to be over. I'll help you finish the job, but you have to allow me to help you." She drove past the county center and its mall.

"You look beautiful, Jan." He stayed quiet until she cracked a smile and looked over. "So, will you help me where I am weak? All right, partner. Let's fark this thing up!" he said, shuffling through some flash cards.

"David! Language," she said with a smile.

Occasionally, he would ask her the meaning of certain words. They drove to a quiet spot in the hills to a local bar and grill called The Launch Pad, which sat across the street from a place called The Rocket.

The surrounding fields looked ready for harvest. The warm clean air and green landscape helped him to relax as they studied together.

Elsa and Jonna neared the Corner Café.

"Oh, that is Paolo!" Elsa said, turning to Jonna.

Jonna took Elsa's cart and started to haul them both in.

"I got this," she said with a wry smile.

"Hello, Elsa!" Paolo exclaimed.

"How wonderful to be known. My sister and I have brought over all of the questionable paperwork. You know, the last season you played was amazing. Why pass on the second down and not run the ball in?" Their question and answer session continued for a short while until Elsa thought it best to join her sister.

Some time passed before a nervous bureaucrat named Ted came up the sidewalk. He paused at the sight of the man whose legs seemed to extend well into the street and looked around at the crowd of people waiting to get in. Paolo tipped up his black, wide-brimmed hat to face him.

"You need something, sir?" he asked with a slight drawl.

"My goodness, you remind me of someone. Honestly, I'm looking for the Dynamic Duo and an errant pair of employees."

"In there, pardna'. Go to the front of the line and tell 'em I sent ya," Paolo said as he turned away.

"And you are?" Ted asked, studying Paolo's attire.

"Paolo. They know me."

Ted looked like electric currents were shooting through his body. He rushed inside as Elsa and Jonna folded up the steel-wheeled carts they'd used to drop off the boxes. Jonna handed over a receipt while accepting a check.

"What is this?" Ted bellowed, almost falling over from a lack of oxygen.

"Who are you?" Ralph demanded.

"These ladies work for me and those boxes belong in my office! Hand them over."

"I just paid for them. It's evidence legally obtained through discovery," Ralph said, leaning back to reveal the nickel-plated .45 beneath his jacket.

Ted began to stammer. "What's this? You're going to shoot me?!"

"If you touch a box, I will." Ralph raised his right hand.

Ted turned around just as Paolo came up behind him.

"Do you have any discovery for us? We're working for the new owner of the Land Sakes Company."

Ted stumbled around Paolo and ran for the door.

"I guess he's not staying for lunch." Anna said.

When the nervous laughter died down, a young man spoke up.

"I got a loan from the Land Sakes Company. I've since learned that the land and all of the equipment I purchased is under water. I owe a lot more than it's all worth. I just want out. What are you going to do to me now?"

Paolo removed his hat. "Sir, the new owner wants equity for everyone. I'm encouraging a restructure of all current debts in order to allow keeping what you have viable. There's no need for you to make a decision for now. Yes, many will just walk away and that'll be accepted with no strings attached." The room was silent.

"This new owner could change his mind. Are you Paolo, the Train?" the young man asked.

Paolo smiled and nodded. "I am. The new owner is going to conduct his first meeting with the CEO and board, if they have one. His name is David Dryer. He used to be my coach and grew up right here in Leduc. We will make written offers once control of the company becomes official. I don't have any influence in changing his mind." The room erupted in laughter.

The young man was suddenly cheerful. "We all know David Dryer. You say you never changed his mind? The Train never made Double D man change his hard head about anything?" he asked with a wry smile.

The room shifted its attention from the man to Paolo. He had to think. *Yes, the wedding!* He suddenly remembered. "I got him to buy a suit once."

The crowd once again burst into laughter.

He waited for the cacophony to settle down before speaking. "I want to make sure everyone understands they are not to settle until given a written offer. Ignore the pay up or quit notice. It's nothing but bullshit," he finished, placing the hat back on his head and walking out.

The conversation between David and Jan left behind the flash cards.

"You're a fabulous student, David, and one hell of a fighter. I think you can see why we're doing this. You see your role now, don't you, David?"

"Jan, you're a wonderful reason to finish this." They made their way into the car and began to drive off.

"I understand the idea that the shareholders will demand Bob leave and that I come in with a newly appointed board. I also understand that a sizable chunk of my money may already be gone." The sun showcased its final display in the horizon. "I want to make sure you and I never miss another sunset together." He stared into the distance as his lower lip quivered.

Jan remained silent.

Dr. Fisher's new physician sat in silence. She was the best in her field and sought the expert opinions of only the very best. She wanted to call John, but decided to wait. The man she knew as a real father could wait one more day for the results.

Jan dropped David off at his house. "My love, when you are ready, come on over. I'll wait for you. I have awesome movie food. I would love for us to just spend time together, no more flash cards."

"That's an offer of a lifetime! Let me compare notes with Paolo, and then I'll be right over."

"Hey there, Double D man!" Bosche yelled. The small crowd joined in the vocal celebration.

Paolo came downstairs in a pair of sweatpants.

"Thanks for returning to normal, son," David joked. Everyone in the room laughed. "And I'd like to thank everyone here for assisting me in bringing a lawsuit against myself."

"Hey, we have to get him and Jan out to the Country Kick!" Bosche said, turning to Cathy.

"I'm done. I just wanted to talk things over with my son before I leave for my date. Thank you again, everyone," David said with a nod to Paolo.

They left the house together and walked out onto the curb. "Son, I get what I'm supposed to do. The thing is that you and I know I'm not suited to run a corporation. I don't want to, anyway. So what happens after the meeting and the turn over?"

"You and the shareholders can elect a board. They will do a proper job of communicating to you and the rest what they are doing. This will include hiring a new CEO." He beamed down at David.

"Okay, son, I just want to retire, with Jan." David looked down at Paolo's near naked feet. "They make flip flops in your size?"

Paolo smiled. "John says you're taking the driving test tomorrow. Don't stay out too late." He went back into the house before David could say another word.

Snacks, Steve McQueen, and snuggles were the theme of their movie night. David knew he was in love. Jan felt right. He held her as she slept in his arms.

The next morning David's feet carried him but with some effort. It was a lonely run. He turned down Cause Way and was in the fields at an extremely fast pace. He ran hard every time something worried him. He completed another lap through the fields. There was no room left for worry by the time he came back. He slowed himself to a cool down pace by the time he reached Jan's house. She stood outside in the same sweatpants as the night before.

"John says Cathy is snoring in the living room." She motioned for him to come inside. He could smell breakfast and coffee.

"I did my warm-ups and some burpees. If you can slow your pace down a bit, I would love to go for a run with you." She directed him to a place at the table.

"Interesting that movie, 'Bullet'. That McQueen guy does a lot and says very little. Nice preparation for my I-move-to-elect-a-new-board speech. Jan set a plate of eggs, toast, and sausage in front of him. "Hey, thanks."

"My pleasure. John said to go straight to his house. He is going to take you for your test today." Jan sat down to her plate.

They ate happily and shared little conversation. David thought this would be a nice way to start each day for the rest of his life.

"Another man!" Cathy said with bleary eyes as David came in.

"Why, Cathy, you look country kicked." David walked past her, looking for John. He found him sitting in the backyard. John stood, walked with David to the garage, and got into the passenger side of the Model A.

"You'll have to drive today, David," John said gravely.

David got in and started the car without being shown how to do it. John smiled proudly. David still remembered everything he heard and saw.

The cat shot up out of its bed when the puppy ran up and barked at it furiously. Iada laughed and shook her head at the cartoon playing in the limousine. "That's our little Davey growing up. He can't leave well enough alone and has to put things to the test like that right there." The cat descended from the ceiling, stopped, turned over, and landed on its feet.

Josephine used the multi-buttons to adjust her plush leather chair. Her phone call to John went straight to voice mail. She thought that was odd. She sent emails to Paolo and the Dynamic Duo, and she began to wonder how the end run would work. Could they or should they be keeping David away so much? Her thoughts turned heavy when it came to worrying about the orphans.

"John, will you turn that off, please?" David pleaded.

"No, let's go!" John got into the back seat. There was more leg room back there and it reminded him of his childhood.

"My good man, I'd like to have a double launch, if you please. Let's make haste." John flipped his hand in a forward direction.

David still looked stunned that he'd passed the driver's test. "I'm not any better than I was yesterday, John."

"Laddie, I must smite mine hunger. Go forth. Ye know the way. To the launch pad!" John leaned back.

At first, David drove with a nervous smile, then a hawkish look. John knew he would settle down. His brother would be an overly cautious driver for a while. He felt drowsy and a little guilty. He should not have brought David out for the test. He was in no condition to drive and should have been ready to take over.

The mild weather and easy handling of the car brought back memories of his father driving him and Uncle Wellington around. The front of the car was narrower than the rear. Wellington needed a seat and a half. He did his best not to occupy much of the driver's side. When his father went to shift gears, his uncle would shrink away the best he could. John noticed there was still a polish on one side of the stick shift. The sweet smell of pipe tobacco also seemed to linger.

They ate their lunch outside. John ordered the biggest plate they had with a shake and some onion rings. The pills Dr. Fisher gave him worked. "So David, let me hear what you're supposed to say at the shareholders meeting."

David looked like he was reading poster boards in his mind. He gave a short dissertation and then shot a relieved look at John. "Anyway, that'll wrap it up. The idea is to elect another CEO so I don't have to do anything."

"Except marry Jan," John reminded him.

"What do you think about proposing to her in the park?" David asked with excitement.

"Just make sure it's not more than three words."

He paused for a long while. "John, with all of your skills, kindness, and such, why did you never marry?"

"I can't have normal intimate relations, David. I'm a man. I just don't function the way normal men do," John said bluntly. *Was that the drugs talking?*

"I was told a long time ago it wasn't my business. I just thought it strange to hear the marriage speech coming from you. Paul and Gaul, they chose their lives. I always thought you'd make the best father. Come to think of it, you've been one to so many people." David stared off into the horizon.

"I never would have made it here without you. You've been my brother and protector when I needed you most," John said as he struggled for words.

"The happy kids, the teaching, everything would not have been possible without you!" David bent his head.

"It is not my place to give you relationship advice," he said, looking at David. "I see how happy you make each other."

"Yeah, well, I'll do it anyway," David said, jingling the keys. "Drive you home?"

John got up and climbed into the back seat. He sprawled across the seat and took a nap. He began to stir when he felt the downhill slope of First Street and inhaled the familiar scent of Leduc.

"Could you drop me off at the clinic?" he asked.

David obliged and drove the car back home.

Saturday provided a break from running. The incoming crowds at the Corner Café finally abated. Jan managed to get John and David into the Model A and took off to the county mall for lunch at the jungle-themed restaurant. John seemed down and nothing they said perked him up. After lunch, they stopped at the market for groceries and then drove home.

Everyone helped prepare David's house for the get-together. Maureen brought over a new BBQ. Paul loaned them some of the church's folding tables.

After everyone arrived, the party kicked into full swing. There was more than enough food, laughter, and drinks to keep everyone satisfied. The chatter reached a crescendo and then subsided once people began to leave. There was no doubt in anyone's mind how much of a family they were to each other.

Earlier that night Anna ran about making copies of papers and photographs. She also took extensive notes. In the end, John, David, Paolo, the Tolsons, Iada, Josephine and Maureen were the only ones who remained.

"Tarnations, John! I never would have seen you this way, but for some damn reason you're the elephant in the room. We're as tight a family as you're going to get. What has you wrapped around the post so hard?"

"I have six months to live," John said, sounding calm.

"Not you, my brother," David said in disbelief.

John nodded. With pleading eyes, he looked at Jan, then at David. "Hey, it's late. I'll tell you all about it tomorrow, my brother. Jan needs to get home now."

David nodded slowly. He looked around for Jan and escorted her home. She stayed with him until he fell asleep on her couch.

The next morning, he made his way home. He felt mournful. Lack of sleep and severe depression made his legs feel heavy.

"Where've you been?" John asked, walking up from behind.

"I've just come home from Jan's. John, what can I do?" He still felt stunned.

"I'm not dead yet, my man. Get in the house. C'mon, you lead ass." John poked at him.

As they stepped inside, they found Paolo seated at the end of the dining room table. Ralph and Cathy were helping themselves to coffee.

"T'ma, John thought it best for us to do a practice run of the shareholders meeting. Just do your best as we anticipate what to expect," Paolo said with a smile.

Hours went by as David spoke confidently when pressed, objecting as he was told to do and making demands like he practiced from the flash cards.

"I like it! No, I love it!" John said excitedly.

Paolo turned to both Cathy and Ralph.

"That's remarkable," Cathy said. Ralph nodded in agreement. Paolo likewise agreed.

"Confident, unshakeable, ass-kicker! That's my brother!" John said, dancing around as though he were shadow boxing.

"Bob Lundberg, get ready to be buried!"

David placed a loving arm around John and took him home. They spent the better part of the day just talking. David suddenly wished they had made more of an effort to do so during their past.

27
FINALLY

The suit fit perfectly and flowed with David's every move. The ride in the executive helicopter was a lonely one without Jan. He made a commitment in his mind that it would be his last helicopter ride without her. The idea that it was lonely at the top began to sink in. Such a terrible feeling.

Once the helicopter landed, he walked to the black SUV waiting to carry him to the board meeting. David appreciated the silence. It was only a short trip from the helipad to the conference, but he used the time to regroup and organize his thoughts. He went over the game plan Paolo and the Dynamic Duo had created for him, hoping he would not disappoint them or the thousands of people relying on him.

In the conference room, he made his way up the center aisle that was flanked on both sides with plain tables and cheap folding chairs. He saw familiar faces; Anna, Jack, and some plaintiffs like the young man and the couple with the baby he'd held in his arms. Maureen was also there, wearing a fierce look on her face. Josephine was present without Iada. There were less than 100 attending.

He turned to Paolo and the Dynamic Duo as he joined them in the front row.

"Fine Hotel. What's with the cheap accommodations?" He looked at Paolo, who did not respond.

A young man in a dark suit and tie stepped up to the podium.

"I am here to represent my client, the owner of Land Sakes Company." He opened a notebook he placed on the podium and turned on the light that was mounted on a bendable chrome arm. "As a proxy, I am authorized to answer all questions from the attending shareholders. Please identify yourself in full before submitting your inquiry."

David was confused. Bob was to speak first, then the board, and in closing any objections. He turned to Paolo. Paolo wore an expression he had never seen before. It was stunned anger.

He turned towards David and got in his face. "Let him have it. Don't sit down again until he folds."

David shot out of his chair. "Objection! The full board and CEO are to be present or the demand letter is not satisfied."

The young man paused and turned to him slowly. "Sir, I asked that everyone identify themselves in full before questions can be asked."

"You can cram that language, kid." The room burst into cheers and hollers. "This is a publicly traded entity. No board meeting has ever been documented. No report has ever been issued to the shareholders. The only CEO mentioned in legal documents is Bob Lundberg. Go get him, or would you like to be arrested?" The room burst out again. "Stop pretending you don't know me. I'm David Dryer, majority stockholder. Go get Bob!"

The young man walked away. A few minutes later, he brought in an old, shaky-looking gentleman. He fumbled with the microphone and looked over at David, who remained standing.

"Sorry about being tardy. Okay, let's all just sit down and be comfortable. I can assure you will be satisfied. Perhaps we can even answer some questions. I'm Bob Lundberg, CEO of Land Sakes Company, the holder of lands and mineral rights," he said, thumbing clumsily through the binder in front of him.

"You're here to answer questions, Bob," David said in a menacing tone. "Questions such as why a report was never issued. Where is the board of directors, Bob?" He thundered. The murmur of the crowd became louder.

Bob looked at David in shock. He shook his head, and his face turned red. He leaned on his heels, took a deep breath, and finally spoke. "I have a report to give. Come to order!"

The young attorney stepped alongside Bob. "There are many points to cover before a proper question and answer session can begin. Sir, please sit down."

"You shut your ass! This is out of order. I nominate Anna Tolson as secretary for the meeting. Do I hear a second?"

"Oh, yeah! I'll go for that. Second! I second that!" Maureen shouted above the crowd.

"All in favor?" David looked at the crowd.

The room exploded into cheers. Anna stood up.

"I accept," she said proudly and took her place at the front of the room. She then set up a video camcorder to document the meeting. At the end of the table where David stood, she set up her computer notebook.

Bob stammered and spoke loudly to the young attorney. He turned to David.

"Want to find out what it takes? Go ahead!" He turned and set his gaze on Josephine. Before storming out, he glanced at David with a smirk.

David noticed his menacing stare. He pushed his way through the crowd, trying to catch up to Bob. Paolo stopped him in his tracks.

"You've done it, T'ma. Please," he said, forcing David into a chair.

Cathy made her way through the crowd, but in the direction of the young attorney and an unidentified man who stood next to him. When she finally reached them, she shoved a thin binder into the young lawyer's chest.

"I have you being paid four ways past Sunday, boy." She got in his face. "Attorney-client privilege has its limits!"

The man standing with them was the same Senator who had met with Bob at the corner penthouse.

"I'm your Senator, counselor." He locked eyes with the young man. "As a shareholder and a person who knows all about Bob, I can assure you a congressional hearing is forthcoming, so don't bother falling on a sword." He let the young man scurry past him.

The Senator greeted Paolo, David, and a few others. He exchanged information and left with a relieved smile.

"Well, shit. Now what?" David asked.

"Language!" Maureen shouted amongst the crowd.

David fumed as he sat alone in the Corner Café. Jan was suddenly so curt. She no longer wanted the warm embraces or long looks into her eyes. She felt distant.

In a few weeks, control of the Land Sakes Company was about to be legally turned over to him. He would personally see Iada and pick up her endorsement letters. Josephine ran that show. What a smart, beautiful lady.

Jan was a smart and beautiful woman. She was helpful. What happened to that woman? His official housewarming would be later that night. He would happily skip it for a movie night complete with her falling asleep in his lap. *That's it.* He thought to himself. *Go to the General Store and see Maureen.*

School was in session, so there would be no chance of running into Jan. He tossed some bills on the table, enough to cover the tab plus tip, and rushed out.

Bob's sons stood around nervously. They had both been beaten before, but not as adults. Their father was handing over neatly bound bricks of cash to men they'd learn to call 'operators'. After the operators left, Bob walked up to them.

"I want Josephine delivered to that office on Sunday. Not Saturday. Sunday. Don't be early and don't be late." He turned and walked off into the dense fog towards the field office.

The older brother slapped his younger brother's bowed head and motioned to the car. They drove off into the eerily quiet darkness that lacked the smell of rotten eggs. The government inspectors had ordered all of the gas wells to be turned off.

In the cold, empty office, Bob pulled out a box of pills and the dope he confiscated from his sons. It was still easy to drag a confession out of the young one.

"Jan, come with me to Iada's this Saturday. We'll spend a night and do some fishing." David sent his text and felt comfortable about being so direct. The near two-hour helicopter ride would be epic, he thought. Jan would love flying close to all the trees with their fall colors against the rolling hills. She loved the movie *Out of Africa* and the scenes where the airplane had flown over the savannah. His fervent pacing could be heard throughout the entire store. It was as if his thoughts were connected to his feet, rushing about here and there with a mixture of anger, hope, and anxiety. His spastic gait continued along the slightly worn carpet and wooden floor adjacent to the large picture windows that ran the length of the store. He turned to look over to where Big Jake used to hang.

"Will you stop that, David!" Maureen shouted from behind the counter.

David spun around. "What do you expect?"

"Expect about what? Oh that, ssssh..." Stopping mid-sentence, she shook her head.

"Language" he said with a smile.

"You're here for the ring." She slowly reached into the cabinet and placed the simple gold band into the shabby envelope it had rested upon for decades.

David observed her actions. "Where are the guns?"

"Your big boy bought them. I have no idea what Paolo is going to do with a pair of six shooters, but they're his now." She handed him the envelope.

"So you're saying to marry her and that should fix everything?" David said with a melancholy tone.

"No, but marry her on a good day. Not even a lifetime can fix everything between a man and a woman. You will both learn to drop certain issues. As a couple, you will find that the issues you face as individuals do not always apply as a couple, so be prepared. The store will not always be open. That'll be $60." She said, closing the glass cabinet.

"It used to be $20. Gold appreciates in value that much?" David asked in a slightly cheery disposition.

"The band is $20. The advice $40," Maureen said with a wry smile.

David handed over the money and left.

Jan arrived early to David's house for the housewarming party. She gave him a quick kiss and a hug, looking away immediately to head into the back yard. Jack and his twin sons were stringing lights from the back porch cover to short poles poking out from the top of the fence. They formed three lines of white lights that met in a point.

David followed her out. "I don't know if it's work, but you've been rather distant," he said, walking up to her.

She looked up and they stared at each other before she turned towards the kitchen. Again, he followed her.

"Is this right?" he asked, getting closer. "Is this the way you want to tell me something's wrong?"

She shook her head. "Just let me know when it's all over."

"Life doesn't work that way. We work together. It's over when we're dead."

She looked away. "I'm not one of your players," she said angrily.

"Thank God for that. At least, they'd listen to me."

"I know you've never been with a woman, David, but don't ever bring up team or coaching with me ever!" she seethed.

"You started this. No, I'm not a virgin except in the newborn way that I am. I have never bothered to work on a relationship this hard or this long. In terms of being a coach, it sure taught me a lot of things. Things I don't hear out of you."

"This'll be good, like what?"

"Like the fact that it takes a combination of different types to make a great team. Even the team that coaches the team is composed of different types. A couple is the most intense team on earth. Both people work off of the other to become one cohesive unit. If only we should be so lucky."

"Oh and am I lucky... wait, did you say you're not a virgin?" She looked incredulous.

"Is that what kept you around?" he asked, genuinely surprised at the idea.

"You're an ass. Should have known. Big coach, big player, boinking all of the cheerleaders."

"No, bad back kept that subdued until I reached 30. Since then, I've been through three failed relationships. Are you enjoying this honesty thing? I'm not, but it's the most conversation I've had with you all month," he ended, shrugging his shoulders.

"I don't think you're ready for a real woman. I need a real man, or do you think you might grow into one soon?

"I think this isn't a relationship. Not a healthy one, anyways. I may lack experience in these things, but this town, the city, the country, even the world, has opened up so much for me since I've been able to travel. Whatever this is, I don't want any part of it," he said, running out of steam.

Jan stormed off. David's emotions swirled with an equal amount of sadness and resolve. He did his best to accept his decision as the right one as his emotions rapidly churned inside of him. He took in a deep breath. It hurt like hell.

The plain green sedan turned down First Street and made a right on Starling. The operators noticed a woman in her early forty's walking along the sidewalk, her head hung low. They stopped in front of the school and watched her enter the house they had marked as their target. The driver turned to the other man, and they traded knowing glances. They drove back out of town.

David noticed that John seemed to be aging at a rapid pace. He put a plate of eggs and sausage in front of him. "Is there anything you want me to take to Iada, John?" David asked, sitting down with his own plate.

"No. I know you and Jan will work things out. I have it on good measure that I'll be around for that." John stared at his plate.

"I love you, my brother. I really do. I'll be back tomorrow afternoon and see her then. I have the goods if she settles into a fine mood." David pulled out the old envelope from his pocket. He shook it close to John's face.

John leaned back and smiled. The pain he was in looked like more than just cancer.

————

The Model A worked like normal. David kept sounding the horn as he drove off. He knew John enjoyed it. After arriving at the airport, he parked the car in a shady spot, grabbed his bag, and walked to the waiting helicopter. This would be his first trip sitting up front.

"This is odd. Why the covers? Don't you want to see all of the screens?"

"Nah man, I don't even want to discuss what they do," the pilot said, winding up the engine.

Leduc faded away from sight. Trees of yellow, red, and brown covered the rolling hills to the Southeast. David thought of Jan and it pained him. Up ahead, the great cabin loomed. There were no cars parked in the clearing out front. He could see Josephine waving to him from the porch. She went inside and shut the front door.

"Thanks, see you tomorrow," David told the pilot.

"Cool deal, man. Did you install that app like Josephine told you?" he asked.

"Yes, the call for help button." David held up his smartphone.

"It's also a tracking device, but don't tell anyone about it. Cool, bro?"

"Do you surf?" David looked perplexed.

"Whenever I can, dude!" The pilot smiled.

David walking into the great cabin and shut the doors behind him. The helicopter blades wound up and the sound quickly faded.

"Hey, Josephine! Where's Iada?" David beamed at her.

She pointed towards the kitchen and took his bag.

David went in and spotted Iada standing with her coffee and uneaten biscuit. "Is this late for you?" he asked, looking at her hopefully.

She did not respond immediately. He observed the entire kitchen and people in it. It was filled with a diverse group of teens with African-American, Caucasian, Mexican, Asian, and other ethnic descent. They were chatting excitedly about attending college in the coming year. David did not know they were new to the kitchen staff. Iada finally turned and look at him.

"You a good, strong man. No one gonna call ya boy evah 'gin."

He paused, watching her face as she looked into the distance past the young ones preparing lunch.

"You can call me your boy whenever you like!" He grabbed her biscuit and dashed out.

"Rascal!" she shouted with a sudden glee to her voice.

He came back to the area inside the great double doors. Persian carpet decorated the vast room. On the side of the doors, there were hooks to hang jackets and hats and benches to sit and remove shoes. It was much bigger than the entirety of David's house.

The ceiling was made out of rough-cut timber, the kitchen located on the left. On the right, a smaller set of doors led to a hallway where the first set of sleeping quarters were located. Straight ahead, two other huge doors with ornate glass decorating the bottom led to the porch. It overlooked the deep, slow-flowing river that murmured unhurried conversations for anyone who cared to eavesdrop.

Alone on a polished antique table which seated around 50 guests, a boy sat quietly trying to eat his meal. David sat down next to him. "Hello, little man."

The boy barely looked at him. He seemed frightened.

"Sorry if I frightened you. Would you like to eat alone?"

The boy shook his head slowly.

"Can I sit with you?"

The boy looked as if he wanted to smile but wasn't permitted. David then realized how thin he was. His large head held slightly sunken, hollow eyes. He noticed they were the same color as Jan's. His skin was the shade of white one acquires from hiding in the shadows. The boy held his utensils like he had never seen anything like them before.

David placed the biscuit on the boy's plate. It was eaten quickly. He knew how to eat with his hands. Time passed quickly as David asked him if it was okay to show him how the fork worked, how to cut his own sausage, and how to eat like everyone else. David's instinct for allowing the boy the freedom to refuse worked. His coaching taught him to let him try on his own and wait to see if he wanted more help.

Shortly thereafter, the boy began to look sleepy. David picked him up and laid him down on one of the long sofas in front of a window that overlooked the river.

Iada came in, sat close to David, and handed him a small, warm blanket.

"The found him a few days ago. Dead mother. No sign of a fatha. Some kid teased him about eatin' with his fingers, so we let him try and eat alone. You da first to get him to try a fork. You something, David. John right about you all along. It's not much effort ta make a child's life good. Let 'em become something, then show 'em right. Don't kick 'em down, but lift 'em in da right direction. You know that as a coach. Easy to convert into a father," she said, looking down at the sleeping child. "Josephine got me to sign everything. She'll hand it to ya when ya leave. She out to see the Tolson boy."

David turned to her. "Jack's twin brother? How is he?"

"He's good, David. Josephine is the only other person that can understand him. He keeps her safe. He can't have no roof. Josephine was like him, a young brat always runnin' off. I was surprised she came home from the University and wanted to live here. She's the one that kept Land Sakes Company from taking this land after it came to light I wasn't payin' the proper taxes. Now you and your team have the Senator saying the taxes don't belong as they do. Well, you saved all this." She patted David's leg and left.

David listened to the old river talk while the boy slept. He felt languid, sleepy.

The first attempt failed. Josephine was faster than the youngest of Bob's sons. He reached her again as she spun around, connected a fist into his lower jaw, and sent him back. Erick Tolson grabbed him with one arm and flung him into a tree.

He did not move after that. She ran up to him with a horrified look on her face.

Erick did not hear the nun-chucks flying through the air. The lead-filled wood split the skin on the side of his head where an old scar had previously been made from a whipping chain many years prior. He was on the ground long enough for Bob's eldest son to apply a stun gun to his neck.

Josephine rushed forward to help him and was whipped in the face, falling over backwards. He stunned her as well. He went to check on his younger brother and noticed his cracked head and the way his spine was bent at the neck. He left the bodies and picked up Josephine after binding her hands.

"Mister, your crappy life has come down to one decision. I can blow your soul right to where it belongs without blinking an eye. Keep your hands up," Maureen growled. The side-by-side shotgun was pointed at the man's midsection near his heart.

The operator held Jan from behind and kept pushing her towards the car while the other operator held the trunk opened. They both wore long coats with weapons on belts attached to them.

"Excuse me," Paul said from behind one of the men.

The operator near the trunk spun around. Paul punched him so hard, he fell over into the street.

Gaul walked around Maureen, moving her shotgun away from Jan. He grabbed the arm gripping Jan's neck and whipped the man around, freeing Jan to run towards Maureen. Gaul held onto his arm while pounded his head with his free hand until the man went limp and crumpled to the ground.

The other operator stood up and tried to pull his firearm. Paul grabbed it and had it disassembled within two seconds, dropping the pieces on the ground. The man rushed him while taking out balisongs. There were blades protruding from each hand as he attacked the brown man wearing a priest's collar. Paul deflected the blow and countered with a quick punch to the face. The man came at him again with the same result.

"Knock that shit off!" Gaul said with disgust.

"Language!" Maureen shouted.

Paul kept his eyes on the man as he lunged for him once more. Paul brushed him of and landed a solid punch to his face. He fell into the open trunk.

Gaul pulled out his phone. "Hey, send someone for David right now. They came after Jan."

A sudden energy woke David from his sleep. Looking around, he saw a large man holding onto Iada with bloody hands through the huge window. Ignoring his ringing cell phone, he jumped up from the couch and ran through the open door towards them. He recognized the bloody face of Jack's twin brother. Iada turned towards him with a terrified expression.

"They have her! My Josephine!"

He heard the sound of an incoming helicopter and turned to run through the house. He got close to one of the older looking teens. "Shut the door behind me. Don't let anyone out until the copter leaves." The teen nodded. He pushed the button on the desktop of his smart phone. "Land hot. I'm jumping in!"

The helicopter circled twice and landed, barely slowing down the engine. David got in and strapped himself in, giving the hand gesture to take off. The pilot reached over and tossed a headset on his lap.

"Hey, bro! Take off those covers I told you not to touch." David complied. The pilot lifted the bird quickly.

David noticed that the ride was rougher than before. "Wow, is this turbulence?"

"No man. We're like at the red line, so the lady gets a bit grouchy dig?" David nodded. "Okay, man, see those buttons in the upper right of each screen?" Again David nodded and pressed them. The three screens came alive. "So what we have here is real time, high resolution, broadband viewing like infrared and so on all mixed together. Remember, bro, none of this exists and you never saw any of it unless you want some strange men showing up at your wedding to take you away."

"How did you know I was getting married?" David asked.

"Nah, it's just a manner of speech, bro."

David nodded. He listened and learned how to spot people in vehicles. He practiced and became skilled at zooming in.

"Hey, bro, we're getting grounded in two-thirds of the way. We need the fuel anyway, but the FAA is grounding everything for the Presidential fly around."

When they landed at the small airport, David noticed he had some missed calls. He returned the one from Jan.

"Love, what's going on?" he inquired.

She quickly relayed what had happened.

He filled her in on what was going on at his end. "Okay, I'll come home as soon as I can," he said.

"No, help Josephine, David. I'll be here," Jan sobbed.

They endured a short, miserable nap in the pilots' lounge. A pulsating thought pushed all of the rest from David's mind. *Kill Bob Lundberg.* A voice broke into David's fuzzy awareness.

"Dude, we can roll now," the pilot said.

He got up and followed the pilot to the helicopter. They quickly became airborne and made their way through the thick fog. David focused on the screens like a hawk.

"Okay, bro, looks like you got your skills on. Remember what I said about all this. Without it, we would have no chance to maneuver where we're going. There's like this coordinated effort with law enforcement, so we're going into a hot zone. Just zoom in when you think you have something. Let me worry about a safe landing pad."

David nodded, keeping his eyes on the screen. They were flying blind into the night with only the assistance of what they could see on the screens. Finally, the pilot spoke again.

"Dude, this is it. What's that you're concentrating on?"

"That has to be the field office. Someone's lying down inside. I see a car with a hot engine and an open trunk. A big pick-up is rolling towards it. Two people are inside. I think I know who they are," David said.

The pilot maneuvered away from the area and landed. They jumped out into the cold fog after the helicopter wound down. The pilot pulled out his pistol and placed additional magazines in his pocket. He tried to hand David another pistol. David shook his head.

"Okay, bro, but let's go easy."

They crept towards the field office and heard the familiar sound of a diesel pick-up. As they got closer, they could make out an outline of the building, the sedan with an open trunk, and the now parked pick-up. David recognized Jack as he jumped out of the truck. Bob came out of the office. David could tell he had a gun in his hand.

Bob's son rushed up behind Jack, who quickly spun around. Grabbing him, he hurled him into some nearby machinery as though tossing out a trash bag. He turned back to Bob.

"Scudder! What did you do with Josephine?!" Jack barked, running at him.

Bob raised an arm towards Jack, pointing the gun at his upper body. David bent down, picked up a rock, and in one fluid motion sent it flying at Bob. It hit him in the jaw and nearly knocked him over. Bob recovered, aiming his gun at David. His head snapped backwards, blood streaming from a hole just above his ears. His lifeless body fell to the ground.

Cathy came out from the other side of Tolson's truck, keeping her pistol steady in front of her.

"Dude, she's got skills," the pilot said.

Law enforcement began to roll in as they checked on a very groggy Josephine.

Jack stayed at the field office with Cathy. David and the pilot were allowed to fly Josephine to a hospital. Hours after they arrived, they were given the good news that she would be fine.

David felt a new level of tired as he texted Gaul. *Josephine will be fine. Coming home soon. OAO.*

28
RESOLUTION

"Jan, I have to go pick up the papers from Iada. Come with me. Call in sick. Do what you have to," David said, waiting at her front door.

Almost an hour went by. Jan came out. "What are you doing?"

"Waiting. I'm going to wait until you talk to me."

"Grrrrr," she said in exasperation as she stepped onto her porch.

"Where are you going? I can at least drive you there."

"I'm going to Iada's house. Because of everything that happened, I left the papers there. I wouldn't mind having some help shoe-horning John into the helicopter." He looked at her like a hungry child.

She shook her head as she pulled the door closed. "Really, David. I'll go with you to John's house." She walked past him.

"I'm glad you're okay. Please tell me what the biggest issue between us is and we'll work on it," he said, walking next to her.

After turning up Cause Way, Jan stopped. "You were supposed to retire."

David drew her close to him. She did not resist, nor did she return his embrace.

"Love, I can love you. I have retired. I want to stay in Leduc. When I leave, I want you with me." His body shook ever so slightly. "Do you know how I felt when I thought you could be hurt? I've been beating myself up over the thought that you would have been safe if you had just come with me and that no one would have been able to harm you?"

She looked up and began to cry with him.

"If you were here, nothing would have happened." She buried her head against his chest and embraced him as hard as she could. They cried together for a short while. The sounds of Leduc began to come to life around them. The gentle winds of home enveloped them.

"I wish something would happen to keep you here in Leduc indefinitely," she said with sad eyes. "Okay, let's go see John. Breakfast on me?" she asked with a weary smile.

He nodded and held her close, kissing her until he knew she would give in and accept his heart the way it was. He stopped and pulled back enough to see her swoon. She batted her eyes slowly, embraced him, and held his hand as they made their way up the street; neither one caring about their red faces or puffy eyes.

"Jan, I intend on getting involved around town as a volunteer. I would like to have something legit to do. Will you help me figure it out?" he asked, turning to her.

She smiled, her face instantly becoming bright and cheerful.

"I'm just going to have a chat with him about being a bully," Gaul said to Paul as they waited at the bus stop.

"I don't think it's our place this time. No one said he was a bully, just scary and not nice," Paul said.

"Hey, David and Jan are coming." He nodded downhill as the cheery couple walked up, swinging hands.

The sounds of the bus snaking its way around town caught everyone's attention. Some of the local children waited around with Paul and Gaul.

David looked at them. "Hey, what are you guys doing? Haven't you had enough trouble?"

"New quarterback on the bus is scaring some of the kids. I just wanted to introduce myself," Gaul said, trying to sound nonchalant.

"Yeah, like you did with that guy who abducted Jan?" David asked sarcastically.

Paul interjected. "I think he's a good young man. He just needs a proper father figure. You know, David, he might take the team to state. It hasn't been done since you were quarterback."

David stood there, looking back and forth from Paul to Gaul.

"David? Really? Did either of you think about talking to the coach first?"

David felt a sudden electricity between he and Jan. She looked excited.

"As experts go, Gaul, I think we have the best right here!" She pointed at David. She turned her attention to a young woman walking up the street in their direction.

"Beatrice! My girl, how are you?"

"Ms. Milnarcheck, good morning. Mr. Dryer," Beatrice replied with a slight nod.

"Please, just Jan. You're like family. Beatrice, I hear you want to stay in Leduc, but need a full-time job first. Is that right?" Jan asked, twisting and tugging on David's hand.

She looked around at everyone who began to smile at her. "Yes, but someone would have to leave," she said mournfully.

"I have it on good authority that may happen." She pulled David's hand, making him look at it and then at the perplexed faces of Gaul and Paul.

"Let me call you about that later. Could you do me a huge favor and let the principal know that I won't be in today? Can you help run the class for me today and maybe for the rest of the week?"

Beatrice became excited. "Of course! Oh my, that money will really help with Christmas just around the corner!" She left in a hurry.

The men stood there stunned as the bus suddenly came to a stop. David looked at Jan, who looked close to bursting with excitement, and at the flummoxed priests.

"I got this, Gaul. Jan, please excuse me." David released her hand and walked onto the bus.

Gaul and Paul stood there silently, looking at Jan who had become as bright-eyed and bushy-tailed as if she'd just won the lottery.

The bus driver looked at the oncoming passenger. It took him a while to recognize him.

"Hey, Coach Dryer!" He turned around and addressed the rest of the passengers. "Everybody, this is Coach Dryer. The last time our high school went to state he was the QB. Hey, Coach, right here in front row is our new all-star QB. Christopher, say hello."

"Chris-man, sir." He looked up at David, who now stood next to the seat he shared with no one.

David sat beside him, making Christopher slide over. David observed his wiry, slightly bony frame. The young man held as much fear as he did anger in his eyes.

"May I call you Chris?" he asked, looking over. The young man nodded and relaxed. "Chris, people helped me. I didn't pop up out of a sock drawer and just walk out on to the field. I want to help you. It may not always be about football, but if that's okay with you, let's meet here tomorrow. Sound good?" He waited for Chris to nod. "You're the big man, Chris. Try to let the little ones know that with you around no bullies are allowed. It will really help establish you as a leader. The one you will need to be in order to take this team to state. Okay?" Chris nodded again, a little confused. "Did you forget your lunch?" David asked. He noticed the aged shoes and over worn Jeans.

"No, it's okay," Chris said, sounding less than confident.

"Sure, here." David handed over a $20 dollar bill. "Make sure you eat and if possible, take an early bus into town. I'm up at 5:00 a.m. every day and will look for you on one of the buses that comes through town every morning. I don't know the numbers, but you can find them in the library. Students ride for cheap, but in case you get mistaken for an adult, here." He handed him another bill.

Chris took both bills and put them into his pocket.

David stood up, turned to Chris, and said quietly. "You're a good man. This I know." He stood up and addressed the rest of the bus. "You guys will see me around the campus. I think we have our man to take us to state." The students erupted in cheers as David turned to get off. The children that were waiting stepped into the crowded bus. David noticed Chris inviting one to sit with him.

The driver made unneeded pulls on the air horn. He could be heard shouting, "STATE! STATE!"

"Excuse us, Preacher twins," Jan said, grabbing David's hand as they walked away.

Paul and Gaul stood there for a while, trying to sort out what happened. "Well, whatever that was, it's fixed now. Wonder when the wedding will be?" Paul asked.

"Soon. Better prepare for the ceremony. It's going to be big," Gaul said, walking uphill towards the church.

"Looking forward to marrying them?" Paul asked.

"Seeing you marry them, yes," Gaul said, continuing toward the church.

"Pastor of the church does that."

"Yes, Pastor Paul of the Leduc church," Gaul said. After a pause, he turned and saw the look of confusion on Paul's face.

"I'm retiring. You get to stay. I can't be CEO of the halfway house with Maureen while running the church. Let's go. I got the papers." He turned Paul in the direction of the church.

———

"You two can go." John scraped some hash browns and gravy.

"Nice scrapings sauce," David said sarcastically.

"Ew, scrapings sauce?" Jan grimaced.

"Yep, we were eating off campus at a place that had to have made the gravy from whatever was on the floor," David said as John nodded in agreement.

"So there is a dive worse than the Launch Pad?" Jan asked.

"In Los Angeles there is," David recalled. John continued to eat.

"I need you to go, John. It's a nice helicopter ride, only 90 minutes." David said.

"Well, David, you said John was going. If he's not, I might as well stay," Jan said feigning disinterest.

David exaggerated his glances at her, then at John. "You're causing me problems, man!"

John put up his hand and cracked a smile.

"So we're on then?" David asked hopefully.

John nodded.

———

They lifted off 20 minutes later. Jan sat in front and John in back next to the window. David heard Jan make comments about the fall trees over the hills. She was smiling in a way only she could, as if sunshine were born on her face.

It all seemed to fly by so quickly, and soon they stood inside the great cabin. Aside from her swollen jaw, Josephine looked healthy. She embraced Jan longer than expected. Being survivors, they shared an unspoken kinship.

Lunch was served. At the end of the table sat the boy who had learned how to eat with David's help. David tapped Jan on the arm and walked towards him.

"Hello. Do you remember me?" He smiled down at him.

"Yes! I'm Edward, but like to be called Ed."

Jan touched David on the shoulder. He turned around. Jan stared at the boy, who looked as though he could be hers.

"Ed, this is Jan. Can she sit with you?" David asked.

"Oh, yes!" He beamed at them.

David pulled over a chair and motioned for Jan to have a seat. He kissed her, excusing himself as he went over to Iada and John.

"Tomorrow night," he said to both of them. They looked confused.

David pulled the shabby brown envelope out of his pocket, showing them the contents inside. Iada smiled and shook her head. John looked like he might start crying.

David stepped aside and let them observe Jan as she talked to the boy. "I was supposed to wait until the right moment, so I have to avoid any screw-ups until tomorrow at sunset in the park on Tolson's bench."

"That's very specific, my David," Iada said. "Tolson's bench?"

"David helped steal a tree. I'll explain later." John looped an arm around Iada. He would later recant the story of Pete's father-in-law, who died soon after David helped to plant a certain tree.

Dawn broke in Leduc. David was out of bed, downstairs, and looking out the door. He planned to ask Jan to marry him that night. He poured coffee into a travel mug, dressed, grabbed his phone, and shot out the door, coffee in hand.

He heard a bus driving into town. He dashed past the Corner Café and an old man, the latter moving as if he walked barefoot on a bed of nails. He did not recognize John.

Chris stood there with a look of wonder on his face. David noticed the lights in the General Store were starting to come on.

"Chris, nice to see you." David's cell phone rang. He answered it, looking across the street as instructed. *That was John!* He turned back to Chris, observing the old shoes and second hand clothes.

"My man, a detour before breakfast." John explained that Maureen had the store ready for them both. They crossed the street and stepped inside the General Store.

"Good morning, my love. Hello, Chris. Please, this way," Jan said after giving David a proper kiss. David followed and watched Jan as she instructed Chris to try on the short stack of shirts and pants that were set off to the side.

"Shoes will be next. We can do more later, but this is enough and won't crowd out his locker." She smiled at David, kissing him liberally.

The trio came out of the General Store and began to walk to the Corner Café. A man approached David from a parked, but still running, large box truck just outside the General Store.

"Sir, do you know where I'm supposed to set up?"

Dr. Fisher spoke before David could answer. "I can help you. Good morning, everyone. See you later." Dr. Fisher waved them off.

The trio continued across the street as David noticed pyrotechnic images on the side of the truck. They came across John, who sat on a bench outside of the café. "Hello Chris." he said, motioning for him to sit down.

"Jan got the messages, David. If you would have checked your phone, you would have known that instead of zipping past me this morning." He smiled.

David noticed how dry he sounded and how skeletal his facial features appeared. *Just bring him life.* "Well, pardon me!" David joked.

At breakfast, David tolerated every story John had to tell. Chris ate two full breakfasts while hearing tales of the early days and what the 80's were really like.

After letting the younger children on first, they finally watched Chris board the bus with his new wardrobe in tow. He was invited to sit next to several kids.

"Jan, thank you for opening the store early. I don't know what to say."

"See you at my door by 6:00 p.m.?" She smiled.

David nodded as she left and proceeded to walk John home. They stopped on his porch. "My brother, thank you for everything. I have to rest, so I'll see you later."

David watched him go inside. He looked exhausted. Suddenly, David felt tired and decided to head home.

The alarm went off. David struggled to get out of bed. He spent a restless day. He went through his checklist after a shower and then headed for Jan's.

They walked hand-in-hand past the school, making their way up First Street, then finally heading into the park. He felt oddly cold; colder than he should have felt after the walk and the way he was dressed. They strolled over to the bench and sat down.

The sun was already kissing the top of the horizon. They sat in happy silence, holding hands. David noticed that the park was crowded, yet no one greeted them.

They began to make small talk. David felt as if they both needed this relaxing moment. He began to wonder if it was right time. He snapped inside.

"My love." He came off of the bench and got down on his knee in front of her. The lingering glow of sun was already fading, but the glow on her face made it seem much brighter to him.

"Will you marry me?" He fumbled with the envelope and pulled out the ring. She could only nod in tearful reply. She helped him place the ring on her finger. He returned to his place on the bench, wrapping her in his arms and crying happily alongside her.

A small, glowing orb shot up from the grassy playground of the school. It soared above the town and exploded. The boom was heard all over town. Cheers broke out all over the park. David and Jan laughed in unison when they realized everyone was in on the surprise fireworks display.

It started slowly. The big bright ones came on a half hour later. For an entire hour, the uncoordinated display brought out every resident. David turned and noticed the old man seated beside him. He gripped John's hand, too, as the trio watched the display.

It took an hour for David to get Jan home as they made their way through the crowd of people who wanted to take pictures, shake hands, and offer hugs.

"Remember, this is a special occasion, so you're Edward today. Okay?" Ingrid asked, helping him with his tie. He nodded with a smile.

"You guys get close together," Ahnee instructed. She took their picture. Edward was halfway in size from P to Ingrid. They wore matching suits, and Ingrid matched her mother.

David hung out in his garage, waiting around with Paolo, Ralph, Farouk, Christopher, Jack, and Piedmont. He was staring at the sign he nailed up, Main Street. It used to be on a pole a block up, but was replaced with Wellington Street.

Wellington Street had been decorated and prepared to handle the massive crowd. A connecting set of open long tents had been set up. Jan would come in from the backyard of the church while David approached from Wellington Street with his groomsmen. John felt weak, so he waited in the church with his mother and Iada.

When the time arrived, the men walked up the block and into the church. They stood in formation near the altar and waited for Jan. Suddenly, the music began to play, which signaled the procession was about to begin.

The bridesmaids began their slow journey to the front of the church. Following the bridesmaids was Ingrid, who was then proceeded by Edward, and then P, who followed closely behind. When they were almost at the altar, Ingrid stopped. She handed the ring to Edward, who took a few more steps forward and paused. He then handed the ring to P, who carried the ring to his father.

The music shifted and whispers could be heard all around the church as Jan prepared to make her entrance. The entire congregation stood, except John, who needed to remain seated. On her way to the altar, Jan paused, turned to John, and thanked him.

David managed to keep his head clear. Paul read from the Bible and mentioned something forever this and that or worse. He suddenly realized he was supposed to say something.

"I certainly do!" he nearly shouted. Everyone laughed.

"I do, too!" Jan said when it was her time to respond.

Their reception was nearly a riot. Jan and David were allowed to change and then mingled throughout the rest of the celebration. Someone left the garage door open and everyone began to fill it with gifts.

Just after sunset, Jan excused them both from the festivities. David looked completely worn out. She had never seen him look so tired. Jan allowed David to rest as she lay against him on their wedding night.

At 3:00 a.m., Jan's cell phone rang. It was set to allow only one call to come through and this was it. She managed to get David out of the house and into a waiting SUV. They arrived at the hospital a few minutes later. She took him to the room where John had been taken soon after the ceremony. Iada and Josephine were there with John's mother.

"Oh, my brother, what a day." John lifted up a hand.

David went to him and held it. "Hey, how long do you have to be here?"

"This is it. I'm not leaving. I witnessed your happiness. That's good enough." He gave David a wry smile. John was hooked up to a lot of wires. Oxygen was being pumped into his nose and an I.V. strapped to his arm.

"There's more to do, John. So much more," David said.

"Tell me all about it, my brother. What are we going to do?" John asked as his eyes became heavy.

David talked about helping with the high school football team and his ideas of John being the track supervisor. He informed him of the Olympic sized pool that was going to be built.

"I mean really, John. Don't you want to rest before I go on?" David said, looking down. Something warm and electric flowed through him.

"Not dressed like this, I'm not," John said, on his feet and staring at the people gathered around his bed. A familiar laugh and then another caused him to turn around.

"Now that is something, eh?" a large presence said.

"You are free, son. See the man next to you?"

John finally recognized them. Wellington and his father. He turned to the swarthy looking man who stood near him and spoke in song. Love glowed and soothed. John understood he should follow this figure out. He turned back and saw the confused look on David's face. He wanted so much to comfort him.

The musical voice told him, without words, the purpose. He realized Jan would be able to help him in the best way.

They came to a bluff overlooking the world. It was solid, it was cloud, it was an idea, it was a beginning and an end.

"He starts every day. We decide what to do with it from there," Wellington said.

Dr. Fisher turned off the machines, drew up the sheet to John's neck, and removed the nasal cannula. He stepped back. Iada, his mother, and Josephine leaned over to kiss and embrace him one last time.

David released his hand and patted it. Jan leaned over, kissed John on the forehead like the others, and accompanied David to the waiting SUV.

Jan gave instructions to the driver. Soon, they arrived at a clearing on the eastern face of a hill. She struggled to get David out. He got to his feet and plodded towards a crowd. He saw Danielle with Gaul, and Paul with many others from town. Jan directed him to a spot just behind the front row. "Just follow along, love, you will see."

On the bluff overlooking the world, the man who spoke only in song raised his hands. Chariots appeared, pulled through the sky by horses and driven by children. In the back, child archers began to aim earthward. Wherever an arrow hit, sunlight kissed the surface. After many arrows, the world began to light. John took the arm of the man and followed them around the rise of the new day.

"Here it comes!" Danielle squealed. She raised her arms and began to flap.

Everyone joined her. On the hospital rooftop, Dr. Fisher and others began to flap as soon as they saw the dawn break. Ralph and his family began to flap their arms when they saw the sunlight coming. On the front lawn with his family, Paolo and neighbors began to fly, too. Around the world, the ceremony was carried out by everyone familiar with John's story.

Summer had just begun. Leduc was a fine place to raise kids, David thought. Jan was training teens to help cover the General Store. Gaul was with Maureen at the Walker House, helping Bosche and Cathy as they restored it.

David took Ed and the other kids from the tyke brigade up the hill to get them some exercise. They came to Tolson's tree. He looked out over the town and took in its sweet air and sunshine. The sky was filled with poufy little clouds.

"Hey, do you guys want to know how to tell if the earth is round?"

"Could we rest first?" his new son, Ed, asked.

"Sure we can." David sat with his back to the tree he'd helped to plant so long ago. It was big enough for shade, just like Phil's father-in-law said it would be when he retired. Edward sat on the grass and used his shoulder for a backrest. The other kids lay sprawled on the grass, using his outstretched legs as headrests. He began to think about John and all of the lessons he'd somehow managed to teach. Maybe he would have to wait for the right time.

He became drowsy and fell asleep to a warming thought. Yes, at some point, when they are ready, everyone needs to learn how to fly on the ground.

THE END

AUTHOR'S NOTE

I have lived David's life and have crossed past the ending. There are vivid details and of course language. I say what things are since I lived them. I cannot write any other way.

ABOUT THE AUTHOR

Born in the mid-sixties, I grew up with a house full of books. They ones I liked had facts in them like the dictionary or encyclopedia. For some reason listening to what someone else thought made me nuts. One day I picked up a science fiction paperback and discovered a boy like me, one who didn't belong here. That feeling generated by ADDHD is common among us so afflicted, but there was no word in my extensive vocabulary to deal with it. I did however find kinship in those stories and often dreamed of a world where my abnormal was seen as a benefit. Not among children it isn't. I was laughed at once for using microscopic in a conversation. I had no choice but to render my taunters pointless wanderers in the vast desert of stupid and walked off.

Fast-forward 40 years to the middle of my current career as a crime scene photographer for the LAPD. I was chomping at the bit for something fulfilling to do. I read a few self-help books, and it dawned on me that I was a storyteller. "What use is that?" I floated to God. "Christ was pretty good at it," quietly the answer floated back. Suddenly I realized that to communicate took facts yes but to touch another heart took story. After an 8 year journey with the help of Mike Foley of Writers Review and Laura Taylor, I was able to go from average to awesome. I thank both for helping me turn pro. My wife, whom I met at a writers' meeting, encouraged and left me alone while I pursued this.

www.facebook.com/flyingontheground

MORE BY THIS AUTHOR

Coming soon: *Ultracycle*, a tech thriller

www.ingramcontent.com/pod-product-compliance
Lightning Source LLC
Chambersburg PA
CBHW020800250626
47155CB00003B/1164